Mirror Me

Mirror Me

Yvonne Navarro

Overlook Connection Press
2004

Published © 2004
Overlook Connection Press
PO BOX 1934, Hiram, GA 30141
http://www.overlookconnection.com
E-mail: overlookcn@aol.com

Hardcover
ISBN: 1-892950-69-3

Book Design: David G. Barnett of Fat Cat Design

The publisher would like to thank the following for their help in the publication of this novel: Yvonne Navarro for writing it. Rick Sardhina for his inspired cover. Dave B. for making it look good. And LeeAnn Barnett for proofing it!

For:
Weston Ochse
BTAM with Kung Fu Grip

In no particular order, thank you to:

My Dad, Martin Cochran
Weston Ochse
Rain Graves
Dimitri Gennetti
Brian A. Hopkins
Don VanderSluis
David McKoy and Patrick Kelly of the Chicago Fire Department
Richard Glasser of the Chicago Police Department
Anne Lesley Groell

Mirror Me

Yvonne Navarro

"If you were to kill me now right here...
I'd make you wear me like a scar."

—Suzanne Vega, In the Eye

Prologue

The things they did in the dark to the baby were unspeakable.

The older one had been watching crime shows on television, and so he knew about things like fingerprints and bits of skin that might be found under fingernails. It was high summer in the poorer part of Cicero, Illinois, hot and green, and beneath the heavy, pre-thunderstorm clouds and the whine of insects buzzing in the humid air, everything around the yard was open—the garage, the rickety gardening shed, the side door to the house. They'd gone scavenging in secret and picked up things like a couple of sets of dirty gardening gloves, rusty trimming shears, a hand-sized hoe-fork, a partially used roll of duct tape and a flashlight from the garage. Then, while the mother was in back hanging the wash on the line—trying to save electricity and keep the ancient dryer from dumping more heat into the small, shabby house—they went into the house and took the eighteen-month-old girl from her crib.

And when they saw that the mother had left the five-year-old girl to watch over the toddler…

Well, they took her, too.

Nineteen Years Later
Friday—September 29th...

He is waiting for the woman in the hallway of her building when she gets home.

It is, he thinks, as if the universe has conspired to make this, his little act of revenge, easy for him. The building where she lives is an old brick three-flat and her apartment is on the second floor, but he is not concerned with that. What he does find helpful is the foyer, which is shallow but wide, with a deep, handy "blind spot' on each side of an entry door that only has glass in the top half and bears a lock that is pathetically easy for him to slip. There are heavily frosted windows to each side of the door, but they aren't wide enough to cause any problem—he can easily stand beyond where his shadow might show against the outside glass.

His emotions are a mixture of cool calculation and anger... no, rage. *It expands and contracts inside him like a red spider working long, prickly legs every time he hears the words she said to him on the telephone that last time—*

"Listen, you lying son-of-a-bitch, because this is the last time I'm going to tell you this. Don't call me, don't talk to me, don't even *think* about me. If I pick up the phone and it's you just one more time, I'm going to call the police. They'll take care of you once and for all."

—and then the red spider inside him actually bites down, filling him with venom at the memory of the final words she said before she slammed down the phone—

"I don't know you, and I don't want to. You are one sick fuck."

No, he thinks as the door opens and she comes inside, you don't know me at all. The door eases shut behind her and she is looking toward the mailboxes on the west side of the foyer, so she doesn't see where he waits a few feet away, like a giant, silent version of the vicious spider inside his mind. There will be a second or two when the spider, this dark, vengeful side of himself, is visible to all in the window of the entry door, but that cannot be helped. The mailboxes have doorbells below each and he must move her to avoid the chance that she will slap her hand against one of them as he performs his task.

Keys in hand, she is reaching for her own mailbox when he darts forward and clamps his left hand hard across her mouth. Her keys drop as he drags her backward and spins her toward the interior entry, bending low to avoid the window in the door behind him, using her body weight and momentum to slam her against the wall on the opposite side. There is a narrow wooden table there and the jarring movement bounces it away from the wall and leaves an eighteen-inch space; she is too stunned to resist as he forces her to bend over the tabletop, pressing against her from behind as he shoves her head and shoulders down and into the gap, keeping her pinned against the wall. He lets go of the back of her head, quickly reaches into the deep right pocket of his black windbreaker, and brings out his weapon. The knife is a beautiful K2K Folder with a drop point and a serrated edge, slightly more than two and a half inches of deadly stainless steel blade. Revenge would be, as they say, a much sweeter thing if he had the time to enjoy it; he does not and so without wasting any more movement he reaches under her neck and draws the blade left to right across her throat.

She thrashes and goes deeper into the space, voiceless, and he holds her there, keeping the spray of blood directed toward the left outside corner of the foyer and away from his clothes, sees it splatter against the wall like an abstract scarlet painting. Warmth covers his hand, seeping through the heavy latex glove he's stretched up and over his wrist to protect the cuff of his windbreaker. When her struggling stops, he lets her fall, not caring about the awkward position of her body or the leather purse that drops to the side of it. He backs away, pleased when he sees that he hasn't stepped in any blood and so he won't have to use the bottle of ammonia in his other pocket to wash away any footprints. There is an arc of ruby-colored liquid climbing across the wall and ending midway on the east pane of frosted glass, so he wipes the blade of his knife with the gloved, bloodied fingers of his left hand and puts it away, then reaches up with his right and loosens the dim, bare bulb overhead.

The foyer drops into darkness and he stands at the door for a moment, studying the sidewalk out front. It is dark and comforting, lined with thick-leafed maples that rustle in the pleasant fall evening and scatter the already weak glow of the overhead streetlights. No one is out there and he quietly pushes the door open and slips onto the porch, quickly stripping the latex gloves inside out and pocketing them before descending the stairs and strolling, unconcerned, to where he's parked his car beneath the elevated train tracks only a block to the west.

The trauma team at Illinois Masonic Medical Center was waiting when the Chicago Fire Department ambulance, lights flashing and siren screaming, careened into the driveway and lurched to a stop beneath the protective overhang at the entrance to the emergency room. The men and women—two doctors and two trauma nurses—were experienced and capable, and no one among them had been with the group for less than a year, plus they'd gotten a heads up from the driver, so they all knew what was coming, had all the equipment ready.

That she was alive, still, was a shock.

"Female, early twenties, knife wound to the throat!" one of the EMTs shouted as he and his partner propelled the Gurney out of the back of the bus and into the half dozen reaching hands. There was blood everywhere, and beneath an oxygen mask the victim's face was as white as the marble cross that hung in the chapel in another wing of Illinois Masonic. Over the past several years, Dr. Ireta Tansey had seen that cross many times, *too* many, and she had also seen this young woman before.

"Ready the suture tray," Dr. Tansey ordered. As the patient was rushed into the ER, she paused only long enough to shoot a question back to the paramedics who stood stripping off blood-soaked gloves and looking disgusted at the mess inside their vehicle. "ID?"

The older one jerked his head toward a police car swinging over to the curb at street level. "Randall's got it."

The doctor gave a crisp nod. "Tell him to bring it in, stat. This girl's been here before and we can look up her records, save time on the blood type."

He turned and headed toward the cop as she slammed back through the ER doors and followed the trail of blood into chaos.

The trauma team had put the woman in the crash room, on the right and closest to the entrance. Everyone was moving at once, juggling IVs, hooking up blood pressure and pulse sensors, hands changing off holding a wad of scarlet-soaked gauze in place over the gaping, happy-mouth of a wound that nearly circled her throat as tasks were switched back and forth.

"Pulse is fifty-nine, respiration is steady, and blood pressure is holding at… one-twenty over seventy?" Jeremy, one of the trauma nurses, scowled. "What the—that *can't* be right!"

Before the doctor could make her way up to the examination table, everyone in the room just… stopped. And stared.

"Move your asses, people," Dr. Tansey snapped as she strode forward. "Unless you want this girl to bleed to death in front of you!"

"I don't think so, doctor," said Camila, the other nurse. Still, at least the others were moving again, if only to step forward and peer at the ivory-skinned girl lying quietly on the table. The other doctor, a young man named Sajag Bharat, looked back and forth from the monitors to the patient, then cautiously lifted his gloved hand from her throat. It came away filled with sopping red gauze, but there was no fresh red pulse behind the material. "She's stopped bleeding on her own."

"What?" Dr. Tansey scooted in closer and leaned over the victim. The cut on her throat was fresh and deep, the edges separated enough to show muscle and the thin, creamier-colored layer of adipose tissue. If it hadn't been for the steady *beep-beep-beep* of the heart monitor, Tansey would have thought the girl was dead—at least that would have explained the abrupt halt of the blood flow.

"Her name is Hannah Danior," the charge nurse called from the doorway. Dr. Tansey glanced over and saw the older woman flipping rapidly through a bunch of cards obviously just handed to her by a policeman a few feet away. "Here—she's got an IM card. I can pull up her data on the computer." She shoved the rest of the cards back into the policeman's hands and disappeared down the hallway.

Dr. Tansey straightened, feeling the gazes of the rest of the team. She knew what to do next, of course, but for the first time in her career she couldn't explain what had just happened on the examination table in front of her.

"Maybe it wasn't as deep as we thought," Jeremy suggested. He sounded as unconvinced as she was, but at least it gave them all something to grasp, a lifeline in the midst of inexplicability.

Dr. Tansey stared at the young woman, her eyes narrowing. Yeah, even without the records pulled up, she remembered this patient. It had been awhile, back in the spring perhaps, but recollections like that didn't die easily in someone trained to hang onto the most minute of details, and when she brushed the girl's hair away from her jaw line, the doctor's memory was confirmed.

"Stitch her up," she said abruptly. She pulled off her gloves and tossed them into the waste receptacle, then pushed back the strands of streaked blond hair that had fallen across her own forehead. "Make sure she's stable and have her transferred... into the psych wing."

««—»»

"Welcome to another exciting Friday night."

As he climbed the steps of the apartment building, Detective Greg Jedrek raised one eyebrow at the nearly light-hearted sound of his partner's voice. Maybe it wasn't going to be so bad, he thought... then again, a homicide was a homicide, and what could ever be good about something like that? When Greg didn't say anything in response, Tony Rutland regarded him impassively. The blue bubble lights atop the three squad cars parked in front cut across Tony's face at half-second intervals. "Where the hell have you been?"

"Got my taste of that Friday night spirit you're so excited about," Greg retorted. "It's called DePaul traffic. Must've spent fifteen minutes stuck on Fullerton between Clark and Lincoln—nobody gives a damn about lights and a siren anymore."

Tony nodded, then stuck a cigarette in his mouth and lit it. He jerked his head toward the porch of a small brick apartment building at the end of the short walkway behind him, where a couple of uniformed cops stood unhappily flanking the entrance. Dim light bled out of the doorway and lit two murkily-textured windows on either side of the door; something dark was streaked in a semi-circle across the one on the left. "Well, wait'll you get an eyeful of what's up there," he said as he ran a hand through his hair. "I bet it makes you wish you were still sitting on Fullerton and listening to the radio."

Greg bit back a sharp reply and shouldered past the older man, who made no move to follow. "Aren't you coming?" Greg finally asked as he paused on the last step.

Tony shook his head and one corner of his mouth turned up in a vaguely cruel smirk. "No, thanks. I've already seen enough to make me blow dinner. Your turn, farm boy. Enjoy."

Greg turned back toward the entrance to the building and said nothing despite his annoyance. What was the use in arguing? Some people were just how they were. Tony wasn't that much older than him but he'd been on the job here in Chicago a lot longer, had been exposed to levels of brutality that Greg would readily admit hadn't been found in his hometown of Grinnell, Iowa. Maybe it was the job that had made Tony the way he was, a young guy who radiated the same emotionally-dead spirit that Greg had so despised in his own father. In a comparison like that, Tony came out the winner—at least he had a reason for the way he was; Boyd Jedrek had made a lifetime career out of turning away from his wife and children, fine-tuning the art of cold-shouldering his loved ones.

The beat cops by the door nodded to him and stepped aside as Greg moved toward the entry door. He frowned when he saw it was open but there were no telltales smears of print dust on it.

"Evidence techs are on the way," one of the uniforms told him before he could ask. "I don't know what they'll be able to salvage, though—the lady who lives on the third floor found the victim, said she had her hand all over that knob when she opened the door. The light was out, too, but she reached up and tapped it with her newspaper and it came on. That's when…" He shrugged.

"Damn it," Greg muttered under his breath. Louder, he said, "What else?"

The older of the two took a deep breath. "Female, middle twenties. We can't tell from the position of the body, but the amount of blood makes it look like her throat was cut. Her clothes are intact and her purse is still inside." He jerked his head toward Tony, still standing and smoking calmly at the foot of the porch. "Rutland already snapped a couple of Polaroids, but nobody's moved anything."

"The woman upstairs—she found her?"

The policeman nodded. "The victim's name is Eloise Addison. The neighbor was a friend of hers, so she's pretty freaked. Couple of the guys are up there with her now. Rutland said you'd do the interview."

Greg nodded. Yeah, Tony would have left it to his softie partner to question the crying witness—which was fine with Greg. If there was ever a classic good cop/bad cop twosome, they sure filled it; too bad they didn't actually get along and make it a perfect match. "I'll get to her in a minute," he said, and toed open the door.

As places to off someone went, this had been a good choice—very little visible from the outside and plenty of space to work with inside. He watched where he was stepping, but the killer had made a clean exit and there were no footprints to worry about. On the floor beneath the mailboxes was a set of keys, and it didn't take much brainpower to guess the victim had been about to open her mailbox when she'd been grabbed from behind. He could see a line of envelopes behind the slots of the box marked ADDISON. She hadn't made it that far and had probably been grabbed and pulled to the other side so she couldn't ring any of the bells.

Greg ground his teeth, then turned to look at the other end of the foyer.

At first he didn't register what he was looking at, then Greg realized what the murderer had done. Mindful of the pool of blood around the small, wooden table over which the corpse was bent, the detective stepped closer. There wasn't much he could see until the body was moved, and they wouldn't do that until the techs got here and bagged the victim's hands, dusted the keys and the other surfaces in the foyer. Lying on its side in the blood beneath the table was a black leather handbag, its zipper closed and clotted with blood—no robbery motive here. Eloise Addison's skin was a dull, bled-out gray and her eyes were slightly open; she'd had her hair, long and dark, twisted into some kind of a chignon and part of it had come loose and was now covering most of her face. From what Greg could tell, the dead woman was wearing an expensive navy blue business suit under a lightweight London Fog trench coat; the coat had gotten tangled to the right when her head and upper body had been forced between the table and the wall. Her skirt and stockings were still intact and tear-free, so there'd been no rape. The atrocity that had been committed here had gone down fast and, for what it was, neat.

The inside door on the right was slightly open and beyond it Greg could see a stairway leading up. He nudged the door with his shoulder so he could get inside, though he knew the neighbor had probably turned the doorknob when she'd run to her apartment to call the police. The detective climbed the stairs slowly, his mind turning over what he'd seen so far. No robbery, no rape, no break-in. What was the motive here?

When he got to the third floor landing, that door was also open so Greg walked inside without knocking. It was a nice place and probably had the same layout as the victim's directly below, but they'd have to contact the landlord to let them in before they could look around down there—that was standard procedure, and no doubt one of the uniforms had already called. He was standing in a living room that had been painted a cheerful yellow to complement a feminine-looking living room set. Vases with silk flowers were set here and there amid lots of floral paintings and china and crystal knickknacks, Victorian lace curtains and embroidered pillows. Nice place but it made him nervous; he wasn't a big man, but he felt like he could move the wrong way in here and break something without even trying.

He heard voices down the hall and turned that way, followed an oak-floored hallway to a kitchen that could have come right out of a Martha Stewart magazine. More yellow—lots of it—trimmed with a generous motif of tiny pink and white roses. A border of the stuff encircled the room at the juncture of the wall and ceiling and on one wall hung a four foot square cabinet with an exhibit of collectible miniature teapots and matching plates. The counters showed off an assortment of carefully placed cookie jars and serving dishes in colors that matched the kitchen and the ruffled, painfully floral curtains at the windows. By the time Greg's brain had taken in all this, he'd resigned himself to dealing with someone his grandmother's age.

But the woman who sat clutching a cup of tea at the table was only a few years older than the victim, in her mid-thirties at the most. Built a little round at the edges, her attractive face was pale and streaked with tears below a messy head of reddish curls that fell to her jaw line and she'd thrown a dainty crocheted sweater over a ribbon-trimmed dress that Greg wasn't surprised to see was in another heavily flowered pattern.

When he saw Greg, one of the officers in the kitchen stepped forward. "This is Mary Kidman," he said. "She found the victim."

"Eloise," Mary Kidman said. Her voice was a little loud and brittle, like little pieces of wood being shaken in a bag. "Her name was *Eloise.* She was my best friend."

Ow, thought Greg, but Mary didn't lose it. "I'm sorry," he said simply, then squatted in front of her. "I'm Detective Jedrek. Can you tell me what happened here?"

Mary shook her head. "I don't know." Her eyes, strikingly gray beneath reddened lids, filled up and a double line of tears joined the moisture already on her cheeks. "I just... found her like *that*, in the hallway, when I came home. I didn't see anyone and I could tell that she was—" She gulped air and dropped her hands to the twisted Kleenex in her lap, then managed to keep going. "She was already dead."

Greg nodded and gave her a second or two before asking his next question. "Do you know if there was anyone who would do this to her? Was she married, or did she have a boyfriend?"

The woman worked her fingers together. "She wasn't married, and she didn't have a steady boyfriend." She bit at her bottom lip for a second. "There was this one guy she had a little trouble with, but I don't think he knew where she lived—she said she'd never told him and her phone number was unlisted. And she hadn't heard from him in almost two weeks, since she told him off."

Greg's eyes narrowed and he pulled a small notebook from his breast pocket, flipped it open and readied his pen. "What kind of trouble? Did you meet him?"

"No. And I just know what she told me." She dabbed at her eyes with the tissue.

"And what was that?"

Mary frowned as she tried to remember. "Eloise was an account executive at Leo Burnett Advertising," she told him. "They're downtown and she met this guy, Blake, in line at one of those fast-food places everybody goes to for lunch. They had lunch a couple of times—nothing more serious than that—then she couldn't go the next time he called her at work and asked her out. She was busy and wanted to call him back, but he wouldn't give her a number, said he wasn't reachable because he was out in the field or something."

Greg scribbled a few notes on his pad. "Where did he work?"

"I don't know. I remember it was some kind of security company, but when she called there, they told Eloise they'd never heard of him. So she put it all together and decided he must be married, and when he called her back, she told him not to call her again." Mary looked vaguely embarrassed. "Eloise was rather... *outspoken* sometimes, and I'm afraid she was rather crude when she did it."

Greg resisted the urge to smile. There wasn't anything about this that was funny, but he found it amazing that the fragile Mary Kidman could be best friends with someone like Eloise Addison, whom he suspected had been a polar opposite. "Then what happened?"

Mary blinked. "He kept calling her, at work, at home, at least twice a day. Finally she told him that she was going to call the police on him if he didn't stop."

"And did he?"

She nodded. "Yes. Eloise was on edge for a couple of days, but her threat must've worked. She never heard from him again."

Oh, yes she did, Greg thought without looking up. One last time. "Did she mention what he looked like?"

"She said he was tall, with dark hair and blue eyes. Handsome."

Just like a million other guys in Chicago. "All right, Ms. Kidman. Thanks for your help."

She looked up at him, her wide, gray eyes penetrating. "I wasn't really much help at all, was I?" Her voice trembled.

"Don't be so certain of that," he said, but it was an automatic response. He'd run the Addison woman's phone records, but the wannabe boyfriend had likely called from pay or untraceable cell phones, especially if he had murderous tendencies. Greg glanced at the two uniforms. "Is there someone you can call to...?"

She sniffed. "I already did. My fiancé will be over as soon as he gets off work." She looked at the two officers. "You can go ahead and leave—I'll be all right. I think I'll just stay in here until..." Her words faded and she stared at the floor.

Greg knew exactly what she was talking about. "That would probably be best. If you think of anything else, you can call me at this number."

He handed her one of his cards, then headed back downstairs, stopping at the second landing when he saw the door to Eloise Addison's apartment was open. There was a heavyset middle-aged man standing just inside, shock still etched into the lines of his face. Greg could hear noises from deeper in the apartment. "Who are you?" he demanded. "And who else is in here?"

"I'm the landlord," the man said, stepping back at Greg's sharp tone. "The detective downstairs said to let him in—that's all."

Greg relaxed a bit as he registered the crowded ring of keys in the man's hand. "It's fine," he said, not bothering with any more of an explanation. He hurried down the hall—a matched layout to the Kidman apartment upstairs—and found his partner in the bedroom, methodically looking through the dresser drawers. "Find anything?"

Tony shrugged. "Bunch of frilly underwear, socks, sweaters, the usual. Nothing kinky. The super says as far as he knows, she never gave anyone else a key, not even that woman upstairs. Seemed to like her privacy."

Greg looked around the room thoughtfully and left Tony to his search, though he had a hunch the other man wouldn't get much out of this place. No number for this Blake guy, no last name, no employer; he'd do a follow-up with her coworkers and a canvas of the neighborhood, but he was betting no one but the late Eloise had actually seen him. When he passed the techs on the way outside, they looked at him and shook their heads—that meant no fingerprints or, at least at first glance, anything else usable. Guy had probably been wearing gloves.

He sighed and went down by the car to wait for Tony. Too bad they didn't have anything to go on, but at least they weren't dealing with a serial killer.

Saturday—September 30th...

Hannah opened her eyes and found two men staring down at her.

Early morning sunlight, bright enough to fry her eyeballs, leaked through half-closed blinds across the small room, but she forced her eyes to stay open. She tried to speak, but for a few seconds nothing worked. Her throat hurt monstrously, like someone had wound it with barbed wire, then twisted the ends nice and tight. She'd endured what she had come to call her *Affliction*—in her mind, she always thought of it with a capital "A"—off and on for most of what she could remember of her life, but this year it had gotten worse... much, *much* worse. She'd thought the time last April, which had also landed her here in Illinois Masonic, had been painful enough to make her think she was going to die, but waking up in a bed this morning in the psychiatric ward when the painkiller had worn off was a rude reintroduction to just how bad life could be.

Hannah tried again, swallowing around the band of fire that had settled between her chin and her collarbone and trying to focus her eyes past the medicine-grit that had settled in their corners. "Who are you?" she finally managed to croak. She was thirsty and she wanted to wipe her mouth but the staff doctor had ordered her hands strapped down. The level of compassion around here was absolutely mind boggling.

The two men standing a few feet away were both tall, one dark-headed and one blond and wearing glasses, slightly shorter than the other. It was the blond who stepped forward and regarded her with calm, light blue eyes; the other one stayed back, and for a moment Hannah thought she saw an expression of raw surprise on his face. What, she thought crankily. He's never seen a woman with her throat cut before?

"My name is Detective Jedrek," said the blond. He pulled one hand out of his pocket and showed her a gold badge encased in leather, politely holding it in front of her eyes where she could see it without moving her head—like she could, anyway. He nodded at the other man, who was still standing a few feet away, as though he was afraid she'd suddenly spray blood all over him—brave cop. "This is my partner, Detective Rutland."

Hannah could think of a hundred replies, and most of them had the phrase 'so go away' neatly tacked onto the end—*I don't want to talk to you, so go away. I don't care, so go away. Leave me alone, so go away.* Unfortunately, she wasn't in the best position to be insistent about it, so she tried a different approach. "What do you want?" Maybe it wasn't barbed wire encircling her throat after all... crushed glass glued to the inside of a wide band of sandpaper seemed more like it.

Detective Jedrek didn't waste any time. "You're Hannah Danior, right?"

"What's left of me is."

Jedrek ignored the crack. "I'd like to talk to you about who attacked you, Ms. Danior. I—"

"I don't remember."

Damn—even though her voice was barely above a whisper, she'd said the words too quickly, and now Hannah could tell he didn't believe her, could see it in the way his eyes narrowed. "Well, that's unfortunate, Ms. Danior. You see, there was another young woman attacked in the same manner last night. When the report on your incident came out this morning, we saw the similarities right away—we're estimating that the two attacks may have even occurred one right after the other." He paused and the look he gave her was penetrating. "I'm sorry to say that the other young woman didn't survive, so any help you could toss our way would be appreciated. We wouldn't want this guy to try it a third time." He looked at her expectantly.

Hannah started to repeat herself, then stopped as someone strode into the room. A doctor... yeah, Tansey. She recognized the woman from the emergency room last night. And, of course, last April. "Hannah," she said, "how are we doing today?"

Hannah grimaced. "I don't know how *we're* doing, doc, but *I* feel like hell."

Dr. Tansey smiled vaguely, then her gaze fell on the straps around Hannah's wrists and irritation flitted across her face. "I think we'll take these off now," she said.

"Changed your mind about me?" Hannah rasped.

"Why was she strapped down?" Detective Jedrek asked. He flashed his badge at the doctor before she could ask and Hannah snatched at the momentary pause to answer the question herself.

"They think I did this to myself," she said. Her voice was working a little better, still sore but using it was getting rid of some of the stiffness. "Body art, maybe."

Dr. Tansey frowned and studied Hannah as her fingers undid first one strap, then the other. "You have to admit there's a history, Hannah."

"I have never tried to hurt myself!" she said hotly.

"Then explain it to me," the doctor shot back. "All of it, right now."

Hannah flexed her wrists and turned her face away from the accusing stare of the doctor, reflexively brushing back the hair that had tangled around her face and neck. Too late she remembered the thick, puckered scar just beneath her jaw on the left side of her neck, too high up to be covered by this newest round of bandages. When she turned back, she saw the sharp eyes of the detective move from that to the pale, inch-long scar through her right eyebrow. Battle wounds from wars in which she'd never fought, but how could she make them understand that?

She couldn't.

So she said nothing.

"Just a minute," said the other detective. What was his name? Rutland, that was it. He stepped up to the bed and stared down at her. "You're saying she tried to commit suicide?" Hannah started to scowl up at him, then found herself shuddering instead as she met his gaze. His eyes were blue like his partner's, but a deeper, darker shade that made her feel like a trapped animal and made her want to look away. There was something disconcerting about his voice—

"There was no weapon found at the scene," Detective Jedrek said, fragmenting her train of thought. "Either by the bookstore owner who discovered her, or by the paramedics or police." He raised one eyebrow and Hannah thought she kind of liked the derisive tone of his voice. "Since you shipped her off to the psych ward, I'm assuming you had her personal belongings searched?"

Dr. Tansey shrugged and Hannah knew that meant yes. What a life—

head home from work, then wake up in the ER and have strangers pawing over your body and your private stuff. She didn't want to think about the part in between the ER and here, not yet. "I didn't do this to myself," Hannah said to the physician. "For God's sake, if I was going for a permanent check-out, don't you think I'd have picked someplace more private than my own fucking front doorstep?"

The doctor rubbed her forehead and said nothing, and Hannah glared at her, hoping she was getting a migraine. The woman deserved one for leaving Hannah tied up in this bed like some unruly nutcase. Okay, maybe she had a *history*, as the doctor had said, but her past had never included attempted suicide... though, really, if they knew the truth, could they have blamed her if it had?

"Listen," Hannah said. "I have pets at home, dogs that need to be walked. There isn't anyone else to take care of them. *Please*—I don't need to be here. Let me go home."

The doctor shook her head. "Absolutely not—you've sustained an extremely serious injury. I'll allow that it may have been a misjudgment to have you placed in the psychiatric ward, and I'll have you moved within the hour. But you need to be hospitalized for at least two more days—"

"I'm almost healed!" Hannah protested.

Detective Jedrek look at her in surprise, then at the doctor. "What's that?"

"I said—"

Dr. Tansey cut Hannah off. "The young lady heals at a... remarkable rate," she said carefully. "But it's still not so rapid that you don't need medical supervision."

Hannah scowled. Damn it—if this had happened after she'd gotten safely inside her apartment, she'd have woken up this morning, cleaned up the mess, and gotten on with her life after wrapping some gauze around her throat and putting on a turtleneck. "I can't stay here," she said again. "I *won't*. I have responsibilities."

Dr. Tansey gazed down at her and smiled gently. Hannah saw the woman's eyes glint, then realized that of all the things in the world she could have let come out of her mouth, that had been the absolutely, undeniably, *worst*. "I'm sorry to hear that, Hannah. That makes me believe you're a danger to yourself, and as the physician in charge of your case, I'm afraid that means you'll have to remain on the psych ward—where we have locked doors and guards—until I deem you well enough to be signed out."

Hannah's mouth dropped open as the doctor tucked her clipboard under her arm, turned, and started to walk out.

"No!" Hannah struggled to pull herself upright, fighting against the sheet and the rough hospital blanket. "I won't—"

"Unless you want to be restrained again," Dr. Tansey commented as she stopped by the door, "I'd strongly suggest you calm down and remain in that bed."

Hannah froze, then slowly sank back onto the mattress as she and the detectives watched the stiff-backed doctor stride out. Jesus, this was terrible—she'd never been in this deep before. What was she going to do about Knothead and Puddles?

"Miss," said Detective Rutland, "we really need you to try and recall something about the attack. If you could think back to right before it happened... was anyone following you or—"

"My dogs," Hannah said miserably. "That damned woman has me locked in here—who'd going to feed and walk them?"

Rutland made an exasperated sound. "Tough luck about the animals, miss. But can we get back to why my partner and I are here?"

"I'll do it," Detective Jedrek said.

Hannah blinked and turned her head to look at him. "What did you say?"

The blond detective flipped open a small notebook and checked it. "You live over on Belmont, right? Near Sheffield. I'm pretty close to there. As long as they don't bite me when I go in, I could handle it."

Hannah stared at him, betting her own expression was a close match to the look of incredulity on Rutland's. "You would? *Why?*"

"Ditto," Rutland said.

Jedrek shrugged, suddenly looking self-conscious. "Can't just leave 'em stuck in the apartment like that. I like dogs a lot, but I can't have one in my building."

Hannah twisted the sheet nervously and thought about this. He was a stranger... but he was a cop. What if he was crooked? And if he was, what would it matter? She had nothing of worth to steal. All she cared about on this planet were those two spoiled animals, and the only friend she had who liked her enough to help out, Winnie Harbin, was fiercely allergic to dogs—it was a given that she started sneezing just from being within two feet of Hannah's front door. But nothing ever came without a price. This man, this *cop,* would want something in return. But what?

Whatever it was, she would give it, because she had no choice. Knothead and Puddles couldn't feed and walk themselves, and no one else would do it. She'd be out of here in two days, and while that slice of time would mean a mess and a couple of hungry pooches who were getting thirsty toward the end of it, two days wouldn't be the end of the world. Unless…

Her *Affliction.*

It was happening more often now. Less than two weeks ago she'd been standing at the bathroom sink and brushing her teeth—with a sniffling, sneezy Winnie leaning in the doorway and talking to her—when she gotten a nasty three-inch slice across the line of her right collarbone. Before that had been less than six months, and before that it had been, literally, *years.* The time periods were getting shorter, *really* shorter.

So what if something happened to her tomorrow, or the morning after, something that kept her sad and sorry butt locked in this place for another week, or two? Or worse… what if the next time her Affliction actually *killed* her?

Someone should know about her dogs, and the way her life was going, Hannah would have to grasp the offered kindness of a stranger.

"The keys are in my coat pocket," she said. It sounded like someone else's voice, small and tired, a woman she didn't know giving up a measure of hard-won control. A woman *surrendering.* "In the closet over there."

Hannah turned her head away as Jedrek went over and opened the door, then dug around in the closet until he found her keys.

She would not let them see her cry.

«««—»»»

Hannah Danior lived above a bookstore called Stars Our Destination on busy Belmont Avenue. Greg had never noticed the place before, but it looked like a great way to burn up a lazy afternoon—thousands of new and used genre books and a friendly-looking staff who acted like they really enjoyed what they were doing. Posters on the picture window advertised everything from new releases to the store's upcoming annual Halloween bash. The roar of traffic on Belmont Avenue might be a downside to Hannah's address, but maybe living over a shop like this made it worthwhile.

The slightly recessed door to the upstairs was off to the side, barely noticeable except for the dark, circular stain on the concrete in front of it—undeniable evidence of Hannah's attack. Strange, Greg thought as he stared at it. Horns blared from the street and people walked by in a steady stream. This stretch of Belmont, especially on weekend nights, was crowded to the point of chaotic. No criminal with a quarter-brain's worth of caution would attack a woman in a place so much out in the open, and so populated.

When the detective let himself in, he found a narrow hallway dark enough to make him grimace—now *this* would have been more to the tune of a rape and/or robbery. Yet that hadn't been the case here; the police report clearly specified that Hannah hadn't even gotten her key in the lock, and the bloodstain out front supported that. She'd still been clutching her purse when the paramedics had arrived. The old wooden steps creaked beneath his weight as he climbed, his ascent taking him onto a landing that was a bit more well lit by a small, dusty window high on the eastern wall. Not much to see up here beyond the door to Hannah's apartment, and as Greg stepped up to it, he grinned at the snuffling and low whining coming from the crack at its bottom.

Hannah had assured him that her two dogs weren't the attack type, but then did she really know how they were going to react to a stranger walking in? "Well," he muttered, "Here goes nothing." He pushed her key into the lock, turned it, and opened the door.

Two shapes—one dark, one light—zipped past him and into the hall as he stepped inside. Then the dogs twisted around each other and came back in, circling and bumping against his legs before finally moving back and forth in front of him in little excited hops. He was relieved to hear no growls or grumbling from either of the well-cared-for animals fidgeting in front of him. "Okay, gals," he said. "Leash?"

Both of them rocketed away, heading for the shadowed recesses of the apartment. Greg closed the front door and followed, watching his step. There was a mess in here somewhere—he could smell it—but that could hardly be helped. Even the most well-trained dogs weren't built to hold it for nearly twenty hours; he'd walk them first, then come back and clean it up. The dogs didn't come back and he found them sitting skittishly by the back door, each offering well-worn leather leashes. He took the somewhat gooey leads and snapped them onto their collars, then led the pooches outside. As he passed, Greg snagged a couple of plastic bags from a bunch hanging on a hook on the porch and marveled that although they were excited and obviously anxious, the dogs still didn't yank him off his feet as they all clambered down the back stairs. It didn't take long—all of twenty seconds—for both dogs to get down to business; Greg cleaned up after them, then went for a nice, twenty-minute trot around the neighborhood.

They were a pair, all right. Before he'd left the hospital, Hannah had told him the older one was Puddles, a black Lab so named because a puppyhood kidney infection had made house-breaking a true challenge. The other one was Knothead, and it was obvious from the little pointy spot on top of the Golden Retriever's head where the name had come from. Together they were a silly duo, nipping good-naturedly at each other's tails and toes, pouncing on blowing bits of paper, *woofing* when they saw another dog or cat peering through a window. Happy, healthy, and not a mean bone in their bodies, and Greg was glad they hadn't been left stranded in Hannah's apartment until God only knew when.

Back inside, Greg found the pups' dishes and gave them fresh water, then refilled the dry dog food in the all but empty bowls. He hunted down the accident—only one—and cleaned it up, amused that both dogs sat and watched him the whole time, each looking so ashamed that he wouldn't have known which one to blame. The entire walking, feeding and cleanup took less than forty-five minutes, and there was really no reason to stay beyond that.

Except, of course, the dogs kept following him around and nudging his hands, leaning against his legs, and bouncing playfully around him with toys in their mouths, silly plastic things that made plaintive squeaking noises every time they bit down. Greg knew they had to be lonely, missing Hannah and starving for human companionship, so he finally just sat on the floor in the kitchen area and played with them, tossing the toys, doing the tug-of-war thing with a well-chewed rope toy Knothead brought him, teasing Puddles with a ridiculous, big blue rubber pacifier. Both dogs were so funny that he found himself laughing out loud as each tried to outdo the other for his attention; ultimately they crawled up on either side and simply snuggled close.

"Good girls," he said as he stroked their fur. "Don't worry. Hannah will be home soon, you'll see." Now that the dogs had calmed, Greg glanced around the place absently, noticing the sparseness of the furnishings. There wasn't much in the way of knickknacks in what was essentially an oversized long studio, but there *was* a bit of clutter—small piles of magazines here and there, a bundle of some kind of knitting on one side of the couch, stacks of obviously used books. The bed was straightened rather than made, but it didn't look like the dogs were inclined to get on the furniture; rather, there was a large, heavy oval rug in front of the oversized window at the north end of the apartment—the place's only significant source of light—that seemed to be where Knothead and Puddles slept for any length of time.

Extracting himself reluctantly from the dogs, Greg stood and wandered around Hannah's place. Clearly there wasn't a whole lot of income going on here—tips probably weren't high dollar at the Classics Diner down the street where she worked as a waitress. Helluva note, that—only a block and a half to walk home from work Friday night and look what had happened. There was a double row of closets with flimsy folding doors across from the bed in the center of the apartment and he opened them both without thinking about it, then felt vaguely guilty as he stared at what was inside. Not much—in the first was a handful of sweaters and a few pair of jeans hanging alongside a winter coat, an extra waitress uniform, and two dark-colored dresses. He found himself wondering how Hannah, with her pale skin and wispy, equally light brown hair, would look in them. But the vision was too much like funeral attire, and he scowled as he pushed the doors closed. The other closet was surprisingly bare except for t-shirts and underclothes folded on a couple of shelves and one of those plastic filing crates, the cheapie things you could buy at Wal-Mart for a couple of bucks. It held no more than a dozen folders, each neatly marked—ELECTRIC, GAS, PAY STUBS and the like, and the only one that caught Greg's attention was labeled TRINITY MHC. What was that?

He took the crate out to where he could see better and, telling himself he'd been planning on checking her background anyway—it was part of the job—Greg flipped through the contents of the folder, raising an eyebrow when he discovered that the "MHC" part on the label referred to "Mental Health Center." There weren't that many papers inside, but their titles gave him a load of info—dateless form copies of things like *Patient's Release Instructions* and *Outpatient Help* seemed to corroborate Dr. Tansey's inferences back at Illinois Masonic. He paged through everything twice, but there was nothing else in the folder that was informative, except for a business card that he almost missed. On it was the name and telephone of a psychiatrist—Dr. Guido Gorrado—from Trinity Mental Health Center, and when Greg turned it over he saw that someone, Hannah perhaps, had written the man's home telephone number on the back in a feminine hand. He fingered it thoughtfully, then tucked it in his pocket; he'd check it out when he ran the background on Hannah, then put it back in the folder the next time he walked the dogs.

With a start, Greg realized it was getting late. Knothead and Puddles had abandoned their scrutiny of him for the comfort of the oval rug below the window in the living room, where they now lay curled around each other like dozing puppies. Greg checked the locks and let himself out with a final glance around Hannah's place. A bit more spacious than his own, but it was... emotionally bereft, nothing more than a box where a troubled woman lived and which would have been cold and empty without the presence of the two large and loveable dogs. The worn couch and inexpensive television, the small, no-name stereo setup on a beat-up bookcase next to it... all of this said something deeper and far more heartbreaking than financial poverty. If it hadn't been for the limitless affection offered her by those two animals and the love she obviously had for them, Greg might have thought Hannah had, indeed, tried to cut her own throat. But if people who truly wanted to die were worried about what was going to happen to those they left behind, animal or human, they generally made arrangements for them before taking that final step.

No, he thought as he went down the stairs and stepped outside and into the Saturday afternoon traffic now clogging the sidewalk. The apartment he'd just left was barren, but it was also incomplete... waiting, *wanting.* Instinct told him that Hannah Danior didn't want to die at all.

She wanted very much to live.

«««—»»»

"Hey, hey, if it isn't St. Gregory."

Sitting behind his desk, Greg looked up as his partner shoved a pile of papers aside and settled on one end of it. "Done with your do-goodly-doggy-duty for today?"

"For now," he told Tony. "I'll stop by and walk them again late tonight."

Tony raised one dark eyebrow. "So what's the deal here? You got a thing for this Hannah? I think she's weird as a three-headed frog—did you see those scars?"

"No, fool, I don't have a 'thing' for her." Greg tapped the file on his desk. "Quite an interesting history on her though. Did you see it?"

"No," his partner said and folded his arms. "I thought we dead-ended yesterday with her insistence that she doesn't remember anything about the attack. Anything else is a waste of time and energy."

"You give up too easily." Greg pulled out the business card he'd filched from Hannah's files and pushed it toward Tony. "I talked to this guy's assistant. She'd only tell me a few things over the phone, but said if we go out and talk to her, where she can see that we really *are* cops, she's positive the doctor himself will want to speak with us."

Tony looked surprised as he checked out the card. "Well, that *is* interesting. None of the usual patient confidentiality crap?"

"Nope. The impression I got was that if we identify ourselves and they're satisfied, they'll open wide."

"Uh-huh. And exactly why is it we want to drive all the way to—" He peered at the address. "St. Charles?"

Greg leaned forward. "Come on, Tony. Are you trying to tell me there's nothing strange about the way Hannah's injury *exactly* matches Eloise Addison's?"

Tony stood and handed back the business card. "I never said that."

"But…?"

"But I think you're trying to climb cobwebs here. I mean, it can't be more obvious—the guy who killed Addison went for Hannah, but just didn't quite hit his mark."

"Maybe." Greg tidied up the papers on his desk. "But there isn't any connection between the two women, and Hannah told us she hasn't dated anyone since she arrived in Chicago. It's also a completely different crime scene—one hidden and well-planned, the other in front of God and everyone else on the street."

Tony's expression was dubious. "So what's your point? We probably just haven't *found* the connection yet."

"I don't know," Greg said thoughtfully. "I guess I'm wondering if maybe she knows the killer somehow, maybe there's some kind of twisted relationship thing going on here that—duh—she isn't telling us about, a kind of kinky pre-crime practice-on-me type of thing."

"That'd be different," Tony said. "Do me first, then do someone else? You really believe that?"

"Find me another way to explain the wounds. Hannah's injury is like a mirror image of Eloise Addison's." He swept up the folder and tossed it into one of the desk drawers.

Tony was silent for a moment. "All right. When are we going to St. Charles?"

"Monday," Greg told him. "Dr. Gorrado doesn't do Sundays. Big surprise there."

"Okay." Tony brought out his notebook and jotted it on his schedule. "So what are you up to tomorrow?"

"Day off," Greg said. "Keeps me sane. Training in the morning, then I'm gonna come home and stay around the neighborhood. Check on Hannah's dogs now and then."

As Greg picked up his jacket, Tony fell into step beside him. "So how's it going with that martial arts stuff? You've been doing it for how long now—couple of years?"

"Yeah," Greg said. "It's going well and I like it a lot—it's a real stress reliever, good workout and great people."

"Plus they teach you how to kick ass, huh?" Tony grinned.

Greg smiled ruefully. "Self-defense, Tony. Not offense. And respect."

"Sure." His partner sounded anything but convinced and Greg knew from dozens of conversations just like this one that there was no convincing Tony otherwise.

"You should try it sometime," Greg said. "It would teach you how to deal better with people—"

"There's nothing wrong with the way I deal," Tony said flatly.

Oops—hit a nerve there. "Of course not," Greg said smoothly. "But it's a great way to stay in shape, lots of fun."

"Nice try, farm boy." Tony glanced at him out of the corner of one eye. "But I got a wife and kid who suck up every spare bit of time and money I get my hands on. And I'm not exactly packing any extra weight."

True enough. Tony was tall and lean, with dark good looks and an athletic build that always caught the eyes of the ladies. Tony, of course, played up to the attention constantly, and sometimes Greg wondered just how faithful he was to Dara, who seemed to worship him and tolerate a lot more of Tony's biting sarcasm than Greg would have ever taken. Then again, Greg's mother had suffered through his father's coldness without comment. Was that what marriage was all about—endurance? No thanks. "So," he said, curious despite himself. "What are your big Sunday plans?"

As they pushed through the doors of the 19th District Police Station, Tony looked sideways at him. "Not much. Hey, maybe I ought to ask around on your girlfriend's case."

Greg sent his partner a sharp glance. "Don't get stupid on me. I'm just helping out because it's convenient and I feel bad for the dogs—there's no other connection."

"Sure," Tony said with a rare and utterly false show of amiability. "Anyway, I'll check stuff out, see if anything else comes up."

Greg nodded. "Let me know if you find anything interesting."

"Should I call you at home or at… Hannah's?"

"Very funny."

Tony laughed and slapped him on the back. "You're too easy, Greg. See you."

Greg managed a half-hearted smile and watched him stroll away. Maybe Tony was right—he *was* too easy, a no-miss target for Tony's constant needling. But there was a difference between pals who teased you because they liked you and someone who did it only to see how much they could aggravate you. What, he wondered, would Tony do if he actually did blow up at him? Perhaps it was a test, a competition thing… or was Tony simply looking for an excuse to get physical with him? Or maybe it was nothing but Greg's own psyche inventing causes and effects that simply didn't exist; some people were just born jerks, harmless but constantly annoying. He couldn't explain it, but Tony had hit a bit of his own nerve with this Hannah thing. There was nothing there beyond the animal lover in him—first and foremost, Hannah was a case to him, a number in the assault with a deadly weapon statistics.

Then why did the idea of Tony asking anyone, any*thing* about Hannah Danior, leave a taste in his mouth like three-week-old milk?

Sunday—October 1st...

Classics Dinner was a 1960s-style restaurant on the corner of Belmont and Sheffield, done up in the appropriate black, white and red color scheme and sporting lots of checkerboard patterns and chrome, with little replicas of the old-fashioned button-type jukeboxes on the walls by every booth. The place was hopping on this early Sunday afternoon, with a constant stream of customers and a harried, overloaded wait staff. Tony thought it might have been a better idea to come by on a slower weekday, but that was too bad. Hannah might be released by then and he wanted to check things out with her employer before that happened. He didn't for a moment believe Greg's far-fetched speculation that she was involved in a perverted game of imitation murder, but there *was* another connection. The exact nature of that—the hows and whys—remained to be discovered, but he was damned well going to figure it out.

Ignoring the surprised looks of the workers, he pushed through the EMPLOYEES ONLY door and headed for the small, glassed-in manager's office he spotted off to the right. The guy inside, who wore a name tag that said MR. ZUBRO, MANAGER, was short and a little on the heavyset side—too many of the big burgers served in his own place. He was wearing a shirt with the sleeves rolled up, and Tony could see blotches of moisture seeping across the fabric under the arms and at the sides of the loosened tie around the man's neck. More than that, the cranky expression on his face when he saw Tony gave evidence he wasn't fond of his little place off the heat of the kitchen.

"Hey, what are you doing in here?" Zubro demanded. "This is an employees only area."

"Consider me a temp," Tony said and held out his badge.

Zubro's eyebrows lifted and he put down his pen. "What can I do for you?"

The detective dropped onto a metal folding chair that had been crammed into the small space between the front of the manager's desk and the wall. "I have a couple of questions about one of your employees, Hannah Danior."

Zubro nodded. "Yeah—of course you do. Helluva thing, that attack. Winnie tells me Hannah's still in the hospital."

"Winnie?"

Zubro waved toward the restaurant. "One of the waitresses. She and Hannah are chummy."

Tony made a mental note to talk to this woman after he was done here. "So what do you know about Hannah?"

The manager shrugged and pulled a key ring from his pocket, swivelled on his chair and unlocked a file cabinet behind him. After a few seconds, he selected a manilla folder from the drawer and opened it, but there wasn't much inside. From where he sat Tony could already tell that there was zip to see on the employment application. "I know what she looks like and what's in here," he said. "And that most of the time she shows up for work when she's supposed to. Other than that, I don't get involved with the help."

Zubro shoved the folder toward Tony and the detective glanced through it, noting that under both 'Previous Address' and 'Education' Hannah had written only St. Charles, Illinois. No work experience, no next of kin. "Didn't give much in the way of references, did she?" he said and tossed the file back on the desk.

Zubro gave him a bland look. "I needed a waitress, not a rocket scientist. As long as she knew how to add and could remember what hamburger went to which table, things were copacetic."

"Uh-huh." He wasn't going to get anywhere here. "This Winnie person—"

"Winnie Harbin. She's out front, short black hair, brown eyes." Zubro was anything but pleased. "Don't keep her too long. I've got a full Saturday crowd here."

"I'll keep her as long as I need to," Tony said without missing a beat.

He rose and walked out, grinning to himself when he heard the man cuss under his breath. There were damned few people in this world whom he'd allow to order him around, and this fat, scummy little manager sure wasn't one of them.

The diner was a swirl of motion, people moving in and out from the kitchen and behind the counter, voices calling out, plates rattling and old music blaring from the ceiling speakers. It reminded him of a beehive—at first glance there didn't seem to be any particular order to anything, but no one collided or hindered, and everything got done the way it was supposed to. The Harbin woman, pretty in a petite, slightly boyish way, was standing at a booth by the west window taking a food order from four teenagers who were trying to flirt with her but probably wouldn't leave over a dollar's tip between all of them. Tony caught her when she hustled up and shoved the ticket onto one of the fry wheels then made for the soda machine.

"Winnie Harbin?"

"Who wants to know?" she asked without actually looking at him. She loaded a tray with plastic water tumblers, silverware and napkins, then started filling over-sized glasses with Pepsi, deftly avoiding getting the soda spray on her white uniform.

Tony took out his badge and waved it between her and the soda machine. "Detective Tony Rutland. I want to ask you a few questions about Hannah Danior."

Now Winnie Harbin did glance at him. "Ask away. Kind of busy, so you'll have to fit it into the gaps."

Tony frowned. "Would you just stop for a minute?"

"No," she retorted. "I'll be glad to tell you whatever I can, but in case you haven't noticed, I'm trying to scrape out a living here." Without waiting for a response, she hoisted the now full tray and headed back to the booth.

When she returned, Tony tried to block her way with his body but she ducked around him to get to the food window. He had to admire her speed. "Listen," he began. "I don't want to have to—"

"I know you're a cop," Winnie interrupted, "but I never believed that crap about how the word is a synonym for asshole. You gonna prove me wrong?"

Tony started to snap at her, then stopped, unable to halt the grin that wanted to tug at the corner of his mouth—he didn't know whether to like or smack this scrappy little woman. "I just want to find out who attacked Hannah Danior," he said. "Preferably before he targets someone else. But Hannah isn't talking."

"Because she doesn't remember," Winnie said.

"I don't believe that."

Winnie shrugged, her movement never stopping as she pulled plates off the window and compared them against a ticket in her book. "Believe me, if she knew how it happened she'd tell you."

Tony stared hard at the waitress. "How?"

"How, why, whatever." Winnie hesitated. "The girl has problems, okay? That's all I can say. If she wants to tell you about them, she will. Otherwise…" She shrugged again.

"These problems have anything to do with Trinity Mental Health Center?" he asked.

Winnie slammed a plate onto her tray, then spun to face him. "Are you *trying* to get her canned? Maybe they are, and maybe not, but you can bet King Zubro'll use any excuse he can to bounce Hannah because of the work she's missed. He can't do it because of the attack, but he'll damned sure use that Trinity business if he finds out about it." Her expression was furious. "What the hell's the matter with you? Hannah's the *victim* here, not the criminal. A little sympathy wouldn't hurt."

Tony smiled darkly. "That's not in my job description."

"Call me surprised," Winnie said as she lifted her filled tray. "I don't know anything to tell you and I've got nothing more to say anyway, except that if you blab about that Trinity thing to Zubro and Hannah loses her job because of it, I'll call your Sargent or captain or *someone* and do my part to make you just as miserable."

He nodded and leaned back so she could pass him in the cramped space behind the counter. "I understand, *Miss* Harbin."

She gave him a dirty look but said nothing. He let her get almost out of range, then eased one foot out and hooked her right ankle as she stepped forward. In an instant, both Winnie and the full tray of food went crashing to the floor in a spray of broken stoneware and french fries.

Several employees hurried over to help her up and clean up the mess. Tony just stood there, looking down as she glared at him and brushed herself off.

"My, my," the detective said gently as he turned to leave. "Looks like you really need to watch your step."

«««—»»»

If I wasn't insane, this place would drive me to it, Hannah thought for at least the tenth time that day.

The door to her room was open, and she could hear wailing down the hall. It was a non-stop thing—forty minutes now—full-throated and with barely enough time in between for breathing. She still wondered where the man or woman (she couldn't tell) found the lung power, but she'd given up on speculating as to the cause of the cries. As she well knew, life gave you plenty of reasons to protest.

Early this morning Hannah had tried, stupidly so, to sneak out, so Tansey had gotten nasty and ordered her put back in restraints. She'd been placed in a rare two-bed room, one of those medically-oriented ones generally reserved for the more seriously physically injured among the psych patients, and right now she was the only patient occupying it. Hannah supposed she was lucky—right after that detective had left with her keys she'd gotten a roommate, a not-heavily-enough-sedated woman with vacant eyes and a face and hands that were cut in a dozen places and pocked with big, purplish-black bruises. She was gone now, transferred to a private facility this morning by an absentee husband, and just in time, too—one of the duty nurses had come in response to Hannah's shouts and found the woman leaning over Hannah's bed, drooling and smiling as she mindlessly wound the cord from the unplugged hospital bed around Hannah's eyes.

The restraints had been removed, but Hannah had learned her lesson. Everything around here was locked and guarded, and no matter how much she wanted out, she wasn't going anywhere until Tansey allowed it. She didn't know why the doctor had taken this personal interest in her—vendetta was more like it—but as with a lot of other arenas in her life, she was helpless to do anything but wait out the storm and hope she'd get a break at the end.

The voice of the unseen wailer was joined by someone else's, this one a man who started screaming—*"Shut up shut up shut up!"*—hysterically. Hannah winced; surely to God the staff hadn't left some poor schmuck tied down in the same room with that motormouth.

"Christ on a scooter, this is a noisy place," said a familiar voice.

Hannah grinned as Winnie sauntered in and her spirits lifted for the first time since getting stuck in this miserable ward. The racket from outside the room abruptly ceased, and for a moment the silence was disconcerting. Then Winnie raised an eyebrow. "I gave'em that age-old hint: *Duct tape is your friend*," she said. "Guess they took my advice to heart. Or mouth."

Hannah laughed and Winnie dragged an ugly, plastic-covered chair over to her bedside, unmindful of the screech and the long black marks it left on the linoleum. "I had a balloon," her friend told her as she dropped onto the seat. "Big red thing with a yellow Tweety Bird on it. But they wouldn't let me bring it in—said it might scare some of the patients." Winnie's smile was wicked. "Too bad, huh? I was thinking you could suck on the helium and screw with their minds."

Hannah chuckled. "You're nuts. They should put you in this bed, not me."

Winnie tilted her head. "I'm just exploring all possible avenues of entertainment." She studied Hannah, her gaze lingering on the bandage wrapped around her throat. "So what happened this time?" she asked bluntly. "I mean, I knew it was bad when a jerk-off cop came by the Diner, but Christ—your *throat?*"

Hannah blinked, surprised. "This cop was a jerk? Was he a blond guy, named—"

"Nah. Dark-hair. Nice looking but what a bastard. He never said his name."

"Huh." Hannah sat up and swung her legs over the side of the bed. "He was here with the other guy, but I don't know much about him—well, either of them, really. His partner's okay, though."

Winnie leaned forward, interested. "What's this? A spark?"

Hannah glared at her. "Don't be an idiotic. He's just walking the dogs for me."

Her friend's mouth dropped open. "You gave him the key to your place?"

"What was I supposed to do?" she demanded. "You'd end up in an allergic coma or some damned thing, and there wasn't anyone else. Besides, he offered."

Winnie made a disbelieving sound in her throat. "Guy could be going through your stuff right now, everything you own—"

"And we both know what a storehouse of wealth my apartment is," Hannah reminded her with a tinge of sarcasm. "There's a whole box full of cash, jewels and bearer bonds I never told you about."

"Fine." Winnie sat back again. "Just watch out for the other one." She held up her palms and Hannah saw they were scraped and nicked. "Would you believe the bastard tripped me at work when I said I didn't have anything to tell him? He thinks no one saw him but one of the busboys told me later that he did—course he doesn't have a green card, so he's not saying anything. Anyway, I dropped a full tray of food and Zubro docked me thirty bucks out of my check."

"What! He can't do that!"

Winnie waved off her protest. "What am I gonna do—go on strike? Whatever. But I could swear the guy was threatening me. He told me to watch my step or something like that."

"Man," Hannah said. "That's *awful.* I can't believe he tripped you—I wonder if his partner knows about this?"

"Probably," Winnie said without hesitation. "He might be just like him—how would you know?"

Hannah thought about this. She wouldn't, of course, even though Jedrek seemed totally different. Plus, it didn't make any sense to bully Winnie—that certainly wouldn't get… what was his name? Rutland, that was it. It wouldn't get Rutland any information. Hell, if she knew the answers about where her injury had come from, she'd gladly tell them everything.

But she didn't.

"So this time it was your neck?" Winnie asked again, as if she could sense the direction Hannah's thoughts had taken. "Must have been pretty bad to land you in here."

"Yeah." Hannah stared at her fingertips, which were cracked and dry from having her hands wet too much at work and never using lotion. What was the difference, anyway? She was going to look like Frankenstein when this bandage came off, even more so than she already did. "Stitches almost ear to ear. I don't even know how many."

"Christ," Winnie said softly.

She didn't say anything else and after a few moments Hannah looked up and gave her friend—her *only* friend—a wan smile. "Thanks for believing me, Win."

Winnie flushed. "We're gal-pals, remember? Been there, seen that." She cleared her throat. "So when do you get free? Hell, I can't even call and talk to you here—the only phone's at the nurses' desk."

Hannah made a face. "I don't know. It's the same doctor as last April.

Dr. Tansey, remember her? So she's all weirded out about it, thinks I'm suicidal."

"Uh-oh."

"Yeah. I tried leaving and ended up strapped to the bed like a mental case."

Winnie's eyes widened. "No shit? They tied you down?"

Hannah held up her wrists, showing pale skin striped with bruises where the leather had cut into her. "Guess I won't try that again. Being the only sane person and strapped to the bed while the maniacs drool on your face ain't fun."

Her best friend's face twisted in helpless anger. "There's got to be someone I can call about this," she said firmly. "Some social agency or—"

"Forget it," Hannah cut in. "I'll be out of here in no time." She prodded gingerly at the wrappings under her chin. "I think they're just waiting to make sure this heals up—it was pretty deep and they kind of freaked."

"All right." Winnie stood, then stepped over and gave her a gentle hug. "I've got to go meet Rex, but you call me when they let you out. I'll come and get you, okay?"

Hannah cringed inwardly, imagining a bumpy ride to her place in Win's ridiculously battered and tiny Fiat Cabriolet. No doubt her boyfriend would be in the cramped backseat and bitching the entire time about how bad the car's shocks were, his charming English accent the only thing making his overly loud tirade bearable. "It's only a few blocks and they always let you out during the daytime," she reminded Winnie. "I can walk it."

"Excuse me, am I speaking alien here?" Winnie rolled her eyes and pointed at Hannah. "You patient, me taxi. Got it?"

Why fight it? "I'll call."

"Home *or* at the Diner. I don't give a shit what Zubro says." Winnie gave her a peck on one cheek. "And for Christ's sake, watch your back around here. It's full of crazy people."

Hannah giggled and watched Winnie leave, grateful for her friendship and, above all, her faith.

Monday—October 2nd...

"Well, it just figures this place would be in a 'burb that's nowhere near an expressway."

Greg glanced over at his grumbling partner, who was staring out the window at the scenery along Route 64. It was actually a pretty nice day, and a pretty nice drive—only a few weeks into fall but it seemed the seasons were changing a bit early this year, the heavy trees already well on their way to shades of red and gold. "We're almost there," he said reflexively. "Maybe another fifteen minutes."

"Didn't you say that a half hour ago?"

"C'mon," Greg said. "Look at it as a rare chance to get away from the crowds and traffic in the city. And all the exhaust fumes."

"Until it's time to go back and we find ourselves smack in the middle of rush hour," Tony retorted. "Then you can sing to me again about exhaust-free air."

Greg chuckled and nodded at the dashboard clock. "It's still early. If we're lucky, we'll miss that by a mile."

"Luck?" Tony pushed his hair back, his jerky movement more telling about his mood than anything else. "Luck is a nasty old bitch with a shriveled heart who likes to stab people in the back. You want luck, you have to make your own."

Greg glanced at Tony, amused. "So what did you step in on the way to work, chum?"

"Same old stuff," his partner answered. "A list of things to do eight miles long—drive Ben here, pick up this there, what time are you going to be home, on and on. The joy of marriage."

Greg held his comments, but couldn't help wondering about Tony's attitude. He'd only met Dara and Ben once, Tony's wife and eight-year-old son, but both had seemed a little too reticent to be as demanding as Tony often described them. While it was true that Greg wasn't high on the marriage concept himself, Dara Rutland had seemed attentive and considerate of her family, and it was clear that she adored Tony and wanted only to please him. Greg was having trouble putting that memory together with the harpy that Tony insisted he had waiting for him at home every night. There was also the minor thing that Tony seemed the least likely person in the world to tolerate a spouse who fit the description he kept trying to convey.

"Route 25," Greg said suddenly, glad for the chance to change a subject he should have known better than to address anyway. "We turn here, and it should only be another mile or so to Trinity Boulevard. Then we turn left and we're there."

"Great," Tony said sourly.

"Nice out here," Greg tilted his head at the hundred-year-old homes they were driving past, all set on spacious, neatly manicured lawns big enough to hold small Chicago apartment buildings. Late blooming flowers bordered porches with rocking chairs, and old-fashioned lawn ornaments—wagon wheels, quaint antique wheelbarrows and the like—further added to the ambiance.

"Yeah," Tony said. "Whitebread America. Ain't life grand."

Greg pressed his lips together—so much for his attempt to find the blandest, safest topic of conversation. "Here's our street," he said and turned his car, a 1998 Jeep Cherokee, abruptly to the left. Tony swore when his elbow banged against the door and Greg thought it served him right; it wasn't often that he let his partner get to him, but damn… today Tony was just being a pain in the ass. He hoped the ride home wasn't as long as this one. "That's it up there."

"Where'd you learn to drive?" Tony demanded, rubbing his arm. "Race track?"

"Something like that," Greg said with a forced grin. His gaze stopped briefly on the other man's left hand, where a splattering of bruises showed across the knuckles. "What happened to your hand?"

"Banged it in the garage," Tony answered vaguely.

"Huh." Greg turned the wheel again and swung into a wide driveway next to a discreetly-sized maroon sign with white letters that read *Trinity Mental Health Center.* "We have arrived."

"Let's park this black buggy and find Dr. what's-his-name." Tony dug into his shirt pocket and came out with a piece of notepaper.

"Gorrado," Greg finished for him. "Guido Gorrado."

"Now there's a name," Tony said sarcastically.

"Whatever." It was all Greg could do not to snap as he rolled the Jeep into a spot, but no—he'd be damned if he'd take on Tony's shitty attitude. "Let's just find his office. Come on."

Tony got out and followed him up the walkway without saying anything else, apparently giving up on his attempt, for now, to goad Greg into a verbal contest. The building in front of them was as old or older than the houses they'd passed out on Route 25, but big and imposing, built back when dark red brick and ornate, stone-rimmed windows had been all the rage. It would have seemed more fitting beneath a sky laden with thunderous clouds, perhaps on the set of some cheesy horror flick, than here, sitting serenely below a sun-filled, gorgeous weekday. A thousand mini-panes of glass sparkled down at them, and it was only when they got closer that Greg saw the metal mesh embedded in each, the sole outward indication that here was anything more complicated than a hospital, or perhaps an expensive private school.

Inside, at least in the overly large reception area and waiting room, was the same calm and cool atmosphere. Lots of varnished oak woodwork and lamp lighting around comfortable looking stuffed chairs and couches—whatever dirty work happened in the mental world didn't occur in the quiet expanse out here, beneath the scrutiny of God or anyone else. The floor was covered by an elegantly-patterned area rug and their footsteps managed to sound offensively loud when their heels tapped on the two-foot hardwood space between the door and the rug.

An older woman with expertly coiffed silver hair looked up from, of all things, an issue of *Scientific American* and gave them a professional smile. "May I help you?"

Greg pulled out his badge. "Detective Gregory Jedrek. My partner and I were told to come out this morning and ask for Dr. Gorrado."

She studied the detective badge carefully, as though she were used to such things being forgeries, before nodding and reaching for the telephone. "Have a seat, please. I'll page his assistant."

They did what they were told, with Tony keeping mercifully silent. The wait wasn't long—no more than five minutes—then a door at the other end of the room opened and a young woman stepped through and gestured at them. "Detectives," she said cordially. "I'm Ms. Tuwile, Dr. Gorrado's assistant. If you'll follow me, he's waiting for you in his office."

"Thanks," Greg said, amused when his partner made a *Wow, do you see this?* face at him behind the woman's back. She *was* lovely—tall and slender, with her auburn hair cut into a businesswoman's classy style and light blue eyes. An expensive suit completed the no-nonsense picture, but its forest green color only highlighted an exceptionally pretty face, one that obviously had his partner's total attention.

Proving this, Tony lengthened his stride until he passed Greg and could speak directly to their guide. "So," he said in a completely different tone of voice than the one Greg had endured on the trip out here, "Tuwile—that's an interesting name. I don't believe I've ever heard it before."

She led them to an elevator and pushed the UP button. "It's not very common," she said without further explanation, and Greg almost grinned. Tony ought to know better—working in a mental health center, the woman was probably an expert at keeping personal information from strangers, and she looked way too smart to be dazzled by a cop's badge. Tony, however, was undaunted. "Tony Rutland," he said and stuck out his hand, knowing she'd have to take it or seem impossibly rude. She did so, and Greg had to admire the way she kept her face impassive when Tony obviously held on too long. "My partner, Greg Jedrek." Greg nodded and touched a finger to his forehead, sparing her a repeat handshake. Tony looked at the pretty young woman expectantly, waiting. "Janice," she finally said, but with clear reluctance. "Janice Tuwile."

"That name again," Tony said with an engaging grin.

"My husband's family name," she said cooly, and Greg almost laughed. He saw Tony glance automatically at Ms. Tuwile's left hand and frown because she wasn't wearing a ring. She could be lying about being married, but Greg would bet she wasn't. She wasn't wearing earrings—maybe she simply didn't like jewelry. Or maybe she simply wasn't interested in Tony. As he often did, Greg wondered again about his partner; was this just a harmless flirtation, or was Tony not the best of family men? In any event, it wasn't Greg's job to judge his partner, so it was best he just stayed out of it.

Tony started to say something else, then the elevator door slid open and they joined a couple of other staff members inside. A stop and a start, then a final stop, and they stepped off the elevator into an office area that was quite a bit busier and more crowded than the hushed reception area on the first floor. "This way, please," Janice Tuwile said and led them to an open office door. "Dr. Gorrado is waiting for you."

Before either of them could so much as thank her, she slipped down the hallway and turned the corner. Tony's look of frustration wasn't lost on Greg, although he thought his partner deserved the woman's rather cold exit in return for his blatant and manipulative behavior. "The ice queen cometh," Tony muttered under his breath.

"Looks more like the ice queen goeth," Greg shot back.

A pleasant, rich voice cut off what would have been Tony's retort. "Gentlemen, please come in and have a seat. I'm Dr. Guido Gorrado."

The man who rose from behind a desk to greet them was a handsome black man in his late fifties with a high forehead and a beard below short hair gone a distinguished white. Dressed in high-money casual, Greg could see the muscles of an athletic build moving beneath the doctor's expensive brown sweater, and when he shook hands with Greg, Gorrado's grip was firm but calculated not to be too strong or overwhelming, as if he were very aware of his own strength. Faint traces of an Italian accent cut through his speech, giving, perhaps, some groundwork for the man's name.

Greg introduced himself and then Tony, and the two settled on small but comfortable leather chairs across from the doctor's paper-crowded desk. The office wasn't large but it wasn't tiny, either, and it was clearly the work space of a man more concerned with results than appearances. A laptop computer in standby mode was pushed off to the side next to a pile of patient files and legal pads crammed with writing, more files were lined up against one wall below an arrangement of degrees and certificates. The wall behind the doctor's desk was divided by a tall, arched window through which Greg could see only the heavy foliage of a golden-leafed maple swinging in the outside breeze.

"I understand you want to know about Hannah Danior," Dr. Gorrado said, getting right to the point. "I have her case history right here. There's a lot you might find interesting."

Greg nodded, momentarily taken aback. "I… have to say, doctor, that it's rather unusual to get this kind of cooperation in the medical field," he finally said. "We usually run into the doctor-patient confidentiality thing." Tony gave him a sharp look, as if to say *Don't remind him of it!* but Greg ignored him.

Dr. Gorrado nodded, but still brought up a file, easily two inches thick, then spread it open on top of the papers already littering the desk's surface. "True, but that attitude is generally used to protect a patient whose history or disclosures may endanger his or herself—surely in your profession you realize this. With certain patients there are times when the doctor may choose to divulge information because he feels it may be of benefit." He regarded Greg with clear brown eyes. "This is my feeling with Hannah. I haven't been able to reach Hannah—I understand she's being temporarily held in the psychiatric ward at Illinois Masonic—and I've received only the most cursory information from the office there, so first I'd like you to explain what she's doing there and why it prompted your trip out here."

"She was attacked," Greg told him without hesitation. "Her throat was cut very close to the time when another young woman died of injuries she received from the same kind of attack a couple of miles away." He went on to give the psychiatrist as much of the details as were pertinent, ending with Dr. Tansey's speculation that Hannah had injured herself and Hannah's insistence that she remembered nothing about the crime. "Her history here at Trinity came up," he said carefully, "so that's when I called you."

Dr. Gorrado raised an eyebrow and Greg had the distinct impression the intelligent man knew he hadn't come by the Trinity "history" in the more accepted manner, but he didn't push it. "I worked with Hannah for nearly twelve years," he said, "so even without seeing her recently I feel fairly confident that this injury was not self-inflicted. I also believe her statement that she doesn't remember the attack."

Greg blinked. Twelve years? "What—"

Dr. Gorrado pulled a yellowed piece of paper from the back of the file and pushed it toward him. "I think this will answer about ninety percent of the question you were about to ask."

Greg took the paper and Tony leaned over to read it with him. It only took a few seconds for what they were reading to sink in. "Whoa," Greg said.

Dr. Gorrado gave them a couple of more minutes to study the text, then folded his hands and sat back. "As you can see, that young woman's start at life was rather challenging, to say the least."

Greg rubbed his forehead, noting that there were two more pages to the report that he had yet to read. "The child in this police report is the same Hannah Danior?" he asked. "It's hard to believe *anyone* could recover from something like this."

"Wait," Tony said, still straining to read over Greg's shoulder. "I only got part of what this says—"

"Let me summarize it as best I can," Dr. Gorrado said. "When Hannah was five years old, she and the eighteen-month-old daughter of her foster parents were abducted from their house while the mother was in the backyard. In the police hunt that followed, Hannah was eventually discovered in a small cave by the railroad tracks in their town, where she'd been sexually assaulted and tortured by a pedophile drifter. The toddler's body was also found, buried off to the side in the cave, and an autopsy revealed the toddler had undergone the same fate."

Greg nodded and fast-flipped through the paperwork, then scowled. "But this says there was no conviction on the murder of—what's her name? Amy Terrell."

"While they had clear medical evidence that the drifter had assaulted Hannah, they could not prove that he had ever done anything to Amy Terrell other than bury her body, which he claimed was in 'his' cave—along with Hannah—when he returned to it. According to forensics, although he never had gloves, apparently he picked up the corpse by wrapping it in a dirty shirt—he never even so much as came into contact with Amy's skin. Some of the implements used to torture Amy and Hannah—various gardening tools—had clearly been handled by the accused, but some had *not*… yet all were stained by blood from both children."

"Then someone else was involved," Tony said.

Gorrado nodded. "A further examination revealed that Hannah had been enduring sexual abuse for several years at the time this happened. The gardening tools were found to belong to her foster father, Boris Terrell."

"You just gotta love that foster care system," Tony said caustically. "What about DNA testing?"

"At the time it was nearly-new technology," the doctor told him. "Expensive and not widely used. Two years after Scott Cutler—the drifter—was incarcerated, he was killed in prison, so the option was never explored. Boris was charged but later acquitted because the bodily fluids found on both children did *not* match his, but it still left him under suspicion. There were two other foster children in the family, Hannah's brothers, and they were immediately removed from the family and put back into the system."

"Where were they when Hannah and Amy were taken?" Greg asked.

"The foster mother had sent them to the park to play, and the police retrieved them as soon as she called about the missing girls."

Greg flipped through the pages until he found what he was looking for. "'Butch and Carl, ages ten and twelve,'" he read. "'Found making mud pies in Clyde Park.' Where are they now?"

"Not a clue," Gorrado said. "I tried to find them when Hannah was thirteen, but they'd been adopted and the records were sealed. Given the violent nature of the family's past, I deemed it better not to pursue the matter. Hannah's natural parents are dead."

Tony looked from the report to the psychiatrist. "Wait a second. She was thirteen? Why did you wait so long to do that?"

Dr. Gorrado regarded the two detectives calmly. "Because Hannah Danior was catatonic for seven years after she was rescued from that cave."

Greg stared at him. *"Catatonic?"*

"Completely." The doctor took the old police report from Greg and tucked it in the back of the folder, then skimmed further through the papers. "Suffice to say we tried various methods of treatment, some perhaps a bit on the radical side, but all without success."

"What finally did the trick?" Tony asked.

Dr. Gorrado lifted his chin. "Frankly, we don't know, but I suspect it was a trauma very much like what she endured at five years old. The night duty nurse discovered Hannah crying but fully lucid on a Saturday night. Her throat was severely bruised and a further examination suggested she'd been raped, but there was no actually physical *evidence* of the attack—no semen or flakes of skin, nothing. It caused quite a scandal at the hospital—all the male patients were checked, and all the orderlies as well—but ultimately no charged were brought against anyone."

"And she didn't remember this either?" Tony looked skeptical.

"According to Hannah, she woke up in the dark feeling bruised and sore, but there was no one around. Since she was only thirteen at the time and we felt her mental status was fragile at best, we opted to focus on rehabilitation rather than reexamining and emphasizing the traumas she'd suffered."

A reasonable thing, Greg thought. "And since then?"

Dr. Gorrado was silent for a moment, as if thinking of how best to explain. "As you might expect, it wasn't easy," he said at last. "She had nightmares constantly, was extremely paranoid, slept very little during the first year after she came out of her state of shock. She had daily counseling and one-on-one tutoring, and getting her to the point where she could be around other people without being terrified was quite a feat. Medication helped, but it also slowed her ability to comprehend, and she was already seven years behind in her mental and educational development, not to mention having to undergo physical rehabilitation—when someone doesn't use their muscles for seven years, they have very little body strength. She wasn't able to attend a normal high school, but she did test for and earn her GED at age twenty." Gorrado looked pleased at the memory. "At that point she made the decision to discontinue her anti-depressant medication and try to live a normal life. I haven't seen her in nearly two years, but she does call now and then." He smiled briefly. "I more or less promised her free telephone counseling for the rest of her life. From what I could tell, until this incident on Saturday, she was doing well, even taking a couple of college courses per semester. I recall her telling me her goal is to be a special education teacher."

"Uh-huh." Greg steepled his fingers together for a moment, then reached into his back pocket. "You say you haven't seen her for some time."

"That's correct."

"Well, Dr. Tansey—the ER doctor at Illinois Masonic—has," he told the psychiatrist. "As a matter of fact, she says she saw Hannah six months ago for another injury. Here's a copy of her patient summary." He handed it over.

Gorrado studied the paper with interest, his pleasant expression slowly morphing into a frown. "Well, this is disconcerting. According to this report, Hannah has clearly been the victim of multiple injuries. 'Heavy scarring on upper left chest consistent with stab wound, scar through right eyebrow, scar of unknown cause on left side of neck beneath jaw line, fresh scar of indeterminate origin across left collarbone.'" His sharp gaze found Greg's. "Still, 'consistent with stab wound'—these are *not* the types of wounds a person usually inflicts upon themselves, even a seriously mentally ill patient. Those are generally more ritualistic and planned. Someone else is causing these injuries. Are there accident reports on file for any of these? Crime complaints?"

"Not a one." Greg folded his arms and looked from the doctor to Tony, then back again. "For most of them there aren't even records that indicate any medical treatment at all. This means that whatever she's been going through—if someone is hurting her or if she's somehow hurting herself—she's been dealing with it completely and utterly…

"Alone."

Tuesday—October 3rd...

Winnie Harbin had two undying passions in her life: books and music. Well, okay, she had a *lot* of undying passions in her life—after all, she was a well-rounded person—but those were two of the main ones. Music she got on a regular basis by taking guitar lessons at the Old Town School of Folk Music down on Lincoln Avenue. Books were a double treat—usually, anyway—because she got her supply of readable goodies at the Stars bookstore, conveniently located directly below the apartment of her best friend Hannah. In fact, they'd met in the store, reaching for the same book, and Winnie still grinned at the memory of how surprised Hannah had been when Winnie had shrugged and handed it over. Right now her pal was unfairly locked up in Illinois Masonic, so Winnie was going to have to be content with wandering around the bookstore alone for awhile, then heading home sans her usual ten minute stopover at Hannah's place, about all she could take because of the dogs.

Winnie loved this bookstore, much more so than the big chains or shopping at the mega-online booksellers. Anonymity wasn't something she particularly cherished—she got enough of that in her day to day world. The Diner was a great place for it, in fact; there she was the faceless waitress that most customers would never see again, and who gave a bat's ass if they left her a fifty-cent tip on an fifteen-dollar check. She wasn't a person with rent and bills and a piece of crap car that might or might not start. She got that same treatment at the grocery store, the gas station, and a thousand other places. But not here at Stars.

"Hi, Win. How are you?" Alice, the owner, looked up and smiled cheerfully from behind a counter crowded with papers, stacks of books and a tangerine-colored Mac. Photos of all sizes were taped to the wall behind the counter, and somewhere in there was one of her and Hannah wearing ridiculous costumes, taken at the last Stars Halloween party. Winnie had borrowed a friend's gown and made herself up as a vampire Countess Elizabeth Bathory, but Hannah's outfit had been a scream. A parody of the Bride of Frankenstein, Hannah had plastered white goop all over her face, blacked out her eyes, then wound her hair into in a hundred bobbing bits of tin foil. Bride of Frankenstein? She'd looked more like the Bride of *Beetlejuice*.

"Same as always," Winnie answered.

"Say," Alice said before Winnie could make her way any farther into the stacks. "How's Hannah doing? She looked in pretty bad shape when the paramedics packed her up."

Winnie stopped. "She's okay. Ought to be home in a day or two. A good thing because—" She stopped and they both looked up as something thumped hard across the ceiling. There was a scattering of sounds, running, then unmistakably the sound of someone walking.

Alice glanced at Winnie. "Funny… I'd assumed you were taking care of the dogs."

"Not unless I can do it while wearing a respirator. Hannah's got some friend of hers doing it." It was the easiest way she could think of to explain it. Winnie stood there for a second, then turned and headed for the door. "Think I'll go check upstairs and meet this guy."

Alice looked delighted. "Guy? Hannah's got a guy?"

"He's just a friend," Winnie said automatically, because she knew Hannah would want her to. "Some dude walking the pooches for her, that's all."

Still, as she stood outside and fished Hannah's extra key out of her bag, Winnie couldn't help fantasize a little. Hannah'd been through such a hellish existence, would it hurt the freakin' Universe to send a little happy in her direction? She let herself in and climbed the narrow staircase, then unlocked the door without bothering to knock. As she stepped through, too late she realized the noise might not be coming from the dog-walking cop, after all. It might be the other one, the asshole who'd tripped her at work. Hell, it might even be a burglar, or someone—

"Hi," said a male voice. "Can I help you?"

Her heart stuttered for a second, then calmed a bit as she stared at the guy standing at the end of the coffee table, a tug-of-war dog toy gripped in one fist. Knothead and Puddles whirled and saw her and she back-stepped instinctively; before they could ambush her, the man dropped the toy and snatched at their collars, holding them fast.

"I'm Winnie," she said. "Hannah's best friend. I was down in the bookstore and I heard noises up here. You must be—"

"Greg," he said. "I'm looking after the dogs for her."

"Right." For a moment neither of them said anything and Winnie grabbed the chance to scrutinize him. Nice-looking, in an all-American sort of way—short blond hair going a bit toward the spiky style, yuppie-style glasses, blue eyes, maybe six feet tall with an athletic build. He could've passed for a computer geek instead of a cop, and maybe that was intentional—all in all a bit too clean-cut for Winnie's tastes. But he looked safe enough for Hannah, and after all, he was a cop. Then again, so was that other moron.

"So," he began, "you—"

She sneezed.

"Uh-oh," he said.

"I'll be all ri—*ahhh-chooo!*"

"You were saying?" he asked mildly.

"I'll be downstairs," she managed, then sneezed three more times before getting the hell out of there. He must've stirred everything up, been playing with them for awhile—Hannah usually made a point of dusting and vacuuming if she knew Winnie was coming over, plus she'd send the dogs to "their rug" and tell them to stay put. Amazingly, they always obeyed.

By the time Officer Greg—as she'd already begun to call him in her mind—joined her on the sidewalk in front of Stars, Winnie had her sneezing under control, or had at least outlasted it. The "fresh" air of Belmont Avenue had cleared her sinuses of dog dander, doubtlessly replacing it with an unhealthy but at least tolerable level of carbon monoxide. Now she could expect to sneeze once or twice every ten minutes for the rest of the day. No biggie.

"Feeling any better?"

A bit surprised by the genuine concern in his voice, Winnie regarded the light-haired man curiously as he came out of the entry door, then automatically turned the knob to make sure it had locked behind him. "Yeah."

"You want to have a cup of coffee?" he asked. "We could go by the Diner—"

"Anywhere but there," she cut in. "It's not like I own stock in the place, you know?"

He grinned and glanced up the street. "What do you suggest?"

"I could do nachos," she said promptly. "Mexican place right up the block. How about it?"

He motioned at her. "Lead on."

Winnie did, but it was a short walk, only a couple of doors west. It wasn't long before they were settled amid a colorful array of painted wooden tables and chairs and waiting for a iced teas, both deciding against the choice of early-afternoon alcohol. People chattered and waiters moved constantly—the place was a kaleidoscope of color and noise. Still, it made Winnie feel comfortable, sort of like the Diner but not, full of a protective bunch of people but without the spying, prying eyes of a fat, greasy boss.

"So you and Hannah are best friends," the cop said after the waiter had taken Winnie's order. "Known each other awhile?"

"Not so long," Winnie answered, and took a sip of tea. "A little over two years. We met at the bookstore."

He smiled. "Seems like a fun place."

That was obvious, so she didn't comment. Instead, she said, "It's awfully nice of you to do the dog-duty thing."

This time his smile was more pronounced, crinkling up the corners of his eyes. "No problem. She needed a hand, and the pups and I are having a good time with it."

He didn't say anything for a few seconds, then his expression changed as he focused on her. Okay, she thought, here it comes.

"I'd like to lend a hand with something else, too," he said. "I'd really like to find out who attacked Hannah in front of her doorway."

"If she knew, she'd tell you," Winnie said carefully. She picked up her water glass and took a sip, giving her eyes somewhere else to look besides into his.

"Really." Officer Greg folded his arms. "And what about you—if you knew, would *you* tell me?"

"Of course."

He leaned forward. "Because I get the feeling that there's a whole lot more going on here than she's willing to admit."

"Look," Winnie said impatiently. "She doesn't know who's doing this stuff, okay? If she…"

Damn.

Nothing stupid about this man—the way his gaze zeroed in on her, she knew her slip of the tongue hadn't gone unnoticed. "What I meant—" she began.

"No good." Before he could continue, a waiter appeared carrying a platter of nachos heaped high with salsa, sour cream, and jalapeño slices. Whew—saved by the taco chips. The guy added a couple of small plates and napkins, silverware, then checked their water supply, and Winnie hoped that it would be enough to derail Greg's train of thought. Hungry, she dug in immediately, savoring the spicy flavor of the peppers and seasoned ground beef despite her nervousness over what she knew was coming. The cop gave her a few moments, loading up his own plate but fussily picking off all the sliced jalapeños.

"Don't like peppers, huh? You're gonna have a hard time getting Hannah to back off the hot food when you guys eat out," she commented.

Incredibly, Officer Greg blushed. "I don't know what you're talking about," he said. "I'm just watching her dogs while she's laid up."

"Isn't denial fun?" she asked mildly. "Some people—"

"Speaking of denial," he interrupted, "what did you mean when you said Hannah didn't know who was doing 'this stuff?' What 'stuff' would that be?"

"My tongue got twisted up, is all," she said quickly. She shoved a double-loaded chip into her mouth, effectively ending her answer.

"I saw the scar on her neck," he said abruptly. "And I read Dr. Tansey's report. Did you know her body is covered with them?"

Winnie stopped in mid-crunch. Sure, she knew about the scar on her neck—hell, everyone could see that one—and the one across her collarbone, too. But… there were more? Somehow she managed to mash the food in her mouth enough to swallow it, a mistake when it lodged somewhere in the middle of her esophagus like a wet lump of dough. "I knew about… a few."

"Where are they coming from?" Greg asked intently. "Who the hell is doing this to her, and why is she—and maybe you—working so hard to protect him?"

"She—*we*—don't know," Winnie insisted. "Listen, I already told this all to your partner. Wasn't that enough?"

Caught off guard, Officer Greg blinked. "You spoke to my partner? When was this?"

"So he didn't mention it?" Winnie's mouth twisted, but she managed to stop herself before her opinion of that jackass came out. After all, they were probably the best of pals, and Lord knows, she didn't need to get this guy pissed at her, too. "He came by the Diner on Sunday. I told him the same thing." She tilted her head at him. "You remember that part, right? That would be where *we don't know.*"

The cop surprised her by grinning at her sarcastic tone. "Yeah, I remember that. Vaguely. But I'm sure I'll forget it by the end of the meal."

"Then I guess we'll have to remind you."

"You do that." He swiped at his mouth with the napkin and stood, swiping the check off the tabletop as he did so. "In the meantime, I've got to head out—no, no, this afternoon snack's on me. Enjoy your peppers. And mine, too."

"Thanks." She reached across the table and plucked a finger-full of the ones he'd pushed aside from the edge of his plate. "Don't mind if I do. Waste is a terrible thing."

"True," he agreed. "I'll be around with the dogs if you get a sudden flash of recollection. Any idea when Hannah'll be released?"

"Maybe tomorrow, maybe not." Winnie frowned. "That doctor doesn't like her."

"I think it's more likely that she's worried about Hannah rather than something personal," Greg said.

"Aren't we all," Winnie said.

"Yeah." He threw a ten dollar bill on the table, then added another couple of bucks for the tip, unconsciously scoring brownie points. "We are. So keep in touch."

Winnie nodded automatically and watched him go, then almost laughed outright when she realized she'd been trying to imagine what he and Hannah would look like as a couple—what, suddenly she was having matchmaker urges? From the blush she'd seen earlier, Hannah didn't need any help with this one, although she wasn't at all sure how her friend would, or even if she *could*, handle a relationship with a guy. She didn't know all the details, but Winnie had the impression Hannah's growing-up times hadn't been so hot; the girl *never* talked about her past and that much secrecy usually meant a lot of pain and no gain in bringing it up. Unfortunately, it also usually meant a hard time in the here and now.

Winnie looked down at the table and saw that Officer Greg had also managed to drop one of his cards on the table without her noticing. She picked it up and fingered it thoughtfully. Had she really seen what she thought she'd seen that day a couple of weeks ago in the bathroom at Hannah's? So much had happened since then, Hannah's attack included, that it was hard not to doubt her own memory. The mental images she'd thought were so burned in her head were fading fast, worn away by the work and stress of everyday life, the recent increased worry about Hannah. Still, a few were hanging in there, unpleasant and, perhaps, unwanted—

Standing outside Hannah's bathroom door, giggling over something inane, some stupid blond joke about a woman getting off a bus and walking down the sidewalk, not realizing her left breast was hanging out of her blouse. Hannah was listening and laughing around a mouthful of toothpaste, rushing through the ritual because she knew that even though the dogs were banished to their rug and the place was vacuumed, Winnie was apt to start spewing snoze at any second. She'd just said the punch line—

"And so she says to the cop, 'Oh my God, I left the baby on the bus again!'

—when a thin line of red, shocking and growing wider with every slow-motion blink that they stared at it, appeared literally out of nowhere and swept across Hannah's right collarbone. Hannah dropped her toothbrush into the sink and winced, then slapped her hand against her shirt as the red spread through the fabric like a streak of scarlet paint. Her finger fumbled at the buttons and she peeled it away, revealing a fresh three-inch wound, weeping crimson tears.

"What the hell?" Winnie demanded. "How did this happen?"

"It doesn't matter," Hannah said grimly. She quickly stripped off the ruined shirt and tossed it in the wastebasket. Lines of red dripped down her thin chest and she swiped at it with one hand, trying to keep it from reaching her bra. Her clean hand yanked open the medicine cabinet and pulled out a box of gauze pads. "Here—open a couple of these."

Winnie did as she was told, then watched as her friend took the wad of gauze and pressed it against the wound to slow the bleeding. "Hannah—"

"I can't explain it," Hannah said grimly. "And if you think about it too much, it'll do nothing but make you as crazy as I am." She slammed the door to the medicine cabinet hard enough to make Winnie cringe, then fixed her with a haunted stare. Hannah's voice softened. "So just pretend you never saw a thing, okay? It's just... easier that way."

But pretending wasn't easier, it was *denial.* Now Winnie turned the card over and found another number handwritten on the back, probably the cop's home phone number since he'd taken such a personal interest in Hannah. Winnie had been telling the truth when she'd said they didn't know who was hurting Hannah, but if she ever somehow found out…

Well, then, she damned well *would* 'keep in touch.'

Wednesday—October 4th...

Hospitals, Greg thought, had changed a lot over the years. He remembered the one from his youth back in Iowa, and he supposed it hadn't been much different from those anywhere else. In past decades, the walls had been a pale industrial green, or maybe a sort of dull cream, yet another semi-gloss shade of industrial nothing designed to hide the everyday dirt and stand up to infrequent scrubbings with harsh detergents. Cheap white sheets gone gray and thin from a thousand launderings, faded metal blinds that the professionally distant staff never raised.

On the surface, things were different now. Someone "in charge" of such things had decided that a cheerful environment was more conducive to healing the body, and the industrial hallway green paint had been replaced by earthy textured wallpaper and flowered paper borders that followed the edges of the ceilings into the rooms with lines of gentle color—roses, soft yellow daises and the like. But still, that was just help on the surface, a little spit and polish to supposedly bring some cheer into the dreaded hospital stay. Beneath that color, it was still the same: pain, suffering, fear, and all of it undercut with an aura of desperation and the desire to leave.

And nowhere was that more prevalent than in the psych ward.

It made Greg wince to think of Hannah Danior, as fragile and tiny as she was, held in this place against her will. But maybe she wasn't as breakable as he thought—after all, according to all accounts, the young woman was a walking, talking testament to the power of the human body and mind to withstand physical and mental abuse. She should have been nothing to him but a name and a statistic on a crime report, but what she had gone through was so abhorrent that he found himself amazed that she had survived and now seemed at least marginally normal… all of her injuries notwithstanding. Walking the dogs for her and poking around in her apartment had unwittingly given him a closeness to her that was not only unusual but probably undesirable in his line of work, but it was there nevertheless. He felt drawn to her, interested in who and what she was beyond the name on the assault form; if they'd met in the Diner because he stopped in for lunch, would he have found a way to ask her out? He wasn't sure, but he liked to think the answer was yes.

Showing his badge got one of the nurses to buzz him in although it wasn't officially visiting hours. Even the walk to Hannah's room was unpleasant; no amount of pretty wallpaper or pastel colors could lighten the dismal mood of the psych ward, and it certainly did nothing to muffle the variety of sounds along the way—everything from soft babbling to one nearly screaming argument at the far end. Hannah's door was open and she was sitting on a chair by the window, staring morosely at the world through the wire mesh.

"Hi," he said. He stopped at the doorway, waiting for her okay.

She turned and her expression brightened when she saw him. "Hi," she said back. "Come on in."

He did and was slightly gratified to see that she wasn't restrained in the chair—at least they'd stopped that nonsense. "How are you doing?"

Hannah shrugged. "I want to go home."

Greg nodded. "I'll bet." He glanced around the room and spied another chair, ugly pink plastic. He pulled it to a spot in front of her and sat. "I was kind of hoping I'd find you ready to go now."

"I think Tansey signed the release order for tomorrow." She looked at him eagerly. "The dogs?"

"They're fine," he told her. "I've been stopping by three or four times a day."

Hannah's cheeks pinkened a bit. "Oh, you don't have to do it so much—"

"Avoids a mess," he said simply. "Besides, I don't think it's healthy for an animal to try to hold it all day."

"I owe you a lot," she said. "This is a huge favor, and I don't know how to repay it."

"No need." He hesitated. "So… tomorrow, huh? I could give you a ride."

"That's okay. Winnie's going to pick me up. I don't have a phone in here, but the nurse said she'd call her as soon as she got the paperwork from the doctor."

"I met Winnie," Greg said. "She was in Stars yesterday and heard me walking around upstairs, so she came up."

Hannah grinned. "She's a character, isn't she?"

He smiled back. "Yeah. We went up the street and had nachos, talked for a bit. She said you still don't recall anything about the attack and mentioned she'd met my partner at the Diner."

Hannah's face darkened. "Yeah? And what else did she say about your partner?"

Greg frowned. "Nothing. Why?"

Hannah shrugged again. "Never mind. I guess it's not important or she would've said something herself."

He folded his arms, too curious now to let it go. "Obviously it's important enough for you to bring it up. Spill."

Hannah chewed her lip nervously. "Winnie said he… got kind of pissed when she couldn't tell him anything. Said he tripped her."

Greg's mouth fell open. "He *tripped* her?"

Hannah avoided his gaze by studying her fingernails. "Yeah. She went down with a full tray."

He frowned. "Maybe it was an accident."

"Maybe."

But she sounded anything but convinced. They sat there in silence for a few moments while Greg turned this over in his mind. Tony hadn't mentioned anything about Sunday and Hannah's case, so Greg had assumed he'd come up with zip. Bad enough he was keeping Greg out of the loop, but would Tony actually do something like that? Hard telling—loyalty made him want to say 'no,' but his partner was sometimes… inexplicable. Harsh, unrelenting, unforgiving. But outright mean? Maybe.

"So," he finally said. "How's the throat?"

Her hand went instinctively to the bandage around her neck, and he saw that the wrapping wasn't much—a few token pieces of thin gauze without even padding beneath it. "Almost healed." She hesitated for a second, then hooked a finger around the front of it and tugged downward. "Look."

He leaned forward and his eyes widened. "Wow." A mild word for it; she was scarred—no way around that—yet less than a week later, that was *all.* Not even a scab or evidence of suturing remained, just an eighth of an inch wide angry red scar running ear to ear beneath her jaw. "What happened to the stitches?" he asked.

Hannah let the bandage slip back into place. "With the rest of it almost healed, they were afraid of infection so they snipped them out this morning."

"Ah. So when do you think you'll go back to work?"

"Friday," she said without hesitating. "Bright and early. I've missed too much already, and Zubro's always looking for a reason to thin the herd." She glanced out the window. "I missed two nights of school, too."

Greg thought Hannah sounded more upset about missing the classes than work, and he figured it was safe to assume that Zubro was the manager at the Diner. "School," he said. "What are you taking?"

"Basic psychology, English lit. I go to Harold Washington College downtown."

"That's off Lake Street, if I'm remembering it correctly. Train runs right there, doesn't it?"

"Sure. Like clockwork."

He tried to hold it back, but finally he had to ask—ever the optimist. "Any chance you've remembered something about the attack?"

Hannah grimaced. "If I knew a thing about it, I swear I'd tell you. In a heartbeat."

Strange as it seemed, he thought she was telling the truth. He couldn't imagine any reason why she *wouldn't,* and his original thoughts about some sick tie-in with Eloise Addison's killer had disintegrated more and more as he'd checked into Hannah's life. There was something else going on here. He wasn't sure what, but sooner or later he was going to dig it out of hiding.

In the meantime, pressuring her wasn't going to accomplish anything. He rose and moved his chair back to its original position. "You sure you don't need a ride home tomorrow?"

"Thank you so much," Hannah said with sudden, sarcastic brightness. "But I'd much rather stuff myself into Winnie's Fiat." When he glanced at her, he saw that her mischievous grin took the bite out of the sharp words.

"Hey, each to their own. You'll need your key—"

"Don't worry about it. I can get the spare from Winnie," Hannah said.

"Well, I'll come by your place and give you back the original after you're released," he said.

"Sure."

"Okay, I'll see you later then."

She nodded. "Thanks for stopping by. And… for taking care of the dogs." Hannah looked at him quickly and he saw in her eyes, which were an odd sort of tannish color, that she was still surprised at that.

"No problem. See you."

And he left. No big hoopla, no fanfare. Completely mundane, an everyday goodbye to an acquaintance in the hospital, without even a hug or a handshake to go along with it.

An acquaintance… a friend? No, not yet. A young *woman*—whose throat had been cut and who had almost miraculously healed in less than a week.

And someone whom Greg wanted on a much deeper and inexplicable level to see in a way that had nothing to do with her case.

Thursday—October 5th...

Hallelujah mama, Hannah thought. Freedom at last!

It wasn't a particularly pleasant fall day outside—cloudy, damp, and chilly—but to Hannah it felt wonderful, smelled wonderful, looked wonderful. Natural light as opposed to hospital fluorescents, the smell of wet leaves and soggy grass rather than medicine and ammonia-laced cleaning solutions—she'd never realized how much she appreciated a simple walk down a neighborhood sidewalk until being locked away in the next best thing to a mental hospital. Life, even one as limited and sometimes spooky as hers, was good.

"Rex's gone to get the limo," Winnie said cheerfully as they stood outside the main entrance. "We had to park over on Oakdale, so it'll take him a minute or two."

"Yeah, well, we both know what a busy schedule I have." Hannah grinned.

Win started to smile back, then her mouth turned down. "Say, you aren't going to work today, are you? Whyn't you take the rest of the week—"

"Tomorrow," Hannah interrupted firmly. "Duty calls. So does the rent."

"Fuck the rent," Winnie said crudely. "You're *sick,* remember? Injured, fileted, whatever. You—"

"Down, girl." Hannah gave her a mild look. "Life goes on, and besides," she pointed to her neck. "Look, I'm all cured."

"An eight-inch scar does not a cure make," Winnie shot back. "For Christ's sake, you damned near died."

"Nah. Didn't even come close."

Winnie scowled at her. "What are you talking about?"

"Didn't I mention it? Stopped bleeding in the emergency room, all on my own, before they got the needle threaded for the first stitch." She peeked at Win out of the corner of her eye. "Just like in the bathroom, remember?"

Winnie's mouth worked, then closed, and Hannah knew that yes, she *did* remember how the blood seeping from the cut on her collarbone had simply... stopped a few minutes after it happened. A few carefully placed butterfly bandages, and voila. End of problem. Well, except for the scar, of course. Another battle token from her unknown opponent. What else was new?

"I still think you should take some time off," Winnie grumbled.

"Hey, I got bills to pay, school tuition, dog food to buy," Hannah pointed out. "You know how that jerk Zubro is—all he needs is an excuse, and where the hell else am I going to find a job close enough to take care of the pooches on break?" She smirked. "Besides, look how long I've been there. I've got seniority."

That made Win laugh as Rex blared the tinny-sounding horn of the Fiat—so much for the *Hospital Quiet Zone* signs posted all around—and swerved to the curb in front of them. "Oh, the *benefits* are just unending!"

Hannah giggled along with her friend, then stood by patiently while Rex and Winnie play musical car seats, insisting that Hannah take the front passenger side. As she'd expected, Rex crammed himself into the Cabriolet's tiny backseat and griped about the car and the work it needed the whole way, engaging in the usual good-natured argument back and forth with Winnie. It wasn't a long ride but Hannah had grown expert at tuning them out; she watched the houses pass, marveling at the upscale surroundings and the crowds. She still found it amazing that she'd found an affordable place to live and that the landlord hadn't raised the rent on her—maybe he'd forgotten she lived above the bookstore. She hoped so, because she didn't have a lease and every time she wrote that cheap monthly check she prayed she wouldn't get a call notifying her that the rent was going up to "keep pace" with the rest of the neighborhood.

"Hannah!"

She jerked, realizing that Winnie must have said something that required an answer. Oops. "What?"

"You know," Winnie complained, "a person gives you a ride home from the hospital, you could at least pay attention to them." Still, her voice wasn't unkind.

"Sorry," Hannah said. "I was thinking about my rent."

Half turned toward Win, Hannah saw Rex make a face. "Bad choice of thoughts, I'd say."

"What did you—"

"I asked if you talked to your boyfriend."

Hannah gave her friend a severe look, all the while feeling Rex's interested gaze on her. Gads—matchmakers. Just what she *didn't* need. "Don't act the fool, Win."

"What?" Winnie kept her gaze innocently fixed on the road. "It's pretty obvious he's sweet on you."

"Oh, for God's sake," Hannah said, exasperated. "What is the matter with you? The man is walking my dogs, nothing more."

"And blushing."

"Excuse me?"

"I said he's blushing. When he talks about you."

"Well, why are you asking him about me, anyway?" Hannah demanded. In the back seat, Rex, usually such a busybody, was keeping carefully quiet, the picture of neutrality. "He doesn't know anything—I've only seen him twice, and both of those times were in the psycho ward. What the hell makes you think he's interested, and besides, I'm not *looking* for a boyfriend or to get involved with anyone. I've got enough stuff going on in my life without having to worry about something like that." She was almost ranting, her words tumbling over one another.

"He probably knows a lot more about you than you think," Rex said suddenly. Hannah jerked around and glared at him, but he only raised an eyebrow. "The man's a police officer, remember? He's got access to all sorts of information."

"I'm just pointing out that the first thing you did was give the guy a key to your apartment," Winnie said. Her voice was almost gleeful. "I mean, come *on—*"

"Hello?" Hannah snapped. "In case you forgot, I was *stuck* there and Tansey wouldn't let me go home. I couldn't let the dogs just starve, you know."

"We'd have figured out something." Winnie spun the wheel and the car lurched into a right turn that would take them on the last leg of the trip home. They were almost at Belmont. "Maybe Rex could've walked them."

Her boyfriend looked at her incredulously. "Me? I detest animals."

"Well, it would have only been for a few days."

"Anyway," Hannah said loudly. "I don't—"

"Parking spot!" Rex suddenly cried, jabbing a forefinger to the left.

Winnie stomped on the brake hard enough to pitch Hannah forward against her seatbelt, then veered neatly into the go-cart-sized space her boyfriend had seen. "Victory!" she chortled as she shoved the gearshift knob into first and cut the engine. "Look how close we are—it must be our lucky day!"

"Yeah," Hannah muttered grumpily as she unbuckled herself and struggled out of the tiny seat. "Maybe I ought to buy a freaking lottery ticket." Louder, she said, "Thanks for the ride."

"And for the hard time to go with it?" Winnie grinned at her over the roof of the car, and Hannah's mouth turned up reluctantly as they came around and fell in step beside her. How could she be angry at this crazy pal?

At her doorway, she stopped. "Want to come up?"

Winnie shook her head. "Thanks, but I got my weekly dose of dog snuff the day before yesterday, when I zipped upstairs to see what Officer Greg was up to." She ran a hand through her short black hair, yanking it back from her forehead and making her 'do look like a badly done boy's cut. "He was pretty good, you know. With the dogs."

Hannah brightened. "Yeah? You think he took good care of them?"

Winnie tucked her arm in Rex's. "He seemed to like 'em a lot, unlike certain Brits."

"A man's entitled to his own preferences," Rex said huffily.

"So true," Win agreed. She looked at Hannah expectantly.

Puzzled for a second, then Hannah realized her friend was waiting for her to open the door. "I'll have to get the spare key from you."

Winnie's eyes widened. "You don't have yours?"

"Greg… er, Officer Jedrek has it."

Win and Rex exchanged knowing glances. "Uh-huh."

"Don't be absurd," Hannah said. "I haven't seen him since Thursday, so I couldn't very well take it back then. I didn't even know for sure when they were going to release me when he last stopped by the hospital."

"Right." She dug the key out of her purse and handed it over. Hannah saw with amusement that Winnie had put it on one of those long and springy hot-pink key chains. "You'll need to get another copy made, you know. So that all three of us have one."

"Damn it, Win—"

Her friend leaned in and quickly kissed her on the cheek. "See ya, girlfriend." She spun and pulled Rex quickly after her, practically dashing away.

"You're a pain in the ass!" Hannah yelled after her.

Still moving at a fast trot, Winnie only turned and shouted back, "But you love me anyway!"

Hannah frowned and pressed her lips together, then felt her irritation melt away.

Damn it again. She just hated it when Winnie was right all the time.

««—»»

Puddles and Knothead greeted her like a couple of semi-hysterical puppies, dancing around her legs in dizzying circles and filling her ears with breathy little yaps and licks when Hannah bent to hug them. There was a vague smell of floor cleaner in the air that told her Greg had cleaned up a mess or two along the way, and she hoped it hadn't been too much trouble.

Happy to be home, Hannah took the dogs out for a long, relaxing walk, letting them jump and play out their excitement at her return and letting herself de-stress from her nearly week-long "incarceration." Even the city alleys, ribbons of cracked, litter-blown concrete lined with trash cans, graffiti-splattered garage doors and ill-maintained fences, seemed bright and cheerful, preferable to the agony-filled rooms of the psych ward. Thank God she was out of there—she'd had her fill of mental institutions during her years at Trinity MHC, and she'd never, *ever* thought she'd have to endure that again. Life was just full of surprises, wasn't it?

Yeah. And holes, too.

Like the one in her mind that was seven-plus years wide.

Hannah didn't do it often, but her little vacation over at Illinois Masonic, coupled with the semi-safe feeling she had now that she was home and back with the dogs, made her force her thoughts backward to a time and place she didn't often visit. There wasn't any sense of flash-back or losing herself and slipping into another time and place; rather, she'd mulled over it and tried to remember it so many times, both privately and with Dr. Gorrado and others, that now she could analyze it, or at least try to, with an almost clinical self-detachment:

The last memory before the blackout, a little muddled but still there, was undeniably of herself. She'd been small, only five, and back then her hair had been platinum-colored, that fine, baby white that so seldom stays into adulthood. Her foster mother kept it cut short and pulled back with two pink plastic barrettes that sometimes pinched a little, but Hannah hadn't minded. She'd been in the big bedroom where the grownups slept, playing house with her rag doll and a couple of boxes, using a shoe box as a couch, a colorful empty cereal box for a bed. She'd even had an old flowered washcloth to use as a bedspread, a handful of baby food jar tops she was using as dishes. Baby Amy was asleep in her crib and the sun had broken through the cloud cover long enough to shine through the thick leaves of the tree outside the window, painting the floor and her dolly's make-believe living room with a pattern of yellow. The wildly dancing spots and shadows from the summer breeze had kept her from noticing anyone's shadow, and of course she'd been singing to her doll—she always did that—so she didn't hear any footsteps either.

Then the hand had closed over her mouth and she'd been lifted up and carried away, and somewhere in her line of vision she saw that the baby was being taken, too. She'd wanted to scream, but then something sticky had been pressed across her mouth, and across the baby's, and then things started fragmenting. Her memories warped and the images that should have been there exploded into pieces of sharp color instead—the hues of summer green and sunshine yellow washed over by watery red and a deeper, shadowed black. There was fire in there somewhere, and… pain? Maybe, maybe not—perhaps the recollection of pain was only because she believed there *should* be such a thing. No, there *must* have been, because in her head, from a very, very faraway place, she could hear screaming. After all these years, she still wasn't sure if it had been her or Baby Amy, if it had been aloud or in her mind. Either way, she was sure they wouldn't have screamed if they hadn't been hurt. So yes, there must have been pain.

She remembered darkness and the smell of sulphur and dirt, other scents less familiar and horribly wrong. After awhile Baby Amy had quieted but her mind wouldn't let her see why, her mind wouldn't let her see, or feel, anything at all because something inside her head had simply decided she was…

Well, safer that way.

And so then there was, quite simply—

Nothing.

For more than seven years. She didn't remember a sound, a sight, the touch of a human hand, even the bite of a mosquito though she'd been told since then that they'd stopped putting her wheelchair-bound form outside in the summer because the 'squitos were using her as a midsummer's feast. She didn't talk, walk, or do much more than inhale and exhale that whole time, until eleven years ago, on a dark March night when she'd vaulted out of the catatonic darkness and clutched at her throat.

No vague recollection there, thank you very much. Sharp, painful detail—she couldn't breathe, she was being strangled, and she couldn't walk either. Her legs collapsed under her weight, the muscles atrophied despite regular passive exercise. The airless feeling was gone almost as quickly as it had started but she'd been left with a line of black and blue bruising around her neck and… other places, none of which the doctors and nurses, a whole mob of which had come running, could explain. All of that notwithstanding, Hannah was, at last, awake and lucid, if still significantly memory-deprived and more than a little behind on her mental development.

Now, steering Knothead and Puddles up the stairs at the back of her building, Hannah thought she'd come a long way from the sickly thirteen-year-old who'd suddenly opened her eyes and been treated to a rude reintroduction to the world. It was Dr. Gorrado's doing, his refusal to accept the opinions of his peers that she was more likely to remain "challenged" for the rest of her life and would be better suited to assisted living. Somehow, he had seen through the shocked outer layer and suspected that an almost-whole person was still in there. His persistence had paid off, both in his career and her life—now she functioned on her own, she had a life, and a future.

Maybe.

As she climbed the stairs, Hannah's hand went unwillingly to her throat. There was still a thin gauze bandage around it, but it was window-dressing; she was scarred and a little sore but healed, nearly miraculously so. The same thing had happened with the cut along her collarbone, and the wound on her neck that she had never quite matched with a possible weapon—was it a puncture wound? Or a viciously deep burn, perhaps by something big, like a cigar or a hot poker? And more—the ragged scar that ran across her left breast and down the center of her sternum, the white one through her eyebrow, countless minor bruises and scrapes that had appeared and disappeared through the years and which she saw and forgot once they were gone.

Well, except for that evening back in April, only a few days before the neck wound that had landed her in the hospital, when for a terrifying twelve hours her entire body—including her face—had turned a mottled black, blue and brown. Staring at herself in the mirror had been like looking at a corpse, and Hannah had wrapped herself in winter-like garments to walk the dogs, then spent the rest of the night as a shut-in, praying desperately that the bruising would go away. It had, but her relief had been short-lived when the horrid neck wound two days later had stunned her into near unconsciousness and sent her to Illinois Masonic and her first encounter with Dr. Tansey.

What's next? she wondered as she peeled away the gauze and tossed it in the bathroom wastebasket. The line of scar tissue, a mixture of raw red and pink, glistened back at her, just another in the road map of marks that her life had left upon her. Or were these marks a paint-by-numbers indication of someone *else's* existence? A strange thought, but one she'd had before. In any case, she'd probably never know. Just as she'd probably never know what happened to her as a child—hell, she preferred *not* to know. Sure, she had the facts, relayed in Dr. Gorrado's careful words throughout the years, but the reality of it had been so terrible that her mind had blocked it out, so why on earth would she want to recall the details?

But…

Hannah lifted her arms and stripped off the sweatshirt Winnie had lent her to wear home, infinitely preferable to the blood-soaked uniform from last Friday. She'd tossed her bra in the trash at Illinois Masonic along with the uniform, sweater and slip, all stained beyond washability. Staring at her body now, in all fairness she had to admit it was no wonder Dr. Tansey had been suspicious. She traced the scar around her neck, then touched the others, one at a time—her eyebrow, the horrid, thick puckering on the side of her neck, the slash that went across her breast and looked like the work of a mad doctor, doubtlessly her own fault for not finding a physician to repair the damage.

But how would she have explained it? Eighteen years old, she'd barely been on her own after her time at Trinity Mental Health Center when she'd woke in the middle of the night in agony, literally covered in her own blood. But she'd never lost consciousness, never not been able to function, and by the time she'd sopped up the worst of it, the bleeding had stopped on its own. By the time morning crawled along, she was striped by a long, nearly black scab almost a third of an inch wide. Hannah had kept her silence, terrified that Gorrado or someone else would use this as a reason to bring her back to St. Charles and keep her there. A week later she was healed and if she couldn't exactly wear a bathing suit anymore, at least she was still living on her own.

But for how much longer?

Without warning, fear ran through her, coupling with the cool air in the bathroom and raising the fine hair on her skin. Hannah snatched up Win's sweatshirt and yanked it back on but not fast enough to stop the shudders that suddenly hit her, and it wasn't long before they were followed by sobs, hard enough to knock her first to her knees, then push her back against the wall. The dogs came instantly, cramming themselves into the bathroom to snuffle nervously, lick at her cheeks and push their warm, furry faces under her arms as they tried to give comfort. It was rare when they couldn't make her feel better, but this time she couldn't *not* cry. Like her, they had no one else in the world, no one but each other, and her, and if Hannah ended up back in St. Charles, who would take care of these sweet girls?

Greg.

Stuffed into the tiny room with the two dogs, Hannah's shoulders stopped shaking and her tension eased a little. Maybe he would, and maybe he wouldn't—he had his own life to deal with, things going on, but he seemed concerned enough about Knothead and Puddles that if worse came to worse, perhaps he could find them a good and loving home.

She thought about St. Charles, and her life before, and what it might be like to go back there. About how it would be without the unconditional affection of her two hairy puppy-pals here, sans even the daily aggravation of Zubro and the Diner. In a way it was like facing another wide, black hole, except this one wasn't filled with lost memories. This one was filled with something far, far worse.

Hopelessness.

Hannah put her head on her knees and cried all over again.

Friday—October 6th...

"Hey, Greg," Tony said. "What's new?"

His younger partner glanced up from the paperwork he was doing. "Not much. Just getting the evidence forms on the Deaver case wrapped up," he said, referring to a shooting homicide that had gone down outside a neighborhood bar on the twenty-third beat last night. "Pretty standard stuff—guy's hammered and gets into a fight with another patron, who pulls out a piece and offs him." Greg shook his head. "The kicker? They're screaming at each other about who knocked over a bowl of popcorn on the bar. Idiots."

"Hey, popcorn is a base food of life," Tony said lightly.

"Not funny."

"Oh, take a pill, would you?" Tony swept aside a stack of papers so he could sit in the usual spot at the corner of Greg's desk. "You can't change the world. Why fight it?"

Greg looked like he wanted to retort, then he glanced back down at his forms instead. "Nothing else going on," he said. "How about with you?"

"Car bullshit," he said. "I had to drop the Olds off this morning for an oil change, lube, that kind of crap." He waited a beat, then said, "Listen, could I borrow the Cherokee for a half hour? I need to run by the hardware store and pick up something. Dara just called and said one of the toilets in the house is screwed up. I figure I can get a kit and just replace the whole thing, but my car won't be ready until the end of the day. By then, the hardware store'll be closed. I don't want to have to sign out an unmarked."

"Sure," Greg said. He dug in his pocket and pulled out his keys, tossed them over. "Hardware store? That's what, couple of miles? Don't forget to fill it up with gas."

Tony grinned. "Kiss it, farm boy."

"No, thanks."

"Be back in a little while."

"Wreck my Jeep and I'll beat you within an inch of your life. And fasten your damned seatbelt."

"Yes, Dad," Tony said humbly. "What time did you say curfew was?"

"Get lost."

Tony laughed and headed out. It was another beautiful fall day, with the predicted clouds still nicely absent. Midday traffic wasn't too bad, and he enjoyed the ride in Greg's vehicle, a black 1998 4x4. A nice piece, low mileage, lots of room to carry stuff—he wished he had something like this instead of the stodgy Ninety-Eight he'd bought almost ten years ago, when he and Dara had first started talking about doing the family-style thing.

Speaking of family, he ought to give his sister Carrie a call—he hadn't talked to her in a week and he knew it made her feel neglected. She was always worried about being accepted, standing out in a crowd, yadda yadda yadda, and so he had to pick up the slack in other areas of her life and do the brotherly support thing. Damn it, people were always making demands on him—like Dara, calling him at work with this stupid thing about the toilet. Didn't he have enough to worry about, a stressful job, the standard money worries of a guy trying to support a family on a cop's salary? On the other hand, the last thing he needed was for her to do something Dara-like stupid and call a plumber in at a hundred bucks an hour.

The hardware store wasn't crowded and Tony found what he needed right away, a kit that ought to fix up the problem right now. He spotted a soccer ball on sale and picked it up for his son Ben; the boy was more into computers, but Tony wasn't giving up his efforts to turn the kid's nerd-like attention to the more appropriate athletic pursuits. He was just about to go to the register when he saw a teenager at the key counter in the back, so after a moment's hesitation—a very *short* moment—he made a quick stop there, figuring it never hurt to have a few spares. Back in the Jeep, he thought about running over to Carrie's, but now he was out of time and didn't want to push his luck with Greg—keep the car too long and Greg would find a reason not to let Tony borrow it again, and the next time he might need it for something more important.

Reluctantly, he started up the Cherokee and headed back to the station.

«««—»»»

It wasn't something he would have admitted, but Greg felt a palpable sense of relief when Tony dropped his car keys back on his desk at the same time he said, "And look, Dad—I didn't even hit anything!"

"Thank you, God," Greg said mildly. "You through with all this personal stuff? We've got work to do."

"Lead on," Tony said. "What's the deal?"

Greg stood and shrugged on his jacket. "Right now things are pretty quiet, but since it's Friday, I'm sure the weekend will change all that. We've got a few leads to follow-up on, still trying to make the connection between the Curan woman and the guy who tried to whack her ex-husband. I think if we lean on him a little harder, he'll cave."

"You still think they're a duo?"

Greg nodded as Tony followed him outside. "You bet. But the woman has a temperament like a demon and she'll turn on him in an instant. If we work him a little, he'll see it and realize she's not worth spending the rest of his life in the joint. He just needs an adjustment to his point of view."

"Right. Say, who's driving?"

"You are," Greg said and angled around to the passenger side of the gray sedan they'd been using for the past couple of months. Tony, Greg knew, liked being in control and driving was a small thing that made him feel that way. To Greg, it didn't make any difference—in fact, he kind of liked being able to watch the city and the people go by on the other side of the passenger window. "Seeing as how you got such a good start on it in my Jeep."

"Excellent." Tony slid comfortably into the driver's seat and cranked up the engine. "Anything else? What about that Hannah Danior thing?"

"Nothing going on there." Greg glanced at Tony out of the corner of his eye. "Hey, didn't you'd say something about checking up that?"

"Yeah," Tony answered. He steered the Chevrolet into the traffic on Western Avenue. "But nothing ever came of it—no one knew jack about what happened. I went over to that restaurant where she works and talked to the manager and one of the waitresses who's supposed to be a friend of the victim's. Bitchy little thing, real attitude."

"No kidding." Greg didn't say anything else.

"Yeah," Tony said again. "So where are we headed?"

Greg pulled out his notebook and read an address to him, turning over in his mind the difference between the three versions of Tony's encounter with Winnie Harbin. Winnie, who had elected not to mention her claim that Tony had tripped her; Hannah, angered enough to do just that; Tony, whose take on the whole thing conveniently excluded the incident and who claimed in so many unspoken words that Winnie had been less than a cooperative witness. He'd called the hospital late yesterday and found out that Hannah had, indeed, been released; he hadn't gone by her place, thinking she could use the time to wind down and just enjoy her beloved animals with as little a reminder of a week ago as possible. Maybe after his training tomorrow afternoon he'd stop by and drop off her key, see how she was getting along.

Obviously wrapped up in his own thoughts, Tony didn't say anything more as he drove toward the house where Greg had arranged to talk to a friend of Margaret and Jack Curan, someone who'd called in and put in an unsolicited vote that Mrs. Curan's boyfriend wasn't a boyfriend at all, but a hired gun. All those interesting details below the surface of something, or some*one*; sometimes Greg thought Tony was like one of the puzzles they encountered throughout their "typical" work day—multi-layered, quite different from what appearance suggested. Outwardly, Tony seemed like a red-blooded U.S. of A. family man, a guy who might have been a high-school jock and had opted for a man's kind of career when he'd gotten out of school. Wife, son, nice house in the city, not much different from a couple thousand other cops on the force.

Yet there was something about Tony that Greg couldn't quite connect with, a layer of frustration that kept him from actually *liking* his partner and which was certainly a wall to them actually being friends. While he'd met Dara and Ben, Tony's son, they didn't socialize—in fact, although he'd never really thought about it before, he wasn't sure Tony socialized with *anyone* in the district. But he was personable enough and he did talk about meeting up with friends now and then; combined with family obligations, he had as full a life as anyone else. And as for Greg liking Tony, or really calling him a *friend*… well, a job was a job, and you took the partner you were assigned, and that was that. No one ever said it was a personality match, so end of discussion.

Silly or not, Greg couldn't help but wish for the kind of camaraderie the television cop shows always touted. Maybe it was because he wasn't from around here, but the other guys in his district didn't seem to relate to him. Still, he had a lot of pals where he trained a couple of times a week, a place called the Degerberg Academy of Martial Arts on Lincoln Avenue. Perhaps it was better that way—Greg supposed he liked what he did as much as any homicide detective could "like" the job, but it was just as well that he kept his personal life separate from it. Too many of the guys seemed to mix it up all the time, hanging out at work and afterwards, dragging the job's hard-nosed demeanor around with them like a concrete block at the end of an ankle chain. Tony, for instance, always seemed on edge, not quite satisfied with anything. Thanks, but Greg could do without that.

"Ready?" Tony asked from the driver's seat, and Greg realized they were pulling up in front of the address, a ratty looking apartment building on Broadway and Bryn Mawr.

"As ever," Greg said automatically and climbed out of the car. As Tony followed him inside, Greg thought he looked as calm and relaxed as he'd seen him in quite some time, as though he was having a good morning despite the plumbing difficulties and the annoying automobile-related chores. It was such a difference from the guy who sometimes complained relentlessly about the smallest things, and Greg couldn't help but wonder at this. In an odd way, Tony was like a box with different colored sides—on one day you'd get a cheerful yellow, on another an angry red or a serene blue, on yet another a dark, muddy brown.

And, of course, there was that infamous black side, the one that revealed a Tony Rutland who would do something like he'd done to Winnie Harbin at the Diner. There was no reason for it, nothing to be gained—being vicious to a witness, particularly someone outside the scope of actual involvement, was the last way in the world a cop would ever get cooperation.

It made no sense.

Still, even if the only person who'd said anything about it had been Hannah, there was simply no doubt in Greg's mind that Tony really *had* done exactly that.

Saturday—October 7th...

Hannah knew who it was when the doorbell rang.

There was nothing spooky about it—no mental flash or divine inspiration—but she had to grin to herself on the way down the stairs because she knew that's just what Winnie would have called it had she been there. It wasn't like it was any big secret; Greg—Officer Jedrek—had said he would come by and bring her back her key. He hadn't done it yesterday, or if he had she'd been out with the dogs or whatever, and she wasn't expecting any company. The only person who visited her with any regularity was Win, and while Alice from the downstairs bookstore sometimes came by, she wasn't likely to do that during a Saturday afternoon, which was her busiest time at the store.

When your options were limited, the answers were pretty easy.

"Hi," Greg said when she pulled open the door. "How… how are you doing?" He glanced past her, and she knew he was looking for the dogs. He didn't know their training well enough to know they'd never come down the stairs unless she told them to.

"Fine," she answered, then stood to the side. "Come on up."

"Okay."

He went ahead, but waited politely on the landing. She'd closed the door behind herself and as usual the dogs were huffing and snuffling around the bottom of it. They must have smelled him, because their panting quickly turned to little whines of anticipation. "I think they missed you," she said and pushed open the door.

"Really?" He sounded pleased, then laughed outright when Knothead and Puddles practically leaped on top of him when he stepped into her apartment. "Whoa!"

Smiling, Hannah watched him play with the dogs—or maybe they were playing with him—for a minute or so. "So, you want a cup of coffee?" she finally asked. "Or a soda?"

"Sure," he answered. He stood, giving each of the pooches a final, friendly ruffle on the head. "Whatever's easiest."

"And that would be a ginger ale." She pulled a can out of the frig as he settled onto one of the chairs at the tiny table. The dogs immediately zipped in and huddled at his feet, like two oversized balls of barely-contained furry energy.

"I called the hospital Thursday afternoon and they said you'd been released," he told her. "Figured you could use a little time to unwind."

Hannah rinsed the top of the can under the faucet, then popped the tab and offered it to him, belatedly wondering if she should have gotten him a glass. You never knew about some people and how picky they could get, but Greg took it and tilted it back without hesitation. "Yeah," she said. "It was nice to get home and back into a semi-routine. That place was… well." She couldn't think of any other way to finish.

"I'll bet." His expression was solemn and while he'd probably never experienced anything like it, she had the sense that he still sympathized.

"I don't ever want to end up somewhere like that again," she said, then wished instantly that she could take back the words. Too late; they hung in the air between the two of them, stalling out a conversation already on the verge of awkward.

"It was just a… mistake," Greg finally said. "The doctor jumped to conclusions. It happens."

Hannah chewed her lips and said nothing. Did he really believe that? She didn't know why, but it seemed very important to her that he wasn't just mouthing the words, or trying to placate her. Now, even more than before, she simply didn't know what to say.

Greg put the can on the table carefully, moving as though he thought he might frighten her. "Look," he said, "it's nearly four o'clock. Would you like to get something to eat later, then take in a movie? The Brew & View is showing that Russell Crowe flick, *Gladiator.* I could go home and come back a little later."

Hannah stared at him, completely speechless. What was this—he was asking her out on a date? For God's sakes, *why?* For years she'd thought of herself as "Frankenhannah," and how much more did it apply now, with this fresh necklace of scar tissue in full view? Wait—

It was the case, of course. Her case, *his* case. She was nothing but a means to an end—maybe he thought buying her a plate of food and shelling out a few bucks for a movie ticket would get her to spill that elusive info he was so convinced she was holding back. It made perfect sense, and oddly, Hannah couldn't believe just how perfectly *bitter* it made her feel.

She stood abruptly. "I-I think you'd better go now."

"I guess that means no." He tried to give her a smile, but it came out sort of crooked and he looked genuinely disappointed. "Maybe some other time." He stood and, following their cue, the dogs rose from their curled positions.

Hannah started to retort *Not in this lifetime,* but the words wouldn't quite come out. Maybe it was his expression, or his attempt to be lighthearted in the face of rejection. Was she wrong about his motives? Her personal crystal ball had certainly been skewed on more than one occasion. "We'll... see," she got out instead. "Maybe." She was suddenly embarrassed by her behavior, filled with self-doubt about why he'd asked, aggravated at herself for her indecision and, let's face it, cowardice. There was a whole lot of life facing her. Was she going to run from it forever? "I didn't mean to be rude," she offered. "You just caught me by surprise, that's all.

"No problem," he said quickly. He took a final sip from his can then walked over and set it on the sink. "It was probably a pushy thing of me to ask anyway." He gave each dog a companionable scratch behind the ears, then headed toward the door. "I'll, you know..." He hesitated. "I'll talk to you later."

Hannah nodded, then he stepped out the door and left. No fanfare, no offer to shake hands, certainly no pal-like hug. She heard his rather hurried descent down the stairs, followed by the sound of the door closing at the bottom—a nice firm bang designed to make sure the lock caught and held. For a long second, she stood there, soaking in the returned silence of her apartment, then hearing it fill rapidly with the sounds of the outside world—the traffic on Clark Street, the creaks of the old building, the slightly anxious pants of Knothead and Puddles. Then she turned and dashed over to the front window, squinting through the glare of the southern sun as she tried to spot him on the sidewalk below, like some teenager trying to watch her boyfriend leave after he'd walked her home from school. He was gone though, apparently already far enough down the sidewalk to have angled out of her range of vision. Strangely, she felt about as disappointed as that same fantasy schoolgirl.

Hannah stood there for a few minutes, staring dumbly out at the crowded street. Finally she turned until she was facing the rest of the apartment and let herself sink to the rug; delighted, the dogs were immediately all over her, licking her face and crawling onto her lap, shoving their heads under her elbows and hands in an attempt to cuddle. But for the first time since she'd gotten her two friends as puppies, the place seemed suddenly sorely lacking in something. It stretched in front of her like nothing more than a… long box with a few over-used pieces of fabric and wood in it. Even the bed was rumpled and unruly—she'd never cared much one way or another if the bedspread was smooth, or even if it was on right side up. Which, now that she looked at it… hell, not even close.

Why had she turned him down? Well, obviously because…

She didn't know.

Liar.

Because she was afraid of him.

Not just him, but of human contact, of getting too close to someone, or having someone get too close to her. Did she want to go out with Greg Jedrek?

If she'd known, Winnie would have had a field day teasing her about it, but… yes, Hannah *did.* But a meal and a movie would lead to other things, and she wasn't sure she could deal with even the smallest of those. To the rest of the world, they probably seemed so innocent—holding hands, maybe, a goodnight kiss that might only be on the cheek, the simple act of tucking her hand into the bend of his elbow as they crossed a street. She'd seen it all done thousands of times on television, in the Diner, on the sidewalks of everyday life. If things went well, there might be another date after that, then another, and another, and maybe things would progress from there into something… closer. Would it be so wrong, or hard, for her to do those things, too?

No, of course not.

Liar.

It would be *impossible.*

Wednesday—October 11th...

He couldn't stop thinking about Hannah.

Odd little tidbits floated into his mind now and then, in between paperwork and case investigation, dealing with witnesses and work, the hundreds of other things he did on a daily basis. Greg wanted to know more about her beyond the case and the bizarre attack—whether he wanted to admit it or not, there was something about Hannah that intrigued him. Maybe it was the strength and determination, the warmth, that he sensed beneath the fragile-looking and battered exterior, a personality that made her seem nothing short of beautiful. Admitting such a thing was asking for trouble, though—cops weren't supposed to get involved with victims, and he certainly didn't need Tony getting all in his face with the crude and rude jokes. His dealings with Hannah should be nothing but police business, but hell… he'd ruined that by asking her out on a date. Her refusal had stung but not killed him; the fact that he was the investigating detective on her attack was only the first of a million reasons why she'd balk, but he thought he'd probably grit his teeth and ask again. He wanted to do a lot of things—take her to dinner where she ordered hot peppers and he wouldn't eat them, to a movie where he could hear her laugh, talk with her until she relaxed a bit, and, somehow, help her heal from the horror of her past.

And, because he wasn't quite convinced that things like her past were *over*, he wanted to protect her.

All right, enough of this mooning around. It was a quarter past noon and Tony had gone to meet some snitch on a case who didn't want to be seen or heard by Greg or anyone else. Greg would have normally balked but Tony had said it was in a public place, nice and crowded. Besides, it was good timing—Greg could make a few phone calls about Hannah's case without Tony breathing down his neck and razzing him. Partner or not, the guy aggravated the crap out of him.

Greg flipped open the file on Hannah and scanned through the papers and notes, then found Gorrado's telephone number and dialed it. When Janice Tuwile's smooth voice came on the line, he couldn't help but grin at the memory of Tony practically making a fool of himself over the attractive young woman. "Hi," he said. "This is Detective Jedrek. I was out there a week ago Monday with my partner. I wondered if I could speak with Dr. Gorrado."

The doctor's assistant put him on hold, then a few moments later the psychiatrist's cheerful baritone rang in his ear. "Detective Jedrek, how are you? What can I do for you—is Hannah all right?"

"She's fine," Greg assured him. "They finally let her go home and I saw her there a few days ago."

"Good," he said. "I'd hoped I'd hear from her but... it's good that she's well. Then...?" Gorrado let the unspoken question hang in the air.

"I'm calling because I've run into kind of a problem on this case," Greg said. He tucked the receiver beneath his chin and shuffled through the forms until he found what he was looking for. "I've been trying to get the files opened on the adoption of Hannah's brothers so I can track them down, but I'm not having any luck. In fact, I'm kind of at the end of my ideas here, so I wondered if you might be able to lend some assistance. A letter from you supporting my request might be just the thing to push it through the court system."

There was silence on the other end and Greg knew the doctor was thinking this over. Still, he'd been so convinced about this that when the psychiatrist's refusal came, he was completely unprepared for it. "I'm sorry, Detective, but I can't do that. This was a terribly traumatic time for Hannah, and I just don't see the point in revisiting it. It's taken her a long time to recover to the point where she can function normally, and unless you've come up with some stunning revelation, I believe that reuniting her with that part of her past can only have the most dire of consequences."

"But I really think it will help us in this case," Greg protested.

"In what way?" Gorrado shot back. "Hannah has a documented history of not remembering bad events. It's much more likely that faced with her past, she'll fall back into a retreating mode in an attempt to avoid recalling or reliving it. I'm sorry, but I can't see how any good would come of this, and unless you can provide me with a more solid reason why I should do so, I won't be part of an attempt to open those records. Frankly, I think they're better off sealed."

Greg opened his mouth to argue, then ground his teeth, thanked the doctor, and hung up. He wasn't going to win here—he'd already talked to a friend of his, a judge in family court, who'd pointed out that there simply wasn't any compelling connection from Hannah's past to the present day crime. It had been his suggestion that a letter from Hannah's psychiatrist might, *might,* help, but that option had blown up in his face. For now, the whereabouts of Hannah's siblings was going to remain as much a mystery as who had attacked her in front of her own door.

As much a mystery as the cause of the rest of those scars that Hannah didn't know he knew about?

Greg closed the Danior file and set it aside, but he knew it wouldn't stay that way for long. One way or another, he was determined find out what the deal was there, why she kept getting hurt, and who the hell was doing it.

«««—»»»

He comes here for lunch once in awhile. It's smoky and dark, and they serve great hot corned beef sandwiches on rye with pepper jack cheese. Years ago there used to be a liquor store at the corner of Clark and Lake that had a deli counter, and the sandwiches here remind him of that. They put bowls of popcorn around this place, too; stuff is a little on the stale side but he doesn't mind too much.

There are a few empty booths along the back wall, but he picks one of the high, round tables instead, settling on one fake leather chair and tossing his bag on the other. He orders his sandwich and a beer, then asks for another beer when the sandwich arrives. There's a guy across the room who keeps looking his way, and he smiles at him a couple of times, hoping he'll decide to come over and talk. It doesn't take long.

"Hi," the guy says. "Mind if I join you?"

"Not at all." He moves his bag off the chair but the floor's too dirty,

so he shoves it onto his lap beneath the table. They chat for awhile about mundane stuff like the weather and sports—there's a college football game on the wall television but he hasn't been keeping track of the scores, certainly not the players or teams. He thinks things are going pretty well until some gesture he makes—he's not sure what—pisses the guy off and makes him suddenly decide he doesn't like the package he thought was there for the taking, it's not what it appeared to be, and so now he's going to go the self-righteous blabbermouth route. The fellow's expression turns ugly and he decides to leave. Before he does, he can't resist mouthing off, some sarcastic, mindfucking and clichéd remark about what you see isn't *what you get. No biggie—he's certainly been insulted before—but then the bastard makes this lewd and rude gesture toward his crotch, and everything just kind of goes red for a second inside his head. Before he can think about what he's doing, or rather what he* shouldn't *be doing, his hand slips inside his bag and returns with his knife, a handy little Camillus Lev-A-Lok, and then it's open and his hand flashes out and there's the sound of fabric whispering apart and the guy is staring down in amazement at a four-inch stripe across his thigh. A heartbeat later and the edges of the wound stretch open and gush blood, and the guy starts to scream in a high, feminine voice like the dickless little weasel he probably is.*

Satisfied, he folds up the knife, picks up his bag and walks out, but not before he throws a twenty on the table. Pretty big tip, but after all, he's left a big mess for the bartender to clean up.

Too bad he won't be able to come back. He really liked this place.

««—»»

"What the hell happened to you?"

Hannah winced at the sound of Zubro's voice and pressed the wad of paper towels harder against the cut across her thigh. "Clumsy," she said quickly. "Knife slipped out of my hand and landed the wrong way. No big deal—it's just a scratch."

Her manager frowned at her, squinting piggy-looking little eyes as he tried to put what she'd just told him together with the bloody paper towel. Before he could comment further, Hannah took a chance and pulled it away, letting the skirt of her uniform drop down before he could see anything. "See? It's not even bleeding anymore. I'll be back on the floor as soon as I wash my hands." She spun and ducked into the Employees Only washroom, shutting the door behind her and leaning against it. Her heart was pounding and her leg pulsed with pain, reminding her to get the towel against it quickly before she started dripping crimson all the way down her leg.

"Make it fast, Hannah," Zubro grated on the other side of the door. "Customers are already screaming for you on the floor."

She doubted that, and wasn't he just the temple of sympathy? But she gave herself a rictus grin in the smudgy wall mirror and called, "I'll be right out." A quick check of her leg revealed that enough of the bleeding had stopped so that she could trade the saturated paper towel for a couple of the scratchy brown towels from the dispenser. She folded the new ones into a makeshift bandage and slid it between her undamaged nylons and the cut, which went at an angle horizontally across the meaty part of her right thigh. It hurt like a sonofabitch, but there was nothing to be done about that, and of course she had no sewing kit or butterfly bandages handy so she could count on another wide and oh-so-attractive scar. And here she'd been thinking how stuff seemed to finally be getting back to normal, she was back at work, her neck was healed, blah blah blah. What a trusting little pushover she could be sometimes.

Hannah scrubbed the blood off her hands then quickly dried them. She could ponder the mysteries of the universe and her life later on; now it was time to get back to work, before Zubro started bitching all over again. A pull on the doorknob and—

"Hannah!"

Caught.

"Where is it?" Winnie demanded. "Zubro said you cut yourself."

"Not now," Hannah tried to say. "I've got customers waiting—"

"I did a quick pass and everyone's set," Winnie said. "Now tell me what happened."

"Nothing," Hannah said desperately. "A scratch."

"No shit," Winnie said. She pushed past Hannah into the bathroom, then caught her by the wrist when she would have ducked back toward the dining room. Trapped in Win's grasp, Hannah could only watch as her friend reached barehanded into the wastebasket and pulled out the wad of paper she'd thrown out, holding up the obviously blood-soaked sheets. She wagged it in the air a couple of times, then tossed her prize back into the trash and stared hard at Hannah. Suddenly she reached over and yanked up Hannah's uniform. "If that's a scratch, I'd hate to see what you call a cut."

Hannah pulled free and slapped her skirt back down. "It doesn't matter. Duty calls."

"Damn it, what *happened?*" Win was right on her heels.

"Don't ask."

"I *am* asking, and I'm not going to *stop* asking until you answer me!"

Hannah scowled and stopped long enough to face her. "Fine. Then if you really *must* know—" She pushed her face close to Winnie's.

"I don't have a clue."

And she did the only thing she could: she walked away and left her best friend standing there with a shocked frown on her face.

«« — »»

"Jedrek."

For a moment, Winnie couldn't say anything. She felt like a traitor, as though she might as well be wielding the knife that had sliced into Hannah's leg.

His voice came back on the line, sharper but not impatient. Curious. *"This is Detective Jedrek speaking."*

"Yeah, uh… this is—"

"Winnie Harbin."

Well, if she'd been thinking of backing out, there went any chance of it. He was taking being good at your job way too far on the serious side; then again, he *was* a cop. But was he… did he *want* to be, anything more, maybe to Hannah? Someone had to figure this out, someone had to *stop* it, or sooner or later her best friend was going to wake up dead. And Winnie just couldn't take that.

"Yeah," she said. Her voice came out nervous and raspy, and she tried to clear her throat without it seeming obvious. "Yeah."

"What can I do for you?" He paused and she heard his sudden intake of breath. *"Is something wrong? Is Hannah all right?"*

She still had doubts—how could she not?—but the tone of his voice, even through the forced distance of telephone wires, conveyed a world of concern. That more than anything made Winnie plunge ahead. "She got hurt again," she blurted.

"Where is she?" Jedrek demanded. *"The hospital?"*

"No—no. Work, she's still at work." Winnie's words tumbled over each other when she realized what he must be thinking. "She just patched herself up and kept working."

"What happened?" He sounded a little calmer, but still wired enough to blow up the receiver in Winnie's sweating hands.

"I don't know," Winnie answered honestly. "It's a cut, big—like four inches long—across her right leg. She wouldn't leave work. I guess compared to… other stuff that's happened to her, she doesn't think it's that bad."

"Did she say who did it?"

Winnie was silent for a long moment. "I don't think anyone *did*," she finally told him quietly.

And because she just didn't feel like arguing about something she couldn't herself explain or understand, she very carefully hung up the phone.

««—»»

Greg sat there and drummed his fingers on his desk, then realized he was hitting the metal desktop so hard that his nails were starting to ache. Hannah'd been hurt, but how bad could it be? Bad enough; he didn't think Winnie was the type to tattle on her pal for a scratch or a skinned knee. Still, if she'd stayed at work then at least it wasn't life-threatening. What he most wanted to do was get the hell over there and see the damage for himself, but there was no way he could that without compromising Winnie. So here he was, stuck, worried about Hannah, and with just enough info to make him go a little crazy.

Had they filed a police report? Of course not—Hannah would have downplayed this as much as possible. Despite this, Greg's fingers pecked out a search request on the computer, more out of something to keep his thoughts from tumbling around than anything else. Today's date, search on the word assault, north side. His request had been broad enough to generate thirty-two returns; just for giggles he narrowed it down by age range of the victim, which dropped it to seven cases. Winnie had said Hannah's injury was on her right leg, so he looked for that, not expecting to find—

Bingo.

Wait—nope, not quite it. The neighborhood and locale was right, a dingy bar down on Clark a few blocks north of Belmont, but that's where any similarity ended. Most of the rest was just off.

> DESCRIPTION: Victim states that at approximately 13:20 he approached a woman eating lunch at another table and asked if he could buy her a drink. She accepted but an argument later ensued and the woman pulled a knife from her purse and cut victim across the upper right leg. Victim was treated for a four-inch gash at Illinois Masonic and released. The attacker was not apprehended.

A four-inch gash on the right leg… strange. Same leg, same type of wound, even the same size as what Winnie said had happened to Hannah. Coincidence? Of course, and this was just some little tiff that would never be solved—no beat cop was going to bother trying to track down this person and the detectives had bigger perps to bag.

Still…

Four-inch gash, upper right leg.

Greg scrawled the victim's address on a piece of notepaper, snatched his jacket off the back of his chair and headed out the door.

««—»»

Jack Iserson was an oily-looking blond guy with sprayed hair, hooded hazel eyes, and deep acne scars. He answered Greg's knock with a beer in his hand and waved him inside with barely a glance at the detective shield. Not much to see in the man's place—the guy was a bachelor and a mess, plenty of crumpled fast food bags and dirty clothes. It was dark and warm inside, the steam radiators going full blast, and Iserson was wearing only a pair of rumpled, too-long gym shorts. Greg could see the white of a bandage just below the fraying hem of the right leg.

"So I didn't expect you guys to do anything about this," Iserson said as he plopped onto his couch. "Have a seat, why don'tcha." Beer splashed onto his hand and he shook it off, then pushed a bunch of stuff on the coffee table aside so he could elevate his injured leg. Greg saw a cockroach skitter off the edge of the table and disappear under the couch.

"Thanks," Greg said, "but I just want to ask you a few questions then I'll be on my way. It won't take long."

Iserson shrugged and took a drink from his can of Bud. "What do you want to know? I told the uniforms everything I could think of."

Greg nodded. "Sure, but a lot of the details didn't get put in the report. There was another incident similar to yours, and I just want to make sure we're not talking about the same attacker."

Iserson perked up. "No shit? Some other sucker fell for it, too?"

"Fell for what?"

Jack Iserson lifted a eyebrow. "Well, I wouldn't admit it to my buddies, of course, but I think that bitch I bought the drink for was a *guy,* one of those fucking cross-dressers. I ain't no pansy boy, Detective. That's what we argued about—I told the faggot he ought to give me my beer money back. That's when she—*he*—pulls out this blade and slices me." Iserson hiked up the leg of his shorts so Greg could get a full view of the narrow bandage going diagonally across his thigh, about half a foot above his knee. "Got me good, too. Took twenty stitches to close this up so it won't leave a big ass scar."

"What did this person look like?"

Iserson shrugged. "In the bar? Hell, it was dark enough so that I thought it was a nice-looking woman, you know? Kinda tall, short blonde hair, dressed nice. I think her eyes were dark blue." The man gave Greg a sidelong glance. "She had tits but I guess they were fake."

"Uh-huh." Greg made a few scribbles in his notebook, then shut it. "All right. I'll ask around, tell the beat cops to keep their eye out. We'll let you know if we come up with anything."

"Yeah, right. Like you got a snowball's chance in the sun of finding this queer. But hey—" Iserson lifted his beer can in a mock toast. "Thanks for trying."

"I'll let myself out," Greg said and did just that, thankful to feel the fresh air and fall sunlight on his face. Total dead end—the odds of catching the perp weren't high to begin with, but he'd leave that problem to the street cops. If there was a connection between this and what had happened to Hannah, he sure couldn't figure it out. And how was he going to deal with Hannah, find out what exactly *had* happened to her without letting on that Winnie had ratted her out?

One step at a time, he thought as he went back to his car. He *was* going to figure out what the hell was going on with Hannah Danior.

Just for professional reasons, of course.
Of course.

Thursday—October 12th...

"Hey, babycakes, how's the leg?"

Hannah couldn't help grinning at Winnie's nickname for her, though God knew she'd told her best friend a hundred times not to call her that because it sounded so silly. Hell, maybe she secretly liked it—no one else had ever given her a nickname. No one else had ever had enough affection for her to bother.

"Okay," she said as she worked at filling up the little ceramic sugar holders. At two-thirty the worst of the lunch rush had dissipated, giving her a chance to catch up on her side work. "Almost healed."

At first Winnie shot her a mystified look, then her gaze shifted over Hannah's shoulder and her eyes gleamed a bit. "Hey, you got a customer on your station. Booth two."

"Thanks." Winnie snatched up a glass of water and a roll of silverware, turned to step around the counter, then hesitated. Greg Jedrek was sitting patiently in the booth, watching the Belmont Avenue traffic through the big front window. Maybe someone else could take him—

Stop it, she thought sharply. This man did you a tremendous favor and you can't even take his lunch order? What's up with that?

Come on. You know you wanted to see him again.

The thought came from no where and everywhere, what she'd heard a hundred people refer to as "left field." It brought heat to her cheeks and Hannah was grateful that Winnie had gone on about her work—she would have surely seen and capitalized on it. Rather than dwell on feelings she couldn't explain, Hannah took a deep breath and headed to the booth.

"Hi," she said brightly when Greg looked up and saw her. "My name is Hannah and I'll be your server."

He grinned. "Hannah, huh? I never would have guessed."

She put down the water and silverware, watched as he fiddled with the paper ring holding the napkin in place. "So, how are you? I mean…"

"You mean what am I doing here?"

"Well, yeah. That too."

"Lunch," he said and plucked the menu from its stainless steel bracket. "That would be a great start. Plus I just wanted to stop by and see how you are."

"Ah." For a second Hannah didn't know what else to say, then she went for the mode she knew well. "Would you like something to drink?"

"Coffee," Greg said. He barely glanced at the menu. "And a bleu cheese burger."

"French fries with that?"

"Sure."

"Okay. I'll be right back with your drink." Hannah scooted off and put the order in, then got his coffee. Such a mundane series of events—like he was just the latest of half a hundred customers she'd wait on over the course of today. She reached for the coffee pot and glanced over at him, inadvertently met his eyes when he was staring at *her.* This time, *he* blushed and looked away—not a very cop-like response.

"Your burger'll be up in a few minutes," Hannah said when she set his cup in front of him.

Before she could turn away, he touched her wrist. "So, you're okay?"

Hannah frowned. "What do you mean? Of course I'm okay."

Greg shrugged. "No more… attacks or anything like that?"

She stared at him. "Attacks? What are you talking about?"

He shrugged. "Just checking. Whoever did this is still on the loose, you know." He glanced at her, then away.

"If you're thinking he'll come back and finish the job, I doubt it," Hannah said. He glanced back at her, his gaze sharp, and she could have kicked herself. "I mean, I didn't see him or anything, so why would he?"

"Why would he attack you in the first place?" Greg retorted.

"I have to get back to work," Hannah said abruptly.

"Of course—sorry."

She went back behind the counter in a little bit of a daze, half angry that the conversation had gone back to her incident, half regretful. Damn, did her entire life have to revolve around her *Affliction?* Bad enough she might turn around and have some new wound just *appear* somewhere on her body, but worse that when there was a guy in her life, that's all he and she talked about. Wait—*guy* in her life? Since when? Greg was just the detective who'd come to question her on a case, that's all.

Aggravated at herself, aggravated at him, she stalled on bringing him his food then felt guilty when she realized it was barely warm. Greg didn't complain, just thanked her and started eating, intentionally focusing his attention on the food and the street outside the window. When she came back with the check, he took it and smiled at her. "Hey, how're the dogs?"

"Good," she said. "Same pain in the neck they always are."

The detective chuckled. "They wouldn't be any fun if they weren't."

"Come by and play with them anytime."

Greg's look of surprise was masked as quickly as it had appeared, although Hannah wondered if she had done as well at hiding her own surprise. Another "left field" thing, this time blurted out of her mouth with no way to take it back. And how could she have, anyway, when his expression changed to one of obvious delight?

"Well, great—I'd love to."

"You, uh, have my number," Hannah managed. "Call first, make sure I'm around. Sometimes I have class or whatever."

"Great," he said again. "And thanks." He stood, letting her off the hook. "I'll be in touch. Take care."

Hannah nodded, then left him to take his check up to the register. It all sounded so normal, so everyday. *Hey, come by and play with the dogs. Thanks! See you later! Okay, bye!* Like they were just two people who knew each another, Dick and Jane or Bob and Mary or Jack and Stella. She stared after him as he left, wanting just that—normalcy—but knowing it just wasn't *so.* The reality was that he was a cop, a homicide detective, and she was… well…

A victim.

Greg Jedrek lived in a black and white world—no, a black, white and *red* world. One filled with broken laws and blood, and the constant search for why those things happened. Her own world was anything but black and white—gray was more like it—but it sure was *red.* She couldn't explain the things that happened to her, and if she kept seeing him, even as innocently as in here, sooner or later he and her Affliction were somehow going to cross paths. The things happening to her were increasing and the law of averages was against her—that something had happened right in front of Winnie proved that. She needed to stay away from Greg Jedrek, if only as an effort to keep what little peace of mind she had intact.

Then why on earth had she just given him an open-ended invitation to come and see her?

««—»»

"Come on, come on," Tony muttered. "Answer the fucking door, would you?"

Finally he heard footsteps, Carrie's heavy tread coming down the steps of the interior hallway. She wouldn't use the buzzer to let him in—too paranoid for that. When she peered through the curtain and saw it was him, she smiled. "Hey, Tony. Come on up. It's good to see you."

"Yeah," he said, making no effort to disguise the gruffness in his voice. He wasn't that happy to see her, but at the same time, he was—it was a love/hate sort of thing. The truth was that he had liked her a lot better the way she used to be, back before—

Well, no sense in thinking about *that.* He'd gone through the counseling with her, listened to all the doctors and their monologues about leaving the past entirely behind, moving on and into her new life with her. He thought it was all bullshit—the past was there and nothing you could do would change it or make it go away. He'd been perfectly happy with his life and it hadn't been his choice to turn everything on its head. Carrie had done that, and now *he* had to live with her in the new life. What a crock. But like the rest of it, the fact that she had done what she had done was also in the past and couldn't be changed.

Carrie was wearing some ridiculous workout thing, some kind of hot pink leotard with flesh-colored tights and fuzzy leg warmers, a daisy-patterned bandana wrapped around her hair like a leftover hippie from the sixties. The television screen showed a tape on pause, one of those stupid hip-hop workout videos that his wife Dara sometimes used. He despised them.

Carrie hugged him before he could pull away. "What are you doing here?" she asked. "Did you just miss me or do you need something?"

"Nothing in particular." He stared at her, then realized what he was doing and glanced around the apartment instead. "Just wanted to check on you and see how things were going, make sure you're staying out of trouble."

Carrie shrugged. "I'm doing okay." She picked up the remote and switched off the television. Thank God—Tony didn't think he could have stood it if the fresh-faced girlie on the screen had started babbling at him to "Push it up, down, one-two-three!"

"Yeah?" Tony headed toward the kitchen without being invited. "What have you been up to?"

"Same old stuff," Carrie said and followed him.

She didn't say anything else, just leaned against the doorway and watched as Tony poked around her kitchen. He thought she seemed nervous, like a dog waiting for its owner to realize his favorite shoes had been chewed. There was something in the sink and he glanced at it, then looked again. It was a knife, one of those "fake" switchblades with a thumb lever that kept it legal where a button wouldn't have. When he looked closer, he saw red crusted around the base of the blade, a stain on the white porcelain below it where it hadn't been rinsed. He picked it up. "Staying out of trouble, huh?"

Carrie shrugged. "It's just a pocket knife, Tony. What's the big deal?"

"Yeah?" He carried it over to her and held it up. "What's this red stuff at the base?"

Carrie's look was sly. "Ketchup."

"No shit." He stared at her, then his left hand whipped out and he had a good fistful of her hair. He yanked her closer to the blade and held it in front of her face. "Then you won't mind licking it."

"No—stop it!" she cried. She tried to twist away, ineffectively slapping at his hold on her hair and pushing at him. "That's dirty!"

"But it's just *ketchup,* remember? What's the big deal?" He let go with a sneer.

Carrie grabbed at the knife and he let her have it before she did something supremely stupid like cut herself. "Asshole," she snarled as she threw it back in the sink, then turned on the water and grabbed up a soapy sponge. "Why do you even come here anymore? You don't like me. Why don't you just leave me alone?"

"Because you're still blood," he said flatly. He watched her as she scrubbed at the blade, knew she was trying to erase he last traces of red. "So who'd you cut, anyway?"

"Nobody you know," she retorted.

"Kill someone?"

"Don't be absurd."

Well, that was something anyway. Tony didn't think his sister had the smarts to do something like murder and get away with it, but a little knife fight… yeah, she could probably handle that. He decided to drop it; the less he knew, the better. Awkward silence then, and when she finished washing the knife and tossed it into the dish drainer, he saw her eyes had filled up with tears. The sight made him cringe.

"Tony," she said pleadingly. She stretched a hand toward him. "Can't we just get along? You're my big brother and you know I love you. You used to love me—can't we just go back to the way we always were?"

He folded his arms, staying out of reach. "Little problem with that."

"I want to see Dara, and my nephew. I'm still the same—"

"No," he interrupted. "And you aren't—not by a long shot. Just look in the mirror."

"Inside, I *am,"* she insisted.

Tony snort. "Yeah, whatever. Tell me another story." He turned his back and headed toward the front door, heard her following. "Anyway, like I said, I just came by to check on you."

"I'm fine," she said brusquely. "Don't worry about me."

They stared at each other for a moment. Carrie leaned forward and held the door shut before he could pull it open. "I love you no matter what, you know. No matter what you think of me, no matter what you do. I'd do anything for you. You'll always be my brother. And I'll always be your—"

Tony slapped her, hard, before she could finish.

Then he walked out and left her crying behind him.

Wednesday—October 25th...

Tony, still bleary-eyed with sleep, poured himself a cup of coffee then headed into the living room to watch the morning news.

Where he found his son Ben wearing a lime green fairy outfit.

And the morning went to hell in a handbasket from there.

Dara, sewing pins sticking out of her mouth, was on her knees next to Ben, fiddling with the material. She looked up in surprise at her husband as Ben beamed at him. "Daddy, look at my Halloween costume! Mommy's almost finished with it and on Monday we get to—"

"Take that thing off of him," he ordered before Ben had a chance to finish.

Beneath dark hair like Tony's own, his son's face immediately went red, and the tears weren't far behind. "But Dad, I'm Peter Pan!"

Dara straightened and put a hand on Ben's shoulder. "Tony, it's just a costume," she said. "Come on, you remember the movie Peter Pan, don't you?"

Tony slammed his cup down on the end table and grimaced when hot coffee splashed on his fingers. "My memory has nothing to do with this. I won't have my son wearing something that makes him look like a little green faggot. Get rid of it."

"No!" Ben yelled. His voice was piercing. "It's *mine* and I like it!"

"Oh, for God's sake, Tony." Dara looked at him in exasperation. "You aren't starting that garbage again, are you? This is your son you're talking about, not—"

He jerked a finger up and pointed at her, its tip stopping only an inch from her eyes. "Don't *even* finish that sentence," he hissed. Tony could tell his wife wanted to say more, then she wisely closed her mouth. Still glaring at her, he reached down and got a handful of that ugly green material, the spiky collar flap hanging over Ben's shoulder, and gave it a hard enough tug to rip it free. "Get in the bathroom and take this *off,*" he said. "Don't make me tell you again."

"Dad, you tore it!"

"I'm going to tear it right off of you! Now what did I tell you to do?"

"Dad!"

Wrong answer. Tony grabbed the boy's shoulder, spun him, and smacked him hard on the butt. "What'd I just tell you?" he yelled as Ben began to screech. "See what happens when you don't *listen?"*

"Tony, stop it!" Dara cried. She levered herself between Tony and Ben, and when Tony lost his grip she pushed Ben toward the other room. "Hush up and go take off the costume. We'll make you another one—you can be Captain Hook." The child looked like he wanted to argue, but the words stayed unspoken when he saw his father's furious expression. Sobbing, he ran out of the living room.

Before Dara could continue, Tony had her by the forearm. He dug his fingers in as hard as he could, then twisted her arm behind her back and slammed her into the wall. She cried out but low, trying to muffle it so Ben wouldn't hear. "Don't you ever come between me and my son again," he growled at her. He pushed against her, increasing the pressure on her shoulder and letting his fingernails sink into the skin of her arm until he heard her whine. "And if I ever catch you dressing him like a queer-boy again, I'll beat you so badly your own mother won't recognize you. Get it?"

Another upward jerk and she gasped and nodded. "Y-Yes! Yes!"

He pulled Dara off the wall and pushed her away from him, shooting her a contemptuous look as she banged one shin into the coffee table. Rubbing her arm, his wife didn't look at him as she hurried to her son's room to change his outfit.

Good. She'd damned well think twice before she did something as stupid as put Ben in a pansy-ass costume again. Pirate? Fine… though a baseball or basketball player would be better, football player best of all.

Yeah, Tony thought, and decided to go tell Ben that he wasn't going to be a pirate either. A football player. I'll pick up the costume after work and bring it home tonight.

«‹—›»

Hannah was almost dressed, just slipping her uniform over her head, when it happened. A suddenly harsh stinging along her left forearm, followed almost instantaneously by a muscle-wrenching ache in her shoulder. Twenty seconds later, a lump, bruised green and black, rose like a quail egg in the middle of her right shin.

"Ow—what the *hell?!*"

She clamped her right hand over her forearm and went to her knees on the floor, folding over on herself and willing the pain to subside, the massive throb in her shoulder to lessen. After a couple of minutes the agony lessened to bearable and she saw Knothead and Puddles hovering nervously outside the bathroom door. Sweat trickled down one side of her face as she gave them a rictus smile. "It's okay, gals. No problem."

Sucking in air, Hannah grabbed the edge of the sink and pulled herself up, then examined her forearm. Black, purple and yellow, the smeared but still quite discernible print of a large hand tipped at the fingertip ends by crescent-shaped gouges that stopped just a hair's breath short of bleeding. The knot on her shin was more of an annoyance than anything, but her shoulder was another matter. She'd need to cover the arm by wearing a long-sleeved top under her uniform and pulling that over her head was a new lesson in the ways that a woman's shoulder muscles could scream.

"Marvelous," Hannah muttered. "Just marvelous." She got herself redressed and downed a couple of aspirins, hoping that would help. The long-sleeved top was okay, though a couple of finger-shaped blotches still peeked from beneath the sleeve's edge. Nothing to be done about that but head to work and hope no one noticed.

No one, of course, being Greg.

«‹—›»

"Good morning."

Greg smiled at the sound of Hannah's voice… funny how he'd gotten used to it over the last couple of weeks. He hadn't really meant to come into the Diner every day, but somehow that's how it had worked out. Most times just coffee, but now and then he'd opt for a full breakfast, sit for a half hour or so even though she never had the time to talk. He'd only taken her up once on her offer to play with the dogs; then, afraid he was making her too nervous, he'd stayed maybe ten minutes, no more. He told himself it was all work-related, he was keeping an eye on her to make sure she was all right, Eloise Addison's killer was still at large, et cetera, et cetera. Business, that's all.

Yeah, right.

"Hi, Hannah. How's it going?"

"Okay." She smiled at him but there was something off about it, strained. "Coffee?"

"Oh, yeah—my morning jumpstart." He studied her for a second. He'd grabbed a bowl of cereal at home this morning, but suddenly he wanted an excuse to stay a bit longer than he'd planned, see what was up in Hannah's world on this late October day. "And maybe a… bagel. Yeah, a bagel would be good."

"Got it," she said and scribbled on her pad. "Back in a flash."

She turned away and that was all it took—that flash—for Greg to catch his first clue. He stayed where he was, resisting the urge to get up and go after her, throw a dozen questions at her before she could even get back to the coffee pots. But he was damned sure ready when she came back with his cup; the instant it settled on the table Greg reached over and pushed up the sleeve covering her left wrist.

For a second she froze and they both stared at the ugly bruises.

"Where'd that come from?" he demanded in a low voice. "Who did it?"

Hannah hastily pushed down her sleeve and glanced around. "No one," she said. "I banged into the door when I was walking the dogs."

Greg scowled at her and at least she had the grace to look almost comically embarrassed. "Come on, Hannah—that's the best you can do?"

"I have customers, Greg."

He let her go, content to know that she had to come back. It wasn't in her nature to totally abandon him, and by now everyone in the place knew—he'd made sure of it—that he only wanted her to wait on him. To everyone but Hannah and Winnie, he'd become all but invisible, like part of the restaurant furnishings. Hannah had never said anything about the cut on her leg, and he'd never let on that Winnie had ratted on her. Now there were more bruises, this time around her wrist. Was there someone else in her life, someone he didn't know about? An abusive boyfriend, or someone taking advantage of her past fear and hurting her now? Just the idea of it infuriated Greg, but if she wouldn't admit it, or wouldn't ask for help—

"Why am I not surprised to find you here?"

Damn—Tony.

Somehow Greg managed to give his partner a wan grin. "Hey. Have a seat."

"Don't mind if I do." Tony looked around, his gaze taking in everything. "Still after that Hannah Danior, huh?"

"I'm not 'after' anyone," Greg retorted. "I'm just keeping an eye on her. In case it slipped your mind, her attacker's still out there."

"Nothing wrong with *my* memory, Greg. Blank spots are your girlfriend's specialty."

Greg let the crack slide, knowing it would accomplish nothing to argue. Tony just liked to bait people, get them all riled up for the fun of it. Greg had other things on his mind right now.

"Long time no see," Tony said cheerfully when Hannah brought Greg's bagel. "Cup of coffee when you get a chance, okay?"

"Sure." Before she left, Hannah shot Tony a look that Greg couldn't have described as anything but cautious.

When she went for the joe, Greg leaned closer to Tony. "Check out her left wrist when she comes back," he said. "She won't spill, but someone's been laying hands on her."

Tony raised his eyebrows. "No kidding."

Hannah was back in a few moments and Greg had to hand it to his partner for tact; Tony moved this and that on the table, all the while keeping up a light chatter just long enough to give him a clear view of the bruises on Hannah's arm. When she was done and gone, Tony looked at him and shook his head. "Yeah, you weren't kidding. Looks like a hand print." He was quiet for a few seconds as he mulled this over. "What do you think—a gift from a boyfriend?" He grinned suddenly. "Not to break your heart or anything."

Greg shrugged, unwilling to let on that the thought disturbed him. A *lot.* "I don't know. She won't say."

His partner stirred sugar into his cup. "Then work on her. Turn on some of that Iowa farm boy charm. She likes it."

"She's not exactly talkative."

Tony regarded him solemnly. "Whether you want to admit it or not, she *owes* you. And she *likes* you. If she didn't, you could come in here from now until all your hair fell out and she wouldn't so much as bring you a clean spoon."

"I suppose." Greg glanced around until he spotted Hannah. She didn't seem particularly busy, but she wasn't coming over to talk to him, either. Why—because he'd asked about her wrist? Or because his partner had shown up?

Tony took a sip of his coffee and grimaced. "Nasty shit. How can you drink this?"

"What's wrong with it?"

"Army sludge." Tony tossed a dollar on the table and stood. "I'll see you back at the station. Don't screw off here too long."

"Hey," Greg protested. "I'm not—"

Tony waved a hand. "Save it, lover boy."

Greg scowled after him, but his expression smoothed out as Hannah edged toward the table, one eye on the kitchen door in case Zubro showed up. She held up a coffee pot invitingly. "More coffee with your bagel, sir?"

"Sure." Greg grinned, but that faded soon enough. "Hannah, tell me what happened to you last night—or this morning. Whenever it was."

She hesitated, then shook her head. "It's nothing, Greg, really. Is your… partner coming back?"

"No. Why?"

"He makes me nervous," she blurted, then looked embarrassed. "I don't know why. I'm sorry—you guys are probably best friends or something."

"No," Greg said honestly. "We're not even close."

"Ah." She sounded strangely relieved.

"Well, hey," he said jokingly. "I guess the idea of a double date is out the window."

Hannah looked at him with such a shocked expression that he couldn't help bursting into laughter.

And after a long moment of staring, she actually joined in.

Friday—October 27th...

"Okay, what's up with you two?" From her spot on the couch, Hannah folded her arms and regarded Knothead and Puddles. Friday night was her chill-out time, an evening of cheap and easy food—usually frozen pizza—and three hours of her favorite TV series, *The Fugitive, CSI,* and *Nash Bridges.* It let her unwind and forget about her problems, work, and school, plus it gave her a little "safe" excitement via the fantasy of television—just the way she preferred excitement in her life, thank you very much. But tonight the dogs were being a pain; for the last forty-five minutes all they'd done was pace between the couch and the north-facing window, whining and snuffling. The evening was unseasonably warm, nearly seventy, so she'd opened the window just enough to let them stick their heads through. Hannah liked the fresh air, but if this was their reaction, she'd just as soon shut it again.

Finally, during a mid-CSI commercial, Hannah lost her patience. "You guys get down," she ordered. "Right now." Both dogs spun and looked ashamed, then immediately went back to jockeying for a spot at the window. "Between you and the traffic, I can't hear a thing on the television," Hannah said crankily. She hoisted herself up and stomped to the window, grinning when the dogs high-tailed it. "What the hell is out there anyway?" A rhetorical question, but she glanced down at the street, just because.

Just in time to catch a glimpse of a familiar face scanning the sidewalk from a car in a parking spot across the street.

Greg.

Ten seconds later Hannah was headed down the stairs, pausing only to snatch her keys from the top of the television. She barely checked for traffic as she stormed across the street and got a couple of horns blown for her effort; the noise made Greg glance her way; in an instant, his expression went from curious to caught-in-the-headlights guilty.

"What the hell do you think you're doing?" Hannah demanded. The car was a dark gray, four-door sedan, standard CPD undercover issue, and she slapped one hand angrily on the top of the car's roof. It made a satisfying noise, right up there with how mad she was right now. "Who said it was all right to spy on me?"

"Hannah—"

"Get out of the car! Get out, right now!"

Obligingly he opened the door and stood, looking like a strange cross between a boy caught doing something naughty and a stubborn-faced adult. "Now what?"

She planted her hands on her hips and glared up at him. "How long have you been sitting down here and watching me, huh?"

"Just a little while," he said, but his tone was too defensive, the words too quick. He might be a great detective with the bad guys, but she wasn't a bad guy. He wasn't going to get away with this. "Not long."

"Almost an hour," she snapped. "That's why the dogs have been so antsy. Which, by the way, is an hour *too* long." For a long moment she was so furious she couldn't speak or move, then on impulse she lashed out and kicked him in the ankle with the toe of her sneaker.

"Ow!"

"Go home, Greg. Just... go *home.*" Before he could respond, she whirled and darted back across the street, jammed her key into the lock and stormed back upstairs. Too late she realized she hadn't pulled the door tightly enough behind her; when she turned at the top of the landing to go back down, Greg had already closed it solidly behind himself and was headed toward her. Angrier more than ever, Hannah unlocked the door to her apartment and went in. The dogs foiled her attempt to slam it shut when they darted through the opening and zipped toward Greg, whining happily. "Damn it, get back up here! When did you two start misbehaving? Traitors!"

"My fault," Greg said as he led them back inside. "I guess I spoiled them."

"You sure did." Hannah stomped her foot. "And you can just turn right around and get the hell out of here!"

"Hannah, what are you so angry about?"

She stepped toward him and was pleased to see him back out of range. That would teach him. "You can't sit around and spy on me and expect me to think it's okay," she raged at him. "I'm entitled to some privacy, you know. Some peace of mind and a *life—*"

"Well, of course you are." Greg's expression was bewildered. "For crying out loud, I only did it because I was concerned about you. I just wanted to make sure you were all right, that's all."

"And that's why you've been coming in the Diner every day?" she demanded. "Out of concern for my welfare? When did you change careers and become a social worker?"

"I just wanted to make sure you were all right," Greg repeated stubbornly. He stepped toward her with a hand outstretched. "It's no big deal."

Hannah waited until he was within range, then balled up her fist and whacked him on the shoulder. "I'll give you a big deal! I will not be *watched* all the time!" She swiped at him again but he deftly leaned backward and she got nothing but air for her effort. She was so enraged, she was nearly crying; now he was backstepping as she flailed at him and the dogs circled them both anxiously. "I will not be treated like I'm a—a *patient* or something, *monitored—*"

A sidestep and a duck too fast for her to follow and then Greg had her by both wrists. She tried to kick him again and he forced her backward, then brought her down on the right side of the love seat with her legs pinned beneath his left knee. "Hannah—Hannah, *stop it!*"

"Let me go, damn you!" She struggled but his grip stayed firm and pain-free, then he crossed her wrists over one another and trapped both her elbows between his left arm and rib cage. Now she was solidly stuck.

"Listen to me," he said. She had tears streaking her face, her nose was all plugged up, and her hair had gone wild. With his free hand he brushed it out of her eyes. "I'm *sorry*—I never meant to make you this upset. I swear it."

"I won't have you *monitoring* me," she said fiercely. More tears spilled from her eyes, and she damned herself for her show of weakness. "There's nothing wrong with me, damn it!"

"It wasn't like that at all," he said calmly. He hesitated then leaned forward and slipped his right arm across her shoulders, pulling her to his chest in a light hug. When he spoke again, his voice was muffled against her hair. "I was just… afraid for you. Afraid that someone would hurt you again and there would be no one around to help you. I just couldn't let that happen. Because I care about you."

Hannah stopped struggling and sat there, very still. Was this true? Or was it some kind of a game to him, a cat-and-mouse detective thing where the cop would use any ploy to get the bad guy?

But she *wasn't* the bad guy, and she was betting that Greg Jedrek knew that.

Although he didn't let go entirely, Greg's hold on her loosened enough for her to sit back a little and stare at him. So much time around him the last few weeks or so, but she'd never been this close to him before, never noticed how light blue his eyes were or the small but deep scar that ran diagonally across the right side of his jaw, probably some childhood injury. "Greg," she said hesitantly. "I'm not—"

He leaned forward and kissed her before she could finish.

Greg's lips were warm and soft, the whole sensation was dizzyingly sweet—she'd never been kissed like this before. His arms felt as warm as his mouth, and where his hands rested lightly against her back and shoulder raised sudden, ferocious heat. Pecks on the cheek, a neutral pat on the back from a doctor or nurse; the only truly affectionate touch she'd ever gotten had come from Winnie. All her air disappeared, as though Greg had somehow found a way to let the oxygen out of the balloon that contained her life's supply. She gasped against his mouth and he pulled back; she found a place to hold onto his jacket and followed, letting herself flow with the feeling for just a few more seconds before they separated.

Greg's face reddened. "I'm sorry," he said. "I shouldn't have done that."

Hannah smiled, felt her own cheeks fill with heat. "There are worse things in the world than a first kiss, Detective. Come on." She grasped his hand and pulled him to his feet, willing herself to ignore the tingle his touch woke against her skin. These feelings and sensations—this *attraction*—was way too new to her, strong and out of her league to deal with. Part of her screamed for more, for discovery… but another part shied away from the big unknown and filled her with fear. She would have to be very, very careful about this. "I'll make you a cup of coffee or something. If you insist on watching after me, you're going to have to do it from *inside* my apartment from now on."

Saturday—November 18th...

He's had a good day—hell, he's had an excellent *day. He's spent most of it shopping at the Harlem & Irving Mall, going from store to store and buying stuff for himself, little things that no one else would ever buy him and he usually wouldn't buy for himself. Stuff like soap that smelled good, a soft, pale green sweater, an over-sized bath robe, a coffee cup with a cat on it that he found appealing even though he didn't particularly like animals. Not a care in the world, no problems, everything is just right—*

Until he opens the passenger side door of his car, flips the seat forward, and leans in to put his packages in the back.

Obviously aiming for a private romp and stomp in the backseat, the guy grabs him from behind and tries to push him inside, then come with him. But the attacker has sadly misjudged the strength of his victim; he braces his left leg against the body of the car and levers himself backward, leaving everything in the car but his own hands. He still has that great Lev-A-Lok knife, his favorite, but this time it's tucked in the side pocket of his slacks—he would never think of being alone in someplace like a dark parking lot after shopping unless he can get protection safely and instantly into his hands. By the time he turns, the knife is out and open.

The man who's grabbed him is Puerto Rican and slightly taller than him, and he can see the surprise blasting into the guy's dark eyes as the knife drives home—once, twice, three times. He's always had good speed with a weapon. The attacker goes down soundlessly, the pain of his wounds sucking away any air he might have had for a scream.

His heart is pounding fearfully as he glances around—no witnesses, thank God. Still nervous, he nudges the still form with the toe of one shoe, ready to jump out of range. But the guy's eyes are open and staring somewhere into infinity—nice and dead, thank you, over and out, amen. Chewing the inside of his cheek, he briefly considers checking the man's wallet and pockets for cash, then decides against it—too much of a chance he'll get blood on his clothes or someone will show up, and then all kinds of shit will hit the proverbial fan. Instead he carefully pushes at the the body with his foot until it rolls partway under the driver's side of the car next to him. Then he leans down and wipes his knife on the man's pants leg before slipping it back into his pocket, climbing into his car, and quickly driving away.

««—»»

"Where'd you say we were going?"

In the living room of Hannah's apartment, Greg scratched Knothead's ears and grinned at Hannah's question. "I didn't."

"Come on—'fess up. What if I don't like it?"

"You might not," he replied. He gave each pooch a pat on the butt, then sidled up to the bathroom door and peered in.

"I see you," she said. It didn't stop her from applying a light coat of lipstick. "As a stand-in for *The Invisible Man*, you're a flop."

"I'm crushed."

"So—"

"Mama Desta's," Greg answered before she could ask. "It's on Clark Street. Down home Ethiopian."

That got her attention. "Ethiopian?"

He raised one eyebrow. "How do you know you won't like it unless you try it?"

She shrugged, but he could see the curious sparkle in her tawny-colored eyes when she glanced at him, then looked back at the mirror. Each day that sparkle extended a bit, and maybe it was ego but Greg liked to think he was the reason for that, the way that over the last three weeks he'd implemented what he privately called *The Attention and Careful Handling of Hannah.* There was no doubt that he'd fallen for the girl, *hard*—he thought she was gorgeous—the light brown eyes, the wispy, shoulder-length pale brown hair that shimmered to gold in the sunlight, her fragile, almost butterfly-like build… all of it suited him perfectly, filled some visual, physical and emotional need he hadn't even known had needed filling until the night he'd impulsively leaned over and kissed her. He still saw her scars, of course, but now they didn't really register—they were as much a part of Hannah as the way she tilted her head and looked up at him from below her eyelashes when she laughed. Hannah was Hannah, and the scars just… *were.*

She reached for a comb and he left her to finish getting ready, afraid she'd feel like he was hovering. He probably was, just because he was so crazy about her. The way she talked and laughed, the way she moved and chastised the dogs when they were naughty—that Please-don't-let-them-see-I'm-laughing expression. There'd been so much hell in her life that Greg sometimes felt like he was holding onto some impossibly breakable piece of blown glass, so easy to destroy but so worth the struggle not to, especially when he saw how she'd relaxed around him, almost blossomed. The smallest things were so telling, like the new white knit sweater she'd bought to wear tonight; probably a thrift shop special but it looked lovely on her and even bargain shop clothes were hard to fit into Hannah's budget. Proud, as stubborn as he was at times, she would have never considered him helping her out in the money department—the most he'd gotten away with was buying groceries since he was spending so much time over here.

"Almost ready?" he called. "If we want to catch a movie at the Brew & View at nine-thirty, we should get a move on."

"Yeah, yeah, yeah," she answered good-naturedly. "Hold onto your—"

Whatever she'd meant to say ended in a strangled cry of pain. Greg registered the clatter of the plastic soap dish as it hit the tile, was already scrambling into the bathroom by the time Hannah thumped to the floor.

"Hannah, what happened? Are you all right?" She was lying on her side with her back to him, facing the bathtub and curled into a fetal position. He knelt behind her and touched her shoulder, heard the dogs circling and yapping anxiously outside the bathroom as she groaned. He tugged on her arm and she rolled toward him and onto her back. "What—*Jesus!*"

Where she wasn't pressing her hands over her stomach and chest, the front of her new white sweater was soaked with blood.

He pushed her hands aside and yanked up the sweater, then gaped at the three deadly-looking puncture wounds. Two at a diagonal to each other in her abdomen, the third—and worse—on an upward angle in the center, just below the sternum. Black-red liquid—heart blood—pumped sluggishly out of the inch-wide hole. He yanked the sweater back down and pushed her hands back over it. "I'll call an ambulance," he said hoarsely, but before he could get to his feet Hannah's scarlet-soaked hand clutched at the sleeve of his shirt.

"*No*—I'll be all right."

"Sure, you will," he said automatically, but he couldn't get up without jerking her—she was still holding on with surprising strength, this time with both hands as she abandoned the pressure on her wounds. Incredibly, she tried to sit up.

"What are you doing? Hannah, stay *still*—for God's sake, keep pressure on the wounds!" Greg wanted to push her down but he didn't dare be too rough—Jesus, there was so much *blood.* He'd seen countless crime scenes, but this was different, this was Hannah, someone he cared about. He felt like he was falling and panicking and screaming inside all at once, yet over all of it was the need to function efficiently and get her some help.

But damned if she wouldn't let him.

"I'll be *okay,* Greg." Her voice was a croak but she kept her grip on his arm with one hand, then reached up and clawed at the rim of the bathtub. Because he didn't have a choice, Greg helped her sit up, amazed that she could talk, amazed that she was still breathing let alone moving and making him kneel here and do nothing.

"Hannah, *please.* Let me get you some help!"

She grimaced and closed her eyes momentarily, then actually managed to smile a little. He saw with a sort of detached horror that there was blood inside her mouth, that horrid telltale sign of internal injuries. "Just give me a few minutes, would you? Then if I'm not better, you can call. I promise."

"In a few minutes, you'll be—" He choked off his own words, could've strangled himself for what he'd almost said. But damn it, if he didn't do something, and *fast,* Hannah was going to die on this stupid bathroom floor.

She blinked and inhaled, winced, then inhaled again. Blood had pooled beneath her and the knees of his jeans were soaked with it. "Better," she said breathily. "Definitely better now."

"Better than *what?*" he demanded. "You're probably just numb. Honey, we have to get you to a hospital! No… no! *Hannah, don't!*"

No good—he might as well have been shouting into the sink drain for all the attention she paid him. Greg would never understand how, but one way or another she got her legs under her and actually *stood*, one hand hanging onto him and the other putting a smeary red hand print on the edge of the sink. He came upright with her because he didn't know what else to do; he wanted desperately to run for the telephone in the other room, but he didn't dare let go of her. Was she insane? Was *he?*

Ten seconds, then twenty; she stood there and panted and didn't do anything else. Back in Iowa Greg had once helped a woman deliver a baby on the side of Interstate 80, and that's what Hannah sounded like now, little *whoo, whoo, whoo* train noises tumbling out of her mouth. Then, incredibly, her breathing evened out, she let go of the sink, and she let go of his arm.

"Help me get this sweater off," she said hoarsely.

"What?" He couldn't seem to move.

"It's ruined," Hannah said. She grasped the bottom of it and tried to pull it up, then hissed with pain. "Come on, Greg—help me, damn it."

He obeyed, pushing her hands aside and trying to ease the crimson-stained fabric upward as gently as possible. It took the longest half minute of his life, but Hannah finally stood there minus her once-white sweater. Her skin and the fabric of her bra, which had also once been white, was as covered in blood as everything else in the bathroom seemed to be, and adding to that were the three puncture wounds. Greg stared, unable to believe what he was seeing—they were still there, of course, but now they were partially… *closed.* The surrounding skin was bruised black and swollen, but the wounds themselves had nearly stopped bleeding, were now oozing only the barest hint of fresh fluid.

"What the hell is going on here, Hannah?" He dropped the sweater on the floor and kicked it aside, letting it pull part of the puddle of Hannah's blood with it. "What did you do?"

Perhaps it was shock and loss of blood, perhaps it was anger, but Hannah's face was gray-white. "What did *I* do?" Her mouth twisted. "You think I did this to myself? *God.*" She griped the sink and stood there, staring into the splattered porcelain. Then she actually laughed. "You and Dr. Tansey. I should have known."

Greg frowned when he realized what she'd said. "I don't have anything to do with Tansey," he said. "Don't make me the bad guy in this."

"Define *this*." Hannah glared at him, then gestured at herself and shook her head. "*This* is me, Detective. Who I am. *What* I am." A little unsteady, she still turned to face him. "These three are new," she said and pointed to the brand new injuries. "But here's your chance to get an eyeful of a few others you didn't know about. Here," she said and wiped at the smears of blood on her chest to reveal a pallid scar, thick and twisted, that ran across what showed of her left breast above her bra. "And here." Another scar, this one long and thin, followed the line of her collarbone. "They go with the ones on my neck, and my face, and my leg."

"But… *why?"*

Hannah didn't answer right away, just stared into space. "I've wondered about that for a long time," she finally said. "And I can't answer it. All I know is that I don't die from what happens to me, and I heal fast—*really* fast."

His hand was trembling, but Greg stretched out one finger and traced the heavy scar that ran around her throat. "Eloise Addison," he said softly.

"Who?" Hannah pushed lightly at him and he stepped aside so she could sit on the closed lid of the toilet and rest. Her injuries had stopped bleeding entirely now, but Hannah looked exhausted and bled out, anemic from loss of blood.

Greg pulled a washcloth off the rack and moistened it, then began to carefully wipe the blood from Hannah's torso. "The woman who was killed the night your throat… was cut. Remember?"

She sat very still, letting him minister to her. "I never knew her name," she said softly.

Greg nodded. "Actually, she wasn't anything like you," he told her. "Long, dark hair, brown eyes, probably fifteen or twenty pounds heavier. Older, too." His gaze went again to her throat, then he rinsed the washcloth and went back to work. "But the injuries—yours and hers—are *exactly* the same. I know—I studied the coroner's photographs."

"Exactly?" Hannah asked faintly.

"Yes." He met her eyes, then looked away. "Your throat, it's like a… photograph of what happened to her. Or maybe a mirror image."

"Mirror me," Hannah whispered, and for some reason, the phrase raised chill bumps along Greg's spine. All these injuries of hers—was that what they were? Mirror images of things that happened to other people? If so, who were the others, and why them? Why *Hannah?*

"Those poor people," she said, suddenly lifting her head. "If what's happened to me has happened to someone else, imagine the pain they went through."

Greg opened his mouth, then shut it. The pain *they* went through? Each individually, while Hannah had taken all of it on herself, *by* herself, as fantastic as that sounded. But… who were *they*? His gaze went to the hideous scar across her upper chest, the puckered, cigar-shaped circle just below the line of her jaw. Some of these he hadn't known about and, like the throat wound, at least one other could have undeniably been fatal, but what was the connection? With a little computer detective work, he must might be able to find it.

"I'm tired, Greg," she said softly. "Can we skip dinner tonight?"

Greg gaped at her. "Well, *duh,* Hannah. You're not going anywhere like this." He checked her wounds gently; not bleeding, but definitely still painful. If he hadn't seen it himself he wouldn't have believed she could still talk, let along stand of her own volition.

"I want to brush my teeth," Hannah told him. "My mouth tastes nasty."

Yeah, it would. He just hoped that her insides repaired themselves as quickly as her outside; otherwise, she could be spitting up blood for weeks. He helped her stand, then stood next to her while she scrubbed with her toothbrush and rinsed until the water ran clear again. Afterward, she gave him a wan smile. "You don't have to stay, you know. I'm fine."

"Oh, I think I will." His tone must've conveyed the futility of arguing. He glanced down and saw her jeans were soaked with a lot more blood than his. "I'll bring you some clean clothes, okay?" he suggested. "I'll throw those in the sink in some cold water."

"Yours too," she said.

He chuckled. "Not unless I want to drive home in my underwear."

"Then stay here tonight," she said. His eyes widened and she blushed. "Not like *that*, just, you know…" Her words stumbled off.

"That's a great idea," Greg said quickly. "I'll feel better being around tonight, anyway. And I'll order a pizza from Leone's—no, you have to eat," he added when she started to protest. "I'll clean up these pants after it gets here." Finally she nodded and he reluctantly left her alone in the bathroom while he phoned the pizza place, then found a pair of soft, flannel pjs for her to change into. "You okay?" he called through the door.

Hannah opened it a couple of inches. "Sure," she said through the crack, but he could see smudges of dark color below her eyes, the tell-tales circles of exhaustion. She'd lost so much blood—it was incredible that she wasn't comatose. "Almost done." She took the pajamas he offered. "Thanks."

A few more minutes and he got her settled on the couch beneath an afghan, saw her shudder now and then, chilled by the blood loss. The pizza came after awhile and he paid for it downstairs, staying back in the dark so the guy wouldn't see the mess down the front of his jeans, ignoring the deliveryman's puzzled expression at Greg's abattoir scent. Back upstairs Greg got out of his jeans and wiped down his legs, then wrapped himself in a towel; he and Hannah ate in silence, neither having much of an appetite. He put the leftover pizza in the frig and it wasn't long before she started to nod off, so he shut down the lights and helped her to the bed. He would have taken the couch except she didn't seem much inclined to let go of his hand.

Too wired to sleep, Greg lay in the semi-dark apartment and watched the traffic lights move across the ceiling, feeling guilty about having searched the bathroom in vain for a weapon but knowing it was something he'd had to do. She was in danger—that much was obvious. But with nothing in there to find, he had no earthly idea how he was going to protect Hannah.

Or even what it was he had to protect her *from.*

Sunday—November 19th...

Greg got up and walked the dogs in the morning, then left Hannah curled under the blankets on the bed after waking her up once and making sure she was okay. To keep from disturbing Hannah, he waited until he was at his own place to shower, then he headed to the station house to do a little research. Tony wasn't around and for that much he was grateful; he knew the other guys wondered about the two of them, why they weren't tight like partners usually were. What could he say? The luck of drawing a partner wasn't an absolute guarantee that the two of you would end up blood brothers, and he just didn't much care for Tony Rutland. Still, he didn't have to like someone to work just fine with him, so he could deal.

Greg stared at his computer screen, then tapped in a few search fields. The incident at Hannah's had happened at a little after seven o'clock, so he decided that was as good a place as any to start. On anyone else—hell, on *everyone* else—Hannah's wounds would have been fatal, so he added that to the search criteria, too.

SEARCH:
Type: Homicides
Sex: All
Age: All
Day: Saturday 11/18
Time: 18:00—21:00 hours
Area: All

It didn't take long for the system to offer up a list of three, and Greg called up the info on the computer and checked it. Two men, and one woman—the woman had been raped and strangled in the Robert Taylor Homes, one of the men had been killed by a shotgun blast to the chest in a liquor store robbery. The computer report indicated that the other man, however, had been found dead of three stab wounds to the chest.

"Pay dirt," Greg muttered. He'd gotten all he could from the data on the system, but a phone call to the 16th District in Jefferson Park got him one of the detectives, who gladly filled in the details.

"Dead guy's name is Raymond Cespedes," the detective in charge of the case told him. "Hispanic, twenty-six years old, record of petty robbery and a couple of attempted rapes. No big loss to the community, I promise."

"You got the report in front of you?" Greg asked. His mind still held a disturbingly clear image of Hannah's injuries. "Can you tell me where he was stabbed?"

"Yeah, hold on." A couple of moments of paper fluttering, then the cop came back. "Here, three times. Couple of punctures in the belly, but the coroner's note says the fatal one was the one in the center. Whoever whacked him caught it on enough of an upward angle to hit the heart."

"Got it," Greg said. The description sounded like an exact match, and it took an immense effort to keep his voice level when his mind kept comparing the dead man's wounds to Hannah's. The final stab had hit the *heart?*

"So what's the deal?" the detective asked. "You got something to share?"

"Nah," Greg said. "Just got a stabbing in the neighborhood and wondered if there was a connection."

"I doubt it," the other man said promptly. "Coincidence is all. Parking lot perps generally operate on opportunity. This Cespedes guy just had the bad luck to be in the way." The 16th District cop laughed wryly. "Who knows—maybe he tried to grab someone himself but found out he was overmatched."

"Could be," Greg agreed. "Well, thanks for your help." He hung up and sat there, half stunned. If he considered the leg wound that Winnie had told him about and his subsequent talk with Jack Iserson, this made three crimes with injuries he could match to Hannah. Iserson was painful but no big deal in the scheme of what had happened last night, but what about the rest of Hannah's scars? The cut across her throat, the huge, jagged scar across her chest, a half dozen others. Jesus, was this going to happen to her the rest of her life? And if so, how in God's name would she keep from going absolutely insane?

"Hey, Iowa. How's it going?"

Greg glanced up as his partner settled on the corner of his desk. "All right. You?"

Tony shrugged. "Fine. What are you working on?"

Greg hesitated, then turned his computer screen so Tony could see the statistics he'd pulled up. "I was at Hannah's last night when she got 'hurt' again," he said. Tony raised one eyebrow, but for once didn't come back with a sarcastic remark. Greg went on to tell him how Hannah's injuries seemed to be an exact match for the dead man's as well as Jack Iserson's, then capped it by bringing up the murder of Eloise Addison. "So what do you think?" he asked when he was finished.

"I think this is the weirdest fucking story I've ever heard," Tony retorted. "You been watching too much *X-Files* or something?"

"Maybe," Greg said. He should've known better. "It was a long shot anyway."

Tony gave him a sidelong glance. "Yeah. Like on another *planet.*" He stood. "I'm going to grab a bite. Want to join me?"

Greg shook his head. "No, thanks. I've still got some paperwork to catch up on." Tony gave him a mock salute in goodbye, and Greg's eyes narrowed as he watched the other man stroll away.

Funny. He'd known from the start that Tony wasn't going to believe him, but he really had expected more of a protest than that.

«««—»»»

Not wanting the number on his cell phone records, Tony made the call from a Convenient Store on Western Avenue.

"Yes?"

"Seems you were out and about last night," he said harshly. There was silence on the other end for a long moment.

"I don't know what you're talking about."

"Bullshit," Tony hissed into the receiver. "Parking lot at Harlem and Irving? Tell me I'm wrong." More silence, this time stretching out until Tony thought he'd lost his connection.

"How did you find out?"

"I have my methods," Tony said. "But you wouldn't believe me if I told you what it is. In case you care, the guy you iced? His name was Raymond Cespedes."

"I don't."

In spite of himself, Tony grinned. "I didn't think so. Just keep a lid on stuff, would you? And stay the fuck out of any more trouble."

"How did you find out?"

More insistent this time. Tony couldn't help glancing around the store, unconsciously making sure no one was within earshot, although who would have known what he was talking about anyway? There wasn't a soul within two aisles but he still lowered his voice. "It's the kid," he said. "She's back."

The sharp, indrawn breath on the other end was enough to tell him his info had hit pay dirt. *"Does she know? Did she recognize you?"*

"No," he answered. "Not yet, anyway."

"You should take her out."

Tony stared down at the floor and scowled. His fingers ached from gripping the receiver so tightly but he kept his voice light. "I don't think that's necessary. She doesn't know anything. If she did, she'd have said so already."

"You always did have a soft spot for her."

"That's not the point," Tony said shortly. "She's a nut case—doesn't remember a thing."

"Then how did you know what I did last night?"

"It's… hard to explain," Tony hedged. "Most of it was a wild guess, anyway." His voice hardened. "But I'm not screwing around here—right now we're okay, but step out of line and she could be a rope right to your door.

"And around your neck."

Tuesday—December 19th...

Greg pulled into the driveway at Tony's house and put the car in park. He started to honk the horn, then decided against it—Tony ought to be looking for him by now, so why annoy the neighbors? Personally, Greg thought car horns were the modern symbol of impatience personified, and he despised them.

Waiting, he studied the house. Tony wasn't the sociable type and Greg hadn't been here in awhile, since sometime last summer when he'd stopped by for...well, the same as now, some automotive malfunction with Tony's Oldsmobile that had made his partner beg a ride to work. Then the lawn had been green if a little shaggy around the edges; now there was a layer of unshoveled snow, not too deep, along the walkway and on the steps to the front porch. A line of Christmas lights blinked around the living room's picture window and Greg could see more lights flickering on a good-sized Christmas tree—of course, Tony and Dara would decorate the place for their son, Ben.

A silver Ford Windstar pulled up next to his jeep and Greg saw the door open, then something sailed up and over the roof of his car before the van pulled away. A half second later, the plastic-wrapped morning paper buried itself in the bushes at the side of the porch—lousy aim. If he didn't dig it out, the Rutlands would never find it.

Greg cut the engine and got out, made his way carefully along the slippery walk. Tony really ought to shovel before someone slipped and broke something but he doubted it would ever happen. He couldn't decide if it was laziness or egotism that made Tony think he was above bothersome chores. Retrieving the paper from the bushes, he brushed off the snow and climbed the steps. He was reaching for the doorbell when Dara Rutland opened the door and without looking up, stepped directly into his path.

"Good morning," he said pleasantly.

She jerked to a stop. "Oh!"

"Sorry," Greg said. "I didn't mean to scare you." He smiled at her, then found his expression freeze in place at the sight of the heavy purple bruise along her left cheekbone. She also had the small but unmistakable beginnings of a black eye.

"I r-remember you," she stammed. "You're G-Greg. I didn't see you. I…" She glanced nervously over her shoulder. "I'll—I'll get Tony."

"I brought up your newspaper, Dara." He held it out, but when she tried to take it from him, he didn't let go. Instead he looked pointedly at her face. "Are you all right?"

Her head bobbed up and down. "Oh, sure, of course." Another semi-frantic nod as her fingers went to her face. "This? I just… you know. Wasn't, uh, watching where I was going." She smiled thinly. "Call me clumsy."

Greg let go of the newspaper. "That's fine," he said easily. "As long as that's *all* it is. Otherwise, you call me. You know where I am."

She stared at him for a moment, then jumped when Tony's voice called out from the darker interior of the house. "Dara, what are you doing?"

"Greg's here," she answered before Greg could say anything else. She stepped inside but turned back before he could follow. "It would be best if you just waited in the car," she said.

He nodded and watched her hurry inside, then turned and went back down to the car. He could imagine her lying right now—*I went out to get the paper and saw Greg waiting in the car.* She wouldn't want her husband to know Greg had seen his handiwork. And that bruise, he'd seen it before. The same size, shape, and color, the previous night when he'd stopped by Hannah's apartment on the way home from work.

"Hey, what the heck is that on your face? And under your eye?"

"Beats me. It was there when I got out of the shower an hour ago. It's sore, but hey—at least it's not bleeding and it's not going to leave another scar. I can live with that."

I can live with that, Greg thought. As was Dara Rutland.

He shivered and started the engine, then turned the heater on high. Bad enough that Hannah endured what she did, but how could he live with actually knowing the person she was… what had she called it? *Mirroring.* As far as he knew, this had always meant that somewhere out there a stranger was being hurt, but now… God. If this connection were true, what was he supposed to do when he couldn't stop the cause?

Greg started when the passenger side door opened and Tony flounced onto the seat. "Hey, buddy."

"Hi," Greg said.

"Dara said she met you on the porch." Tony shot him a sidelong glance.

So she hadn't lied. Probably hadn't wanted to take the chance. "Yeah. I saw the paperboy throw the *Trib* into the bushes and got it out for you."

"Did you see her face? Man." Tony shook his head as Greg put the car into reverse and backed onto the street. "Unbelievable. She's cleaning out the basement and this box falls on her. Who the hell cleans out a basement at this time of year?"

"Maybe she was looking for Christmas stuff," Greg said. Better to play along—the more Tony thought Greg believed him, the less trouble Dara would face on the other end.

"Yeah." Tony sounded relieved. "That's it exactly."

"'Tis the season," Greg said, but his light tone sounded false and neither man said anything for the rest of the ride to work.

Monday—December 25th Christmas Day...

"I know all about you, you know."

He's filling the meds for the last round of his shift when Connie DuPree, one of the nurses from the other side of the floor, steps into the pharmacy lockup and closes the door behind her. He gives her a what-kind-of-shit-is-this? glance and keeps on going down his checklist. On the outside he is cool, calm, unconcerned; on the inside, his heart is thundering and a nasty layer of sweat has instantly gathered under his arms. He has to be careful not to screw anything up on the meds, a patient could die if he does and there won't be hiding that, now will there?

"Don't you have anything better to do?" he asks Connie. "Like take your catty little bitchself back to the gossip lounge? I don't know what you're talking about, anyway."

"Don't try to change the subject," Connie shrills. "Don't think for a moment that I'm not going to tell Rodney. He has a right to know."

"What difference is it to you?" he asks. He still keeps his vice carefully calm, no indication of the fear and rage building inside him. "Rodney made it clear months ago that he doesn't want to see you anymore."

"Only because he doesn't know the truth about you!" Connie glares at him vindictively. "But I know how to fix that. I'm calling him later this evening, you know. And once I tell him, you can kiss it all goodbye."

Connie turns and stalks out and he watches her go without saying anything else, then rechecks the meds he's laid out. No mistakes—good. He doesn't know exactly what she's found out, but he can't let that little whore get to him. She's a problem, yes, but he can deal with it, he's done it before, he'll probably have to do it again.

He does his rounds, doles out the meds, fills out his charts, checks the vitals of the nine patients under his care this shift, another day-in-the-life-of except this one ends on a holiday morning. Every now and then he sees Connie DuPree doing the same, coming to or from some mundane chore in the course of her day, the triumphant Little Miss 'Oh, by the way, I'm going to ruin your life today.' He will do what he has to do and it is not that job that makes his palms perspire and his blood pressure hike, but the fact that he must do it so close to where he works, to 'home', as it were. Still, sometimes situations are what they are.

And so he is waiting in the deserted employees' parking lot at the side of the building, crouched behind Connie DuPree's car when she steps up to her passenger side door at the end of her shift, which ends an hour later than his. Never let it be said that he doesn't learn from what others have taught him, and when she opens the driver's door, he shoves her forward, hard, then goes in on top of her. He is considerably heavier than her five-foot-two frame and it is easy to jam his legs between hers and pin her with her right arm beneath her while he leans his elbow on the back of her head, pushing any screams she might make into the cold vinyl of the passenger side car seat. His trusty knife is already out and he catches her scrabbling left hand in his, yanks it upward and faces it toward the floorboard, then slices her arm open vertically from wrist to elbow. The flesh separates easily and so does the artery beneath, flayed apart like a filet of fish. She tries to scream louder now, driven by pain, but he pushes as hard as he can on the back of her head, smothering the sound. The rest of this messy chore is easy, and it takes hardly any time at all for Connie DuPree to bleed to death and be still in the front seat of her car.

When she is finally still, he crawls backward off of her and checks his clothes, is pleased to see that he doesn't have any blood on them. He had the good sense to slip on surgical rubber gloves while he'd waited for her so there are no worries there; the knife he cleans on the slacks of her uniform before folding it away. He gives a moment's thought to leaving her there, relishes how humiliating it will be for her to be found with her legs splayed wide in her car, but he quickly dismisses the idea.

Better to conceal the killing as long as possible, so he folds up her legs and rudely shoves until her body, the white of her nurse's uniform conveniently covered by a dark woolen coat, is crammed into the space of her shadowed front seat.

Satisfied now, he stays low as he relocks the car, then quietly closes the door after tossing her keys inside. Swing-shift changes are always going on, and he can see a few people headed down the walkway toward the employee parking lot. He crab-walks to his own car four rows over, ignoring the ache in his thighs and keeping a close watch to make sure no one surprises him, or vice versa. Inside his car, he puts the gloves in a plastic grocery bag, which he will dump in the trash bin of a service station on the way home as he stops in to buy a little gasoline. He'll pay cash and be pleasant and completely anonymous with the cashier, then go home to his apartment and have a nice, relaxed Christmas breakfast, sleep a little, get up and take a nice long shower.

And later on he'll call Rodney and they'll get together for Christmas dinner. He has the menu all planned out.

««—»»

Hannah inspected the gift she'd just finished wrapping and smiled. Not bad for someone who seemed to possess four thumbs when it came to things in life requiring manual dexterity. To a lot of people, it might not seem like much, but Hannah had been hoarding her tips and budgeting for a month so she could get Greg something nice for Christmas; the soft cotton shirt and the accompanying teal-colored sweater in this box were easily the nicest thing she'd ever bought, and she couldn't wait to see him open it.

No tree, but she had picked up a glittery gold garland and a cheap little Santa Claus figure at dollar store. The garland was draped over the bookcase below the fat Santa, and she carefully placed Greg's gift next to it, finally positioning it on its edge to make it more noticeable. The whole idea that she was buying a gift for a boyfriend was simply amazing—who would have thought that a young girl, formerly comatose and once nearly insane, could have an almost normal life? One that included a job, a slow but steady regime of college courses, and yes… even a man.

A normal life.

Dr. Gorrado had told Hannah, in very small, carefully controlled, and non-detailed doses, about the things that had happened to her. *Kidnaped. Sexually abused. Probably tortured.* But they were just scary words—oddly, they held no real power in her existence. Was it because she had endured and survived whatever had taken place? Or was it because she continued to endure and survive the rest of it, the unexplainable injuries and scarring that, before Greg, she had been convinced would control her for the rest of her life?

But not now, not anymore.

It was Christmas morning, Greg was on his way here, and it had been over a month since anything had happened beyond the occasional quickly-disappearing bruise. Hannah didn't believe in God, but she did believe in trying to get along, and that people could sometimes, given the right season and circumstances, lighten up on the awful things they did to one another. This was that time, Christmas, and no matter if she followed its religious aspects or not, if there was ever a time for hope, this was it.

She walked the apartment end to end, the dogs following happily as she made her final circuit. Everything was clean and neat, the furniture was dusted, the floor swept and shined. Even her bed was made, but she paused and tugged at the bottom corner anyway. Would it happen later tonight—would she and Greg finally become intimate? She'd read the magazines and listened to the talk—nowadays to wait this long in a relationship for that final bond was almost unheard of. Then again, she wasn't exactly the common American woman, and Greg had proven time and again that he was, in his patience and his faith in her, nothing short of extraordinary.

But intimacy…

The idea brought a strange amalgamation of emotions with it—excitement, anticipation, curiosity… *fear.*

Hannah sighed and checked the kitchen counter, then glanced at the clock. Greg had brought over a bottle of Merlot a couple of nights ago, and it waited next to two exceedingly expensive Kmart wine glasses; their big Christmas evening plans included that wine and *A Christmas Story*, which was airing all day on channel thirty-two. She'd offered to cook but he'd said no; they would take it easy and he would treat for Christmas dinner at Ann Sather's up the street. She was more than ready for the evening to begin—

Fire ripped up her left forearm.

She cried out and thrust her arm away from her body, instinctively stumbling toward the sink. Knothead and Puddles spun and erupted in a series of panicked barks, hopping anxiously around her legs. Bent over the sink and gasping with pain, Hannah groped for the water faucet with her right hand and twisted it; a half second after the cold water splashed onto her arm, the flesh split wide and blood sheeted onto the white porcelain.

"*Damn* it, it's Christmas day!" The pain was incredible, the cut deep into the muscle and lengthwise down the artery. She ground her jaw and kept her arm in the sink with the wound facing downward as she twisted sideways and snagged the dishtowel to her left, fought to get it around the arm and close up the gash. She would *not* make a mess in here, bad enough this was happening today of all days, but everything was ready—

The doorbell rang.

Greg.

"Damn it," Hannah whispered again.

And with the towel wrapped around her forearm and already soaked through and dripping, she could do nothing but wait for him to come up the stairs and find her.

««—»»

"Come on, Hannah," Greg grumbled to himself good-naturedly. "It's cold out here."

Please—he was so *not* cold. He was far too happy and excited to be concerned about the twenty-degree temperature, or the slush on the sidewalk, or much of anything else that was going on in the rest of the world. What he did care about was that the daisies he'd bought at a package store on the way here were going to get frosted before he could do the boyfriendly thing and give them to her along with a nice big box of chocolate-covered cherries. He'd also gotten her what she'd asked for—a new bedspread (okay, so he'd gone a little overboard and gotten her a whole comforter set)—but he'd thought that as a gift, this was way too neutral; the flowers and candy would put the personal back into it.

Greg pressed the bell again, wondering if it was working, then realized that below the traffic he could hear both the dogs barking. The noise made him frown, then step back and reflexively peer upward at her window. What was this? They never barked at the doorbell. Juggling his packages, he dug out his keys and found the one that fit Hannah's front door; he'd never gotten around to giving it back to her and she'd never asked. But he'd also never used it since her time in Illinois Masonic Hospital.

He could hear the barking more clearly when he got into the front hallway. It put a rush in his step and on the landing he abandoned the flowers and packages altogether, shoved the key into the lock and pushed through without bothering to knock. "Hannah?"

The most obvious thing was the dogs—neither ran to meet him. He turned to the left and saw Hannah at the far end of the apartment. Her back was to him and she was bent over the kitchen sink. Knothead and Puddles yapped and circled at her knees like a couple of hovering kids.

"Hannah?" he repeated. She glanced at him over her shoulder and even from where he was by the front door he could see that she was crying. "Honey, what's wrong? Did something… happen?"

Well, of course something had happened—Greg knew the answer when his stride took him to the halfway point and he smelled the blood. He found her holding the kitchen towel wrapped around her wrist and forearm like a sopping, scarlet bandage, her face nearly gray from shock, pain, and blood loss. "Jesus."

"I need a clean towel," she said, and he was vaguely amazed that her voice, while tired, could sound so normal. It wasn't until he hurried to the linen closet and came back with a fresh towel that he realized she'd somehow managed to keep herself and the floor from getting splattered. "Thanks."

"Thanks?" Greg repeated. *"Thanks?"*

"Well, what do you want me to say?" she asked. Hannah unraveled the first towel and let it fall, revealing a gaping slash that ran from the center of her left wrist nearly to the inside of her elbow. Blood pulsed sluggishly from the wound, but the volume had obviously slowed. Still, he thought it looked like most of what had been in her body had gone down the drain with the running faucet.

"How long has this been bleeding?" he demanded. "You need stitches. And maybe a transfusion."

"No." She softened the flow of the water, then passed her arm beneath it, hissing from the sting. When most of the red had been rinsed away, Hannah carefully pressed the clean towel in place, the wound it around her forearm. "I'll be fine. I'll close it up with little BandAids, butterfly-style."

"It'll leave a bad scar," he said. "You should—"

"Big surprise there."

He glared at her, a dozen different emotions churning in his head. Fear on her behalf because, God, it had to have hurt so *much*, amazement because he couldn't believe this had happened again, even anger—how the hell could she be so damned *blasé* about it? "Hannah, how did this happen?"

She leaned on against the counter and rested her injured arm next to the sink, staring at the crimson-splattered porcelain. "How does it ever happen, Greg?" She sounded worn out, but she still used her other hand to swish the water around in a half-hearted attempt to clean up. "It just *did.*"

"Right along your wrist." The words were out before he had a chance to think about them, a classic case of *Make sure brain is engaged before opening mouth.* Any quarter-wit could see there wasn't a bloody knife or razorblade anywhere around, and the expression on her face said it was way too late for backtracking. "I'm sorry, I didn't mean it to sound like—"

"Then what *did* you mean?" Hannah demanded. The bleeding had stopped enough for her to straighten and she cradled her arm and glared at him. "You think I did this to myself?" Her mouth worked, then she looked away from him and shook her head. "God, and here I was just a half hour ago, walking around this place and thinking how neat it was that my life was almost fucking *normal.*" She took a step toward the living room and staggered a little, but when he reached for her, she jerked out of range and angled instead for the kitchen table. "What a *fool.*"

Greg followed and pulled out the chair across from her. "Please, honey—I was just so *shocked.* I really didn't mean that the way it sounded." He leaned toward her. "Look at it from my point of view. These things that happen to you, the way you get hurt—it's your own body but most of the time you can hardly believe it yourself. Don't you see how hard it would be for someone else to process this?"

"I need some aspirin," she said instead of answering. She sounded as normal as she could given the circumstances, but he could tell she was angry by the way she wouldn't meet his gaze. "This hurts. A lot."

"I'll bet." He smoothed her hair briefly, then went and got a couple of

Excedrins from the bathroom medicine cabinet. She downed them with the glass of water he offered, then sat back against the chair. To Greg, she looked like a flower that had been left in the heat too long, wilted and on the edge of total collapse. That image made him remember the stuff he'd left in the hallway. He didn't want to leave her, but except for the obvious soreness in her arm, Hannah actually seemed okay now. "Be right back."

Despite the nightmare of only a little while ago, he knew she was all right when the dogs left her to come to the door and see what he was doing—he knew from experience that they'd have never done that if she was in less than functional shape. It seemed like such a long time go, but it was only five weeks previous that she'd mirrored Raymond Cespedes's injuries; for the ten or twelve hours following that, Greg had nearly had to drag Knothead and Puddles outside to do their business. Now Puddles sniffed curiously of the slightly drooping daisies, then shook her head and sneezed comically; Knothead seemed much more impressed with the foil-wrapped box of chocolate-coated cherries.

Back inside, Greg managed to fit the candy and the big box containing Hannah's gift next to another gift on the bookcase. The sight of the clearly masculine paper made him smile—he'd told her not to buy him anything, but he'd known she wouldn't listen. When he made his way back to the table she was sitting there with her eyes closed and her chin resting on her chest, nearly asleep. Moving quietly, he found a tall plastic glass and used it for a vase, then left the flowers sitting next to the wine and stepped up to Hannah's chair.

"Come on," he said. He took her by the elbow and tugged her gently to her feet. "We'll get that arm bandaged the right way, then how would you feel about a little nap?"

"A nap? But it's Christmas day—I can't sleep it away." She tried not to do it, but there was no missing the quick, wistful glance she sent toward the bed.

"Half an hour," he suggested. "Just to get a little strength back. Besides, it's still early—you sleep, I'll make a few calls to the family, extend the expected holiday greetings."

She nodded at last and let him pull her into the bathroom, then sat on the edge of the tub while he peeled away the now-crusty towel and inspected the underside of her forearm. The wound was nasty and deep—nearly seven inches long—but at least it wasn't bleeding anymore. He cleaned it gingerly, acutely aware of her every wince and indrawn breath when he used eight of the smallest BandAids to pull the edges together and keep them closed. That done, he wound the whole thing lightly with clean gauze—Hannah had long ago learned to keep a lot of the stuff around.

She still wasn't talking much and Greg didn't known if it was because of his idiotic semi-accusation or exhaustion. He didn't force things, just led her to the bed and watched her crawl on top of the covers instead of under them, then roll on right side and face away from him. He stood there uncertainly for a moment, then eased down behind her. He was *not* going to let their first Christmas together be completely destroyed, even by the strangeness that had insinuated itself into Hannah's existence. "I'll just lie here with you for a few minutes," he said softly. "Okay?"

After a few seconds, she nodded, but he could feel the tenseness in her muscles in the way the surface of the bed jerked when she moved. Greg stubbornly stayed where he was, curled loosely behind her like a spoon but not too close; the minutes slowly passed and he felt her relax, bit by bit, then finally he heard her breathing even out as she slipped into full sleep.

She'd want him to wake her up soon, but on that he'd beg to differ—she needed some extra sleep time to recuperate. For God's sake, how many times could one small-boned, lightweight woman recover? He stayed there with her for another fifteen or twenty minutes, then pulled away and got up, folding his side of the bedspread over her when she moved and mumbled something at the loss of body heat. He still felt guilty about what he'd said to her, and that was amplified when it suddenly occurred to him that somewhere in the city was someone else who had suffered the same injury that had manifested itself on Hannah's body. Whomever that person was, how likely was it that he or she had the unprecedented healing ability that his girlfriend possessed?

Greg still didn't have a clue what the connection was between Hannah and these other people. The closest he'd come was Dara Rutland—he hadn't forgotten that the bruise on Dara's face had been a mirror image of the one that had appeared on Hannah's. But that had been the *only* clue, and even that had happened two months ago. He stood at the side of the bed and watched Hannah sleep for a little while, letting his mind do the free-association thing while he tried without success to tie something, *any*thing, together. Ultimately, he came up with a big fat zero.

Greg wandered over to the front window where he could get a good signal and pulled out his cell phone. Both dogs looked up at him, tails thumping lightly against the rug until they realized he wasn't going to play. He started to dial his parents' number, then paused. Dara, he thought suddenly. Was she all right today? He glanced at Hannah's sleeping form, then dug Tony's home number out of his wallet instead.

"Yeah, hello?"

"Tony," Greg said. He didn't know why, but he was surprised that his partner had answered the phone. On the other hand, it made perfect sense—Tony liked to be in control of everything, why not the telephone, too? "It's Greg. I just called to say Merry Christmas."

"Well, Merry Christmas to you, too, buddy. How's it going—you at your girlfriend's house?"

"I'm at... yeah." Really, why keep trying to deny it? "I'm at Hannah's."

"You guys having a good one?"

Greg was silent for a moment. "It could be better," he finally said. "Hannah got hurt again a little while ago, this time on her left arm. It was pretty bad."

"Are you serious? Man, that just *sucks.*" Greg heard laughter in the background—Dara—and the television. At least that gave him a bit of relief. "You at the hospital or what?"

Greg shook his head, then realized his partner couldn't see him. "No. The bleeding's stopped and she's sleeping right now. She didn't want to go—you remember her history with that doctor over there. I think the woman's name was Tansey."

"Yeah," Tony agreed. For a change he sounded mellow and happy. "Tansey—I've seen warmer personalities in polar bears."

"Anyway, keep your ears open for anything that matches this, would you? Seven inch slash on the underside of the left forearm."

"Yeah, I got it." There was a pause and Greg thought Tony was going to suggest that Hannah had attempted suicide; if the thought had crossed his partner's thoughts, he had the rare good sense not to mention it. "Too bad your Christmas got screwed up."

"Oh, it's not so bad." Greg's gaze found and rested on the mini-pile of gifts and the candy. "I figure it's got to get better from here out—hell, we haven't even opened presents yet."

Tony laughed. "All right, bud. Good luck."

"Thanks. Have a good one." Greg cut the connection, then reluctantly dialed his parents' house. He might not care very much for Tony Rutland, but that conversation had been downright *affectionate* compared to the one he had with his mother—

"Hi, Mom. Merry Christmas."

"Merry Christmas to you, son.

"How are you? How's Dad?"

"We're just fine. You?"

"Doing great. Well, I just wanted to call and wish you a happy holiday."

"Thank you. Same to you. Goodbye."

Same old mom, same old safety valve—his father must have been standing close by during the entire conversation, not that it had been more than a quarter's worth of Greg's time. He snapped the cell phone shut and hit the OFF button, then stood there staring at the device in his hand. The whole thing left him feeling a little empty, like someone had reached inside his chest and sucked out a part of his emotions. He didn't know why he'd called. Wishful thinking, perhaps, that never-ending hope that some day his mother would realize that even if his dad was determined to die a cold-hearted bastard, she could still be normal, still show the caring, affectionate side of herself that surfaced every time the elder Boyd Jedrek stepped out of the room. God—why had he bothered? It was never going to happen, never—

"Greg," Hannah said softly.

He turned and found her standing right behind him—he'd been so wrapped up in the same useless family thoughts that surfaced every Christmas that he hadn't even heard her get out of bed. It was disconcerting and disappointing to realize that after all these years his family could still affect him like that, still derail him despite the miles and the lifetime he'd managed to put in between them.

"Hi," he said.

She took the phone from his hand and set it on the coffee table, then stepped close to him. She looked better—beneath her sleep-tousled hair there was a little more color in her cheeks and her eyes were bright again. She slid her arms around his waist, careful not to jar the injured one, then rested her cheek against his shoulder. "Can we do today over?"

"I think that's a fine idea," he said. "In fact, I can't think of a better idea."

"Okay." Hannah looked up at him and smiled. "Then let's start right here. I'll go first." She laced her hands behind his back and lifted her face to his. They kissed, just so, for a long, perfect moment, then Hannah let go, picked up her gift for him from the bookcase and offered it to him with a soft smile.

"Merry Christmas, sweetheart."

Tuesday—December 26th...

Greg had gone home last night only at Hannah's insistence that she'd be fine, and as much as he tried, he just couldn't find the humor in her jokes about being Frankenhannah and the woman who wouldn't die. He'd slept lousily and his nerves had done the jingle-jangle until the moment she'd answered the doorbell this morning. Now he followed her up the hallway stairs, happily letting the tension drain from his muscles while he watched the sway of her hips as she climbed and felt a smidgen of deliciously wicked lechery.

"Stop by for your morning caffeine injection, huh?" Hannah kidded as she took out a couple of cups. "Did you eat? I have leftover donuts. Only two weeks old." He gaped at her and she laughed. "I'm only kidding. You're such a victim sometimes, Greg."

"I can't believe I fell for that," he grumbled. He scrounged around in the half-box of Dunkin' Donuts until he found a vanilla-frosted one. "Ah-ha!"

"Pah," she said. "You haven't lived until you've tasted toasted coconut." Grinning, she waved one of the tan-flecked donuts under his nose.

"I don't like coconut," Greg protested. He made a face at her. "Especially cooked. It's dry and—"

Hannah's bottom lip split.

For a frozen moment, she just stood there, blinking in surprise. Then she dropped the donut on the table and her fingers reached up to prod at her mouth; they came away covered in blood, and she stared first at them, then Greg. Below her lip, the skin was already darkening to bruised purple. "Ow." It seemed to be the only thing she could think of to say.

"I'll get you a cold washcloth," Greg said. "Don't get blood on your sweater."

Greg ducked into the tiny bathroom, feeling dizzy and numb all at the same time, almost feverish. He'd *seen* it happen this time, literally been looking right at her when this latest of wounds had appeared out of *nowhere*. He didn't know what was stranger—that he could accept what he just saw as part of everyday existence, or that he actually felt relief that it wasn't something worse, like the hideous cut along her left forearm from yesterday morning, or the three stab wounds of last month. He wished to God he could find a pattern, or a connection—*something* that would let him get to the bottom of this. If... no, *when* he did, he might not be able to stop it, but at least they would understand why.

When he came back out with the water-soaked washrag, Hannah was sitting on a kitchen table, shoulders hunched as she held a paper napkin to her mouth. "I'm sorry," she murmured as he pulled her hand aside and dabbed gingerly at the cut on her lip. "You should go—you don't need to deal with crap like this."

"This 'crap' is a part of your life," he reminded her. "So stop with the apologies. And *I'm* a part of your life. Like it or not, you're stuck with me."

That actually made her smile a little. "Really?"

He kissed her on the forehead. "Yes, really."

"Would you eat a toasted coconut donut for me?"

Greg scrunched up his face. "If I had to... yeah. But only if I had lots of coffee to wash it down." He tried to make his expression as pathetic as possible. "Is that what I have to do?"

Hannah made a show of thinking about as she checked the washcloth to see if she was still bleeding. Not much. "No. Right now, just the coffee part would be good. I suppose it's enough that you would if you had to—you know, if my life depended on it." Her mood had lightened considerably.

Greg's mouth turned up in a smile and before he went to pour the coffee, he reached out and tugged on a lock of her fine hair. "Honey, for you I'd even eat a big crunchy beetle."

But if he'd thought he'd get to her, he was wrong. "Now that's devotion." Hannah meticulously folded up the stained washcloth, then raised one eyebrow and gave him a droll glance. "Just don't expect me to kiss you afterward."

«««—»»»

Someday, Greg thought, Tony was going to get a new car, or figure out what was wrong with his.

He pulled into the driveway of Tony's house and sat there for a minute. The drive and steps were clear, but messy around the edges; something told him the person pulling snow duty here was little Ben. Tapping the steering wheel and staring sightlessly at the holiday lights blinking in the picture window, Greg thought about the split that had appeared on Hannah's lip this morning, and about the bruise she'd had shared with Dara Rutland a couple of weeks ago. Rather than honk the horn as Tony had instructed when he'd called over at Hannah's and asked for a ride, Greg decided to pay an inside visit to the Rutland household. He climbed out of the car and headed up to the door.

Dara answered the door. She managed a smile when she saw him but there was no doubt that it was forced; her face was pale and she looked like she'd been crying not long before. "Greg," she said. "Merry Christmas." She glanced over her shoulder. "Uh, Tony's not ready—"

"Could I come in?" It was pushy of him, but he wasn't about to cool his butt in the car this time.

She swallowed and stepped back. "Of course. Would you… would you like a cup of coffee?"

"That'd be great." He followed her through the house, noting the gaily-decorated Christmas tree and the fastidious way the neat living room was arranged. It was darker than he expected, with no papers or clutter, no empty boxes or toys—not at all what one would expect on the morning after Christmas with an eight-year-old. The dark furniture gleamed with fresh polish while somewhere in the house a radio played, tuned to a news station; other than that, silence.

The kitchen reminded him of something from the fifties, not very big with dark cabinets and a Formica counter. "Tony's still getting dressed," Dara said. She moved around the room like a frightened dragonfly, flitting from counter to the table and back again. Tony's wife was a pretty woman with streaked medium-brown hair and brown eyes; he'd never noticed before, but there were perpetual frown lines between her eyebrows, as though she spent a lot of time worrying. Nothing wrong with her bottom lip and the skin of her arms, visible below the pushed-back sleeves of her sweater, was unbroken. There was, however, a small, white scar through her right eyebrow—

Just like the one that bisected Hannah's right eyebrow.

Greg accepted the cup of coffee Dara offered, barely feeling the sting of the hot stoneware. Did Dara, he wondered, have scars in other places that matched Hannah's? "Thanks," he said aloud. "Where's Ben? He's on Christmas break, isn't he?"

"Yes. He's, uh, probably sleeping late. Yesterday was a big day, what with presents and all."

"I'll bet," Greg said. He took a sip of his coffee—good stuff—and intentionally glanced at the window, trying to put Dara at ease, get rid of the feeling that he was inspecting her. "So what did Tony get you for Christmas?"

"He got me a really nice winter jacket," she said. "And a—"

"Mom, I can't find my Spiderman sweatshirt."

Greg turned his head at the sound of Ben's voice, then jerked when he actually focused on what he saw. The boy was standing in the doorway to the kitchen dressed in jeans and a clean undershirt. His dark hair and eyes made his skin look pale. They also accented the scabbed-over gash bisecting his lower lip and the purple-bruised skin below it.

Dara looked from her son to Greg and back again, her expression absolutely terrified. Greg found his voice first, kept it calm and controlled. "Hey, Ben," he said. "How're you doing? That's some job on your lip."

The boy's hand flew to cover his mouth when he saw Greg, and Greg realized Ben hadn't known he was there. "Oh! I—"

"Kid fell when he was running around the living room this morning." Tony pushed past his son and cut off anything Ben was going to say. "Boy's so clumsy I'm surprised his head doesn't fall off. Isn't that right, son?" Ben nodded jerkily and Tony patted him on the head. Greg could swear he saw the little boy flinch when his father's hand came down.

"Your Spiderman shirt is in the dirty clothes," Dara said quickly. "You'll have to wear something else today."

"Yes, ma'am." Ben turned and disappeared down the hallway.

For a long, awkward moment no one said anything, then Greg stood. "You ready to go? The limo's waiting."

"Yeah, let's hit it."

His partner gestured toward the door, then followed him through the house. Greg paused at the front door and looked back, again struck by how very *un*-Christmas-like the room looked and felt. "Thanks for the coffee, Dara." She didn't answer as he started to step outside, found that his partner wasn't following.

"Something wrong with your ears, Dara?" Tony's voice rose, cutting through the gloomy house. "You didn't hear what Greg said?" He started to take a step back toward the kitchen.

"Maybe she's busy," Greg said hastily. "It doesn't matter."

"She could use a lesson in fucking *courtesy,* that's what." For some reason Greg couldn't fathom, Tony looked absolutely furious.

Dara's strained face appeared around the corner of the kitchen door. "I'm sorry, did you say something? I had the water running in the sink."

Greg tried to give her a reassuring smile. "Just thanks for the coffee. That's all."

Tony's wife smiled, but Greg thought it was like a lot of other things in this house—forced. "You're welcome."

"Let's go," Tony said shortly.

Greg led the way to the car, his thoughts spinning. He believed that little Ben had fallen and busted his mouth about as much as he believed the Statue of Liberty was going to get up and walk away. Still, there wasn't much he could do about it… and why on earth did Hannah seem to have a sort of supernatural connection to this family? She didn't even *like* Tony, for God's sake, had reluctantly admitted that when Greg had suggested they take in a movie with Tony and his wife some Saturday night. That his girlfriend didn't care for his partner didn't bother him in the least, but it *was* interesting given Hannah seemed to be mirroring the injuries that Tony inflicted on his wife and son.

But she did the same for other people, too—Raymond Cespedes, Jack Iserson, God knew how many others… and, of course, the late Eloise Addison. Ben's split lip notwithstanding, both he and his mother seemed fine, so that meant someone else—perhaps someone Tony knew?—now carried a seven-inch gash on the inside of his or her forearm.

"So how was your Christmas?" Greg asked when they'd gotten underway.

Tony glanced at him, then visibly relaxed. "It was good. Kid ran around like a maniac with all the toys and stuff, Dara cooked. You and Hannah were welcome to come by, you know."

Greg ware careful to keep his gaze on the road. "Hannah's not up to the whole socializing thing yet. I think just the Christmas thing with me around is already kind of overwhelming for her."

Tony folded his arms. "Unless she plans on hiding for the rest of her life, she's going to have to face it someday."

"True enough." He decided to turn the topic away from Hannah for now. "So Dara said you got her a jacket? What'd she get you?"

They talked some more about the gifts and whatnot, enough banter to keep them going until Greg pulled into the station's parking lot. Things were pretty calm inside, a couple of domestic squabbles but no serious injuries, all thankfully calm on the post-Christmas front. Greg still had plenty to do—follow-up on unsolved cases, paperwork, new info to track down—but he decided it wouldn't hurt to spend a little time at the computer and see if he could match anything to what had happened to Hannah yesterday morning. This time he changed the criteria a bit, thinking—or hoping—that the injury she'd experienced hadn't been fatal to the unseen victim.

SEARCH:
Type: Assault, Homicide
Sex: All
Age: All
Day: Saturday 12/25
Time: 06:00—11:00 hours
Area: All

"Jesus," Greg said as the search window flashed, then gave him the message *17 matches found*. "People can't even stop beating each other up on Christmas day." What was sadder was that this number represented only the incidents that had been reported—how many never would be?

A depressing thought, but something else he couldn't do anything about. What he *could* do, however, is keep up his efforts to find out why Hannah was enduring what she was, and if someone else out there was falling victim at the same time.

He went through all seventeen listings and found that most of them were the result of domestic squabbles, somebody dipping into the holiday cheer a little too early, a few coming home from the Christmas Eve parties in a fighting mood. Greg found what he was looking for in the next to last listing, though he was mightily surprised at the info:

HOMICIDE REPORT			
Name: Connie DuPree	Sex: Female	Age: 29	
Height: 5' 2"	Weight: 103 pounds	Hair: Brown	Eyes: Brown
TOD: Approx. 0830	COD: Exsanguination	Date: 12/26	
DESCRIPTION: Victim was found 12/26 in a downward-facing position on the passenger side of her vehicle after her work shift when a coworker noticed her car was still in the employee parking lot. Victim sustained mortal injury in the form of a significant knife wound to the left inside forearm, evidence indicates victim was killed while in her vehicle and not moved after death.			
Weapon: Not Found	(List all suspects and witness on page two.)		

The report went on to say that the Coroner's preliminary report indicated bruising of the face and body that indicated Connie DuPree had been held down by someone of significant strength while she had literally bled to death. There had been no witnesses, no other evidence had been found in the car, and there was, as of yet, no discernible motive.

Connie DuPree, Greg thought as he scanned through the rest of the report, had been a night nurse at the University of Chicago Hospital. He'd ask Hannah, but he was willing to bet his badge that this woman was someone whom Hannah had never heard of met. A total stranger.

And a total dead end.

Sunday—December 31st...

She didn't want to go.

Hannah stared at her reflection in the bathroom mirror and sighed, then fiddled some more with the wispy strands of hair trying to escape the glittery mini-butterfly clips she'd used to pull it back. She supposed she looked all right, but God, she was *nervous.* Because of her damnable Affliction, going out in public always made her that way—hell, even the day-to-day necessities of her job and school had the same nerve-wracking effect—but she'd learned to live with that. A woman had to try to make a living and do something with her life. As for the rest of it... well, Greg was a big part of the reason she could finally feel ninety percent okay about taking in a movie or going to dinner. But this—this was a double date, for God's sake. Not only that, but one with Tony Rutland and his wife.

"Ugh," she said to her reflection, then actually giggled when she realized she sounded like some kind of skinny little Neanderthal. At least sounds and looks were different; Winnie had recommended a consignment shop on Lincoln Avenue and Hannah had found a lovely crushed black velvet dress there for only twenty-four bucks. It wasn't hard to see the reason the price was low: Hannah's slight build was teenager-like, and most gals that age wanted to show skin. This dress, with its high, formal collar and long sleeves, kept her wrapped up in a tight, warm package... and that was fine with her. The last thing she wanted was to have to endure was stares from other people.

Still... she didn't want to go. What was it about Tony Rutland that bugged her? She had no idea, but there was definitely *some*thing. As freaked as she'd been, Hannah still remembered the creeped-out sensation she'd had in September when she'd met Tony's dark gaze from her hospital bed in Illinois Masonic. She hadn't seen him much since then, a few times in the Diner with Greg, but that feeling of unpleasantness had never gone away. If anything—and she'd never admitted this to Greg—it had *intensified*, to the point where it was all she could do not to shudder at the mere mention of his name.

Then why had she agreed to party with them tonight?

Because Greg had wanted to, of course.

Had he known the truth about how she felt, Hannah knew Greg would have canceled their plans immediately. But Hannah had made the decision on her own to go, a sort of self-test of her own will and strength. Damn it, she would not waste her time trying to think up excuses for avoiding this man, she would face her fear and conquer it.

Even so, her hands were shaking as she applied the last bit of gloss to her lips.

«« — »»

"Wow," Greg said when Hannah opened the door. "You look beautiful."

She blushed but he could tell she was pleased. "Thanks."

"Are you about ready?" he asked as he followed her up the stairs. "We're supposed to meet them at Stefani's in a half hour and traffic is terrible."

"Just let me get my coat," Hannah said.

She took it from the closet and he helped her slip it on, enjoying her nearness and the scent of the peach body spray she used. The ankle-length black velvet dress made her look like one of those hand-drawn models in the newspaper, impossibly long and slender, elegant. They'd gone out before, sure, but Greg had never seen her dressed like this, had never considered what she might look like if she did.

He felt pulled in two directions tonight—on the one hand, he wasn't such a fool that he didn't realize she didn't really want to go, but on the other, he wanted, selfishly, to show her off to the world. Even to Tony—his partner hadn't seen Hannah in quite awhile and Greg hadn't forgotten the sarcastic comments Tony had made about Hannah early on, cracks that had continued long after Tony had known Greg and Hannah were dating. Tonight would be Greg's version of the nyah-nyah-nyah finger in Tony's face, the *See, I* told *you she was a great girl!* The behavior of a teenaged boy, but there it was.

"All set." Hannah smiled at him and he felt guilty all over again at the sight. It was a little too bright, too big, a genuine I'm-going-to-have-a-good-time-dammit expression.

"You know," he said, and pulled her into his arms. "We don't have to go. Tony's always late—why don't I just call his house and cancel?"

"Don't be silly," Hannah said. "We'll have a great time. I'll bet you a dollar. Come on."

Greg chuckled and followed her outside, where Belmont was already jam-packed with cars and people. He'd gambled on the New Year's Eve crowds keeping the cops busy and his Jeep was parked in the bus stop only a half block away. There had been a dusting of snow on everything this morning, but the day's bustle had long since turned it into a dirty slush that made him glad they weren't walking anywhere.

Stefani's on Fullerton was his all-time favorite Italian restaurant, pricey but worth every penny. He gave the Jeep over to the valet and they went inside, where they were surprised to find Tony and Dara already waiting. Either Tony was getting a handle on his schedule or his wife had overseen the planning for tonight.

"Hey, guys," Tony said cheerfully. "Happy New Year and all that. Greg, you know Dara, of course."

Greg smiled at her, relieved to see her looking happy and relaxed tonight. "Nice to see you again. This is my girlfriend, Hannah."

"Hi," Hannah said and shook Dara's offered hand. "Have you been waiting long?" She sent Greg a sweet smile that made him groan inside.

"Not at all," Dara said, and looked toward the coat check room. "We were just headed over there." Greg and Hannah went with them, and while they waited their turn Hannah's hand folded around his and squeezed. The coat business taken care of, they met the Rutlands in the bar and ordered drinks; reservations or not, Stefani's was always so packed that they knew it would be at least a half hour before they got their table.

The four of them chatted for a few minutes, general getting acquainted kind of stuff, then Greg realized that Hannah had gone silent.

When he glanced over he realized she was staring at the top of Dara's dress, where the burgundy-colored fabric was held in place over the woman's shoulders by spaghetti straps. Wait, it wasn't the dress that had caught Hannah's attention at all… it was the scar along the line of her right collarbone, maybe three inches long and thin, almost healed white.

A picture-perfect match to the one on Hannah's own body.

He saw Hannah's gaze flick to Dara's face and focus on the nearly indiscernible scar through her right eyebrow, knew that she'd made the connection. Shock, first, then she recovered instantly, far too quickly for Tony or Dara to notice. The only problem was when she looked over at him; she was hiding it well but Greg knew her well enough to know when she was mightily pissed. For a second he was completely bewildered, then it sank in. He'd never so much as mentioned his speculation that she was somehow connected to a portion of Tony Rutland's life, and Hannah didn't like Tony to begin with. What had he been thinking to just spring this on her, with no warning? Oh boy.

Still, Hannah held her own during dinner, smiling and laughing, even telling a few jokes. The food was superb as always, with soft roasted garlic cloves to spread on chewy Italian bread, Gorgonzola and walnut-sprinkled salads, rotelle with red snapper sauce, wild rice ravioli with walnut-butter sauce, scallop and cheese tortellini, and more. True to form, Tony ordered a steak instead of something fancier or Italian, but it was just as outstanding as the rest of the meal. They were all far too full for dessert, but they did share a bottle of good champagne. Greg hoped the bubbly would ease Hannah's irritation—he could tell she was still angry by the way she refused to touch him or meet his gaze for more than a second at a time.

Hannah relaxed a little in the car but she still wasn't a hundred percent herself. To hell with this avoidance crap, Greg thought suddenly. Let's just get it out in the open.

"Look," he began. "I—"

He wasn't sure what he'd been about to say, but Hannah didn't let him finish. "You had no right to do that," she said. "Seeing her like that, with the same scars as me, was completely unnerving. To not even warn me was wrong in too many ways to count."

Greg opened his mouth to retort, then shut it again. Yes, he had suspected that Dara might bear more of a resemblance to Hannah than anyone could imagine, but getting defensive wasn't going to help anything. Hannah was right about how he should have told her, and he said so now. "I'm sorry."

"How long did you know about this?"

He ran a hand through his hair, trying to think about that and watch the other drivers, a good many of them half-soused, as he turned onto Southport and headed north. Now he wished they hadn't gone out at all, that they'd just stayed at Hannah's with the dogs and a pizza and a couple of good bottles of Brut. He hadn't exactly planned on bringing in the new year with an argument, and the crude and superstitious part of him was afraid that this was a portent for how their upcoming year would be—resentful and cool-hearted.

"I've suspected for awhile," he finally admitted. "But I wasn't sure until I saw Dara tonight. I'd seen the scar on her eyebrow and a couple of weeks ago she had a bruise on her face that matched yours." He risked glancing at her, found her listening closely. "Then the day after Christmas..." He didn't finish, afraid that Hannah would find the rest of what he had to say too incredible.

"What about the day after Christmas? That was..." She paused, then touched her mouth as the memory came back. "That was the day my lip split down the middle."

Greg nodded. "I drove Tony to work and I made it a point to go inside. Their little boy..."

Hannah's mouth dropped open. "No. Oh, no—you can't be telling me this—"

Greg's mouth was grim. "That's exactly what I'm telling you. Ben's mouth was cracked up exactly like yours. Tony said the boy fell in the living room."

"Do you believe him?"

Greg looked sideways at her. "What do you think?"

She didn't say anything for a long time, just sat there and let him concentrate on negotiating the wet streets and the antics of drivers who seemed suspiciously prone to weaving. The glow from streetlights and neon signs played over her skin and made it sparkle, and as strange as it had been to see his suspicions given weight, Greg found his thoughts turning away from his partner and focusing more on the lovely woman in the car with him. They were turning onto Belmont when he took her hand and lifted it to his lips. "Forgive me?" he asked.

Hannah turned her head and her expression softened. "Yes."

Greg felt his shoulder muscles relax, hadn't even realized he'd been so tense. "I won't do something like that again," he promised. "Never."

Hannah lowered her gaze, but her fingers curled around his and tightened briefly. "Good," she said quietly. "I don't care for surprises. At least not ones like that."

"I'll remember," Greg said. With so many unpleasant surprises in her life, and so often, Hannah certainly didn't need him springing any more into it. The traffic on Belmont was worse than it had been earlier in the evening and it took him awhile to find a spot half into a fireplug zone and behind someone already illegally parked there. They made their way back to Hannah's place with New Year's Eve revelers weaving around them on the sidewalk like ants streaming around a couple of pebbles. He waited while she fished out her key at the front door, unsure about where the evening was going. He'd staved off an argument, but had his little person-to-person comparison of Hannah to Dara ruined the rest of it?

Hannah's words broke into his thoughts. "Come on, silly. Don't stand out here in the cold." She tugged him inside and he followed her dutifully up the stairs, then the two of them went right back out the rear door with the dogs for a quick but chilly late night walk. That done, they pulled off their coats and got rid of their shoes, with Hannah sighing in relief when her feet came out of the unaccustomed high heels.

"Surprise," she said, and pulled a bottle of chilled champagne out of the frig.

"I thought you didn't like surprises," he reminded her.

She grinned "Ah, but this time *I'm* the one doing the surprising. Makes all the difference in the world."

"True." Greg went to the cabinet and got out Hannah's two wine glasses, thinking fleetingly about how comfortable he was here. Of course he was—he spent more time at this apartment than he did at his own place. His digs were nice enough, well maintained and clean, but the place was… lifeless or something. He'd never cared much about where he lived or what was in it beyond serviceability, and most of his furniture consisted of that inexpensive, put-it-together-yourself stuff with fake oak veneer. Hannah's, on the other hand, was filled with warmth—her used stuff was all made of well-polished wood, dog-eared books and rumpled magazines were piled here and there, chewed and mildly gooey dog toys popped up in the oddest places. These were the things that made it more desirable than his own—

Bullshit.

It wasn't the furniture, or the magazines, or the odd little knick-knacks that she'd recently started picking up in the resale shops that gave this place the feeling it had, the *heart.* It wasn't even the dogs.

It was *Hannah* who made this place was it was. For him, it had always been Hannah.

For a moment, as he let the admission wash through his mind, Greg couldn't turn around and face her. When he did, he found her struggling with the cork on the bottle, a look of concentrated determination on her face as she tried to pry it open. Her hair had escaped the hair clips in a dozen places and now made a wispy sort of halo around her face; she looked beautiful, standing barefoot in the black velvet dress with the bottle gripped in slender, pale fingers. "Let me," he said.

She gave the bottle a mock scowl, then relinquished it. "Okay."

"Duck," he said, and twisted the cork abruptly. It gave a loud pop that made Knothead yip and Hannah let out a half laugh, half yelp. Greg quickly tilted the bottle over the glasses as liquid churned out; when the glasses were filled, he offered her one.

"Living room," she ordered and took him by the arm. "Come on."

He snagged the bottle and followed, dimly aware that his breathing had gone short and slightly ragged, as though he were on the verge of hyperventilating. They sat on the couch, then faced each other, raised their glasses to toast. "To us," Hannah said, smiling. "And to a wonderful new year together."

His glass touched hers then he brought it to his lips and drank, feeling the chilly dryness of the champagne coat his tongue and throat. "What?" she asked. Her head tilted, and he knew she had no idea how pretty that little movement was. Her eyes, an odd shade somewhere between hazel and tan, were shining as she looked at him, "No toast of your own, hon? Nothing to add?"

Greg held up his glass obediently, though he had no idea what he should say.

"Will you marry me?"

He didn't know who was more shocked, Hannah or him. Had he really just asked that?

"Oh," she said. "Greg—"

"I love you," he said before she could keep going. More words came out of his mouth, completely unplanned, every one of them true. "I've never said it but you know I do. I don't know if you love me, but I think so. Everything for us is right when we're together, or at least as right as it might ever get. So let's take it the rest of the way."

Hannah sat very still, holding her glass so tightly that her fingernails were white, her wide gaze fixed on him. Then, oddly, she shivered.

"I can't," she said softly. "I just can't… *do* that to you."

"What?"

She set her glass on the coffee table, then took his and did the same. When she folded her hands over his, Greg could feel the coolness of her skin, the way she was shaking. He felt paralyzed, as if he were balanced on a wire above a great abyss, one that was divided by an unseen wall. If he went one way, there would be happiness, for him and, he was convinced, Hannah; if he went the other, who knew? Because really, how could two people stay together if one loved the other enough to need commitment but the other either refused or simply didn't return the feelings? Either way, Greg was going to fall.

"You're right," Hannah said. "I do love you… and that's exactly why I would never tie you to me. It wouldn't be right."

Greg frowned. "What are you talking about?"

She pulled her hands away and stood, as though she couldn't bear to be so close to him and say these words at the same time. "Look at us, Greg. No, not just how we are here tonight or how we were last week, but at the big picture of *us*. You're a handsome guy with a good career. You're young, and you have your entire future ahead of you." Hannah gestured at herself then, and Greg thought he could predict everything else she was about to say, just from the amount of anger he saw in that one, jerky movement. "And then there's *me*—oh boy, what a package I am!"

"Hannah—"

She held up a hand, then left it there and used the other to tick off points in the air. "I was a physically abused child, and so psychologically damaged from it that I walled out the rest of the world for a good chunk of my life. Yeah, I've caught up—I've got a job and I go to school, and I even have two great dogs. But I also have this unexplained tendency to bleed at any moment. It can't be explained, and it can't be scheduled. It just *is*."

"I can deal with it," Greg said.

"For *now*." Hannah hugged herself. "But what if it never *stops,* Greg, not ever? And what if one of these days I don't heal like I always do? What if I *die?"*

"We all die sometime," Greg said stonily. He found himself gripping the couch cushions and was glad Hannah had taken the champagne glass from him.

"Of course we do." Hannah looked at him calmly. "And what if I die because of this nasty little Affliction of mine, *and you get blamed for whatever killed me?"*

He opened his mouth to retort, but nothing came out. She had him there—this was something he'd never considered. What, indeed? "I'll take my chances," he blurted. He jumped to his feet and strode over to her. "It's worth it—*you're* worth it. Damn it, Hannah, what are you going to do? Hide for the rest of your life, however long that is? Or take it day to day and do the best you can to enjoy it?" His hands found her shoulders and rested there, and he could feel the heat of her body through the soft velvet. He ached to hold her.

"Greg—"

"We can do this, Hannah. I know we can. We can have a good life—"

"I don't even know if I can sleep with you."

He sucked in his breath. "We'll get there. When you're ready, however long it takes, we'll get there. I'm not in any hurry."

Hannah stared up at him. He realized her eyes were glittering but not from the dim light in the living room; they were filled with tears. "And what if it's never?" she asked softly. "What if when we try, I…" She swallowed instead of finishing.

"Then we'll try again some other time," he said stubbornly. "And if it doesn't work that time, then we'll wait for another time after that. Eventually it'll happen." He tugged on her upper arms until she was close enough to enfold in a hug. "Sex is great, but it's only part of it."

"A big part," she said against his chest. "Don't downplay something so important."

"Yes, a big part." He paused, trying to find the right words. "But I believe, and I swear this, that it'll happen naturally. I don't think we have to push it, or worry about it, or even think about it."

Surprisingly, Hannah grinned. "Not think about it? Someone once told me that men think about sex once every five minutes. Or was that five times every minute?"

Greg felt a corner of his mouth turn up. "That someone would be Winnie, I bet."

"Seriously, Greg. I don't think we should do this. It could be a big mistake."

Now he did smile, because even if Hannah didn't realize it, she'd softened, gone from 'no' to 'I don't think so.' He might be interpreting it this way only because it was what he wanted, but he'd bet that in her heart, the last thing in the world she wanted was to turn him away. "Tell you what," he said and guided her back toward the couch. "Let's just table the idea for right now. You keep it in the back of your mind that the offer is there and I'll just keep on hanging around, and we'll both see where this goes. No time limit, no ultimatum, no *pressure.* What do you say—toast on it?"

Hannah sat down and took the glass he offered, but her expression was glum. "It doesn't seem fair to string you along, Greg. That's so awful—"

"What's awful?" he demanded. "That because of everything that's happened you're not sure about where to go in the future? Welcome to the human race, Hannah. There are no guarantees for anyone, least of all you or me. Maybe you can work this out, maybe you can't. On my part, I opened a door. I'm willing to wait and see if you decide to go through."

She inhaled, then nodded. "All right. But you might be waiting a long time. And on the other side might be nothing—no promises."

"Fine," Greg said, sounding a lot more glib than he felt. "In the meantime, let's refill our glasses, turn on the television, and watch the ball drop in Times Square."

Hannah's eyes widened and she turned his wrist so she could see his watch. "We haven't missed it!"

"Nope." Greg dashed over to the television and turned it on, then came back and settled next to her, happy to slip his arm across her velvet-covered shoulders. She snuggled close as the old television warmed and brought them an image of the party going down in NYC. He leaned over and kissed her warmly on her forehead. "We haven't missed anything at all."

And when the countdown hit zero they raised their glasses to the new year as Greg vowed to himself that he would find and stop whoever, or *whatever,* it was out there that had such a stranglehold on the woman he loved.

Wednesday—February 7th...

She lives in a duplex in Geneva and he has to leave home extra early so he can get there before she leaves. He's been watching her, wooing *her, for three weeks now, spending as much time as he can learning about her life. Twice he's been at the restaurant where she has breakfast every morning, both times sliding uninvited into the booth with her as if they were old friends. She didn't like it, but she didn't make a scene either, just tried to keep that cool, disinterested composure of hers going. He knows it's just a ruse and she's playing hard to get—that's how they always are with him. At first.*

This morning he wants to catch her before she leaves, actually knock on her door. She's always claimed she was married but he doesn't believe that—maybe he hasn't been here twenty-four hours a day but he has parked down the street quite a bit. In all that time, he's never seen a man come out of the duplex, with or without her. It's just one more facet of her cat and mouse game, but now he's tired of it. She's a beautiful woman and he's ready to move forward in the relationship—he wants to run his fingers through her lovely auburn hair and see those sky-blue eyes of hers widen when their bodies join for the first time.

Yeah, he's definitely ready.

She has a dog, a little thing that looks like a white mop, and she lets it into the fenced yard every morning about fifteen minutes before she leaves for work. This morning he's standing beside her back door when she opens it; the dog runs out then spins and barks at him when it real-

izes he's there. Still, it turns and heads into the yard, not inclined to do anything more annoying.

She gasps when she sees him but he only gives her his most engaging smile. "Good morning," he says. "Can we talk for a few minutes?"

He'd thought that with him on her doorstep she would finally drop the hard-to-get routine, but now her mouth twists in anger. "What are you doing in my back yard?" she demands. "This isn't funny!"

"Hey, relax," he protests. "I just wanted to catch you before you left for work. It's no big deal."

She looks incredulous. "No big deal? You follow me around and then sneak into my back yard, scare the hell out of me when I open my door—that's no big deal?"

She's beautiful even when she's angry and he tries to make his voice soothing. "Come on, it's not like I'm stalking you or anything. I just want to talk—"

She surprises him by snapping, "Stalking is exactly *what you're doing, and I want you to leave.* Now.*"*

"Five minutes," he insists. "That's all, just five minutes."

"No."

He's getting pissed but he knows it's a bad idea to say that. He folds his arms and tries a pleasant smile. "What's the big deal? I only want to tell you a few things—"

"I guess it's time to call the police." She turns to go back in the house and he helps her along, putting a hand in between her shoulder blades and pushing her inside and pulling the back door shut behind him.

She stumbles inside and whirls. "What are you doing?" Her voice is practically a scream.

"Sit down."

Instead of obeying, one hand reaches out and suddenly he has to duck to avoid getting brained by a ceramic jar full of wooden spoons and spatulas. She spins and runs for a doorway, and he knows she's either going to get to a telephone or make it out the front of the house—either way he's in deep shit and this isn't at all the way he'd pictured this going. The time for convincing arguments has evaporated and all that's left, unfortunately is elimination and clean-up. Too bad; he'd thought she'd be different.

People always laugh at actors who drop keys or fall on their faces in movies when they're running away from something. The truth is the odds of going down increase exponentially when a person panics, when they keep looking over their shoulder, when they just generally know *they're probably going to die no matter what they do. She trips crossing the threshold and he's much faster than her anyway; he grabs hold of the back of her hair before she can crawl away and then he's on top of her, straddling her back while pinning her wrists beneath his knees and hooking his feet across her slender calves to stop her from kicking upward. She's face down on a ceramic-tiled floor—they're in some kind of utility room that divides the kitchen from the living room.*

"Please!" she cries. Her voice is nearing the screaming range. "Let me go—you don't have to do this!"

"Now I'm afraid I do," he says calmly. His hand is still tangled in her beautiful, soft hair and while this is not the way he'd always imagined touching it, it'll have to do. Sometimes it just sucks the way things work out.

His hand is between her shoulder blades and he feels her hard inhalation, knows the next that's going to come out of her is a scream. He can't let that happen so he yanks her head up hard, then slams her face against the tile floor. Blood splatters against the white sections and soaks into the grout, and her scream is cut off by a cry of pain. She goes limp for a moment and he uses the chance to grip the sweet curve of her neck roughly with his fingers. He digs in as hard as he can, searching for the fragile windpipe; she struggles but she has no leverage to fight and is trapped by the weight of his body.

It isn't long before her lovely face is marred by the death-shade of blue and her thrashing ceases. He pulls his hands away slowly and sits there, on her back, waiting, for several minutes. Her eyes are open but sightless and she doesn't move; it will be a long time before her body cools and she is warm where the insides of his thighs press against her. The feeling is surprisingly intense, highly erotic.

It's something that he's never thought about doing before, but she is there and won't protest, and he has more time—lots of it—than he had with that Eloise Addison bitch. Smiling, he reaches beneath her and kneads her breasts. They are full and firm, and the blouse she is wearing aggravates him so he pushes it up and out of the way, then unfastens her bra. Everything feels so good—her soft nipples under his fingers, his erection grinding against her. He stretches out on top of her and works her skirt up until he can rip at her pantyhose and underwear. When he gets that out of the way he unzips his pants and slides them down, and after exploring her center for a bit with his fingers, he buries his body deep within her unresisting form.

It's not as good as if she was alive, but it isn't bad—she's still warm and he ends up folding one arm under her rib cage and pulling her up to better position himself. It's strange that she's limp but he doesn't believe this is really necrophilia; after all, she's only been dead for a couple of minutes. The way she doesn't fight when he hammers into her or buries his other hand between her legs excites him even more and he's only good for about two minutes. When he comes, it's like a volcano erupting and filling her with his goodbye gift, all the wishes for the things they could have been.

Afterwards he stands and pulls himself together. The only thing he's touched besides her is the doorknob in the kitchen. He goes back there and wipes the knob thoroughly with the tail of his shirt while glancing around the yellow and white room. It's much too bright for him, too open and... spatial. He prefers his own place, with his roomfuls of comforting, dark wood. He lets himself out without touching anything else, and when the little mop dog comes running up to him, he opens the door and lets it go into the house. It would never do for the neighbors to wonder why she'd left her little dog outside in the cold all day.

That done, this whole nasty business done, he tucks his shirttail into his pants and walks to where he's parked his car about five blocks away.

Then he heads off to work.

As the saying goes, another day, another dollar.

«««—»»»

Greg had, he supposed, been entertaining quite a little fantasy in his head since New Year's Eve. It involved himself and Hannah, of course, and a certain way their existence would and wouldn't go. While things between them might have gotten off to a bumbling start, where it could head from here was straight into the good old American Dream—marriage, a little house somewhere, two dogs (slightly above average), no cats, and two-point-five kids.

Where it *wouldn't* go was where it was right now, since he'd gotten out of Hannah's bed and found her sitting on the couch in the living room and crying.

He hadn't realized it, but each day that had passed had heightened his sense of security with her. It had been forty-three days (yes, he kept count) since anything had happened to Hannah, and he had begun to believe that it was over. He didn't know why, and he didn't care; all that had mattered was that it was. Each day that passed brought them closer to each other mentally and physically, and he had convinced himself that in the not-so-distant future the woman he loved would not only make love with him but agree that they should spend the rest of their lives together.

Kneeling in front of her now, he realized that sense of security had been completely and utterly false, a thin coating of paint spread over something ugly. A pleasant little lie that had worn through all too quickly.

"Hannah?" Greg couldn't see her face but the way she was hunched over and hiding within her cupped hands was a bad, bad sign. He got his fingers around her wrists and tugged; at first she resisted, then she allowed him to see what was wrong. He inhaled sharply when he saw the purple and black bruise that centered on her cheekbone and covered almost all of the right side of her face. The most prominent part of the cheekbone had a painful-looking scrape across it, but at least it didn't seem deep enough to leave a scar.

Then she lifted her tear-streaked face enough for him to see the line of bruises beneath her chin.

"Jesus," he whispered. "That must have hurt." She flinched a bit when he reached out to touch the discoloration and he couldn't blame her. He'd seen enough murders and fights and incidences of domestic violence to recognize the marks of strangulation. There were even finger print impressions, darker and more prominent that the rest of the marks, that showed the attacker had known to go for the windpipe.

"I couldn't breathe, Greg." Hannah's voice was raspy, the words obviously difficult to say. She started crying again. "I couldn't *breathe!*"

He moved up and sat next to her on the couch, then enfolded her in his arms. "It's okay," he said helplessly, then felt immediately stupid for saying something that was so clearly a lie. "It's over now," he added. But it *wasn't* okay, not at all. He'd vowed to find and put a stop to this, but God help them both, he couldn't do anything until, like now, something happened to guide him along the way. It infuriated him that Hannah would have to suffer for him to save her.

If he even could.

For the moment, the best he could offer was to sit and hold her until she healed a bit on her own.

«««—»»»

He hammered so hard on the Rutlands' front door that he bruised his knuckles.

Greg had gotten Hannah to go back to bed and left her sleeping fairly soundly, the pain and exhaustion driving her right back to bed. She was working lunch today and had to be at the diner by eleven, so he'd promised to call her at ten-fifteen to make sure she was awake. It wasn't until he'd started to pull in the lot at the station and seen that Tony's car wasn't there that he'd given in to the impulse to go over to his partner's house and see just what was what with him and his family… specifically with Dara. Was she all right? Or would he find her beaten and battered as Hannah had been early this morning? Or worse—dead, perhaps—since he had enough years on the job to recognize that the injuries on Hannah would have killed anyone else.

He banged again on the door, harder, and heard Tony's irritated voice answering through the wood. "Who the hell is it—damn it, stop that pounding!" That was followed by the sound of the bolt being unlocked, then Tony yanked open the door and stared at him in amazement. "Greg? What the hell are you doing here? What's wrong?"

"I want to see Dara."

Tony's mouth dropped open. "You want to see my wife? Why?"

Greg shoved Tony aside without bothering to answer. *"Dara!"*

"What the—are you out of your fucking *mind?"*

Greg whirled back to face him. "Hannah got hurt again this morning, Tony. And now—yes, I'd like to see your wife. I'd like to make sure she's all *right."*

Each time Greg opened his mouth, Tony seemed more astonished. "Of course she's all right—oh, Jesus. You're kidding, right? You think there's some kind of connection between my wife and your fucked up little girlfriend?" Tony strode back over to the door and yanked it wide, spilling the February air into the dark living room. "Just get the hell out, Greg."

Greg was right on his heels. "I'm not going anywhere until I see Dara, Tony. And no—I don't think there's a connection between Dara and Hannah. I think the connection is *you.* I think she gets hurt every time *you* do something. So what it is now, huh? Did you beat up your wife again this morning, partner? Or did you—"

"What's all the yelling about?"

Greg jerked around to see Dara standing in the doorway staring at them, but the living room was so poorly lit that he couldn't tell anything else. Tony grabbed at his arm but he sidestepped and hurried over to Dara. "Listen," he said urgently. "Are you okay? What did he do to you?"

"What?" Dara looked back and forth between him and her husband. "I don't know what you're—"

Before she could finish, Greg reached up and tugged aside the collar of the light green turtlenecked sweater she was wearing. What he found was the last thing he expected—smooth, unmarred skin. At the same instant, he realized Ben was standing behind his mother; the boy was wearing only pajama bottoms, and he looked frightened but unharmed.

"Are you satisfied?" Tony snarled from behind him. Greg started to argue but Tony was already propelling him toward the door. "Go back to your crazy girlfriend. You found her in a mental ward, maybe you ought to get some treatment yourself."

Greg reached out and snagged the side of the door before his partner could push him totally outside. "Where were you a couple of hours ago?" he demanded. "Just tell me that."

"Right here," Tony shot back. "Where else would I be?" He glanced at his wife. "Right, Dara?"

"Y-yes. Right here."

Greg scowled as Tony crowded him the rest of the way out the door. There had been a definite hesitation in that answer. "I don't think I believe you—*either* of you."

"Ask me if I care," Tony retorted. "Now get *out.* Unfortunately, I'll have to see your sorry ass at the station."

And he slammed the door solidly in Greg's face.

«««—»»»

He had plenty of things to keep his mind busy, but as the day wore on nothing on his list of things to do could keep his thoughts from turning back to Hannah's injuries and the fact that Dara and Ben seemed to have gotten off free and easy this time. Damn it, there was a connection to Tony in there somewhere, but he just couldn't put his finger on the how or why of it. He didn't believe at all that Tony had been home—the agreement that had automatically come from Dara's mouth had about as much truth to it as tap water had color, but there was no way he'd get the truth out of her. So now what?

Tony had become the stone statue toward him to the extreme, not even acknowledging Greg's presence. That was fine with Greg; he'd never liked his partner and he had no intention of apologizing for his accusations, whether or not they had substance. There was too much history there, too many times in the past where he suspected Tony had played punching bag on his wife and son. The thought of apologizing for calling Tony on it made Greg nauseous, and it'd be a hundred degree day in January before that would happen.

In the meantime, he had to try to figure this out. He couldn't just sit idly by while someone, or some*thing* made Hannah's body into a battlefield. How long could she last if this kept up, not just physically, but mentally? She'd already been through so much; it didn't seem fair that the worst portions of the unremembered nightmares of her earlier childhood should come back to plague her.

But where to start? The only notion he had was to go the same route he'd taken in the past—hunt for crimes that had taken place in the right time period with victims bearing similar injuries. This morning had given him something a bit more solid to work with—if Hannah's injuries were really linked to Tony Rutland, then that crime couldn't have occurred that far away. Once Greg found he could snag a few minutes for some personal inquiries, he took a crack at finding some info on the computer. This time, he made a few assumptions based on Hannah's injuries and, well, it was Tony after all. He hesitated a bit over the time, then decided to back up the time frame a bit, working on the assumption that the early morning incident had been keyed in by the clerks.

SEARCH:
Type: Murder
Sex: Female
Age: > 16
Day: Wednesday 2/7
Time: 04:00—07:00 hours
Area: Central and < 35 miles

God bless the age of computers, because the results came up right away: two in the city and one in a suburb called Geneva. He started with the urban ones first, but when he went into detail, neither seemed likely. One was a teenaged girl in the Robert Taylor Homes and the report said it was gang and cocaine-related; the second one was another drug tie-in, where a fifty-six year old woman had been murdered by her adopted son, a junkie whom she'd caught rifling through her purse looking for smack money. But the third one made Greg's eyes widen.

HOMICIDE REPORT			
Name: Janice Tuwile	Sex: Female	Age: 26	
Height: 5' 8"	Weight: 127 pounds	Hair: Reddish Brown	Eyes: Blue
TOD: Approx. 0700	COD: Strangulation	Date: 2/7	
DESCRIPTION: Victim was found in home by husband. Assault wounds to head, bruising around neck consistent with manual strangulation. Evidence of post-mortem sexual assault. Minor evidence of a struggle; however, no forced entry indicates victim may have known her attacker.			
Weapon: N/A	(List all suspects and witness on page two.)		

Janice Tuwile? He knew that name, and it only took a couple more keystrokes to come up with the connection. Jesus, this was Dr. Gorrado's assistant, the gorgeous young woman that Tony had gone so bug-eyed over but called the Ice Queen.

Greg dug around in his drawer until he came up with Gorrado's number, then yanked up the telephone. It rang a few times, then was answered by the man himself. Even through the telephone lines, Greg could hear the shock in the psychiatrist's tone of voice. "Dr. Gorrado here."

"Doctor, this is Detective Greg Jedrek. I was out there once about Hannah Danior, then I talked to you on the phone after that?"

There was a pause and Greg gave the doctor time to get his thoughts to process. The way his voice sounded made it impossible to think he hadn't heard about his assistant's murder. "Yes, I remember. Is something wrong with Hannah?"

"She's fine," Greg lied. "To be honest, I was just going over the area incident reports from this morning and I saw… well, I saw Janice Tuwile on the list."

More silence but Greg didn't push. "Yes," Gorrado finally said. "It's a terrible, terrible thing."

Greg chose his words carefully, knowing that the detectives on the case might not have revealed all the facts to Janice's family and coworkers. "The report says she was attacked in her home?"

"That's what they tell us, yes. I don't know much beyond the fact that when she didn't call in or come to work by ten o'clock, I called her husband at his office. He's an overlap night manager at a film processing plant in Lombard and he works three a.m. to eleven a.m. When he got my call, he left work early and went home, and that's when he found her."

"I see." So Gorrado's call and his coworkers would verify that the husband was at work until ten or later, and the report said the time of death was estimated at seven—the husband was in the clear.

"Rob—that's her husband—is just devastated. They'd just celebrated their first anniversary."

"It's a terrible thing," Greg agreed. "I'm very sorry to hear about this. Do you… do you know if she was having any problems with anyone, an old boyfriend perhaps?"

"Not that I know of—the detectives on the case asked me all that this morning. It's odd I should hear from you, though."

Greg sat up. "Why is that?"

"Well, I hadn't heard anything from Hannah or you, so I hadn't thought about Hannah in quite some time. Then last week Janice mentioned that your partner had called her."

Greg sat very still. "Really? Did she say what he wanted?"

"No, she didn't mention it." Greg started to ask another question but Dr. Gorrado interrupted him. "I'm sorry, but I have another call. Is there anything else?"

"No," Greg replied instead. "Thanks for your time. I hope we catch the person who did this."

"Yes, Detective. I do, too."

The doctor broke the connection and Greg slowly hung up the phone. Tony had called Janice Tuwile last week, and now that young woman was dead… after Hannah had endured one of her Affliction "events" this morning, very likely at the same moment Janice had died. He scanned the homicide report again and shuddered when he caught the part about the sexual assault. If poor Janice Tuwile had been alive when this happened, would Hannah have had to experience that with her? Beneath a haze of fury at his partner, the thought made him want to gag.

Tony Rutland was a killer, of that Greg was absolutely certain.

He just had no idea how to prove it.

Greg dug into his drawer and pulled out copies he'd made of the case files on Jack Iserson, Connie DuPree, Raymond Cespedes and Eloise Addison. Three murders and one attack, but these were the only ones he *knew* about. Hannah had been going through this physical torment for years; how many other crimes had been committed that would never be discovered?

Still, even some of the facts in these cases didn't fit. Jack Iserson, for example, had described a blonde transvestite, tall, with dark blue eyes—could this be Tony in drag? The man had so much hatred for gays that it seemed absurd, yet it had happened during the middle of the day when Tony had been off on one of his errands. Connie DuPree—well, Greg hadn't suspected any connection back then, so he'd never checked or asked. But that murder had occurred on Christmas morning way down in the city, and he'd talked to Tony on the phone too soon afterward for him to have been involved. Anyway, at this point, Antarctica would melt before he'd get any reliable information from Tony or Dara as to whether Tony had gone somewhere during that time period, and the same would apply to the Saturday that Raymond Cespedes had been murdered.

Speaking of, where *was* Tony right now? He'd been in the station this morning, pointedly ignoring Greg, but gone off on his own after lunch, snapping something about some legwork on a couple of cases. Greg didn't know how much longer they were going to get away with this gig—now the other cops were starting to talk and the lieutenant was bound to notice and start screaming about teamwork and backing each other up. The truth was that he and Tony had quietly worked apart most of the time since Greg had started. It was only their growing animosity, brought to a screaming head by Greg's visit this morning, that had suddenly put a big red arrow over them.

A line from an old public service television commercial came floating back to him, and for some reason, he found it unnervingly appropriate when his mind modified the words:

It's three o'clock. Do you know where your partner is?

««—»»

Damn. Tony had never wanted to come here again—it was his great and grand plan to weed his sister entirely out of his life—but here he was. He'd avoided the whole Thanksgiving and Christmas thing with one very brutal phone call, where he'd told his sister that if she so much as tried to set foot on his property he'd call her counselor and find a way to get her detained in a mental facility. That had been a bluff, but it had worked; Carrie had sent a Christmas card and couple of Christmas presents for Ben via good old UPS and let it go at that. She'd gotten brave and called on Christmas Day, but Tony could live with that—the truth was it'd been nice to hear her voice, even if it wasn't the way it ought to be.

Same Carrie as always, coming down to see who it was rather than just buzzing him in. The smile she gave him was tentative, tempered with sadness and longing. Sad, but she'd brought it on herself.

"I have to talk to you," he said before she could even say hello. He gave her a little push to get her back inside, then followed, thinking he'd have to wash his hands now. "I'm in kind of a jam—*we're* in it, actually."

Carrie glanced back at him, puzzled, and he had to reluctantly admit that she looked pretty good for a change. Maybe she'd been ready to go out or something, because for a change she was out of the sloppy sweats or scaldingly bright workout clothes. Still, it made him uncomfortable to note she was wearing a sweater tight enough to show off high, firm breasts.

"Coffee?" his sister offered. "I can make you a sandwich—"

"No," Tony said. He went into the kitchen and dropped onto one of the kitchen chairs. Carrie followed and sat across from him. "I didn't come here to eat. I came because we're in trouble."

"What's wrong?"

"Hannah."

Just saying the name to her made the flesh rise on the back of his neck, and the shock that rolled off Carrie was almost palpable. When she finally found her voice, Tony had to lean forward to hear her words. "Hannah is... *alive?"*

His expression was grim. "She's more than alive. I *told* you this, remember?" His voice turned sarcastic. "Maybe you thought I was talking about a old school chum, dumbass."

Carrie blinked. "I… I guess it didn't really register." Then her eyes almost bulged. "Oh my *God,* Tony. Don't tell me she *remembers—*"

"Not yet. But when you think about it, it's only a matter of time, right?" He picked at the tablecloth, some bright and ridiculous sunflower-patterned thing that matched curtains bearing the same gaudy print.

"What did she say?" Carrie's hands were twisting on the tabletop like panicked snakes.

"She doesn't remember," Tony repeated. He gave his sister a dark look. "We have to make sure it stays that way, Carrie."

She didn't say anything, then she met his gaze. "Are you… are you going to take care of it?"

"No." He reached in his pocket and pulled something out, pushed it across the table. *"You* are."

Carried stared at the small ring of keys on the tablecloth, then slowly reached out and picked it up. "Why me?"

"Because Hannah is my partner's girlfriend," he told her. "He knows something's not right, but not just *what,* not yet. That means I can call you and tell you when and where, but I *have* to be at work and with my partner when it happens. There are… connections here, between Hannah and me—and you, too, I think—that can't be explained, but they all point to one thing: if we don't do something about her, we're fucked. Period."

"What connections?"

"It doesn't matter." One hand shot forward and he gripped her wrist, dug his fingers in hard enough to make her wince. "But I'll tell you this. I am *not* going to see my life ruined because of her, and I'm not going to jail either."

"But do we have to… you know?" Carrie's eyes were wide and pleading.

Tony yanked her toward him hard enough to slam her rib cage into the edge of the table. "You want to take that chance, Carrie? How do you think a person like you will make out in the joint, with those perky silicon breasts and that fake little pussy of yours?"

Carrie jerked away and rubbed her wrist. "Fine. I'll handle it."

"You bet your phony ass you will. And you'll do it without whining, too."

"How—"

"I don't care." Tony stood. "Just get it done quickly and *quietly,* and for Christ's sake, don't let anyone see you going in there or coming out. She lives on Belmont and I'll call you with the exact address. It's a busy street, there's a downstairs and an upstairs door, and I don't know which key fits what. I'm pretty sure they'll only work in the front, so you don't have any choice. Go in the front, come out the back. And don't leave any fucking fingerprints."

His sister nodded as she followed him to the front door. "Got it."

"I got a good life, Carrie. I don't know if yours is good, but it's what you wanted." He looked at her. "If you want to keep it that way, you're going to have to make sure Hannah never opens her mouth again."

Monday—February 12th...

Man, Carrie, thought. Tony wasn't kidding when he said this was a busy street.

He brother had called her this morning and given her Hannah's address and the time he wanted it done. She'd checked out the place from across the street, then decided it would be best if she came up to the door from the east, so she wouldn't have to pass in front of that bookstore window. Now, heart hammering, she walked up to the entry door and quickly tried the keys on the ring, trying to look as though it was the most everyday thing that a person could do. After the second try, she lucked out—the gold key slid in and turned without a hitch. She didn't look around, because she felt that would draw attention to herself; as far as she knew, no one noticed her going inside.

The hallway was nothing special and after she'd closed the door quietly behind her, Carrie stood there in the semi-darkness and listened. She could hear music playing upstairs, not very loud, but it was nearly drowned out by the noise of the traffic outside. Would it be enough camouflage? She hoped so.

She felt oddly calm. She'd expected exactly the opposite—breath-shortening fear, the crazy way her heart tended to alternately thud and skitter at the same time in times of high stress, maybe a shot of adrenaline to push her into turning that final key. But there was none of that. Instead, standing on the top landing and staring at the door she was about to open only brought Carrie a great, deep sense of sadness. She'd always liked Hannah, and while Tony could shrug off the old memories with hardly a thought, Carrie had invariably been secretly ashamed about all of it.

So little in her life seemed to have worked out the way she hoped—her big change, her job, her boyfriends. All that trouble to silence Connie so she wouldn't blab Carrie's big secret to Rodney, and then the guy had never done anything more than have a few dinners with her, eat up her food and then dump her. She'd liked him *so* much—whoever would have thought he was like that underneath his suave and sophisticated exterior? There hadn't even been a hint of interest in her from anyone after that—people just never seemed to be what they appeared.

And now, this. Wasn't it ironic that in the end she, not Tony, had to clean up the mess?

Carrie took a deep, stabilizing breath, then carefully and quietly began trying the other keys until she found one that slipped into the lock and opened the door.

«««—»»»

Hannah was in the bathroom combing her hair when she heard the door open, then footsteps. She glanced automatically at her wristwatch, then frowned. Greg was supposed to be at work and she had to leave for the Diner in a half hour. "Greg?" she called as she put the comb on the sink and stepped into the kitchen. "What are you doing here? Aren't you—"

There was a stranger in the apartment.

It was a woman, tall and blonde. She was wearing a plain maroon jacket and blue jeans—no handbag—and she was moving toward Hannah with purposely quiet footfalls. Already she had closed half the distance between Hannah and the front door, and she showed no signs of slowing.

"Who are you?" Hannah demanded. "Get out of my house!" Instinct kicked in and she went to the right, her goal the back door. Then the woman said something—

"Hannah."

—and she froze.

Gooseflesh rippled along her arms but she didn't know why. For a too-long moment a sort of black *fog* rolled across her vision, blinding her to the present and giving her a glimpse—just that—into memories she'd thought were gone forever. Just that tiny flash, brief but wrought with incredible pain, was enough to make Hannah stagger.

"Who are you?" Hannah whispered. She squeezed her eyes shut briefly, opened them, shut them again. "Why are you here?"

By way of an answer, the stranger pulled something from her pocket and flicked her wrist. A knife sprang into view, and the woman held it in a loose and very comfortable grip. "I'm sorry," was all she said.

Hannah screamed and bolted for the door and the woman leaped heavily on top of her, slamming her to the floor in a painful heap of tangled arms and legs. She got one hand in front of her face in time to deflect a swipe at her throat, felt a strip of fire across her wrist as the blade sliced it open. Still screaming, Hannah punched the woman on the side of the head and heard her grunt. Hannah tried to wriggle free and the woman steadied herself, then brought the knife up again, this time cutting into Hannah's jaw line on the left side, barely missing her throat. Hannah twisted her head away and flailed wildly at the woman's face, then two snarling streaks hurled themselves on top of Hannah's attacker.

The dogs—Hannah had forgotten about them, lying on the living room rug, probably waiting to be told they could check out her unexpected visitor. Now their growls and barks added to her screams, and it only took a couple of seconds for the tables to turn. The woman lashed out with the knife and Hannah heard one of the dogs howl in pain; the other's onslaught increased at the sound as Hannah got a hand in the woman's hair and pulled as viciously as she could.

Suddenly the weight was off her. Hannah tried to sit up and got kicked back down, then Knothead shot forward and clamped a mouthful of teeth around the woman's ankle before her foot could connect with Hannah again. The dog shook her catch furiously, claws fighting for purchase on a floor slicked with blood. Hannah's attacker nearly toppled over and the dog lost her balance and let go. Outnumbered, outfought, the stranger yanked open the back door and fled.

And Hannah was left on the floor to bleed and wonder what the hell had just happened.

««—»»

The phone rang, he answered it.

Then, simple as that, everything went to hell in a handbasket.

"Detective Jedrek." He started to lean back in his chair but by the time the caller, the Sargent out at the front desk, had gotten to the second sentence, Greg was on his feet. "What? *What?"* He made himself listen to the words even as his gaze tripped around the room until it settled on Tony. His so-called 'partner' was at his desk doing paperwork, and had been all morning.

Whether he felt Greg's stare or caught the urgency in Greg's voice, Tony looked up at him quizzically as Greg dropped the phone in the receiver and grabbed his jacket. "Something wrong?"

"It's Hannah," Greg said shortly. "I've got to get over to her place."

Tony raised an eyebrow, then turned his attention back to his paperwork. "She have another one of her whacko sessions?"

Greg didn't have time to trade verbal punches with the other man. "Someone broke into her apartment and attacked her. She wants me to take her to the hospital."

His interest renewed, Tony started to rise. "No shit? I'll go with you—"

"Spare us both, Tony." Greg shot him a withering look right before he stepped out the door. "Hannah doesn't like you any more than I do." He didn't bother to stick around and see Tony's expression, nor did he much care about what the other cops in the squad room thought. Right now his biggest concern was getting to Hannah and making sure she was all right.

The ride to Hannah's took days, or maybe it just felt that way. Every mopey driver in the city seemed to be in front of him, every traffic light seemed determined to mire him in a line of cars with drivers who remained blissfully oblivious to his blue lights and angry pops at the siren. He pulled up in front of the bookstore and double-parked behind the two patrol cars that were already there, then took the stairs three at a time and careened into the apartment. The thing that scared him the most was the Fire Department ambulance parked out front—he'd assumed it wasn't that bad since she wanted him to drive her; apparently the beat cops had disagreed and called the paramedics anyway.

Greg didn't know what he'd been expecting, since they hadn't said how badly Hannah was hurt. He'd never seen this many people in here and it threw him for a moment, then he flashed his badge and pushed through the knot of uniformed personnel. Before he could call out, he heard Hannah's irritated voice rise above the chatter and radio static—

"No, I am *not* going anywhere in the ambulance. I'm waiting for Greg, and we have to get the dog taken care of! *No,* damn it!"

"Hannah?" Greg pushed past the last two guys. "Are you all right? What happened?"

When she saw him, her pale, strained face lit up like sunshine. His gaze went from her eyes to the blood-soaked gauze she was holding on one side of her face, then traveled to another bloody bandage wrapped around her wrist. "Greg, thank God you're here. I know these guys mean well, but we can't just leave Puddles here—she's *bleeding.* Really, I'm not that badly hurt. It's just a lot of blood."

For the first time, Greg realized that Hannah was sitting on the floor with the black lab's head on one knee. She was panting and one of the officers was squatting next to her, his hand pressing a washcloth again blood-soaked fur. Knothead sat at the man's elbow, whining and vibrating like a tuning fork. "We can put the dog in the back seat," he suggested. "I'll take him over to McKillips Animal Hospital on Clark Street as soon as we get you taken care of."

"No," Hannah said stubbornly. "Greg, she's *stabbed.* And we don't know how deep." She looked at him, her eyes wide. "These dogs saved my life today. I'm not going to leave her to bleed to death in a car while I get a scrape or two stitched up."

"Little more than a scrape, lady," offered one of the paramedics as he knelt next to her. He pushed her hand aside to replace the wad of cotton on her face with a fresh one and Greg's stomach twisted when he saw the ragged slash along her jaw line. "If you don't get that taken care of right away, you're going to have a helluva scar."

Hannah looked like she was going to smart-mouth him and Greg cleared his throat sharply enough to get her attention. She closed her mouth, wincing when she did so.

"Tell you what," said one of the cops. "You take your gal to the hospital and me and my partner'll put the pooch in the back of the squad and take it over to McKillips. You can pick her up later."

Greg glanced at the guy and gave him a grateful smile, liking the way he'd played on the assumption that the dog would be all right. "Thanks. I appreciate it."

"No problem." He looked to Hannah. "You got a spare sheet? It'll be easier if we use it as a sling to carry her."

"Second cabinet to the left of the refrigerator," Hannah said. "Thank you *so* much—"

The officer waved her off. "Like I said, no problem. I like dogs. Hell, they treat people better than people treat people."

"Ma'am, why don't you let us take you over to Illinois Masonic?" asked the paramedic. "We—"

"No," Hannah said stubbornly. She shivered. "No offense, but I *hate* ambulances."

"It's okay, I'll take her," Greg put in.

"They'll be waiting for her," said the other one, but he didn't look pleased. "We already called it in."

"Come on, Hannah." He and the paramedic helped her stand as the two police officers carefully slid the sheet under Puddles, then hefted him up. That done, Greg got her coat and he draped it over her shoulders and led her to the door as the rest of the officers and the two medics followed. "What *happened?"*

Hannah looked at him and her expression was still a little dazed. "I heard the front door unlock and I thought it was you. When I came out of the bathroom, there was a woman coming toward me. She pulled out a knife and said 'I'm sorry'— can you imagine that? And then she came at me." Shock was etched in every feature of her face. "*'I'm sorry.'* My God."

"We found a couple good doses of blood going down the back stairs," said one of the two officers following them down the stairs. "We're guessing the dogs chewed her up pretty good. One of the bookstore employees heard the screaming and the dogs barking and called it in. We've got it all written up, notices into the hospitals about people coming in with dog bites."

"Great," Greg said. He handed over one of his cards. "Lock up the place, would you? And call me if you get a lead on anyone."

"Will do."

He got Hannah settled on the passenger side, then hurried around and got in. He'd just pulled away from the curb when she gave hm yet another shock. "Greg, she knew my *name."*

He scowled and gripped the wheel hard enough to hurt his fingers. "She did? How about you— did you recognize her?"

Hannah shook her head. "Never saw her before. She was kind of tall, blonde hair. It all happened so fast I didn't get a much closer look—I don't even think I'd recognize her if I saw her again."

"Tell me the whole thing," Greg said. "Start to finish."

And so she did, but it was a painfully short account. By the time he'd gone the few blocks over to Illinois Masonic and pulled into the ER drive, the story was over and he didn't know much more than he'd already gleaned.

"Oh, Christ," Hannah muttered as someone wearing a white coat hurried over to her side of the car. "Could this day get any better?"

"What's the matter?" Greg asked, then got the answer to his own question when he saw Dr. Ireta Tansey waiting for Hannah to climb out. Her face was stony.

"Ms. Danior," she said. "Follow me, please."

"Shit," he heard Hannah mutter under her breath, and if she hadn't been all slashed up Greg would've grinned at her unaccustomed crudeness. He kept his comments to himself and went with her, mentally preparing himself for what he knew was going to be a fight.

In the examining room, Hannah sat on the table with a pained expression while Dr. Tansey and a couple of nurses examined the two wounds. Both were fairly deep and Greg was surprised to see that neither seemed inclined to exhibit any of the remarkable healing tendencies that usually accompanied Hannah's injuries. There could be only one explanation for that, though it was grounded in about as much reality as anything else that happened to her: since these knife wounds had happened to Hannah directly, she would have to heal at the same pain and pace as any other normal person. That she healed like she did, he realized, was something he—and perhaps she—had come to take for granted.

"I'm going to butterfly both of these so the scarring is minimal. I want you to be very still while I work on your face," Dr. Tansey said. "It wouldn't hurt you to see a plastic surgeon, you know." Hannah was still wearing her blood-stained sweater; Greg knew she didn't want to take it off for fear of what the physician would say when she saw the scars Hannah had added to her "collection" since her last visit to the emergency room.

"'k," Hannah said without moving her mouth. She recoiled when Dr. Tansey when to touch her face. "Sorry—I guess I just wasn't ready."

Tansey waited until Hannah had settled herself, then tried again. This time Hannah managed to keep still, though Greg saw the pain reflected in his girlfriend's eyes.

"So what was it this time?" Dr. Tansey asked. That she kept her voice carefully bland only made Greg think of a placid-looking cat that could reach out and slice a person open in the space of a second. "Did this just 'happen,' too? Like all the other times where you don't remember?"

Hannah looked like she was going to retort but Greg got in there before she could. "She was attacked by an intruder in her apartment," he said shortly. "Her dogs drove the woman away."

"Really," Tansey said. "By the way, Hannah. That's a pretty good scar going up the inside of your left wrist."

Hannah blinked but kept quiet so the doctor could work. Greg could see the dismay in her gaze though, knew she wished she'd remembered about that and kept that arm out of sight.

"I think for your own safety we'll admit you," Tansey said. "Just to keep an eye on things."

"That won't be necessary," Greg said quickly. "She's under my... protection."

The doctor arched an eyebrow as she pressed the last butterfly strip into place on Hannah's face. She opened another packet and went to work on the injured wrist. "Really. And if I recommend against it? On the grounds that this attacker may be only theoretical?"

"Listen," Hannah said acidly. "I know you think you're doing me a favor, but if you could keep your skills to the medical part and out of my personal life, I'd appreciate it."

Greg reached out and squeezed Hannah's shoulder, and the gesture wasn't lost on Dr. Tansey. "Hannah's attacker wasn't imaginary, doctor. The person escaped, but she was bitten by Hannah's dogs. Instead of berating Hannah, you and your staff would be much more helpful if you'd watch for someone coming in here with severe dog-bite injuries."

"And what about all these other injuries?" Tansey demanded.

"Those aren't the focus of this investigation," Greg said. He folded his arms and regarded the doctor dispassionately. "I believe I've made myself clear?"

"Crystal." Tansey finished up with Hannah's wrist, then peeled off her gloves and slapped them angrily on the surgical tray.

Hannah reached out and lightly touched the physician's arm. "Dr.

Tansey, please," she said. "I'm sorry I was sarcastic—this morning just really freaked me out. But I'm okay, and Greg will take care of me. And I swear to you, I'm not hurting myself. I never was."

The woman pressed her lips together but in the end, she had no choice but to step aside. There was, at least this time, no basis to hold Hannah. But no wonder Hannah didn't want to come over here—under the mistaken auspices of having Hannah's best interests in mind, this woman would have her drugged and restrained in a heartbeat.

"Spray this antiseptic on both wounds twice a day," Tansey said brusquely. She handed Hannah a small bottle. "Be sure not to get it in your eyes. The butterfly strips will eventually come off in the shower, but don't rub them— just rinse." She taped a couple of gauze bandages over the wounds, then stared first at Greg, then at Hannah. "I don't want to see you in here again, Ms. Danior. If I do, I *promise* you, I will find some way to keep you for your own safety. For a long, *long* time."

"Thanks for your *help.*" Hannah slid off the table and grabbed up her jacket. "I always look forward to seeing you."

"Anytime." The doctor spun and stalked out.

"Hannah, you're not helping," Greg said sharply.

"Like she *is,*" she said crankily.

"Come on." He started to hold out her jacket but stopped when she moved in close to him and buried the uninjured side of her face against his shoulder. Damn—he was so much the cop, he hadn't even thought to give his girlfriend a little bit of comfort. His arms went around her and he hugged her. "It's okay now," he murmured against her hair. He wrinkled his nose, then realized what was wrong—Jesus, her hair smelled like blood. Suddenly it sank in, really *in,* that he could have lost her this morning, that she could have actually been *killed.* It took him a few moments to get past the emotions that were suddenly stuck in his throat, and he was glad she didn't say anything. "Let's go check on the dog," he said hoarsely.

"Okay." She looked at him, her eyes wide. "Do you think she's okay?"

"Let's hope so," was all he could say, because he didn't have a clue. "It's only a few blocks. Come on."

They didn't talk much on the way, but there was enough time for Greg to turn over a few new and unanswered questions in his mind. Tony, of course, had been in plain sight all morning, but that didn't let him off the hook in Greg's mind. It was too pat, too much of a coincidence that Hannah would get attacked so soon after Greg and his partner had had their little blow up—did Tony have an accomplice? It wasn't a pleasant concept.

He and Hannah were at the vet's within ten minutes and the news was, thankfully, all good. "It wasn't that deep," said the vet as he led a slow-moving but happy Puddles out on a leash. "Puddles here lucked out. The stab wound went only about an inch into muscle and missed any internal organs. A few stitches and she's good to go. Keep her quiet for four or five days, and bring her back in a week to get the stitches out." He was an older man with a reddish, Mormon-style beard. He gave Hannah a serious look, noting the bandages on her face and wrist. "From what the policemen said when they dropped her off, you're one very lucky woman."

"I know," Hannah said softly. She rubbed the dog's head and Puddles leaned against her and whined. "It's okay, girl. We're going home."

At the front Greg ignored Hannah's protest and paid the bill. "Let's just get you home as quickly as possible," he told her. "We'll talk about money later." If he had his way, the subject of the vet bill wouldn't come up again, because as far as he was concerned, these two dogs were worth their weight in diamonds for saving Hannah's life this morning.

He just wanted to get back to the apartment, sit next to her on the couch while the dogs curled up on their rug, and be thankful she was alive and well enough to hold in his arms.

Tuesday—February 13th...

The blood was cleaned up and the locks were changed. Greg had been concerned she would be nervous, afraid every time she heard the smallest thump or bump, but Hannah felt just fine in the apartment. Oddly enough, it was the dogs who were fidgety, lifting their heads at every noise, going to the door and checking out any sound that remotely resembled a door opening. That they were her guardians and had come through so remarkably for her yesterday was precisely the reason she felt just as comfortable as she ever had. Greg already spent most of his time here, and now, of course, he couldn't be pried out of here with a crowbar. Who knew when he would relax and go back to sleeping at his own place; Hannah had only been over there twice, not that long ago, and both times it had looked dusty and unlived-in.

Winnie had covered for her yesterday—thank God, because Zubro always had his eye on getting rid of her— and Hannah was scheduled off today. It would give her a bit of time to heal on the outside, but the inside…

That was a whole different thing.

She had thought plenty of times that she might die of the injuries that just appeared on her body—God knows, so many of them were certainly serious enough. And if she really were a sort of mirror for other people, as Greg had convinced her she was by telling her about all those unsolved cases, then any normal woman would have died. But she hadn't; instead, she had healed, and at a remarkable rate besides.

But not this time.

Hannah's face and wrist were bruised, painful and swollen, just the way anyone else's would have been had they gone through the same trauma. She was used to pain, incredible amounts of it, but she'd also come to assume she could live through nearly anything. This was *different,* so much so that this morning she had woken pre-dawn with a whole different perspective on the Interesting Life And Times Of Hannah.

Greg lay beside her, snoring lightly. She'd never minded the sound, finding it vaguely comforting. He'd gone to sleep in what he always wore when he stayed: gray sweat pants and a t-shirt, as unthreatening an outfit as he could find. When he'd first started sleeping over, Greg had bunked out on the couch; somewhere around mid-December, she told him he could sleep in the bed but warned him that she wasn't ready for intimacy. He had respected that, and despite his marriage proposal, that's the way it remained.

Why?

Yesterday, someone had tried to kill her. Hannah didn't know who or why, only that had it not been for Puddles and Knothead, she could have been lying cold on a slab in the Cook County Morgue this morning. The wounds she'd sustained from the attack were painful and to her mind, excruciatingly slow in the healing process, completely different than the way things healed when injuries suddenly "appeared" on her. For the first time she could remember, she had to take prescription painkillers to help her tolerate the healing. It was infuriating, exhilarating, and terrifying, all at the same time.

Wonder of all wonders, there was a part of her that was actually *normal.* She wasn't invincible, and she cut, bled, and healed just like the next person. She could *die* like the next person, and if that was the case, *what was she waiting for with Greg?*

Maybe she was selfish, but suddenly she wanted it *all*, as much of life as she could get, packed in as quickly as possible into whatever time she had left. Because really, how much time could that be when first she took on other people's injuries, then someone intentionally—that couldn't be denied when the person had known who she was—tried to kill her? Sleeping beside her was a man who loved her and wanted her, and who had shown the patience and self-control of a saint where sex was concerned. Enough of that.

But could she go through with it?

Hannah didn't know. The idea of getting that close to someone physically had always filled her with apprehension, as if the notion pried at doorways in her mind that were best left closed. But she was tired of missing out on the *all* part of life, of dancing skittishly around the final, so-important part of giving herself fully to the future.

Tomorrow was Valentine's Day.

It was as good a day as any to open a road into her future that had been closed for way too long.

««—»»

Tony could have screamed, it took Carrie so long to come down and answer the door. When she finally did, he shoved her back inside and yanked it closed behind him, then spun to face her. "You fucked it up!" he said furiously.

"Tony—"

"I *counted* on you to take care of this for both of us, and you *fucked it up.*" He punctuated each word with another push to herd her further back into her apartment. "Get your ass in there and tell me why."

"You didn't tell me she had those animals!" Carrie cried. "Tony, they *attacked* me! I tried to finish her off anyway, but there were two of them, and they were big!"

"Damn it," Tony growled. For the first time he realized Carrie was limping as she stumbled along in front of him. He pushed her a final time as they crossed into the kitchen, then he dropped onto a chair. "How the hell am I going to fix this?"

Carrie lowered herself painfully to the chair across from him. "She didn't recognize me. She didn't know."

"That's not the point," Tony snapped. "You were supposed to *handle* it, remember? I told you, there are connections, almost like psychic or something, between her and me, her and *us,* that you don't know anything about."

"Then fill me in."

"I'm not going to bother with the details," Tony asked in disgust. "Let's just say she *knows* every time you or I do something we shouldn't. And you—well, you had your chance to help out. I should have known you couldn't pull it off."

Carrie's face darkened with resentment. "You know, you never even asked if I was okay. Those damned dogs of Hannah's hurt me really bad, Tony. I had to go to this sleazy little prick of a failed med school student to get sewn up because I knew they'd send a watch alert into the emergency rooms. I'm gonna miss work, and when I go back, I have to grit my teeth and act like I had nothing more than a bad cold when I had twenty-two *stitches* in my leg and my ankle. I'm scarred for life, and I'm not even sure his damned needles were clean. Is there any compassion at *all* left in you?"

"Not for you."

"Not for *anyone,*" Carrie retorted.

"Whatever." Tony pushed to his feet.

His sister struggled up and followed him as he headed toward the front door. "What now?" she asked anxiously. "Do you have a plan?"

"I'll figure something out," he said in a terse voice. "I just have to find something else for Greg to focus on. Don't worry about it."

"Well, of course I'm worrying about it!" Carrie shrilled from right behind him. "You're my brother—family. No one asked her to come back into our lives and ruin everything!" She clutched at his sleeve. "I'm lonely, Tony. I haven't seen Mom and Dad in years, not since—"

He swatted her hand away. "You made your choice, now deal with it."

"Give me another chance, Tony. I won't mess it up this time."

Tony whirled. "Stop whining at me, you fucking *freak*!" he yelled. He shoved her to put some distance between them, not caring that she gasped in pain as she stumbled backward. "You had your chance! You think my partner's going to sit back while you try the same stupid move? I have to figure out a way to go at this differently now." He glared at her. "Just stay the hell out of sight, and *trouble,* and leave the rest to me."

He slammed the door in Carrie's face, but that just didn't make him feel any better about the disaster his life had become.

Wednesday—February 14th...

Greg had found out time and time again that "life with Hannah" always seemed to hold another surprise, and tonight was no different. Yes, it was Valentine's evening, but it was also the night after she'd been attacked. He'd planned on taking her out to dinner but since these newest wounds showed none of the miraculous healing tendencies of the former ones, she'd asked him to postpone it. Always on the lookout for options, Greg had pre-ordered a couple of rib dinners from Carson's and he arrived at Hannah's fully loaded with food, roses, and a box of Valentine's chocolates.

There was something… *different* about her when she answered the door. He didn't know what it was, but something had changed in her smile and the way her eyes sparkled when she opened the door and ushered him inside, something definitely warmer in the soft, careful kiss she planted on his lips before she accepted the flowers and candy he offered. Whatever it was, it left him a little light-headed and wondering momentarily where his breath had gone.

"What's all this?" Hannah asked as he followed her to the kitchen and dropped the white shopping bags from Carson's on the table. The dogs circled his legs and sniffed eagerly at him and his hands, knowing better than to put their noses onto the forbidden tabletop area.

"Dinner," Greg said. "Since we're not going out, I thought I'd bring it in. Told you I'd take care of it."

"I thought we were going to order a pizza or whatever." She peered into the shopping bags. "God, this smells wonderful, like barbeque sauce."

"Yep. Ribs, baked potatoes, salad, the works."

"Yummy. I'll set the table."

Greg paused in the middle of pulling a covered aluminum container from one of the bags. "The table?"

Hannah grinned at him. "Don't look so shocked. It's this thing here that the bags are sitting on? It's Valentine's Day and you brought us a real meal. We're going to eat it at the table like a real couple instead of like a pair of couch potatoes."

Greg twisted his face into the best imitation of sorrow that he could muster. "But what about the reruns of *My Favorite Martian* and *Mr. Ed*? We'll miss them both!"

Hannah giggled. "I think you'll live. Now come on and help me set this up."

"Oh, all right," he grumbled, but it was a poor acting job and they both knew it—he hadn't seen either show in decades.

It wasn't long before they were seated across from each other, peering around the huge vase of roses that Hannah had insisted be placed on the table. A little wine, a lot of food… but less than he expected they would both eat. Hannah laughed and chatted right along with him, but he had the distinct impression her mind was on something else. Oddly enough, Greg still never felt slighted—just being around this woman always made him feel like he was the center of the universe.

When they'd finished the meal, Greg got up and pulled another container from the refrigerator, a little something he'd tucked in there when Hannah's back had been turned. "Dessert?" he offered. "Strawberry pound cake, but without the whipped cream. I was afraid that would make it soggy."

Hannah inhaled, then shook her head. "It sounds wonderful, but let's wait a bit. I don't want to get overfull."

"Okay." He turned back and slid the box back onto its shelf, then straightened and shut the door. "You want to watch a movie or—"

"No," Hannah said softly from right behind him. Her hands slid around his waist and she pressed herself against him, hard enough for him to feel her small breasts against his back, the flat of her stomach, even her hip bones. Greg found himself suddenly standing very still. "There's something else I want to do instead," she continued. Her voice had dropped to a warm whisper next to his ear. "Something I've… never tried before."

Her fingers found his and Greg let her turn him, then lead him toward the bed.

«« — »»

Hannah had one dark moment of near-panic, a shiver of some unasked-for memory as it tried to rise to the surface of her mind and destroy everything—

She is surrounded by darkness and cold, the smell of damp, wet earth, but the cold isn't enough to stop the fire against her skin as the bright end of the cigarette presses experimentally against it. She's used to pain but this is more than she can stand and so she screams; he clamps a hand over her mouth and she tastes the cotton glove, the one that belongs to her foster father. It's gritty with dirt from the scruffy vegetable patch that man is always trying to grow to save money, and if the glove hadn't been stolen for use by another right now, it would be a good memory. She sees a shadowy figure raise the knife and cut himself and the other one, small nicks but enough to draw blood. Then he turns to the baby and her mouth opens against the fabric once more, wider, but she is tied and helpless to stop him as he draws more blood. Then it's her turn for agony, this time deeply across the palm of her left hand, and he drags her forward to the other and the baby, so very, very still, and he presses all four of their palms together. "I love you, little sister. We're tied forever, so you must never, ever *tell." He grinds his hand harder against hers, mingling their blood, then smears the mixture across her eyes. His hands are on her in the dark, under her clothes and in places where they shouldn't be and she hates it, hates* him, *but this she can endure, she has endured it from him for as long as she can remember. But the other thing, what they have done to the baby—*

"What you've seen here today is our secret forever. Don't ever tell anyone, anything." Beyond the sound of his words, she hears something more than a command. Her mind is young but not stupid, easily influenced, and it buckles under a threat that's meant to last her a lifetime. "Not a word, sister. Just forget you ever saw a thing. We're all tied together by blood, for always."

—and then she forced it away, because the here and now of tonight was so much better than a past filled with atrocities she didn't want to recall.

Now was good, so sweet and incredible. Now was the chilly but candle-lit room and the warmth of Greg's bare chest sliding against her breasts, his gentle hands stroking her hips and belly and beyond, making her want to open herself to him like a flower seeking the spring sunshine. His kisses tasted like barbeque sauce while his skin smelled of clean soap; she felt heat and anticipation everywhere, as though she was standing on a hilltop in the midst of a raging thunderstorm as the electrical field built and the lightning came ever closer to striking.

And when it did hit—when their bodies finally joined as one—Hannah closed her eyes and rode out the storm and the fear and the pleasure, wondering afterward why she had waited so long to share herself with this man whom she loved so much.

Monday—February 19th...

It's the middle of the day, a decent day, not bad, not good, just unremarkable. He's on his way back to work from an errand and even though he doesn't have any pressing problems, any immediate *problems, there's always this other thing preying on his mind, this thing where he ends up feeling like he's watched all the time, like he's under a fucking microscope and the world is hovering over him like a praying mantis reading to bite the head off some poor sucker of a meal. He hates feeling like that, like a* victim. *He's the kind of person who likes to be on the other end of things, the control end where he's the one making the decisions and the other people around him have to do what they're told.*

The more he thinks about how that part of his life has gotten out of control, the more angry he gets. He shouldn't have started thinking about it at all, it was a mistake to let his thoughts go down that road, to let his mind start looking at all the angles which were really nothing more than ways in which he'd recently decided he was fucking trapped *and hadn't yet figured out how to fix it.*

And then he pulls into the alleyway that connects Wolcott to Damen, the one he always uses when he's coming from this direction because that way he doesn't have to deal with the traffic—

And it's blocked by some kid dressed up like something out of a Boris Karloff movie.

Goths—that's what kids like this call themselves. He calls them pallid-looking excuses for human beings, miserable little attitudes with legs and pancake makeup who don't have the sense to get some of the sun God put on this green earth. Under the white and black shit smeared on his face, this boy is probably nineteen or twenty, right at the age where he thinks he knows everything and the universe revolves around him. The little Goth is sitting there in some monstrosity of a car—a puke green 1973 Buick Centurion that's older than him and so full of rust holes it's a miracle it doesn't crack apart going over a pothole. Worse than all that, This big, shitty dinosaur is parked right in the middle of the alley and blocking it completely.

He stops about ten yards away, rolls down his window, and sticks his head outside. "Hey," he yells. "Pull it to the side so I can get through."

Instead of answering, the kid flips him off through the windshield.

For a moment, all he can do is be amazed at the audacity of this nothing little fucker who, in the scheme of the big wide world, is less than an ant under the heel of the boot about to come down on his dirty, black-dyed, spiked-out hair.

Then the blood surges through his temples and wipes out everything with a red haze of anger. This little bastard is just one more symbol of how things in his life have gotten so out of control, how everyone around him thinks they can just fuck with him and push and push and push. Well, his button was just pushed, all right.

He gets out of his car and walks over to the driver's side of the Buick. His steps are calm, measured, never giving away the rage razoring along his nerve endings. The Goth boy in the car is sitting with his jaw resting on his fist. He barely glances at his visitor; obviously he is bored with his existence.

That is a problem that can be rectified.

"Pull the car to the side," he repeats calmly. "So I can get through."

"I'm waiting for someone."

"I'm thrilled for you. Wait for them without *blocking everyone else."*

"Go fuck yourself."

The pounding of his heart increases, not fear but outrage. He slides a hand inside his jacket and pulls out his revolver, presses it against the little jerk-off's temple.

The boy freezes and his eyes widen, then narrow. "You won't do it," the kid sneers at him. "You're just a cowardly poser like the rest of them."

He doesn't feel like arguing, so he squeezes the trigger.

There is a split second in which the boy actually looks surprised. Maybe it's that one instant in which his eyes register movement in the hand at the side of his face, or he hears the mechanisms turn in the gun as its metal pieces work to function as it was designed. He imagines he sees fear cross the rancid little Goth's features, maybe even regret. It's hard to tell, since it happens so fast. Maybe the boy even looks happy—

Nah. Probably not.

He looks at the gun in his hand for a second, then at the kid. There is a hole in his temple the size of a quarter. It has blackened edges and at first glance it looks very neat. But most of his brains have come out the other side of his head and the inside of the car now looks like someone tossed an open can of scarlet paint on the seats. There is a smell already building up—gunpowder, blood, human waste. Then it kicks into his own head that he just fired his gun, this *gun, and boy wasn't that just the stupidest, most assole thing he could have done? That temper of his was going to be his damned downfall.*

There's nothing he can do to fix or hide this—it's broad daylight in the alley. He glances around but all he has left is the hope that if anyone heard the gunshot, they'll think it was a car backfiring… at least long enough for him to beat it.

Hastily tucking the revolver beneath his jacket, he climbs back into his car, backs out of the alley, and drives away.

««—»»

Hannah was sitting at the kitchen table with a cup of Orange Zinger tea, happily looking through a catalog for the next semester of classes, when everything went black.

She came to a minute or an hour or a lifetime later. The dogs were lying close to her on the floor, one on each side like sentinels, and maybe it was the sound of Greg's key in the door that cut through the unconsciousness. She heard the door unlock but she couldn't move; her head ached ferociously, the pain centered on her left temple above the already sore area on her jaw where her skin was still partially butterflied together by Dr. Tansey's ministrations. She thought she should get up and go see about the door but the best she could manage was to push herself up on one elbow. She couldn't even lift her head, and so there she was, reclining on one side, when Greg opened the door.

"Hannah!" Greg ran over and knelt next to her. "Jesus, what happened?" His hands were gentle but they still hurt; it wasn't until he tried to lift her head that she realized the side of her face and the floor where she'd been lying were tacky with blood. "Come on—let me see."

See what? She shoved his hand away and reached for the curriculum catalog that had fallen with her. One whole side of it was smeared with red. Had she spilled paint on it? Why was she on the floor?

"Hannah—"

She blinked at him, then frowned. "Hey, how did you get in here? I locked the door. I *always* lock the door."

Greg jerked a little, then his expression smoothed into forced calmness. "I have a key," he said carefully. "Remember?" He offered her his hand. "You're hurt. Let's get you off the floor."

"I am?" She took his hand and let him pull her up enough to where she could sit on a chair. While he went to get something—a towel?—she inspected her hands and the blood on them, the thick puddle of it on the floor. The dogs had moved off to the side as though they were sure this man would take care of her. His name was Greg… that was it, right? "I gave you a key? Why would I do that?"

He came back with a clean towel and pressed it gently against her temple. "Yes. So I could take of the dogs." Greg studied her for a moment. "Hannah, can you tell me what day it is?"

She frowned at him, was immediately sorry when the movement made pain scissor across her forehead and left eye. "It's…" She broke off. She didn't have a clue.

"We should take you to the hospital," he said gently. "I don't know what happened but this is bad, worse than it's ever been." He tilted her head very carefully, then peered at the wound beneath the towel. "It's stopped bleeding, but it looks like a gunshot wound. You might have a concussion."

Hannah pushed his hand away. "I'm not going anywhere. This is where I live."

"I know that," he said patiently. "It's just that you're not remembering stuff the way you should be. I just think—"

"Stop telling me what to do! I can stay here if I want!"

"Of course you can." He went back to the sink, this time dampening a washcloth. "Tell you what. Let's get some of this blood washed off and then you can just relax for awhile. Maybe you'll feel better then."

"Blood?" Hannah whispered. She took the washcloth and ran it across her sore face, stared at the red stain that appeared on it. God, she must have had another one of her damned events, and here was Greg, coming to her rescue. What time was it? She didn't even remember him coming home. She gave him an ashamed glance. "I'm sorry."

"Don't be. It's not like you planned it." He helped her stand. "Let's go take it easy on the couch. We'll see how you feel in a couple of hours, okay? If you're not better by then-"

"I will be," she assured him. She felt sluggish and off-kilter, but she really *did* feel a bit better. Her mind was finally clearing and she even remembered *not* remembering that she'd given him keys a long time ago, but now it was like she'd watched and heard some other woman say those words. "By the way, it's Monday."

Relief slid across his features and he even managed a tiny smile. "Yes, it is."

"I think I'd rather lie down than sit on the couch," Hannah said. "Find me something to put over the pillow?"

"Sure," he said. "I'll get a clean towel."

She settled on the bed and waited while he covered the pillow first with a plastic bag, then a soft, dark-colored terry towel. Finally, she gratefully lowered her aching head to the pillow and slipped into a healing sleep.

«« — »»

It wasn't until Hannah was asleep and breathing easily that Greg felt his pulse and breathing slow to something vaguely resembling normal. Jesus, but he'd been scared—this was by far the worse episode he'd ever seen her endure. It wasn't even the blood that he cleaned up as she slept, but the fact that she'd been so *out* of it—the memory loss was terrifying, a hint that someday something could happen to her that might leave permanent damage. Really, how much more could she take… and how many times had he asked himself that very same question?

And that wound. God knows he'd seen enough during his time as a cop to recognize a gunshot, and while it had never occurred to him before, there was another just like it on her neck, on the same side. It was faded and pale, slightly smaller, and he'd always told himself in the past that it was probably a cigar burn. Now Greg realized that he'd just been in denial, unable to accept that she'd had to go through something so brutal.

With the mess in the kitchen cleaned up, he rinsed the sodden towels in the bathtub then hung them to dry. After that he changed his own blood-spotted clothes, choosing a clean shirt and jeans from the supply he was slowly building up in one of the closets—the fact was, he'd sort of unofficially moved in after Valentine's Day. His clothes were piling up over here, his videos, books, and various other odds and ends were quickly doing the same. The time with Hannah had been the happiest of his life and he liked to think that it was the same for her, that because of him she could forget how frightening the rest of her life had been. Now he was comfortable and happy and he simply didn't want to leave. And if he had things his way…

He never would.

Tuesday—February 20th...

Greg hadn't wanted to leave Hannah this morning, but she had insisted. She *did* seem like she was okay, but while he wouldn't admit it fully to her, that whole episode of near-incoherence yesterday had terrified him. It hadn't helped that she'd thrown a little temper tantrum last night, apparently triggered by that most innocent of questions—"What do you want for dinner?" In retrospect, it wasn't hard to understand that the whole scene had been frustration at the seeming mismatch of her own strange existence with the necessities of normal, everyday living.

Things were calmer now, as close to that normal, everyday living thing as he and Hannah could currently expect. He'd left her under the watchful gazes of Knothead and Puddles, grinning to himself as she made funny faces in the bathroom mirror and tried to find a new way to comb her hair and hide this newest addition to her skin.

Life at the station, too, was as normal as it could ever get in a squad room. Tony was already there when Greg arrived but neither man acknowledged the other; Greg was through acting like he liked his partner. He didn't, he never would, and he never had.

He went through his in-box but when he found nothing new in his case load, Greg turned to the computer. Someone had died yesterday afternoon, but who? And where? Hannah couldn't tell him exactly when she'd blacked out or how long she'd been unconscious, so he had no idea if Tony was involved or not. Another question had also turned up in his thoughts, brought on by all those other injuries on Hannah. He'd long suspected that Tony had a cohort, someone with whom he was inexplicably linked. If this was true, did Hannah also "present" with an injury if this unidentified person hurt someone? It was a frightening concept, but it would explain how Hannah could end up hurt even when Tony's whereabouts were verified. Conversely, it might just be that Greg was reaching for anything that would help explain this phenomenon.

As he considered that, he brought up the department's search engine and filled out his info—not much to say except that he expanded the injury field to include bullet wounds to the head *and* neck. It didn't take long to get the first of the results, and his mouth dropped open when he saw what came up on the screen:

<table>
<tr><td colspan="4">HOMICIDE REPORT</td></tr>
<tr><td>Name: Steve Genaro</td><td>Sex: Male</td><td colspan="2">Age: 19</td></tr>
<tr><td>Height: 6' 4"</td><td>Weight: 155 pounds</td><td>Hair: Black</td><td>Eyes: Brown</td></tr>
<tr><td>TOD: Approx. 1500</td><td>COD: Gunshot</td><td colspan="2">Date: 2/19</td></tr>
<tr><td colspan="4">DESCRIPTION: Victim was found in his automobile parked in alleyway behind the 4600 block of N. Wolcott. Victim had been shot once on the left side of the head. D/O/A at Ravenswood Hospital.</td></tr>
<tr><td colspan="2">Weapon: Forensics report indicates weapon was .38 revolver.</td><td colspan="2">(List all suspects and witness on page two.)</td></tr>
</table>

Yes, it was true that this was clearly the match for Hannah's injury yesterday, but that wasn't at all the thing that made it so spectacular. No, what did that was the entry down at the bottom of the screen, one he would have missed had he not scrolled down a notch or two:

Investigating Detectives: Anthony Rutland, Gregory Jedrek

"Wow, now *that* takes some brass balls," Greg said. He glanced around when he realized he'd spoken aloud, but thankfully his voice had been low enough that no one else had noticed. Still… *wow.* Tony had literally pulled his copy of the assignment sheet out of Greg's in-box before he'd gotten here this morning. Surely the man wasn't so stupid that he didn't realize the first thing Greg would do following Hannah's injury was get on the computer? Then again, how would Tony even know that anything had happened to Hannah at all?

Before he could think further about that, the computer bleeped at him. More results, this time under the neck wound criteria, and when he leaned forward and read through them, one unsolved case sent up such a red flag that Greg could have swatted himself for not having checked on this before. The report was lengthy and detailed, as cases involving one of the department's own usually were.

<table>
<tr><td colspan="4">HOMICIDE REPORT</td></tr>
<tr><td>Name: Theodore (Ted) Lokela</td><td>Sex: Male</td><td colspan="2">Age: 44</td></tr>
<tr><td>Height: 5' 9"</td><td>Weight: 195 pounds</td><td>Hair: Black</td><td>Eyes: Black</td></tr>
<tr><td>TOD: Approx. 2230</td><td>COD: Gunshot</td><td colspan="2">Date: 4/7</td></tr>
<tr><td colspan="4">DESCRIPTION: Det. Lokela was shot in the line of duty while attempting to apprehend a drug offense suspect. The bullet entered the left side of his neck and severed the carotid artery. D/O/A at Ravenswood Hospital. By the time backup arrived, the suspect had fled and the deceased's partner, Det. Anthony Rutland, was unable to apprehend the perpetrator.</td></tr>
<tr><td colspan="2">Weapon: Forensics report indicates weapon was 9 mm semiautomatic pistol.</td><td colspan="2">(List all suspects and witness on page two.)</td></tr>
</table>

Tony's previous *partner*. Christ, Greg thought, could he have missed a bigger clue? He'd known the man was killed in the line of duty, but he'd never thought twice about it. For that matter, apparently neither had Tony—no ongoing search for the shooter, no regular file review… hell, Tony never even talked about it. Christ, he thought again. Had Tony actually *murdered* his last partner? And if so, why?

It didn't matter, and short of Tony spilling his secrets—fat chance there—Greg would probably never know. If there *was* a tie between Ted Lokela's murder and Tony, it hadn't been found; the case file listed the two detectives assigned to the case, but while their notes indicated a concentrated effort, they'd come up with nothing. If Tony had done this terrible thing, he'd also done a damned fine job of covering himself.

Greg cleared the screen and sat back. Across the room Tony appeared to be working diligently, dark head bent as he concentrated on the paperwork spread across his desk. Greg supposed he could go over and demand to know about the Genaro case, but he really had no proof beyond his own instinct that it was Tony who had swiped the assignment memo. For now, Greg decided, he'd just let it ride. The particulars were firmly embedded in his memory, and besides, he was already positive who had killed the unfortunate nineteen-year-old.

Across the room, his partner looked up from his work and his gaze locked with Greg's.

Yeah, Greg knew who had killed Steve Genaro. He just couldn't prove it.

Wednesday—February 21st...

Greg was with Hannah when the next round happened, and kept happening and happening and happening, and there was nothing he could do but hold her and hope that it would soon be over.

«« — »»

Tony was walking on an invisible tightrope this morning.

Dara Rutland didn't know what had gone wrong, but there it was. She and Tony had been married for over ten years, and she had spent half that time, since her husband had turned around one deceptively bright Sunday morning and slammed a metal spatula into her right eyebrow, walking a tightrope of her own. That scar had faded, but the one it had left inside her had turned out to be only the base for many to follow.

"This coffee is terrible," Tony said. "When was the last time you ran vinegar through the pot—five years ago?"

Sarcasm was a normal thing for her husband, but there was something more under the tone of his voice, something much more ominous. It was that tone, the ups and downs and a thousand other indications, that Dara had used to construct an internal gauge over the years. That same gauge measured the volume and speed of Tony's words, the look in his eye, the way his shoulders hunched over his coffee cup, and told her she was in trouble this morning.

"Not that long ago," she answered carefully. "Maybe it sat too long this morning. Why don't I make a fresh pot?"

"Do I look like I have time in my life to waste waiting for coffee?" he snapped.

"No, of course not. I just thought—"

"Don't think," he interrupted. "You've never done well with that."

Dara started to retort, then managed to lock the words in her throat. It would be unadulterated stupidity to pick a fight with Tony; she'd toss a few words at him, he'd end the argument with his fists. God knows she didn't want that to happen, especially in front of her son. Ben was sitting across from his father and concentrating on his cereal. It pained her to think that the boy had his own childlike version of a danger gauge; he had been very careful to stay quiet and unobtrusive this morning.

"You want me to pack a snack for you?" she offered. "I picked up some nice apples at the Jewel yesterday. They had some great roast beef at the deli counter—"

Before Dara could finish the sentence, her husband picked up his mug of coffee and threw it at her.

It hit her in the right cheekbone and hot coffee splashed across her face and neck. She had a painfully short moment during which she was grateful that the coffee wasn't scalding—Tony had been sitting there and brooding over it long enough for the liquid to cool a bit—before Ben started wailing. "There," Tony said with satisfaction. "Maybe that will get you to shut up."

Somehow Dara kept her silence. She snatched up the dishtowel from the counter and wiped at the coffee on her face, then bent to retrieve the unbroken mug. At least it hadn't cut her. "It's okay, Ben," she said automatically. "Just quiet down and finish your bowel of cereal."

But while her son tried to cut off his sobs, he wasn't quite successful. Three or four sniffles later, Tony lashed out with an open-handed slap that caught the boy squarely across his cheek. Ben screeched and too late Dara realized Tony was on a roll and somehow she needed to get Ben out of range.

She grabbed her son by the arm and yanked him off the chair before Tony could hit him again. Tony was bellowing at the boy to shut up, Ben was screaming as loud as he could, and her own shouting—*"Don't you touch him!"*—just added to the chaos.

"You'll be quiet and take your punishment!" Tony bellowed.

"But I didn't *do* anything!" Ben howled.

Tony's response was to try and grab Ben but Dara propelled the boy behind her and gave him a shove toward the doorway to the hall. "Get to your room, *now!*"

"Don't you stand between me and my son." Tony was so furious his face was nearly purple. "I told you before, don't you *ever* do that!"

"Tony, *stop* it!" Dara said desperately. Her heart was pounding and she was so afraid that she felt light-headed. She couldn't remember the last time he'd been this bad. "Look at yourself—you're angry for no reason. What's the matter? If you'd just talk to me about it, maybe you could calm down."

"I don't need to calm down," he snarled. "And I don't need to talk, either. That's all you ever do—run your mouth. Day in, day out, not a moment of peace and quiet around here." He advanced on her. "Don't you realize you're driving me crazy, Dara? You and Ben and the job—constant pressure and demands, everybody *wants* something, every fucking day. It never *stops.*"

She was out of maneuvering room but at least Ben was safe… for now. She'd told him just a month ago that if Mom and Dad had a fight, one of their bad ones, he should run outside and wait until they stopped arguing, but she thought it was doubtful he'd remember that; he was probably hiding under his bed, or maybe in his closet. The best she could hope for was that with Tony and Ben, it would be an out of sight, out of mind thing. Or at least she could distract her husband, get him to focus on her instead of their defenseless child.

"I'm sorry," she said carefully. The counter was at her back and she couldn't retreat any more, but she had turned away from the hallway door. Tony's gaze had tracked her like a hawk zeroing in on a mouse. "I had no idea you were under so much pressure."

Her apology got her a stinging backhand slap across the face. Her eye swelled instantly. "Of course you didn't," Tony hissed. "Did you ever?" He hit her again, and this time she couldn't tell if it was forehand or backhand or fist.

A whimper escaped and she brought her hand up to cover her mouth. "Tony, please—"

"Please, *what?*" He shoved her sideways and she tried to get away from him. There was a frying pan in the dish drainer but the idea of fighting back was gone as soon as it surfaced; if she raised a hand to him, he'd probably kill her. "Please put up with my bullshit?" he continued. "Please do this, please do that, please please please." His voice had gone into an unpleasant singsong tone, like he'd slid into some familiar internal groove. Did she really sound like this to him, nagging and whining all the time?

No, of course not—he was sick, and cruel, and she should have gotten away from him a long time ago. One of his hands closed brutally around her wrist and he hauled her forward and spun her against the edge of the table; her leg nearly went numb where the muscle connected with the wood. She could feel tears leaking from her eyes, stinging and letting her know that he broken the skin on her face. Her leg buckled and he helped her along with a hard kick that sent her to one knee, added another kick in the ribs that pushed the air out of her lungs. She rolled into a ball and stayed where she was, crying silently.

"Look at you," he said derisively. "You're skinny and ugly and who else would want you, anyway?" He glanced over his shoulder. "And that stupid brat in there—not a brain in his head. Sometimes I can hardly believe he's mine." Her husband stared down at her without saying anything for a moment. Terror jabbed at her; God knew what he would do to her and Ben if he really took to the notion that Ben wasn't his.

"I'm going to work," he said abruptly. "Clean yourself up."

And he walked out.

That was it, the end of the beating, just like that. Over as quickly as it had started, and it wasn't until Dara pulled herself up that she realized that along with the bruises and bumps and scrapes, her husband had also broken one of her ribs.

«««—»»»

Tony felt better by the time he got to work. It was a cold but clear day, the kind he liked best—hell, if he'd looked out the window or maybe gone outside in the sun, he might not have lost his temper with Dara and the kid like that. Not that she didn't need a good smacking around once in awhile, but maybe he'd gone a little overboard this morning—there was no question that was Greg's fault, brought on by the way he was dogging Tony out all the time nowadays. The drive was good despite the morning traffic on Ashland Avenue and by the time he parked his car in the lot, Tony felt pretty much right with the world again.

When he realized that Greg wasn't around yet, that was even better. The animosity between them had grown to the point that others were commenting on it now. Tony didn't know if the other man had put in for a new partner yet; if not, maybe he would beat the guy to the punch and just get it over with. He wished he could just work alone, but there was no way his lieutenant would go for that.

At his desk he went through the paperwork that had to be done to make sure he was caught up—he couldn't stand to fall behind on that crap, have it pressuring him along with everything else. Greg ought to be grateful he had a partner who didn't pile up stacks of uncompleted forms that would get them both constant grief from the higher ups. No, Tony had that under control, just like he had his family life under control. Dara, for instance, just needed a little reminder now and then that *Tony* was the one who made the decisions between them—hell, he just damned well ran the show. After this morning, she wouldn't forget that for awhile, now would she?

Damn it, the only part of his life that he couldn't get a handle on was Greg, and that was because of Hannah. He had to do something about that, fast, or God knew how this little drama was going to end up playing out. He'd be damned if he was going to watch everything he'd built up fall to pieces because of some skinny little ghost who'd popped up out of a past that he and Carrie had been happy to leave behind.

Still, what the hell *was* he going to do about Hannah? Carrie's effort on his behalf had been pathetic, and really, what had he expected from a freak like her anyway? Most of the time it took everything he had just to use the word *sister*, much less to maintain what he felt was just a sick and pitiful denial of what they had been to each other only a few short years ago. Even when—

Forget it, he couldn't think about that right now. He had to focus on ridding himself of Hannah. The option of doing it directly was gone, that much was clear—even if he could get close to the woman, having something happen to her now would only compound the problem, drop suspicion squarely on his head in Greg's eyes. If Tony couldn't take her out, then he had to point Greg's attention somewhere else, find something that would make it seem ridiculous that Tony was in any way involved. Something... *inconceivable*.

He just had to figure out exactly what that was.

«««—»»»

Tony was already at the station when Greg arrived, and Greg hadn't needed a crystal ball to know he would be. He was late, having stayed with Hannah through the invisible attack, watching helplessly as the bruises and scrapes appeared, hearing clearly the horrid *crack* when one of her ribs had broken. If there was a good side to this morning's event, it was only that this time there were no deep gashes and it wasn't natural, therefore, Hannah had already starting healing at that unnatural pace. By the time he'd allowed her to push him out the door an hour after the last of the injuries had appeared, she was sore but functional, left with nothing worse than fading bruises and a rib that would probably be okay by tomorrow morning.

And, of course, the memory of a vicious beating by unseen hands.

Tony glanced at Greg when he came in, then quickly looked away. For a long moment, Greg stopped by the door to the squad room, contemplating whether to go over and confront him. But no, where was his proof? For that matter, just what was it he was accusing Tony of doing? So many questions, but no one would understand that the only answer Greg needed was there as he passed the man's desk on the way to the coffee pot and saw Tony's bruised knuckles. Who'd been his partner's latest victim? His wife? His son?

Back at his desk, Greg set his coffee mug down and tapped his fingers on the blotter for a few moments, then snatched up the handset and quickly punched in Tony's home number. It rang nine times before Dara finally picked up, and the sound of her voice told Greg just about everything he needed to know. Thick and not quite normal, but not *not* normal, a struggle to maintain the everyday illusion.

"H'llo?"

"Dara, this is Greg."

A beat of silence, then, "Hi, Greg. Tony's not here. He should be at work."

Greg took a deep breath. "Yeah, I know where he is, and he doesn't know I'm calling you. I just… wanted to know if you're all right."

A longer pause then, no doubt while she tried to figure out what he knew and how he knew it, what she should say in response. Sadly, she went for the lie. "Of course I'm all right. I—"

"Dara, I *know* he hit you this morning. Don't ask me how I do, because I can't explain it."

"Don't be absurd. He would never do that."

His years on the force and responding to domestic violence calls had taught Greg the futility of arguing. "Sure," he said. "But just in case you ever need it, here's my cell phone number." He rattled off the number, then added, "Call anytime if you need help, or just to talk. Anything."

For a moment, he'd thought she'd hung up. Then she asked, "Can you give me the number again?" Her voice had dropped to a whisper, as if she were afraid her husband could hear her all the way from the office. "I'll just, uh, add it to our address book."

He did, then told her gently to take care and hung up, figuring it was better to end the conversation on that note then to push it. Past that, there was little he could do to help her or Hannah—by association, his hands were bound by that same mysterious force that had put the woman he loved through hell for most of her life.

«« — »»

Most of the rest of the day was blissfully peaceful, with no new murders and only a few caseload things to spin around in his head. Alone, Greg followed up on a few case leads but got nowhere; presumably Tony was doing the same. Perhaps he was even now fabricating information to put in the Steve Genaro file, interviews with witnesses who'd heard the gunshot but saw nothing, dead end ballistics reports. He thought about this all day long but could find no way to solve it—again, no one would believe his story, or Hannah's body even though she was walking, breathing proof. It didn't take a master's degree to know they'd jump to the same erroneous Hannah-as-suicidal conclusion as had Dr. Tansey.

He watched Tony pack it up and leave at around five-thirty and knew Hannah was safely at work at the Diner. It wouldn't keep her out of harm's way, but at least she wasn't alone. Greg fidgeted at his desk for a few moments, then squared his shoulders and went over to knock on his squad commander's door.

"Yeah, come in."

Lt. Jorge Quesada wasn't a big man but he was capable, with an air of authority and a level-headedness that Greg often wished more people in the department would emulate. The dark eyebrow that raised when he saw Greg step through the doorway pretty much said it all—Greg didn't doubt for a moment that Quesada had been monitoring the tension between him and Tony for some time. Now it was time to spill it all out.

"Close the door and sit down," the lieutenant said before Greg could say anything.

Greg did as he was told, then waited, mired by his own indecision about what to say. If he just didn't like the guy, it would be so much easier, but there was so much more at stake here.

Quesada sat back and regarded him cooly. "I'm assuming you've decided it's time to tell me what the deal is between you and Rutland."

Greg decided maybe it was best to just not bullshit. "We don't get along," he said flatly. "I'd like to put in for a new partner."

The lieutenant didn't blink. "You don't have to like someone to work with them, Greg. You two were doing all right for quite some time, then it fell apart. I want to know what you're not telling me."

Greg leaned forward and rested his elbows on his knees, staring at the floor. There was a haphazard pattern of cigarette burns in the industrial carpet to the left of the desk corner, no doubt courtesy of the previous squad commander. The irregular little burns reminded Greg of the way the facts and events that had led him into this room were in his head—mismatched and in utterly random order.

"I don't trust him," he finally said. He couldn't think of anything else that so totally covered what he felt without making a fool of himself.

"Why?"

Greg rubbed his knuckles, thinking about the purple discoloration he'd seen on Tony's this morning, the bruises on Hannah's face, the scars he'd seen not only on Hannah, but on Dara. "I think there's stuff… going on in Tony's life that isn't good," he said reluctantly. "And I have problems with some things I believe he's done…" He didn't finish.

Another arch of a dark eyebrow, a little more sharpness in the tone. "What things?"

Greg cleared his throat. He had to be careful here but he was struggling to find the right words. He couldn't say anything about Hannah or about how or why he suspected that Tony might have done other things. Somehow he had to stay in the realm of believability, stick with what could be digested by the down-to-earth man sitting on the other side of the desk. He couldn't bring anything else into it.

"He abuses his wife and son," Greg said. There wasn't any way to sugarcoat it, and he didn't want to.

The lieutenant frowned and rubbed a hand across his chin. "I'm sorry to hear that," he finally said. "You have proof?"

"I've never witnessed it firsthand," Greg admitted. "But I've seen the marks on both Dara and Ben, on more than one occasion." He cracked his knuckles and the sound was loud in the small room. "I guess I shot my mouth off one too many times and it blew the hell out of our working relationship. He doesn't care much for me anymore."

Quesada nodded. "I wouldn't think so." He scribbled a few notes on a yellow pad in front of him. "His wife, what can we do for her?"

Greg shook his head. "Not much. Right now she's still in denial. I let her know that she can call me if she needs help. For whatever it's worth, she did take my number." He waited.

"All right," the lieutenant said at last. "As of tomorrow morning, you're both working solo until I can do some rearranging. I want to keep an eye on Rutland myself, see what's up with him. In the meantime, you stay out of his way—he's always been a little like a lit firecracker and I don't want him going off on you or anyone else, especially his family, because he's feeling stress from the squad. Got it?"

"Yes, sir."

"All right. I'll see you in the morning."

After checking his desk a final time, Greg shrugged on his coat and took off, leaving the next round to Chicago's finest on the evening shift. The temperature had dropped considerably with the sunset and now it just seemed cold and dark, the kind of evening where he wished he could get back to Hannah's apartment and find her waiting there with the two pooches instead of it being the other way around—him and the dogs waiting for her to get off work. Greg had gotten into the habit of giving the dogs a little extra exercise by walking them up the street to meet her when she got off work, and he knew by the expression on her face each time he was there that she'd come to look forward to the reception.

The ride home was uneventful, the usual traffic-clogged inner-city trek, followed by the standard semi-desperate hunt for a parking space. Knothead and Puddles were bouncing around like a couple of puppies when he let himself in, but he cut their walk short, wanting only to get back inside and, well, mope because Hannah wasn't there. Even with the dogs and the street noise outside the window, the apartment seemed too quiet and empty; he'd come to need Hannah's presence as an integral part of what made him function when he was outside of the job.

Too restless to watch television or a tape, Greg prowled the apartment under the ever-curious gazes of the pooches. There was the usual jumble of thumbed-through magazines piled on the coffee table and night stands, a dozen unfinished crocheting and knitting projects dropped here and there. Greg fingered one of them now, a soft collection of shakily crocheted squares in a pastel pattern that was almost babyish. He'd asked her why she never finished any of these and she'd said vaguely that she got bored with them. Greg, however, had a different notion—he thought she just kept starting over with a new one after working on something because she hoped to get better at it. Privately, he didn't know if she ever would. He'd seen her work at several, tongue between her teeth in concentration as she struggled with the needles and the movements, each time setting the work aside when the small stitches became shakier and more unmanageable. The heartbreak of it was that he thought she was just too full of fear to keep her hands steady for very long.

He paced for awhile longer, then spied a pile of magazines he'd never noticed before, tucked in the bookcase space of the night stand on Hannah's side of the bed. Crouching down, Greg poked around in there, hoping to find something new and interesting. One side of his mouth turned up in a grin when he found yet another assortment of Hannah's usual—handmade this, knit that, even a few cooking magazines although her skills in that department also needed a healthy dose of help. Still, she'd occasionally pick up a recycled copy of *Gourmet* or—

"Hey, what's this?"

It wasn't until the dogs lurched to their feet and padded over that Greg realized he'd asked the question aloud. The thing he'd pulled out of the stack wasn't a magazine; it was a book, not very big, with a pretty fancy textured gray cover patterned with Chinese characters. A diary? If so, he had no right to read it—his days of investigating Hannah's personal past history were over and if he had a question, he'd just ask. Still, he couldn't help being curious. She'd never mentioned keeping a journal and it hadn't really been hidden, just kind of shoved off to the side, as though she'd stuck it in there after the last time she'd opened it.

So what was in it?

I'll scan the first line, he decided. If it looks seriously secretive, I won't go any further.

Feeling vaguely guilty, he opened the cover and glanced inside, quickly, as though what he would see might singe his eyes, Lot's wife turning to salt as she looked back at the doomed city of Sodom.

Hannah's writing, chunky around the edges and a little uncontrolled like her needlework. But it wasn't a diary at all—it was a... schedule. No—a *calendar,* a rundown of all the *events* that had occurred in her memory, a written listing of all those ugly incidents of her so-called "Affliction," dating all the way back to *eleven years ago.*

Greg stared, then kept reading, torn between amazement that she had endured all this, and fury that she should have *had* to—where was it written that someone as sweet and inoffensive as Hannah should be singled out to suffer through this shit? It was obvious that the first of the entries had been written in long after the fact and that there were also small, almost after-thought entries about feeling a stingy slap here, getting a little bruise there, but still... the time period over which this had been happening was incomprehensible.

march — that was the first day i woke up from my coma, all bruised up around my neck and sore in my private parts. i was 13 years old.

may — nothing until 5 years later, when i got a long, deep cut across my chest while i was doing my homework one night. i got towels and went to call dr. gorrado, but by then it had stopped bleeding, so i didn't tell anyone. it healed in only a couple of days.

july, a year later — i got a gash through my eyebrow right out of the blue, no explanation for it at all. that's when i decided i should write these things down.

He skimmed the smaller ones, then saw the longer entries move into last year.

april 5 — i woke up this morning with all these weird bruises on me. at least they look like bruises, except they're all over every part of my body, all mottled yellow and black, like a total skin gone wonky thing. i was coughing, and spitting up horribly too, like i had water in my lungs. i thought i had some kind of disease and called into work, but by the end of the day everything was fine.

april 7 — i was taking out the garbage at the diner when something happened to my neck on the left side. i woke up in illinois masonic and they told me it looked like i'd been shot, but i don't remember it (and i don't think that's what happened anyway—there wasn't anyone else by the trash cans). it hurt horribly and they made me stay overnight, but they let me go the next day when they saw the wound was almost healed up.

september 16 — i had to tell winnie the truth about my scars because i got cut out of nowhere across my collarbone right in front of her while i was standing at the bathroom sink. so now she knows; she's having a hard time accepting it, but she saw it with her own eyes.

september 29 — this was the worst time ever. all i was doing was unlocking the door downstairs, then suddenly i had blood all over the front of my jacket and the door and i passed out. i woke up in illinois masonic's psych ward and they'd said my throat was cut. the doctor in charge thought i did it myself and wouldn't let me leave.

october 11 — got a big cut across my right thigh at work.

Greg remembered that, not because he'd been there—he'd seen the scar since, of course—but because Winnie had called and told him about it. And the calendar went on from there, covering every single time Hannah had been bruised or cut, dates and descriptions, all carefully listed. He knew about the ones after the September throat business, but it was the ones before that interested him the most. They made him feel like an imbecile—why in God's name hadn't he thought to ask her about these before?

Well, he hadn't, and there was no sense berating himself about it. Now, however, he was going to make good use of this information, and he carefully copied down all the old dates and a two-or three-word description of what had happened to Hannah before he tucked the book back where he'd found it.

Yeah, he was going to make *damned* good use of it.

Sunday—February 25th...

He plans it all very carefully, making sure the woman isn't in the house, waiting until she's gone out to the store for a few items, some special recipe ingredients she wants for a family Sunday dinner or some bullshit like that. He makes sure that she knows he's going to be working in the yard, cleaning up the trash and crap blown in over the winter months, finally raking up the mess of rotting branches that collect on their side of the fence because the neighbor has one of those filthy, pain-in-the-ass weeping willow trees planted almost directly on the fucking property line. For years he has thought about going out in the middle of the night and poisoning that tree by driving a copper spike deep into its base, but he's never gotten around to it. Now he sees that procrastination not as an act of laziness but destiny; today he will need that tree to be his alibi.

He makes sure that as she leaves, she knows he is in the yard and not the house, and that the boy is playing in his room. Beneath the grime-encrusted gardening gloves, his own hands are encased in double latex gloves, the kind anyone can buy at any beauty supply house. He figures he can do the job in under a minute and grab a can of pop from the refrigerator on his way out—that will account for his time if any of the neighbors later tell the police they saw him go into the house.

He's thought long and hard about the method, turning over the various possibilities. It has to be neat and dry—he will have no time to clean up, no way to rid himself of blood that won't be found out about later.

Choking, smothering, or perhaps a quick snap of the neck—those are all options. The investigators will look for a motive, of course, and there will be none, especially not from him. It is a big price to pay to turn the suspicious eyes of his coworker in another direction, but he has no choice.

He waits until her car pulls out of the driveway, then sets his rake aside and strolls back to the house. Outside the door, he tugs off the work gloves and sets them aside, knowing he is too far away for anyone to see the latex covering his hands. Before going to the boy's room, he turns the knob on the front door and opens it just enough so that when the woman returns, she will find it open and think, at first, that she didn't pull it shut. He knows her, and she will stupidly blame herself for what's about to happen, and that's fitting, too—she's certainly done her share of adding to all his problems. Then he hurries into the kid's bedroom.

The boy looks up as he enters and smiles at him, says something that he does not hear, and holds out the small metal car he is playing with. He reaches forward, past the toy, and his left hand slides under the small chin. The child's eyes widen as his grip tightens and the toy falls away; before the kid can start flailing, he uses his other hand to slam the boy backward onto the bed.

He tightens his fingers around the skinny throat as hard as he can. The small face goes red first, then a deeper shade of purple, then begins to blue. His young victim struggles but it's pretty useless. In another ten or fifteen seconds, he'll—

"Tony, what the *hell* are you doing?"

He whirled and lost his grip on Ben's throat, heard his son's wheezing, desperate inhalation almost as an afterthought. "Dara!"

The second, just the one, that she stood frozen in the doorway to Ben's room seemed to stretch for an hour. Her horrified gaze flicked from Ben's nearly unconscious form on the bed behind him to the gloves on his hands—

She bolted.

Tony charged after her, his mind already winding around and trying to figure a way to get him out of this mess. He'd have to kill her, too, act like someone had broken in and somehow make it look like he'd fought to save them. He saw his wife careen into their bedroom and slam the door, heard the doorknob lock click and almost laughed—that stupid thing would never keep him out. And how typical of her to run and try to save herself, with no thought for her child. He twisted the knob but of course it didn't turn; without bothering to argue or cajole—what use was that, anyway?—he raised his leg and kicked open the door.

Now it was his turn to freeze. She was standing by his side of the bed, in front of the opened drawer in the night stand, and pointing Tony's 9 mm Baretta at his chest. Her hand was shaking but her voice was eerily calm. "Stop, Tony."

He almost laughed. She wouldn't shoot him, she was his *wife,* for Christ's sake. She didn't have the stones to do something like that. There was maybe ten feet between him and where she was standing, and he lunged forward and grabbed for the gun—

And the last thought in Tony Rutland's mind was how surprised he was that the woman he'd been married to for ten years actually squeezed the trigger.

««—»»

By the time Greg got to Tony's house, it was crawling with cops, the coroner's wagon was parked in the driveway, and a handful of local newspaper and TV reporters were already pushing to try and get more information. He ignored everyone outside and went in, where he found Dara sitting woodenly at the kitchen table, answering questions in a monotone voice while more than a dozen people crawled through the house looking for anything and everything.

"Dara." Greg knelt on one knee next to her.

His voice must have cut through the shock surrounding her, because she blinked and turned her head to look at him. She had old bruises on her face, and they painted her skin a sickly shade of yellowish green. "Greg?"

"I'm here," he said and squeezed her elbow. "What happened?"

"I went to the store," she said. "But I forgot my coupons." Her voice was small, like a child who's afraid she's about to get in trouble. "Tony's always yelling at me that we have to save money, that I spend too much on groceries, so I came back to get them. When I came in, he was in Ben's room, and he was choking Ben."

"He?"

Dara blinked again, but Greg didn't think she was seeing what was in the room right now. "Tony. He—he was trying to *kill* our son."

Greg swallowed. He'd figured it would be bad when he'd gotten the radio call to report to Tony's address, but this… *Jesus.* "And then?"

"He stopped when I caught him. I ran and he came after me. I knew he kept an off-duty gun in the drawer by the bed, so I ran into our bedroom, locked the door behind me to give me enough time to get it. He broke down the door." She sobbed, just once, then laced her fingers together tightly. "I *told* him to stop, but he didn't listen. He jumped at me and so I just, I just…" She didn't finish.

Greg glanced at one of the detectives hovering nearby and the guy nodded, then jerked his head for Greg to come and talk to him out of earshot. "Hang in there," he said to Dara. "We'll get you through this. Where's Ben?"

"The paramedics are checking him out," the cop answered for her. "He's pretty bruised up but I don't think he needs to be hospitalized."

Greg stood and patted Dara's shoulder, then stepped off to the side with the detective, an older man with thick white hair cut short and bags under his eyes. "It went down fast," the guy told him, keeping his voice down so Dara couldn't hear him. "She only shot him once but she got him square in the chest." He hesitated. "It looks like he *planned* this," he told Greg. "She said he was working in the yard when she left and that the door was open when she came back. Said she was sure she'd locked it—we figure he did that on purpose to make it look like someone had come in while he was in the backyard."

Greg frowned. "You'll need more than an open door to prove attempted murder."

"He was wearing rubber *gloves,*" the cop told him. "Two pair to make sure no prints came through. There's enough dirt on the outer ones to show he was wearing them underneath the work gloves he left by the back door—he probably already had them on when she left for the store." The older man shook his head. "I've seen a lot of shit in my years on the job, but a cop who plots to kill his own eight-year-old? What the fuck is *that?*"

Greg ran a hand through his hair. "He was really screwed up, that's for certain. What's next?"

The cop ran his pen down a checklist on his notepad. "Crime lab's almost done, and they're taking the body out in a few minutes. We'll have a clean up crew here in a couple of hours, the commander found someone to fix the bedroom door where Rutland kicked it in. They'll be a routine ballistics check on the weapon, but it's pretty cut and dried. I doubt there'll be charges. Other than the fact that his father tried to kill him, the boy's pretty much okay. But her…" He glanced at Dara and one side of his mouth twisted. "She's probably going to have a few nightmares. This was your partner, right? I heard you guys didn't get along. You want to see the body before they bag it?"

Greg grimaced. "I'll pass, thanks."

The detective nodded. "Well, we've got it under control. I guess Rutland has a sister but they weren't close. We sent a patrol car over there to notify her. Social services is going to work with the wife and the son—they've got some kind of specialized trauma counselor or whatever who's going to stay with them in a hotel tonight, then I guess they take it one step at a time from there."

"Thanks for bringing me up to speed." Greg walked back over to Dara, then pulled out one of his cards. He scribbled Hannah's number on the back, then pressed the square of paper into her hand. Her skin was cold and clammy, but at least she didn't seem so spaced-out when she looked at him again. "Here," he told her. "Home number's on the back, okay? Call if you need *anything*, even just someone to talk to. Social workers are great and all that, but you might want a familiar face. Hannah and I'll be there for you."

Dara managed a ghost of a grateful smile. "Thanks, Greg."

He nodded and made his way outside, wincing as he passed the semi-dark hallway and got an eyeful of what was going on down there—a gruesome shot pattern of blood against the wall, his partner's still-uncovered body sprawled in the doorway, blown halfway back into the hallway. It was only a glimpse, yet it was enough to imprint the image of Tony lying there, his eyes open and looking toward the ceiling but seeing nothing but eternity. Greg wished he hadn't seen it at all.

In the car, he pulled out his cell phone and dialed home, thinking of Hannah and Ben. He dreaded the idea that there might be a connection, but at the same time he almost hoped for it. If there had been such a thing—some kind of psychic tie between the dark deeds that Tony had done—Tony was dead now. Did that mean the connection was finally broken?

"Hello?"

Hannah's voice, but raspy and low, like she had a sore throat. He didn't need to ask to know she'd gone through a mirror image of Tony's attack on Ben.

"Are you all right?" he asked.

She hesitated before answering. *"Yes. Now. What... what happened?"*

He decided not to bother trying to explain over the telephone. "I'll be home in fifteen minutes," he told her. "I'll tell you everything when I get there. But let's just say I've got high hopes that things are finally going to change for the better for you."

He felt incredibly morbid doing it, but Greg still couldn't help grinning ear to ear when he clicked off the connection.

Monday—February 26th...

While a lot of other people in the department were, Greg wasn't a bit surprised when the ballistics report came back on the gun that Tony had kept in his night stand drawer.

"We're going to take a lot of heat for this internally," Lt. Quesada told everyone in the squad room. "We need to make damned sure it doesn't go beyond this room. Am I making myself clear?"

There were shocked nods and murmurs of agreement, and Greg hoped he was doing a good job of looking as startled as everyone else at the news. He wasn't, of course, but he couldn't explain why. From his place at the front of the room, the lieutenant's gaze touched on each and every one of them. "I don't think I need to convey what kind of a pall it would put on this department if the media got wind of this." He held up the ballistics report and the DNA match that had come out a half hour earlier. Greg had suspected all along that Tony had killed Janice Tuwile, and the report had only confirmed it; a second strike against Tony had been a match of Tony's service gun to the weapon that had killed Steve Genaro.

While he wasn't exactly *glad* that Tony was dead, part of him wanted to be elated because of what this might mean for Hannah. But that was it—*might* mean. Not definitely did, but *might.* Because not everything in this added up, there were days when he couldn't be absolutely sure that the events that had happened to Hannah had been Tony's doing.

And if they weren't trackable to Tony, then who else was involved? Who else *could* be?

It was a maddening question and the only way he was going to find an answer was to dig deep. Despite the difficulties he and Tony had encountered, no one else in the squad had been close to him so he'd talked to the lieutenant and gotten the go-ahead to interview Tony's parents under the guise of very carefully looking into these two murders. The paperwork was a nightmare, there were questions of pensions and benefits and how Tony's family would be denied all those things if the man was charged posthumously with two counts of murder. The odds were that the lieutenant would find a way to leave both cases as unsolved or inconclusive, but there were still things he wanted to know.

Tony Rutland's mother and father lived in a rundown section of Zion situated way north on the Edens Expressway. Although rush hour had quieted, it still took Greg an hour and a half to drive all the way out there, a necessary thing since he wanted to see these people for himself and try to get a better feel for what might have been going on in Tony's mind and life that he—and apparently Dara—hadn't known about. Besides, Tony's parents, Bruce and Erma Rutland, apparently weren't much on answering their telephone; the department had finally called the local Sheriff and asked that he pass along the news.

The house was in the unincorporated part of the town. Lots of space and trees, but at this time of the year, with the branches bare and the fields full of matted, dead yellow grass, all it did was add to a feeling of desolation that already permeated the small manufactured dwelling, itself hardly larger than a double-wide trailer. It hadn't been very well taken of; the windows were surrounded by paint that the weather had beaten to an indeterminate shade of gray-brown, there was trash blown under the half-wild juniper business that followed the front of the house, and the pitted, asphalt driveway had long since seen better years. A rusting mailbox leaned away from the driveway, pushed backward by years of having its front slammed shut. Pulled as close to the bushes as possible was an old, black AMC Spirit, itself a testament to what the humid northern Illinois climate could do to neglected metal.

A quick touch on the warm metal of the hood as he passed told Greg that someone was home, but he knocked for a long time before he finally heard footsteps. When the door swung open, the man who stood there looked anything but friendly, and had Greg not immediately held up his badge, he had the feeling Mr. Rutland would have told him to go scratch. "Mr. Rutland, I'm Greg Jedrek," he said, deciding not to give the man a chance. "I was your son Tony's partner. I'd like to talk to you about him."

Bruce Rutland stared at him for a moment, then shrugged and stood aside. "Fine," he grated. "Come on in." Over his shoulder, he yelled, "Erma, we got company!"

More footsteps, faster but no less heavy. When Erma Rutland strode into the room, it was like seeing the female twin of her husband—both were rugged and husky, with iron-colored hair and skin that looked as weather-beaten as the outside of their house. Neither smiled, but with the news of their son's death coming just yesterday, they didn't have much reason to do so.

"This is detective…" Mr. Rutland squinted over at him.

"Jedrek," Greg filled in. "I was Tony's partner on the force."

Mrs. Rutland nodded and motioned toward a worn-looking chair. "Have a seat. I'd offer you something to eat but me and Father were just getting ready to leave for church."

"Thanks, but I'm fine," Greg said. *Me and father?* He couldn't recall the last time he'd been around a married couple who referred to themselves like that to strangers. They were definitely dressed to go out; Bruce was wearing a sensible black suit and Erma had on a plain black dress with a white collar. Near the door was a coat tree bearing several layers of outerwear, all in dark and dull colors. "You must be getting ready for a service for Tony, so I'll try to keep this brief—"

"Daily devotion," Mr. Rutland said. His voice was completely void of expression. "We're not getting involved with services for the boy. Some fellow from the police department called, but I told him that was his wife's place, not ours."

Greg was silent for a moment. "Well, I believe the funeral's going to be—"

"We won't be going."

Greg managed to hide his surprise at Mr. Rutland's statement, but just barely. "I… see."

Tony's mother settled herself on the opposite end of the couch from her husband, adjusting her dress carefully so her knees didn't show. "You say you were his partner," she said. "Then you must have known we hadn't spoken with him in a number of years."

Greg sat back and thought about this. "No, actually I didn't. We hadn't worked together that long and I don't believe he ever mentioned it." No one said anything for a long few moments and Greg tried to fashion a way to ask why. As it turned out, Erma Rutland was willing on her own to supply at least the minimum details... and when she did, they contained more than a few surprises.

"We adopted the boys when they was young," she said. "Gave them our family name and a fresh start—"

"A damned *fine* fresh start," Bruce Rutland threw in.

"—but alls we got in return was a load of trouble." She folded her arms across her chest, reminding Greg more of a prison matron than a loving adoptive mother. "But the Rutlands aren't quitters and so we did our best by them. Raised 'em up as right as we could. How they came out, well... it ain't our fault. Probably bad blood."

Greg resisted the urge to shake his head in an effort to clear out the jumbled facts. "Wait—the boy*s*? Tony had a brother? Older? Younger?"

Mr. Rutland's mouth twisted bitterly. "Younger. I guess Tony didn't mention him. Can't say as I blame him, all the grief he caused."

"What—"

"Gery," Erma answered before Greg had to finish. She scowled. "He's two years Tony's junior. Named him after my grandfather, I did. Poor old man's probably rolling in his grave because of it, too. A shameful thing, but I never meant it to be like that—I pray every Sunday that Grandpa forgives me."

Greg's eyes narrowed. "So was Tony named something else when you adopted him? And he had a brother whose name you also changed?"

"That's right." Bruce lifted his chin. "You give a couple of boys no one else wants a fresh start, then you do it right. Helped 'em leave their pasts behind completely." He shot a glance at his wife. "Leastways we tried."

Greg reached for his notebook. "What were their names before the adoption?"

Erma Rutland frowned slightly. "I can't rightly recall," she admitted. "We didn't read 'em but once or twice on the papers we signed. Gotta figure that was, what, seventeen or eighteen years ago. They came out of one of them county foster homes though—you might be able to look it up or something. We don't even have the papers anymore, tossed out all that trash when Gery graduated high school and moved out."

"Gery," Greg repeated thoughtfully. "You know, Tony never mentioned a brother, but he did talk about a sister. He said her name was—"

"We don't say that name in this house, young man," Bruce Rutland interrupted. His face had gone rigid. "Not ever, detective. I'd thank you to respect that."

Greg blinked and tried to rearrange the question that wanted to come out of his mouth. There was something completely off-whack here… but he had absolutely *no* idea what it was. "Of course, Mr. Rutland."

"*She's* crazy," Erma Rutland said. "Just flat crazy. She's never been around us, and she never will be."

"So you didn't adopt…her?" The woman said *she* as if the word were something dirty, and Greg asked his question before he could think about whether it was wise to do so or not.

"Adopt? No God-fearing person would want to deal with someone like that," Bruce Rutland said. "It's an abomination, that's what it is."

"I'm sorry," Greg said. His pen was poised above his notebook, but the page was still blank. The truth was, he didn't know what to write about all this. "I'm totally confused. I've never even heard of Gery, and I didn't know Tony was adopted. Now I'm getting the impression there's something wrong with his sister. Maybe if I could just talk to them, I could clear up a lot of questions and not trouble you any further."

Bruce Rutland stood and his wife followed suit, signaling the end of their conversation. "I'm sorry, officer, but there's nothing more we can tell you. We had a falling out with both the boys almost six years ago and haven't talk to them since. The sister thing… well, *that* was never part of our plan, and so we stayed away from having anything at all to do with that. And that's all there is to it." Greg stood reluctantly and Mr. Rutland went over and picked up his coat, then handed his wife hers. "We need to get going so's we're not late for church. I don't expect there's any reason we need to see you again."

As dismissals went, that pretty much covered it. The Rutlands waited politely as he stepped out the door, then they locked up and climbed into their car without so much as a good-bye. Effectively cut off at the knees, Greg had no choice but to start his car and back out of the driveway so they could leave. He sat for awhile on the side of the road and tried to sort out the hodgepodge of information, but he couldn't make any sense of it, and he obviously wasn't going to get any help from Tony's parents.

He barely noticed the trip back into the city. *"She's crazy,"* Mrs. Rutland had said, talking about Tony's sister. *"Just flat crazy. She's never been around us, and she never will be."* When the boys had been adopted would have made them around ten or twelve years old. It was a wild thought, utterly ludicrous, but it was there nonetheless. Tony had always said his sister's name was Carrie… then again, his own name had been changed when he was a child. He hadn't talked much about Carrie, and hadn't mentioned a brother at all. What had been the names of those siblings, their *real* names, way back before the adoption? Greg didn't have any inkling about the younger boy—it sounded like no one had seen or heard from him in years. But the sister…

Could her name have been Hannah?

No, of course not. That didn't make any sense, didn't fit in with any history or true-to-life facts in the here and now. There were a few times that Tony had said he was going to see his sister where Greg had known exactly where Hannah had been and what she had been up to at the time.

Hadn't he?

Of course he had—and what about the woman who had attacked Hannah? There was a flesh and blood attacker, with evidence to back up the reality of it—footprints, bloodstains, other people who had heard the commotion. It hadn't ever entered his mind, but maybe the woman who'd come into the apartment had been Tony's sister. He'd have to get her info from Tony's records and question her somehow, without anyone knowing it.

He nearly pounded on the steering wheel, not out of frustration at the unanswered questions, but because he was asking them to begin with. Damn it—he had had his life, and Hannah's, all figured out and under control, he had *trusted* her. He *needed* to trust her, and now this afternoon's visit had unaccountably destroyed that, dumping too many unanswered questions and possibilities into his lap. He wished he could step back five hours and get a fucking flat tire, have the car engine blow, get sent on a case to the other side of the city, *anything* to wipe out all the ugly questions and doubts that were suddenly looming way too large in the front of his mind.

He'd have to figure it out, work through it until he came up with the right answers. And he'd have to do it alone, and in silence, because if he was off track—and he *had* to be—Hannah would never forgive him for losing faith in her to begin with.

«««—»»»

My brother is dead my brother is dead my brother is dead my brother is dead my brother is dead—

Carrie sat at the kitchen table and cried and dabbed at her eyes, then cried some more, like she'd done for a half hour or so every day since she'd gotten the news. The table and the floor were dotted with wadded up tissues splotched with eye makeup, the remains of the liner and shadow she'd stupidly applied this morning in her even more stupid attempt to maintain some retarded semblance of a normal life.

My brother is dead.

Tony… God, what was she going to do without him?

She could see him in her mind, his deep blue eyes and handsome dark hair, the usually cruel smirk that he somehow passed off as a smile. There had been bad times between them for the last six years or so, and she had been the cause of that—*she* had torn the family apart by her decision to flipside everything about her life. Her decision, her consequences, and so she couldn't blame him for his hatred any more than he could fault her for the fact that in spite of it all, he'd still held a spark of ill-kept and unwilling love for her in his cold, cold heart. They had shared so much more in their lives than any normal siblings ever would. Brother to sister and vice versa, brother to brother, brothers to sister—who else in the normal world could ever even comprehend the bond between them? Between *all* of them?

No one, of course. Things had happened among them that could never be told or talked about, and time and circumstance had broken them apart… then brought them back together, to a disastrous end. Carrie didn't know what Tony had been planning or trying to do, but she had no doubt that the story the police department had told her on the telephone about his murdering bitch of a wife was nothing but a lie, facts twisted to sully her older brother's memory. There had been precious little love between that woman and her brother—too often he had complained about how miserable he was—and now wasn't it just *so* obvious that the witch had found a way to end the marriage with speed and blood rather than go the troublesome route of a nasty divorce?

But she would pay. Oh God yes. Carrie would see to that.

She wanted to pace, but she couldn't even do that—the dog bites on her ankle wouldn't allow it. It'd been nearly two weeks since she'd been bit, and she was, finally, on the way to healing after going through a touch-and-go period where the bites had started to get infected. He might be a crappy little low-life, but her doctor knew his stuff and he'd put the fear of Jesus in her, pointing out that if she continued to walk around on it before it was healed she could say hello to blood poisoning and probably so long to her foot. She'd seen him yesterday and he'd told her that tomorrow she could start walking, and if there wasn't a significant amount of pain, she was home free.

She needed to walk, all right. She had a visit to pay.

To Dara.

Dara had called her, but the conversation hadn't gone well. How *dare* that woman cut her off from paying her final respects to Tony, and from seeing her nephew? Granted she hadn't seen Ben since he was a baby and before the big transformation of her life—Tony had forbade it afterward—but he was still her nephew, damn it, her flesh and blood. Carrie didn't know if it was Dara's insistence that she stay away from Ben "until he'd gone through counseling and learned to deal with his father trying to kill him"—clearly some kind of perverted fabrication—that was making her so angry, or the fact that Dara had changed her mind about a service and funeral and sent Tony's remains off to be cremated without even the simplest of memorial services. And all this barely before Carrie had gotten the news about what had happened.

The woman's behavior was unspeakable. *Unforgivable*, and Carrie didn't give a rat's ass what Dara had been through to prompt such a decision. The final blow was that now her nephew's fate and future rested solely in the hands of a murderess, with no one else to watch over him or monitor Dara's behavior. How could the boy grow up healthy knowing that his mother had shot his father? He would never be able to trust the woman, or confide in her—he needed to have someone else take custody of him, someone who could remove him from that house of horrors and give him an unsullied path in life.

Her brother was dead and it was time to change things around, again, in her life. The first part of that was clear: tomorrow morning Carrie would take her first tentative steps outside this apartment since Hannah's dogs had chewed her up. And if things went as well as she hoped, sister-in-law Dara was going to get the visit of her life.

Wednesday—February 28th...

"Hi. Are you Detective Jedrek?"

Grateful for the interruption, Greg looked up from where he'd been filling out a laborious departmental psychological questionnaire that had to do with Tony's death. Standing in front of him was a slightly overweight woman with bright green eyes and streaked gray hair drawn back into a loose, slightly frizzy bun. Pinned to the lapel of a less-than-expensive business suit a few shades darker than her hair color was a CPD visitor's pass on which the Desk Sargent had scrawled *Monica Kenweigh* in black marker.

The woman stuck out her hand. "I'm Monica Kenweigh."

Greg accepted her handshake and said, "I can see that. What can I do for you?"

She settled herself on the chair next to his desk without being asked, then plunked a worn vinyl attache on her lap and began rummaging through it, pausing every few seconds to push her sliding glasses back up on her nose. "Not much, detective. But I might be able to do something for you."

Greg grinned to himself, liking the woman's straightforward manner. "Oh?"

"I'm from the Department of Children and Family Services," she told him as she continued without looking up from her search through the bag's untidy contents. "I'm the DCFS caseworker assigned to Benjamin Rutland, your partner's son." Another nudge on the wayward glasses. "I understand you've been trying to find background information on Anthony Rutland's adoption as a young boy by Bruce and Erma Rutland. I—here it is. Finally. I *have* to get better organized." She pulled out a manilla folder that was rumpled and yellowed with age. It bore a peeling label that had been taped back in place several times and was now once again precariously hanging on. She frowned at it, then reached over and picked up his stapler; a quick snap and the label wasn't going anywhere.

Greg leaned forward, his gaze on the folder as he recalled Gorrado's refusal to give him Hannah's information and his failed efforts to get it on his own. "You managed to get into the adoption records?"

Monica Kenweigh's right eyebrow arched. "I didn't have to get *in* to anything, detective. I have access to that sort of thing, for obvious reasons. It's what I do. I came across your request for information and while normally a request like that would be automatically denied, in these circumstances—quite extenuating—my supervisor and I felt that it might be in the better interest of Anthony's Rutland's son to take a second look." She made no move to hand over the folder. "So, of course, I have to ask. Why exactly were you—or *are* you still—interested in your partner's familial history?"

Uh-oh, Greg thought. *Careful here.* "I've wondered about that for some time because I suspected he was abusing his wife and son," Greg answered carefully. It wasn't a lie, not at all... just a truth devoid of a few essential ingredients.

He hadn't thought it was possible, but the caseworker's eyebrow climbed even higher. "I see. And did you report this suspicion of yours to anyone in authority?"

"I spoke to my lieutenant about it," Greg told her. "I'm afraid I'd made the mistake of confronting Tony and so we weren't exactly on the best of terms. My lieutenant instructed me to step back and he split the two of us up. He was keeping an eye on Tony, but none of us had any idea that he'd gone so far over the edge." Again, not quite the truth, but not a total falsehood, either. He had to fight not to reach for the folder. "I assure you, Ms. Kenweigh, if I'd had any idea that he—"

"Oh, I have no doubt of that," she said. "And call me Monica." Her attention went back to her folder and she flipped it open. Greg wisely let the rest of his sentence remain unspoken; he'd learned a long time ago that prattling on was more a sign of guilt than innocence. "All right, let's see what we've got in here. I haven't looked at this thing in more than fifteen years. My memory's usually pretty good, but to be honest, I can't say that I remember much about it at all, so there probably wasn't much about it that was remarkable."

"Oh?" Greg willed himself to sit still, to wait for whatever information she was willing to impart. He could have cheered when she decided to spread the folder open and display the contents.

"Actually, it looks like we're talking almost twenty years ago." She read from some of the forms, pointing to names and dates as she went so Greg could follow along. "According to this, Tony Rutland started life as Butch Danior. He had a brother two years younger who was named Carl, and they were adopted together by the Rutlands, who subsequently changed the boys' names to coincide with theirs." She frowned. "It's rather unusual to change an older child's first name, but there's certainly nothing illegal about it. It's generally not recommended, though, because it can result in some psychological and identity problems—" She stopped and stared at him. "Is something wrong, detective?"

Too late Greg realized his mouth had dropped open. He closed it with a nearly audible *snap* and tasted blood as he bit his tongue. The sting was enough to clear his mind of the shock that had tumbled into it—

Tony Rutland started life as Butch Danior...

Jesus Christ.

Tony *had* been Hannah's older brother.

There could be no denying it, no bullshit hemming and hawing about coincidental last names, it's a small world, or whatever. *There* was the formerly elusive connection between Hannah and Tony—it was natural and unnatural at the same time.

But wait—Hannah and Carrie were *not* the same person. Somehow, this was all still fouled up.

"Detective Jedrek?"

He cleared his throat and tried to get his thoughts in some logical order. "I see. What... what his sister? Tony talked about his sister."

The caseworker's brow furrowed and she flipped through some more papers in the file. "Sister?"

"He said her name was Carrie."

"I don't see where... oh, wait. Jesus save us from too many cases—I can't believe I didn't remember this."

"Remember what?" Greg asked, although he already had an inkling what she was going to say.

She held up what looked like the oldest piece of paper in the file. "You say he talked about his sister?"

Greg nodded. "Yeah. I got the idea they were fairly close. He'd go visit her now and then."

Monica's eyes widened. "Really? I wonder how he found her." She rattled the paper in her hands. "According to this, the sister was separated from the brothers and the records regarding her whereabouts and any future proceedings or adoption were sealed permanently by the court. She must have gone through something pretty terrible to lock them up like that. Even I wouldn't have access to those." She peered at the paper again and confusion swept across her features. "You said the girl's name was Carrie?"

Greg nodded. "That's what he told me."

"According to the initial report here, the sister's name was Hannah."

For a few seconds, Greg couldn't speak. He'd suspected… no, *known* it, but to have it stated right out front like that, in such black and white fashion…

Monica pushed her glasses up and closed the folder. "I can tell by your expression that the name rings a bell, detective. If you have some link between what Mr. Rutland did and his sister, I'd appreciate it if you'd just spit it out. I don't have time for departmental games or politics."

Greg took a deep breath, trying to give himself time to formulate the right words. There were things going on here that this woman would never understand—hell, he didn't understand them himself. He could still be honest with her… to a point. Ultimately it came out in about as blunt a statement as he'd ever meant *not* to make. "Hannah Danior is my girlfriend."

The caseworker sat up very straight. "Excuse me?"

Greg imagined he could practically *see* the thoughts and the oh-my-God-what-a-conflict theories whirling around in the woman's brains. "I did *not* have any clue about that," he added quickly. "In fact, while I know about Hannah's history, the possibility never occurred to me until a week ago, and if you check your records, you'll see I asked about the adoption way before that."

Monica looked anything but pleased. "This is highly irregular, detective—"

"Greg," he said. "And of course it is—there isn't anything about what Tony Rutland did before his death that *was*." He pulled his chair around until he was almost knee to knee with the older woman. "Work with me on this, *please.* I'm just a cop trying to figure out what the hell my psycho partner did and why, and if he still had any influence on Hannah. There's nothing more underhanded about it than that."

Monica's mouth pressed together, then relaxed. It wasn't much, but it was enough to make Greg think he just might have a cohort here. "I'll… *think* about it. In the meantime, tell me about Hannah."

And so Greg did… well, not *everything,* of course, because no person with a logical mind would believe it. But he came close, neatly editing out the parts where Hannah had apparently been hurt every time Tony had hurt someone else and substituting, instead, what he now recognized had been a pretty obvious hostility on Tony's part toward Hannah. Monica Kenweigh listened keenly, taking a note or two in a sort of sloppy shorthand that looked more like chicken scratch than anything else, but never interrupting.

Finally, Greg was finished. "So that's it," he said, and spread his hands. "Now you know." He stopped before adding *as much as I do,* the honest streak in him stepping in to cut off the words.

"All right," she said slowly. She studied her notes. "If I've got all this down straight—"

"Jedrek." Greg looked toward the sound of his name and saw his lieutenant standing by the door to his office. The man motioned at him. "My office. Now."

Greg frowned, wondering what the deal was. "Would you excuse me for a minute?" he asked Monica. "This shouldn't take long." At her nod, he went over and stuck his head inside Quesada's door, then went all the way in and pulled the door shut behind him at another gesture. "What's up?"

The lieutenant pushed a piece of paper across his desk. "We got results in from some routine computer checks run by the crime lab. It doesn't look good."

Greg lifted the report and read it. "Oh… shit," he said slowly. He'd been worried that he'd have to work to look surprised when the truth—the match on the bullet pulled out of Steve Genaro's head and the DNA match-up to the semen from Janet Tuwile's corpse—hadn't surprised him a bit. He supposed he'd known all along that Tony had killed Ted

Lokela—exactly what he was reading in this routine ballistics report—but seeing it come out in the open actually made it easy to act like he was hearing it for the first time.

"Jesus," he said. "Is this… are they *sure?"*

"Yes." Quesada answered. His face was grim, almost gray around the edges. "I guess you can say that your intuition about not liking the guy for your partner was definitely on track."

Suspicion be damned—all the times that he had been alone with Tony, plenty of them when no one else had known where they'd gone, came filtering back and suddenly Greg felt like he could barely breathe. He really *had* been one fortunate cop.

"I think you can consider yourself a very lucky guy," his lieutenant said.

Greg nodded, then found enough air to speak. "So according to this not only did he kill two people this month alone, but he murdered his last partner?"

"Yes." Quesada's voice was tight. "There was no mistaking the ballistics match between the gun that Tony had in his night stand and the bullet that killed his partner, Ted Lokela, in April of last year." His commanding officer stared at his desk. "Ted was a great guy, and a good cop. All the evidence now indicates that Tony shot him in the neck during a raid on a crack house. There was no reason to doubt his story that Ted was shot by the suspect, who escaped, and tests proved that while Tony's service revolver had been fired—he said he shot at the fleeing suspect—obviously it wasn't the gun used to kill Ted. Now it seems the whole thing was a very careful set-up."

Greg set the report down, then scrubbed at his eyes until he could see sparkles behind the closed lids. There was so much going on here, so much to digest and try to sort out. "But why the hell would Tony want to kill his partner?"

"A cover-up, probably. Maybe Ted found out something about Tony that he shouldn't have and Tony decided the only way to keep him quiet was to shut him up permanently. I don't think we'll ever really know," Quesada answered.

Greg nodded, and thought of all the other wounds that Hannah had endured—knife cuts, bruising from beatings and strangulation. How many other times had Tony killed? The lieutenant had no true idea to what extent the unknown was just that… unknown. He stood. "All right."

Quesada glanced through the window to where Monica Kenweigh still waited beside Greg's desk. "Anything interesting?"

"She's the caseworker for Tony's son. Just following up."

"All right. Keep me posted if anything new turns up. We're trying to keep this quiet… but at the same time, we want to follow-up on any new information for obvious reasons."

"Right," Greg said, then relaxed a bit when Quesada turned back to his work. He walked back out to the squad room, willing his legs not to wobble. He felt like he was in a sort of shocked fog, still thinking about how often Tony had had the chance to put a bullet in *his* head. *Too* often.

"Sorry to keep you waiting," he told Monica.

"No problem," she said. "It gave me time to think, although I admit I haven't come up with any great brain flashes about this. The more I go over it, the more questions I get instead of answers." She pushed up her glasses, then prodded at the space between her eyebrows, as if she had a headache. "You say your girlfriend's name is Hannah Danior, and her history certainly bears that out. She didn't recognize Tony, but that's not surprising. Not only was she just five years old the last time she saw him—and he would have been what? Twelve?—but it was right before she was abducted with her foster parents' daughter. Considering the circumstances and the psychological block she has about the crime itself, it's not so hard to believe she wouldn't have a clue what her older brother would look like as an adult." She snapped the folder shut, then stuffed it into her bag. "I don't have a doubt, however, that Tony Rutland knew exactly who he was talking to the first time he saw her and heard her name."

Greg scowled. He'd been so caught up in his thinking about how everything revolved around Hannah that he hadn't thought of that. "But why wouldn't he say so?"

Monica Kenweigh looked at him steadily. "Because, detective, he and his brother Carl probably had something to do with what happened to her and that baby."

Greg's mouth dropped open. *"What!"*

The woman folded her arms. "I can't prove it—likely no one can now. But I've seen it far too often in my line of work. Children, especially small and easily frightened ones who have been shuffled around by the system, are abused by both those with whom they are placed for care and those whom they trust the most—their parents or siblings. Tony

Rutland didn't just *get* this way as an adult. He was this way because he was a very sick child, and either no one ever noticed or if they did, they never did anything about it. Likely he was made this way by his environment, or by an abusive parent himself. The bottom line? God only knows what he, and perhaps his brother, got away with in regards to Hannah."

"But..." Any argument he might have had about this stuttered away as parts of his conversation with Dr. Gorrado came back. According to the good doctor, the evidence in Hannah's case clearly indicated that someone else had been abusing Hannah for years besides the drifter who'd been arrested. Supposedly, that person *wasn't* her foster father. If that was true, then the only option left was...

Her older brother.

Or brothers.

"Then I need to find the other brother," Greg said. "Carl. And have a serious conversation with him."

Monica Kenweigh nodded. "And there's something else you need to find out, too."

"What's that?"

That right eyebrow again, arching impossibly high. "Just who the hell is *Carrie* Rutland?"

Ah, Carrie, the mystery sister. After all this, there was no way Greg was going to believe that Hannah and Carrie were one and the same. The dates didn't fly, the circumstances didn't jibe... and the physical attack on Hannah couldn't be discounted, although now he could see a possible explanation for the injuries that Hannah would sustain when Tony's whereabouts were accounted for. If this Carrie woman really was a blood relative, might not Hannah have that same unnatural tie to her? Might she not also feel the effects of what Carrie did? It was also to Carrie that Tony had put the dirty work of trying to eliminate Hannah so as to destroy his link to the unspeakable crimes he and Carl had committed so long ago. They were two different people, all right. And now it seems he had a whole new avenue to investigate.

"I don't have an explanation for that," Greg finally answered. "According to all of his personal records, at least the ones I've seen, Carrie is his sister. I've never met her, but there's an address and a telephone number, and you can bet I'm going to."

Monica nodded. "All right. Keep me informed, please? I'm going on vacation—boy, do I need *that*—and I won't be back until the twelfth of March, but I'll definitely be interested in what you find out."

Greg nodded. "Can you be reached in the meantime?"

The caseworker smiled slightly. "I suppose I could, but do you take your police work with you when *you* go on vacation, detective?"

He laughed. "I get your point."

He stood when she did, and they shook hands. "It's been an informative meeting… Greg."

"Likewise. I'll be in touch." Greg watched her stride out of the squad room, then settled slowly back onto his chair. For a few minutes, he just let the shock wash over him—

Hannah and Tony were brother and sister!

—then he shook himself and set about the business of deciding what, if anything at all, he was going to tell Hannah about all of this.

Friday—March 2nd...

Most of the time, Carrie had only good thoughts about her brother. She'd loved Tony fiercely all her life, even though his return of that sentiment had sometimes seemed as fickle as a politician's promises during an election. Her current musings about her dearly departed sibling, however, were about as black as they could get.

"Doesn't this just figure?" she muttered to herself. "Once again I'm the one stuck trying to clean up his mess."

She was parked in the alley behind the Rutland family home, huddled in her car with the engine turned off and the cold quickly settling around her. For once she was glad she'd opted for the whole nondescript package when she'd bought the Acura—silver exterior, gray upholstery, nothing fancy or noticeable. It was snowing, cold, and damp, the kind of weekday where people who were getting winter-weary stayed inside and hid from the weather.

The perfect day to take care of a big problem and not be noticed.

Carrie pulled her black wool jacket closer around her and checked the alley. No one was around, and there were no footprints breaking the cover of newly fallen snow. No dogs, either—she was more than a little paranoid about those damned things since that episode in Hannah's apartment, clearly another time that Tony had sent her to take care of his dirty work…

Then again, if she was to be honest, there had been times in her past when Tony had stepped in and done the 'ounce of prevention is worth a pound of cure' thing. The biggest time, of course, had been last April, when she'd gotten in trouble with that bitch Lanita Gardner. Carrie had never killed anyone before that. Hell, she'd never even *hurt* anyone—that whole, awful thing years ago with Hannah and the baby had *not* been her idea, she'd just gone along because she'd been afraid not to. Connie DuPree might have been a problem, but she had just endangered Carrie's short-lived relationship with Rodney; Lanita, though, had threatened *everything* Carrie had worked so carefully to build.

It pained Carrie to remember the couple of years that she had spent trying to "find" herself, figure out who she was in her soul and in what direction she should take her life. They hadn't been good ones—there had been drugs and sex, and all of it had mostly been bad. Lanita was a part of those bad times, a flamboyant cross-dressing hooker with whom Carrie had hung out and shared more than an unsafe number of needles—dear God, but she had been *so* lucky in that respect. Bad drugs, bad sex, bad times, and Lanita had brought it all back when she'd run into Carrie in the Kmart on Western Avenue. Carrie had been working the morning shift back then and had stopped by the store to pick up a few things on her way home. God must've been laughing His holy ass off to put that homo in the line right behind her.

But there she'd been. The years hadn't been good to the transsexual. Lanita still had the same small bone structure, but her skin was thin and dried—too much hard drinking and drugging—and her scalp was covered by a blond wig that might have once been expensive but was now about as used up as the flesh stretched across her cheekbones. Her mind was still sharp, though, downright cunning; one look at Carrie and her crisp, clean nurse's uniform, that flash of recognition that said Carrie's modest, impeccable makeup hadn't hid anything, and Carrie had practically seen the blackmail dollar signs light up in the hooker's muddy green eyes.

Carrie had paid for her purchases—a stupid tube of toothpaste and a bottle of laundry detergent—and tried to hightail it, but Lanita was too quick for that. Carrie wasn't sure how she did it, maybe Lanita had just tossed a twenty dollar bill at the cashier and told her to keep the change, but she'd been right on Carrie's heels as she went out the door, although thank God she hadn't tried to talk to her in line. Carrie would have been mortified. Now, sitting in the frigid car behind her dead brother's house,

Carrie's face still burned red when she recalled Lanita's words to her in the parking lot, that high-pitched sugary falsetto voice—

"Girl, look at you! Haven't you just made good for yourself? You always said you were going to take it all the way, but when you dropped out of sight, I had no idea *you really had! Come on, let's go somewhere and talk about it. Oooh, I can't* wait *to tell all of our old friends what a success you are! And you're a nurse—why, I bet all those people you work with, all those hunky doctors and orderlies, just have no idea, do they?"*

Carrie had been reading between the lines for years, and it didn't take a Ph.D. to understand Lanita's message. Her life and what she'd gone through and given up to attain it, the years of counseling, hormones and expense, the alienation of her family—the transsexual who stood before her that day was the weapon which would destroy it all. With enough money, she might be quieted... for awhile. But eventually she'd come back and want more, again, and again.

Carrie had smiled and talked to Lanita like they were still old friends. She'd accepted Lanita's invite and driven over to her apartment down around Broadway and Thorndale, her skin goose-pimpling in disgust every time the cross-dresser had reached over and squeezed her thigh with a familiarity that was years out of date. Upstairs she had returned the flirting and the touching, then suggested they share a candle-lit hot bath. Beneath her clothes Carrie was tall and strong and healthy, and Lanita was just a skinny, underfed street hooker; Carrie didn't even get winded when she drowned the bitch in her own bathtub.

That might have been the end of it, it *should* have been. But again, it was the first time Carrie'd killed someone, and she just hadn't had the forethought for murder. When she'd undressed in Lanita's apartment, she had overturned her purse; her card wallet and fallen out, and when she retrieved it, she hadn't noticed that one of her hospital ID cards had fallen out. When the neighbors finally complained about the smell coming from the apartment and the cops were called, the homicide detective who had found the card with her name on it had been Ted Lokela.

Tony's problem-solving had been swift and sure. He'd taken the piece of evidence from his partner with a smile, then destroyed it and written up the homicide report as though it never existed. His partner was a straight-shooter though; he'd given Tony a chance to talk to her about it, but there was no way he was going to let that piece of evidence disappear entirely. Carrie had two days of nightmarish anxiety and then—

Ted Lokela had somehow gotten killed in a drug raid.

End of problem.

Things had certainly changed a lot since then. She checked the alley one more time, then got out of the car and closed the door, softly so that it wouldn't make any noise. There was a time when she would have never imagined she could kill someone, but she was almost numb to what she was about to do—yeah, one more number in the tally. Lanita had been a desperation move, Connie DuPree the same but with a more carefully planned execution. She had no illusions about the fool who had tried to rob her in the underground parking lot at the mall—she hoped he was rotting in his grave right now. Yeah, she was almost numb to the whole messy business.

But not *quite.*

See, there was the thing about her nephew, who would come home from school this afternoon to continue his life with a murderer for a mother. Carrie just couldn't let that be—her brother wouldn't *want* her to. She didn't know if there really was a God or souls or whatever, but if there was, how could Tony rest in peace when the woman who'd killed him raised his son? It was simply unthinkable.

She didn't think Dara Rutland would recognize her, and of course the woman was going to find it strange indeed that Carrie knocked at the back door of the house instead of the front. Despite that, she was pretty sure that once she told Dara who she was, the woman would let her in—now and then, when Tony had been in one of his very rare magnanimous moods, he would let it slip that he had told Dara something about Carrie and her history. The decision to cut her off from his family had been entirely Tony's, and Carrie remembered her brother once saying Dara had suggested inviting Carrie over for the holidays. Not something Tony, with his homophobic tendencies, would have ever allowed, and that had probably been a mistake on Dara's part—knowing Tony, she'd probably gotten smacked for even voicing the words.

Carrie didn't know much about Dara Rutland. There had been Tony's wedding, of course, but things had been different back then, *Carrie* had been different—half zonked on drugs most of the time although pretty good about not showing it, going through a huge mental identity crisis.

It was doubtful, indeed, that Dara would recognize Carrie as the person she'd met at her wedding reception. There'd been the marijuana thing, and the smell of it, and Tony had been livid about that, so to keep the peace Carrie had stayed away for a long time after that. A little over three years later had been the surgery, and the family rift that had come out of *that* was worthy of the halls of history.

The backyard was empty and cold, filled with a sort of loneliness that comes only at certain times of the year, when the land is still trapped inside the frozen grip of winter. Brown patches of muddy ground peeked from between clumps of snow, dead leaves and branches, and made the yard look dirty and unpleasant. The bushes were spiky and leafless, a line of dead-looking wood along the back of the house. She climbed the stairs to the deck slowly, keeping her hands inside her pockets.

At the back door she hesitated, wondering if she was any different from her brother. Probably not much, although it had always surprised her that Tony had married to begin with. He'd always been a player, a womanizer, and the first sign that he wasn't going to do well in that realm—beyond that obvious atrocity when they were kids—had been the teenager in high school, that girl he'd gone off on and ended up dumping, after he'd raped and strangled her, in the forest preserves out in Niles. Tony should have been more grateful about getting away with that, since Mr. Smart Ass had needed help in fabricating his alibi. After awhile Carrie had thought that had been a one-time thing, then Tony had that affair after he'd gotten married—why get married to begin with if you didn't want to stay with one person?—then killed the woman when she'd threatened to rat him out to Dara. That had been an ugly one—Tony had cut the woman open like a slab of beef and he'd been *covered* in gore—and once again Carrie'd come to his rescue, helping with clean-up and a ready cover story, though thanks to whatever he'd done with the body, none had ever been needed.

And now Tony was gone and everything was different. Somehow she'd thought her older brother would always be there. Even if he didn't much like the woman she'd become, Carrie had always thought there would be time to fix that, that the passage of years would close the huge gulf between them. What a fickle, funny bitch fate had turned out to be.

She inhaled deeply, tasting the frigid air and smelling the far-off, faintly homey scent of firewood being burned from somewhere down the block. It took a little effort, but she found the best smile she could and pasted it across her mouth, hoping it didn't look too much like a grimace. The back door had cutesy curtains on it, tied back on each side, and through the window Carrie could see the kitchen counter below dark wood cabinets; on it was a wooden cutting board and one of those fancy wooden block holders where the knives were stored point-first. Finally she raised one hand and knocked briskly on the back storm door, quickly dropping her hand out of sight before Dara Rutland pushed back the curtain to see who was standing outside.

She didn't need her sister-in-law noticing the heavy rubber gloves protecting her skin.

«««—»»»

Man, Greg thought, this is like trying to untangle a ball of yarn after a cat's been playing with it.

He rubbed his eyes and sat back, squinting at the pile of papers on his desk. Tony's school records, work records, damned near his weekly dry cleaning lists, but most containing not much more than public information; all that was topped off by the considerable number of case files on which Tony Rutland had worked over the last two years.

Ordinarily, Greg wouldn't have had access to any of the more personal stuff, but the lieutenant had cleared it by giving him the confidential job of sorting through the mess and trying to piece together exactly why Tony had murdered his partner last April, then tried to kill his own son. But there wasn't a damned thing in here that suggested any answers. He hadn't yet figured out a way to break the news to Hannah about being related to Tony, and he wanted to clear up this Carrie thing first, anyway. He hadn't tried to call her personally yet, but his paper hunt was at a standstill—the address in the files was old, and there was no forwarding one. The phone number on file turned out to be a cell phone linked to a post office box that was paid up but had a registered home address that hadn't been updated in years, and calls to the former landlord had turned up zip. To stick a cherry on top of the whole messy pie, the whereabouts of Gery Rutland was also still a big fat dead end. He hadn't wanted to put Dara Rutland through a bunch of questions about Tony's actions, but he was getting to the point—

"Jedrek." Greg looked up as Lieutenant Quesada stepped out of his office. His eyes were hooded and his mouth was twisted into a scowl. "Get over to Rutland's house right away."

"What—" Greg began, but the other man's words cut him off.

"His widow's been murdered."

«««—»»»

For the second time in a week, the tasteful house on Maplewood was stuffed with cops and forensics personnel.

As he climbed the front porch stairs, Greg tried to remember the last time he'd visited here when it had been a happy home. He couldn't recall—had it ever been? While falling in love with Hannah had dominated his life, she had seemed inextricably tied to Tony, and the more that unwanted bond became obvious, the more displeased Tony had become. Greg had thought that was all over with Tony's death—messy and scandalous, yes, but still over—but apparently that wasn't the case at all. Now here he was again, and in front of him the door had obviously been forced open. Had this been a break-in, a random occurrence? Because of the family's history, that just seemed too far-fetched.

"What happened?" he asked the first person he saw when he stepped over the threshold.

The uniformed cop, a young woman with short brown hair, turned to meet him. Greg held out his badge so she didn't have to ask for it. "The neighbors heard screams and called the police. They met the squad out front and said the noise had stopped, but that they were sure it had been the woman who lived here—apparently they knew her voice from occasions where she and her husband had gotten into it, but they also knew her husband was dead." The officer jerked her head toward the depths of the house. "They got no answer and the house was locked up tight, but because of what happened last week, they went on and forced the door. They found her in the kitchen."

"All right." So, Greg thought as he strode across the darkened living room, no forced entry, as least not any that was obvious. Something caught his eye at the corner of the couch and he paused and bent to look at it. A toy truck, obviously Ben's. What was going to happen to the boy now?

He heard voices further in and followed the sounds, then found the forensics team moving carefully around a kitchen that looked like an abattoir. Dara Rutland lay sprawled face-up on the floor, her body halfway underneath the table with one leg twisted beneath her. Her face looked thinner to Greg, the stress of these last few months eating into her body weight and making her age. Now her eyes were open and staring at things none of them could know, perhaps finally seeing the answers to all the questions the still-living of the world would forever ask.

One of the guys on the forensics team, a fellow named Rick who often worked Greg's cases, saw him and nodded. "Hey, Jedrek. Hell of a thing, isn't this? She shoots her old man, then somebody whacks her a week later. I tell you one thing, though." He bent at one knee and spread Dara's fingers open where they were curled. The palms and fingers were clotted with blood and striped with deep gashes. "Defense wounds—she went down fighting hard."

Greg pressed his lips together. "Yeah, I see. Those didn't kill her though. What did?"

"Probably this one." Rick used a wooden tongue depressor to lift the edge of Dara Rutland's scarlet-soaked blouse. Beneath the fabric was a cut easily two inches wide, its edges gaping and filled with blood. "There are a couple of more like this, but more superficial. We tilted her before you got here, and this one went all the way through, came out the other side."

"Is there a weapon?"

Rick pointed at an oversized knife that had already been bagged and tagged. "Found it right there on the counter. Maybe the killer pulled it out of the knife block. Preliminary check doesn't show any fingerprints, though."

Greg glanced over and saw the slot where the biggest knife, the carver, was missing. "All right." He scanned the kitchen and Rick jumped in and answered his next question before he could ask it.

"They're checking the rest of the place a second time, but there's no sign of forced entry and nothing's taken. The victim's purse is on the table in the hall and there's still money in it, no sign of rape. Hell, maybe it's just a house invasion, a fucked-up coincidence. It wouldn't be the first time."

For a few minutes, Greg just stood there, trying to think and imagine what had happened in this kitchen earlier this morning. Poor Dara—after all those years of putting up with Tony's abuse, she finally freed herself with one heroic act of self-defense… only to have someone else come along and take her out. But who? Who would care anything about an everyday housewife who had no money and not much of anything in the house to steal? Obviously her killer hadn't wanted those things anyway, so what—

Ben.

Greg frowned and worked his way out of the kitchen. The boy's room was down the hall, the second to the smallest in an older four-bedroom bungalow that was pretty spacious. When he leaned inside the open door, Greg found an environment that Dara had attempted to make a lot cheerier than the rest of the house, where dark wood was abundant and the windows were covered by heavy drapes that were usually closed. Here was a true little boy's room, filled with sports toys and memorabilia, dominated by a patriotic red, white and blue theme. Still, there was an air of over-neatness about it, as if the boy had been trained all his life to military standards of organization and cleanliness. That mode was starting to fray a little at the edges—the clothes hamper in the corner was spilling over just a bit, the bedspread wasn't on quite perfectly—and Greg had an idea that while Dara had decorated, when he had been alive, Tony had overseen everything with his custom iron hand.

It was just so obvious. The single most valuable asset in Tony and Dara Rutland's life could easily said to be this young boy.

Where was Ben now? School, of course. The wheels were already in motion and the DCFS probably had a caseworker on the way there right now—not Monica Kenweigh, but whomever was watching over her workload while she vacationed in… wherever that was, Greg hadn't actually caught the location. Ben wouldn't know anything about this, not yet, and God help him when he found out that he'd lost both father and mother in the same week—he'd be lucky not to spend the rest of his life in therapy. With this latest development, the next in line to get custody of the boy, theoretically, was Tony's sister, the ever-absent Carrie. At least there was the absent part; with no address or current phone on file, the boy would slip into the system for the time being. Not such a great place, but when you had members of your family dying at the rate going on here, a few days of governmental anonymity might be a good thing. Greg did *not* want the child given over to Carrie Rutland without seeing the woman in person first, talking to her, *assessing* her.

Jesus. He wondered what Hannah would think when she got home from work and he told her about Dara.

«««—»»»

Hannah heard Greg come in.

He didn't call out for her, of course. Why would he? He thought she was at work, hustling her butt off for her daily bread, bringing burgers and fries and *Hey baby, how about one of them triple thick chocolate shakes?* to the hordes of Friday night customers at the Diner. Well, her days of that were going to be over after tonight's no-show, that was for certain. The telephone had rung four times since her shift started, but she hadn't answered; it was probably Zubro, calling to see where the hell she was, and if she'd answered she wouldn't have been able to talk anyway. It had taken literally hours for her to get enough strength to strip off her bloody clothes and make it into the shower, where she could lean against one wall while the warm water fell on her as gently as she could make the flow.

And Greg was finally home. Any second now, when he walked into the kitchen—

"What the hell—Jesus! *Hannah?!*"

She'd been in way too much pain to clean up the blood, too.

He pulled the door to the bathroom open, then yanked aside the shower curtain. The best she could do was give him a dull look and ask—

"Who died this time, Greg?"

««—»»

What does he see when he looks at me?

The thought kept running through her head as Greg tended to her wounds, carefully rinsing away the clotted blood and inspecting the slashes across her hands, the punctures in her abdomen. They didn't talk about it at first, not until he'd bandaged the last of the injuries and left her to sit on the kitchen chair like some fragile, damaged mummy, with her fingers wrapped in snow white gauze and more strips of the stuff encircling her waist. She watched, helpless and frustrated, while the man she loved crawled around the kitchen floor and sponged up the crimson mess she'd left, and when she could bear to look no more, Hannah's thoughts turned inward and she pondered her own body, how it was a road map for the horrors of her life. Could she really keep subjecting this man, who was so filled with goodness and love, to her personal daily hell?

"I don't want to see you any more."

The words shocked her almost as much as him—had she really said that out loud?

His gaze met hers and Hannah saw him, for the first time, literally shut down a part of himself to her. Self-defense, self-protection—a label didn't matter. He might as well have waved his hand and magically erected a steel wall between them.

"No," he said.

And he went back to cleaning up the floor.

"Greg," she began. "I—"

"No," he said again. "You're not pushing me out of your life. I won't let you." He squeezed pinkish water out of the sponge into the bucket a final time, then rose and carried the bucket into the bathroom to pour the contents into the toilet. She heard him run more water in the bucket and knew he was dropping her clothes into the water, leaving them to soak away the evidence of another go-around with her *Affliction.*

When he came back, Hannah had figured out her next words. "This is never going to stop," she said in a low voice. "*Ever.* Isn't that obvious by now? I can't give you a normal life, Greg, *I'm* not normal. It isn't fair for me to expect you to put up with this shit for... well, *forever.* So I think we should go our separate ways."

The whole time she'd been talking, Greg had been moving, wiping down the front of the sink cabinet where she'd been leaning when the first of this morning's injuries had appeared. When he finished that, he washed his hands and finally turned to look at her as he dried them with a paper towel. "I love you," he said simply.

"That's not enough," Hannah said. "It's not enough to carry you when you don't know from one day to the next what you're going to find when you walk through the door—like today. It's not going to be enough when you look at me in ten years and God knows what my face and my body look like, when I might end up looking like some kind of fucking Frankenstein *monster—*" Damn it, she was crying now, and she hadn't wanted to do that. She'd wanted to be strong, and firm, and not let him see how much this was killing her, how much more painful and worse sending him away was than *anything* she'd ever endured. She tried to wipe her eyes and got a nasty sting when she put pressure on the bandages, and that just made her cry harder. She squeezed her eyes shut and pushed the backs of her bandages into the lids as hard as she dared, trying to stop.

"Hannah."

She felt Greg pull her wrists down and reluctantly she opened her eyes. He was kneeling in front of her, his face only inches away. God, she loved him so *much.* "Greg, please," she rasped. "Don't make this any harder than it already is."

"I haven't even *started,*" he said. He didn't let go of her wrists. "Do I care that this happens to you? You bet I do. Is it enough to drive me away?" He leaned closer, so close she could smell his breath; he must have been chewing on a breath mint in the car, because his words still carried the scent of wintergreen. "Not on your fucking *life.*" His fingers tightened around her wrist, firm but not so much that it hurt. "When I look at you, I see what's *inside* you. I know that you want to be beautiful—every woman does. To me, you *are,* and it isn't going to matter how many scars you have, either now or a decade or five decades from now, or whether they're on your face or your body or inside you. *I am not going away,* Hannah. Do you understand me?"

She closed her eyes again, trying to think of something that would make him change his mind, but the truth was that she didn't really want that, didn't know how she would face tomorrow or any other day if Greg wasn't in her life. When he let go of her wrists and put his arms around her, all she could was hold onto him and hope for the best in the future.

Saturday—March 3rd...

By the time Greg left for the station the next morning, Hannah was, all things considered, doing pretty damned well. All but the worst of the wounds—the one that had gone in the front and come out the back of her left side, and the one that had been fatal to Dara Rutland—had closed, leaving scars that would eventually give way to the familiar angry red scars to mark their passage. The main one, one of the worst that Hannah had ever received, had finally stopped bleeding at about midnight; it hadn't quite sealed itself and was still seeping slightly, a clear fluid that reminded Greg of the protective liquid that builds up in a blister. He figured she'd be normal, or as close as she could ever get, by noon, and in the meantime Hannah had slept so deeply last night that he'd found himself sitting up in the dark periodically and listening for her breathing, searching for the sound of that shallow inhale/exhale that let him know his world was still complete.

There had been a half dozen times last night when Greg had almost told Hannah about her relationship with Tony, just because it would at least explain the thread that had existed between her and Dara Rutland, the one that had caused Dara's mortal injuries to manifest on Hannah's body. But he was loathe to come right out and do it, because he was... well, *afraid.* Afraid that Hannah had been right about the fact that this might never end—this seemed so much an indication that she was somehow tied not just Tony, but to other people with whom the man's life had been intertwined. For who else would Hannah suffer over the coming years of her life?

Work was tense, tempers were high, patience among the squad's members was short. Too many murders committed by one of their own, and now that same fallen cop's son was effectively an orphan—

Sitting at his desk, Greg could have slapped himself. He couldn't believe it hadn't dawned on him before now.

Carrie Rutland couldn't be found, neither could Gery. Bruce and Erma were *not* Ben's biological grandparents. The next best thing in this world to a relative that eight-year-old Ben Rutland had was—

Hannah.

For a few seconds, Greg literally couldn't breath. How would she take this? Did she want kids? Did she even *like* them? He had no idea—for the first time, he realized that, given the outlandish life that Hannah led and her reluctance about marriage, they'd never discussed children. Hell, he still hadn't been able to get her to agree to his proposal, much less tackle the idea of procreation. But now… well, little Benjamin Rutland was her nephew. What in the world was she going to say to that?

Something stung his eyes and Greg realized he was sweating despite the chilliness of the squad room. He glanced around but no one else had noticed—they were all too busy arguing with each other or people on the telephone, fighting with paperwork, generally being pissed off at the world. Suddenly all of this wasn't as important as it had been, not trivial but… not as high a priority either. In his—no, Hannah's—palm, was the life of a little boy, and tonight he would have to go home and tell Hannah one big whopper of a truth… one she might not be prepared to hear.

««—»»

Over the telephone line, Hannah recognized the snap of Winnie's gum even before her friend started speaking.

"Girl, you owe me big time."

"It's nice to hear from you, too," Hannah said mildly. "I was going to call you later today."

"Yeah, seeing as how—*snap!*—I saved your job and all last night."

Hannah blinked. "You did? How?" She had assumed her days at the Diner were history—no manager with a restaurant that busy would tolerate a no-show waitress on a packed Friday night. In fact, she'd felt so guilty and embarrassed she'd decided not to even pick up her last two days' pay.

"Zubro is a dipstick," Winnie said. *Snap!* "When he couldn't get you on the phone, he finally called me. I acted like it was all a big plan, said you had a family emergency and that I had agreed to cover you but couldn't come in until four. Lied my ass off and said I left him a message and he must not have gotten it."

"Oh, Winnie, you did that? And he believed you?"

"Yeah, well, he wasn't too happy, but I'd overheard him complaining to the phone company earlier this week that his voice mail wasn't working right. So I played on it." Winnie paused, and when she continued there was a mixture of irritation and worry in her voice. "Me and Rex, we had good plans for that night. He ain't too happy with me right now."

"I'm sorry." Hannah twisted the phone cord around her finger, then unwound it. "It… it couldn't be helped. I just figured Zubro fired me. I wasn't going to go back."

"Are you all right? Did you get, you know… did, uh, something happen again?"

Hannah hesitated. "Yeah," she finally answered. She didn't want to go into detail, but she'd be damned if she'd lie to her best friend. "Something happened. But I'm over it. It wasn't so good last night, but I'm right as wet rain today."

"Really?"

"Definitely."

There was a pause while Winnie considered this. "So then you're going to go back to work, right? I mean—*snap!* —I put it on the line for your happy little butt. If you don't, he'll know I made up the whole sorry-ass story and he'll probably give me the axe right along with you. You know what a forgiving soul he is."

"Yes, of course I'll go back." Perched on the edge of the bed, Hannah sat up a bit straighter. "You're scheduled for tonight, right? Why don't I take your shift, and then you and Rex can have a Saturday night on the town?"

"Aw, you don't have to do that. I mean, what with you getting hurt and all…"

But Hannah could hear in her friend's voice that she was tempted. "I'm fine," she said firmly. "Come on, I've been through this dozens of times. You know me—I bounce back fast. And I could use the tips to make up for the missed work."

"Well, if you're sure—"

"Consider it done," Hannah interrupted. "What's your schedule for tonight?"

"It's a long one," Winnie told her. "Four to one. Saturday night, you probably won't get much of a break for dinner."

"I'll eat before I go. You and Rex have a great time tonight. If you see a movie, eat double popcorn for me."

A few more niceties, then Hannah hung up the phone and went to change into her uniform. She got a twinge in the left side, but when she lifted her sweater and checked the bandage that Greg had taped in place this morning, it was clean and dry; she decided to leave it in place, just in case. A couple of aspirins to cut down on the achiness in her muscles, caused by spasming on the floor yesterday morning during the unseen attack, and she'd be good to go. She started to just leave Greg a note, then nixed that idea—if he called the apartment and got no answer, he'd probably panic. She dialed him at work and got voice mail so, grinning as she thought of Winnie's lie to Zubro about this very same method of communication, she left Greg a message telling him she was working Winnie's shift for her tonight.

««—»»

Fighting not to be grouchy about it and not particularly succeeding, Greg had the dogs on leashes and was waiting for Hannah when she got off work at one in the morning. She smiled when she stepped outside and saw him, but the smile faded at the edges at his expression. "Hi," she said cautiously. "What's up? Is something wrong?"

"What could possibly be wrong?" he asked, tucking her hand into the crook of one elbow as they headed west on Belmont and back toward home. "You only damned near died yesterday morning, and today you leave me a phone message saying you've decided to go traipsing off to work, where you can be on your feet all day and drag big trays of food around and probably deal with an asshole every half hour. Nothing's wrong."

She gaped at him, then laughed. "Okay, wait—you're mad at me because I got well enough to go to work?"

Greg frowned. "No, of course not.

Hannah rolled her eyes. "Sure sounds that way to me."

"Don't be silly."

"Then what?" She poked him lightly in the ribs as the dogs padded happily in front of them. "Come on—like you said, I've been… what was the word? *Traipsing,* that was it. I've been traipsing around all day, so I'm tired. I'm even a little hungry, if you can believe that the smell of the grease in there didn't completely smother my appetite. I was hoping for a good old-fashioned microwave dinner."

Greg started to grumble some more, then choked back the words before they could escape. She was right—what was his problem, anyway? It wasn't so hard to figure out that it was the Tony thing, and the Ben thing, and wondering just what the hell finding all this out was going to do to Hannah. But he was being selfish, bumbling around and bursting at the seams to tell her when it wouldn't hurt to wait another night or so. Right now Ben was safe in the foster system for a few more days and Hannah was still healing. Yeah, she'd been strong enough—*incredible* enough—to go to work tonight, but despite her light tone of voice he could see the fatigue in the set of her shoulders and the shadowy circles beneath her eyes. Did she really need to get the news about Tony and Ben thrown in her face on top of everything she'd gone through just yesterday?

No, she didn't. He could wait, at least until tomorrow, maybe the day after. He'd checked this afternoon and Ben was doing fine, relegated to a temporary foster home pending final assignment. Another day or two wouldn't make any difference, and he'd make sure that Hannah knew about the boy long before a judge assigned him to a permanent foster-parent situation. This was going to be a big, no, a *huge* decision, and he would give her a little more time to rest and gather herself for the storm she didn't have any idea was headed her way.

««—»»

They've gone now, finally, leaving her behind with the baby. The toddler is silent and still, and that's wrong because after what was done to her the baby should be crying like babies do when they get hurt. But she can't do anything about it because they've left her tied up and with her mouth covered over with tape, so she can't even call out to Amy, try to soothe her a little and tell her things will be all right. Will they? She isn't really sure. She hurts, a lot, and there are noises in this dark, damp little cave, sounds in the shadows but which she can't turn her head to investigate. Rats? Bugs? It's raining outside—she can hear it, a steady, heavier-than-normal downpour that sounds like beans falling on a drum. And beneath that, something else, someone else, *a man mumbling and cursing to himself as he enters the cave amid more noise, the rumbling of paper and plastic bags, the rattle of tin cans. And then—*

"Well, lookit here—someone left me a coupla little presents, ain't that just a peach."

Her hope of freedom disintegrates at the sight of the man swaying from side to side in front of her. He's whip-thin and his clothes are ragged and filthy—he hasn't come to rescue her and Amy at all, and with growing horror, she realizes that this is his *place,* she *is the intruder here, left by her brothers to suffer even more. The stranger turns to where Amy lies on the dirt floor, a loose little bundle of motionless flesh; he shakes his head and gives a disappointed shrug. "That toy's broken." So he forgets about Amy, and he reaches for Hannah instead.*

And Hannah tries to scream for her brothers to come back and get her but her mouth is covered with duct tape. The sounds goes on her in her mind instead, on and on and on—

"Butch!"

Hannah sat up with a gasp, the name still ringing inside her head along with another one. What was it? Carl. Yes, *Butch* and *Carl.* Her brothers, a family never mentioned by Dr. Gorrado because he'd always felt she needed to discover that part of herself on her own.

And oh, she sure had.

Beside her, Greg stirred then opened his eyes. "Hannah? What's wrong?" He pushed up on one elbow. "Did I hear you say something?"

"I have brothers," she said bluntly. Shock creased Greg's face, instantly driving away the soft edges of sleep. "I remember them."

"You do?" He sat up fully, then put a hand on her arm. "What do you recall?"

Hannah shuddered and hugged herself, fingers digging into her own flesh. "Their names were Butch and Carl. They were older than me. They…" She swallowed, then her gaze found the dogs, both of which had come to sit at the edge of the bed when she and Greg had started talking. She focused on them, their soft, friendly faces and liquid brown eyes, rather than allow the horrid memories to replay behind her eyes. "They took me and Amy to a cave and they… did things. Amy was just a toddler, I think. I don't remember everything. But she wasn't moving afterward, or making any noise." Her gaze cut to his. "I think they killed her, Greg."

He didn't say anything but she could see him registering this. There was something else in his expression, something more than the astonishment that she'd expected. He knew her history, so it must be that he'd never expected her to remember the details; well, neither had she. "There was another man who came afterward," she said. Her voice had gone unaccountably hoarse, but trying to clear it didn't seem to work. "He did the same, uh, things that Butch had done to me… for a long time. But I don't think he knew them—I think he was just a crazy person who lived in the cave they'd taken us to."

Greg nodded, then let go of her arm and rubbed both hands across his face. He said something so low that she wasn't quite sure she'd heard him correctly.

"If he was still alive, I think I'd kill him myself."

She shivered again, feeling cold but somehow distanced, cushioned by the years between the helpless little girl she'd been then and the woman she was now. "What? Who are you talking about, Greg?"

He didn't answer right away, then he lifted his face and looked at her. "Tony."

Hannah frowned. "I don't understand."

He swallowed so hard she saw his throat convulse. "Hannah… Tony Rutland was your brother Butch."

««—»»

"If you think about it, it makes a weird kind of sense," Hannah said a little later, when they were sitting at the table in the middle of the night over hot mugs of no-caffeine tea. "I mean, I can't explain how, but I can see the *why* of it."

"All right," Greg said. "If I can't have how, then I'll take what I can get." She nodded and he watched as she held out her left hand, then slowly spread open her fingers. There, on the palm, was a scar; faint, white, more than an inch long. Greg had thought he knew every inch of Hannah's body, but somehow he had missed this one. He didn't remember her writing about it in that journal of hers, either. But he could understand why he'd missed it—from what he could see, it was easily the oldest one she had, so faded that it blended into near-invisibility among the surrounding lines.

Now Hannah pointed to it with her other hand. “This is where he—Butch—cut me,” she told him. “He cut all of us, even Amy, although I think she was already dead by then.” She closed her hand briefly, as if she couldn’t bear to look at the scar now that she knew what it meant. “Then he… what would you call it? Made us all do this like, blood pact or something. You know what I’m talking about—it’s like kids in school, when they do that blood brothers thing.”

Greg sat quietly, trying to imagine what Hannah had endured. As always, he couldn’t; he simply didn’t have the ability to comprehend what could make one child turn so monstrous that he would torture and kill another. But according to Hannah, Tony had been hurting her, abusing her, for years before his big finale. Had Tony—Butch—ever truly *been* a child? Or had he been an animal from the start?

“So it’s like we were bound together,” Hannah continued. “Spiritually or whatever.”

Greg frowned, his mind making connections. “So you’re saying that what Tony experienced, you experienced?”

Hannah shook her head. “No. Exactly the opposite—I experienced what Tony *did* to other people.”

“But Tony is dead.” Greg gave her a bewildered glance. “And you have no blood connection to Dara.”

Hannah looked at him steadily. “But I’m still connected to Carl. Even though Tony never told you about him, it sure seems like Carl’s still out there, doesn’t it, using the name Gery? So I must have this… whatever you want to call it—psychic tie or something—to him, too.”

Greg thought about this. “So you believe he’s the one who murdered Dara?”

Hannah rubbed her hands together, as if they were chilled. “I can’t think of any other explanation. Can you?”

“Tony’s sister.”

She sat back. “I can’t tell you anything about that. I just don’t know. Amy died in that cave, and it’s obviously not me.” She tilted her head. “A stepsister, maybe? From his adopted parents?”

“Not according to the Rutlands, who were quite adamant about how they’d never had anything to do with ‘her.’ Unless they’re lying, but I don’t see what they have to gain from doing so. They sure don’t seem the kind of people to try and protect anyone, least of all the two boys they took into their home."

Hannah was quiet for a couple of moments. "It must have been rough for them," she said at least. "To grow up like that, in a home where there wasn't any affection."

Greg stared at her, then gave a little jerk of his head. "Seems to me they had it better before they attacked you." He couldn't quite keep the venom out of his voice. "If you ask me, they got what they deserved."

Hannah shrugged. "I can't say. It's not for me to judge."

Personally, Greg thought that if anyone had the right to do just that, it was Hannah, but he wasn't going to argue the point. There was something else important that they needed to discuss. He wasn't sure how to bring up the subject, and in the end he ended up blurting it out with no preamble. "Hannah, you know that Tony had an eight-year-old son, right? His name is Ben. That… that means he's your nephew."

Hannah's eyes went wide. "My *nephew?* Oh my God—he is, isn't he?"

Greg looked at his hands. "As it stands right now, if they ask for him, he'll probably go to Bruce and Erma Rutland, Tony's adopted parents." He raised his gaze to hers. "Unless something, or some*one*, stops that from happening."

Hannah sat very still. "Where is the boy… *Ben,* now? Is he with them already?"

"No, not yet. He's in temporary foster care. His assigned case worker is on vacation. When she gets back, she'll make permanent arrangements."

"Wow," Hannah whispered. "Instant parenthood. And to a boy who's already had more than a chunk of grief in his life."

"Yeah." Greg said, and because he couldn't think of anything else to add…

"Yeah."

««—»»

Hannah didn't sleep much the rest of that night. Thoughts of her "new" nephew rolled erratically through her mind, and from one moment to the next she couldn't decide if she was elated or lost in panic. Greg lay beside her, but she could tell he wasn't resting very well either, even though he was better than she was at repressing the tossing and turning—she simply gave in and rolled all night, with every little wrinkle and bunch of the sheet and fabric beneath her one more irritation, another way to distract her from slipping into slumber.

She wondered what little Benjamin Rutland was like, and how he slept tonight, lying on a strange bed somewhere with everything and everyone in his life ripped away. Was he cold? Did he feel safe? Of course not—how could he? His father had tried to kill him only a week ago, now both parents were dead and he thought he was an orphan. As shocked as she was to learn about this, the basic fact was that she was his last true relative. How could she abandon him?

She couldn't.

And by the time the sun spilled itself onto the street in front of her apartment, Hannah was at peace with her decision, and with herself.

Sunday—March 4th...

He didn't know why, but Greg had been dreading making this telephone call. He could have gotten out of it, done the whole 'pass-the-buck, this should be the case worker's job, take it to family services,' whatever thing, but that wasn't the point. In fact, he didn't really know what the point *was,* only that he didn't want to call Zion, Illinois and would have been happy to never speak to either of the elder Rutlands again. It was something indefinable, like psyching yourself up for that call to the bank about the screw-up on your account, how you knew it wasn't going to go well and so you just kept putting it off.

But, of course, you could only procrastinate for so long.

Maybe they wouldn't answer, like before when the department had tried to contact them and let them know about Tony. Maybe—

"Hello?"

Greg winced, then cleared his throat. "Mr. Rutland, this is Detective Greg Jedrek of the Chicago Police Department. You might recall that I came out to your house and spoke to you about Tony—"

"Nothing wrong with my memory, Detective. What do you want?"

Greg realized he was gritting his teeth and tried to make his facial muscles relax. "I'm afraid I have some more bad news, Mr. Rutland. I wasn't planning on breaking it over the telephone, so why don't I drive out there this afternoon?"

"Nothing wrong with my ear against this telephone, either. Whyn't you just say what you have to and be done with it."

It wasn't a request and Greg suppressed a sigh. He could picture Bruce Rutland standing impatiently in his living room, or maybe sitting on that faded old couch while his wife was off doing something in the laundry room. Greg would have bet his next paycheck that there wasn't a bit of emotion on the man's face. "I'm afraid your daughter-in-law Dara was… killed on Friday," he finally said, reluctant to use the word *murdered.*

Of all the things Greg could have imagined Bruce Rutland saying, the words he heard next had never crossed his mind. *"That's too bad, I suppose, but she wasn't any real kin to Erma and me. I know we told you we haven't dealt with Tony in nearly six years, so why are you telling us about all this?"*

Greg inhaled. "Because I still haven't been able to contact Tony's sister or find Gery," he said. There was no sense mentioning Hannah right now, and he felt fairly confident that Hannah was *not* the crazy sister the Rutlands had talked about when he'd visited them in their home. "And as of right now, we have an orphaned eight-year-old boy. Of course, if you feel that there's no relation than I'm sorry for wasting your time." That sounded on the harsh side, but he'd meant it to.

"I ain't surprised you can't find Gery, and I done told you that we don't talk about that sister thing." Bruce Rutland was silent for a moment. *"But this boy… well, I suppose we ought to take him in. It's our God-given duty and all. Can't say we were planning on raising another youngster at our age, but we can bend to the Lord's will. We'll do what we have to."*

Greg leaned into the phone, looking forward to the next part of the conversation for the first time since he'd dialed the telephone. He was going to lie, but sometimes, as Rutland had said, you did what you had to do. "That may not be necessary, Mr. Rutland. While it hasn't happened yet, I do expect to get in touch with Tony's sister within the next day or so. We don't have any reason to doubt she may be willing to take him in—"

"Don't you even think *about such a thing, detective!"* For the first time, there was real emotion in the older man's voice, true anger. *"We done our best by Gery but he was a lost cause—stubborn and ungrateful.* Sick. *There's no changing that now, he's made his choices. Both those boys were out of control almost right from the start, no matter how we tried to contain them. But to put a child into the hands of that, that—"*

Bruce Rutland sounded like he actually choked for a second. *"It's unthinkable, is what it is. Blasphemy. I don't want to hear any more about it. So you just make the arrangements and have that boy brought out here where he can be raised up normal. And don't you be asking me no more questions about that sister again, or about Gery. We done told you we don't know anything about all that."*

There was so much more Greg wanted to say and know, but he knew it was useless. Instead he nodded into the air and said, "All right, Mr. Rutland. I'll pass your information along to the appropriate department and they'll take it from there. I wouldn't expect this to happen quickly though. These things take time and Ben's family services representative is on vacation. Right now he's in foster care."

"How long, then?"

Greg hesitated, suddenly wanting to buy himself and Hannah all the time he could. "I'm not sure. With paperwork and departmental hearings, it could be several weeks. You know how the government is—nothing moves quickly."

"It ought to be run like the church here in town. Then there wouldn't be any of that red tape nonsense."

"Oh, I agree—"

"I can stand here and yak off with you, Detective," Rutland interrupted. *"Mother and I were on our way out the door to Sunday services and you've already made us late. We'll have a cot in the sewing room waiting on the boy when he gets here."*

And Bruce Rutland hung up on him.

Greg pulled the receiver away from his ear and scowled at it. The thought of turning Ben over to these cold people made him cringe inside, but he was also terrified that that was exactly what might happen. There was all kinds of unpleasant business likely to hit daylight when Hannah stepped up to the bat and said she wanted custody of her nephew. What would a family court judge do when faced with choosing a home for this child between the Rutlands or Hannah?

The phone on his desk rang, jarring him from his thoughts. When he answered it, Hannah's voice was shaking in his ear. He listened to her first few words, then cut her off. "I'm coming home," he said. "I'll be there in fifteen minutes. You can tell me this whole thing then, from start to finish. Until I get there, don't answer the phone and make sure the damned doors are locked."

««—»»

"He said 'I'm not through with you, bitch. You helped kill my brother and you're going to pay for that.'"

For as nervous as she'd sounded on the telephone, Hannah felt much better now; she'd called Winnie's cell number right after hanging up with Greg, and Winnie had actually beat Greg to the door—she'd been only a couple of blocks away, rummaging around through the goth and leather shop near Clark Street. Now that she had both her best friend and boyfriend, not to mention the two protective pups, surrounding her, Hannah couldn't really recall when she'd felt safer.

"Did you recognize his voice?" Greg asked.

"No, not at all."

"Maybe it was a joke," Winnie suggested. "Some kid who just happened to hit you at the right time, or read a newspaper article about what happened with Rutland."

"But there really isn't any way to tie Hannah to that," Greg pointed out, knowing that Winnie was more or less aware of the strange things Hannah had been subjected to for most of her life. He also knew Hannah had brought Winnie up to speed, sans the more painful details, of her connection to Tony Rutland. "Sure, the three of us might have our suspicions, but no one else does. It *has* to be Gery."

"But you can't find him," Hannah said.

Greg held up his hands, and Hannah saw frustration etched in the tightness of the lines around his mouth. "I haven't found him *yet*," Greg corrected. His expression was grim. "But I will. Especially if he's the bastard threatening you."

Winnie peered at Hannah, her hands pulling thoughtfully at the short strands of black hair surrounding her face. "What else?" she finally asked. "I can tell there's something."

Hannah hesitated. "It's… it's probably just my imagination."

"What?" Greg asked. "Come on, you're not helping anything by holding back."

"Well, when he said that, the first time, I just kind of… I don't know… automatically said *'Carl?'* For a couple of seconds there was nothing—I thought he'd broke the connection. Then he just repeated himself, before slamming the phone down."

"Sounds to me like the dude got seriously bent cuz you recognized his unhappy ass," Winnie said.

Greg considered this, then had to agree. "Yeah, I think Winnie's right. In any case, I've taken some lost time so you're stuck with me for the rest of the day."

Despite everything, Hannah couldn't help the smile that spread across her face. "Really?"

He grinned at her. "Yeah. Really."

Across the table, Winnie rolled her eyes. "I'm outta here. I don't even want to know what you two are gonna do with the rest of your Saturday afternoon."

"Aw, come on, Win," Hannah chided. "Don't you want to make it a threesome?"

Winnie gaped at her. *"What?"*

"It's so much easier to compare that way," Greg said.

This time Winnie couldn't even say anything. She just fumbled for her backpack, eyeing them both suspiciously. "It'd freak your conservative butts out big time if I said yes, wouldn't it?"

Hannah couldn't hold her laughter in any longer. "Shopping, you fool." She gave Winnie's shoulder an affectionate push. "Maybe Harlem & Irving."

"Whew," Winnie muttered. "Thought you two'd gone prevert on me."

Now Greg laughed. "Prevert?"

"Transposing letters is a mark of individuality," Winnie said smartly.

Hannah planted her hands on her hips. "Spare me any more marks, please. If I want more, I'll get a tattoo."

"I'll second that."

Hannah squinted at Greg. "You want me to get a tattoo? Where? What?"

"Okay, now I really *am* history." Winnie followed that statement with a heartfelt sneeze, then scampered for the door. "Hannah, you call me if you need me—you've got my cell number!"

"Definitely." When the door had closed behind Winnie, Hannah turned back to Greg. "So, we were discussing tattoos, right?"

"Were we?" He pulled her to a standing position and folded his arms around her. She leaned into him and felt his breath, warm and ticklish, on her neck as he exhaled, heard him inhale slowly as if he was enjoying the peach scent she always wore. A warm flush spread from the spot, inching down Hannah's shoulder and collarbone and beyond. How long had it been since they'd made love? Too long—her life was so difficult, and his likewise by default, that the sweeter side of their relationship was far too often pushed away because of weariness or injury or just outright fear on her part.

But not today.

Not now.

Greg was still wearing his holster and she slipped it over his shoulder, then let him take it from her and ease it onto the tabletop. The apartment was cool, as it often was in that odd time that wasn't quite winter and wasn't quite spring, when the thermostat couldn't wrap its mechanical logic around what was too cold but not warm enough. Hannah, on the other hand, felt quite warm for a change, unaccountably *hot.* She'd read in some magazine or another about a method of yoga healing where heat transfer took place through the hands, had wondered at the time what it would feel like to have that kind of warmth emanating from her flesh onto someone else. Now she knew—her hands ached to touch Greg, to share whatever this was she felt churning away inside her. Love, passion… *sharing.*

Their routine, their *way,* was usually slow and easy, Greg always so careful not to frighten or push her in any way. But she had so much sudden need for him that she just couldn't wait. When he started to ease his hand beneath the back of her top, Hannah reached out and yanked Greg's sweater up and over his head. Before he could recover, her hands were pulling on his belt, already getting the clasp undone and apart.

"Whoa," he said in surprise. "What's got into you?"

"You," she said, then added with a flash of wickedness, "at least you will be very soon."

His eyes widened, then he gave her a devilish-looking smile. She felt her feet leave the floor and the room swung momentarily as he lifted her into his arms. "Oh, I think I can accommodate you on that!"

"Well, chop chop," Hannah shot back. "You think I have all day or what?"

He smiled and kissed her as he carried her over to the bed. "There's plenty of time," he said as lowered her to the bedspread. "We've got the rest of our lives."

Monday—March 5th...

Monday morning started with a nasty feeling in Greg's gut, and by the end of the day, staring at the results of his all-day digging into obscure records and closed files and phone calls to every freaking person he could think of, that slightly sick feeling had grown very close to full nausea. The only thing that kept him even remotely calm was the knowledge that little Benjamin Rutland was housed in a foster home, safely out of reach of his Aunt Carrie, or his Uncle Gery.

Both of whom were the same person.

Petition for Legal Name Change pursuant to Illinois Statutes 735 IL CS 5/21-101.

Somewhere around six years ago, Gery Rutland had legally changed his name to Carrie Rutland.

Gery.

Carrie.

Could it be?

More phone calls, but he kept dead-ending at that one critical point: *doctor-patient confidentiality.* No one out there who'd dealt with Gery Rutland, or Carrie Rutland as he... *she* was now known, was willing to cross the line as Dr. Gorrado had for Hannah. So Greg had suspicions, God did he ever, but no definite proof—the missing brother, the mysterious sister that Tony had acknowledged but whom Tony's parents wouldn't talk about. That in itself nearly screamed *sex-change* operation; the Rutlands were self-righteous Bible-thumpers, not particularly prone to tolerance to begin with, and the last thing they would condone was something like that. He was willing to accept that there were people who couldn't accept the sex they'd been born into, but to start life as a child who'd participated in sexual abuse and murder, *then* develop gender identity difficulties—what kind of mentality would a person like that have? Had the change that Carrie had gone through been a result of the murder Tony had involved her in so many years ago?

Who knew? Confused might be phrasing it gently, and perhaps the whole gender reassignment had been Carl Rutland's attempt to escape the darker parts of his past, although he had still held tight to his relationship with his brother. This kind of procedure wasn't performed quickly—there was a protocol of mental therapy and it was expensive. And wasn't there follow-up treatment with hormones? What he knew about gender-changing could fit in half a thimble, so he'd taken things in a direction with which he was more familiar. He had a credit report in the works and there was also a definite paper trail at a number of mental therapy facilities, although again, no one would release any information to him, not even a hint as to whether there had been an actual operation. For now, however, it was enough for Greg that they would acknowledge the existence of files on both Gery and Carrie Rutland.

On his way home, Greg thought again about the threatening telephone call Hannah had received. He'd checked with her a number of times today, but there hadn't been any repeat and she wasn't scheduled to go into work. Fine by him—he liked her being at home, safe and snug with the dogs to look after her when he couldn't. Had her unidentified caller been Carrie? No doubt, and she'd probably been trying to disguise her voice, something which might or might not have been all that difficult, depending, again, on things like hormone treatments.

The dogs met Greg at the door when he let himself in, bouncing happily in front of him as he shrugged off his jacket. Hannah turned and smiled at him from the kitchen end of the apartment, but he could see even from thirty feet away that her expression was strained. "Hi," she said.

"Hey." He walked over to where she stood at the sink and found her smearing some whipped butter on pieces of bread. The smell of beef stew permeated the air; while Hannah really wasn't that great a cook, she could follow package directions as well as anyone and, as she had said on more than one occasion, *Thank you, Lawry's Seasoning Mixes.* "Smells good."

She smiled again, but there were dark circles under her eyes. "Yeah, it does."

Greg glanced at the piece of bread she was finishing, the final one, then frowned. Her wrists were splattered with fingerprint-sized bruises, as though she'd been grabbed and held. "Hey, where did those come from?"

Hannah scraped the side of the knife against the rim of the butter container, then dropped it in the sink. "I guess from the same source as these." She reached up and pushed aside the loose neckline of her sweater. More purplish green bruises, each about the size of a nickel, dotted the pale expanse of her shoulder. Her gaze found his. "I guess Carl's still making his mark on the world, huh?"

"Damn," Greg said. He rubbed his hand gently across the skin and was gratified to see that his touch brought a pleased smile to her lips. "Come sit down and I'll bring you up to date on what I think is going on."

"Dinner's ready just about any old time," Hannah said. "Just fill me in while I set the table."

"Well..."

She gave him a slightly shaky grin. "Come on, hon. I'm a big girl now. After all I've been through, I don't think anything you could say would surprise me."

He pressed his lips together, then took a deep breath. "Carrie and Carl are the same person."

"What?"

"I thought you said nothing could surprise you."

"You're making that up, just because I said that!" Hannah's mouth worked. "Greg, I don't think that's funny at all!"

Greg sat up straight. "No, I swear it—I would never do something like that."

She stared at him, then seemed to get her bearings and start moving again. "Are you saying Carl is a cross-dresser?"

He shook his head, then decided to get up and help arrange their small dinner. He was much too antsy to sit and watch her work without helping. "No. Look, I don't have any proof yet—no one will let me into the medical records, although I haven't stopped trying. But they all point to the same thing: a sex-change operation."

"Are you serious?" Suddenly Hannah's eyes widened. "Wait—that almost makes sense. Remember that woman who came in here, how she said my name? Like she knew me?"

He nodded. "Exactly."

Her face darkened. "But why would he... *she* want to hurt me, Greg?"

He reached out and pushed a wispy strand of hair out of her eyes. "My theory? I think Tony told her to—he knew you had that connection to him and he probably figured it was only a matter of time before we would able to really get him on something. The man was a wife-beater and a murderer. God only knows what he got away with that we'll never be able to trace to him. He wanted that connection eliminated."

Hannah put a couple of paper napkins next to the bowls she'd set on the table, then slowly lowered herself onto a chair. Her eyes were a little too bright, starting to fill with unshed tears. "But Carl was never like that—he wasn't the one who killed Amy or hurt me, not ever. Why would he start now?"

"Because Tony told him to," Greg told her quietly. "If I'm right about this, it seems pretty obvious from the way they've acted that Carl—Gery—was disowned by the Rutlands because of his decision to have the operation. I knew Tony well enough to know that he despised gays and transvestites; whether this grew out of his brother's gender-change, I can't say, but my guess is that Carrie would have done anything to try and keep his affection. Including murder you, if he—*she*—had to." He regarded her solemnly. "I think your phone caller was Carrie, and I think she's starting to crack under the pressure."

Hannah was silent for a long moment, then she held up her wrists. A single tear spilled from one eye and slid down her left cheek. "And someone out there is paying the price."

Tuesday—March 6th...

"*Detective Rutland, this is Monica Kenweigh. I have to say that after all we discussed, I find it pretty hard to believe that you didn't at least try to contact me before allowing the Rutland boy to be placed."*

Holding the receiver next to his ear, Greg said the first thing that came to his mind. "Monica? I though you were on vacation."

"That's a damned sorry excuse to use to put a boy in a situation like this. We talked *about this—"*

"Wait a minute," Greg interrupted. "*What* situation? Ben Rutland is in temporary foster care."

"No, he's not. I decided to call the office this morning to monitor a couple of files—his was one of them—and the intermediate case worker, a raving idiot *if you ask me, who's supposed to be fielding my cases told me that his aunt showed up on Sunday afternoon to claim him."*

"His *aunt?"* Greg almost couldn't get his next words out. "Jesus God, they gave the boy to *Carrie Rutland?"*

"They most certainly did—apparently it was all right there in Tony Rutland's file that she was the next of kin after his wife."

"But this is a *murder* investigation!" Greg exploded. He was so angry it was all he could do to keep from slamming his hands against the desktop. "They're supposed to go through channels, talk to the investigators. There was no current address or phone for Carrie, and I was stalling on processing his adoptive parents' request for custody because

Hannah was going to request it. I figured we'd find Carrie and get any threat to Hannah taken care of first—I didn't think they would release the child until you returned! For God's sake, Monica, I found out that Carrie and Gery Rutland are likely the same person, thanks to an operation. They'd need interviews, evaluations—"

"I'm just a county grunt, detective. Take me out of the governmental wheel and no one even misses me, much less thinks to ask me before screwing with my cases. I filed some report requests and they came through while I was gone; there were occasional local complaints of abuse to the boys by the Rutlands, but nothing the small town department would act on—mostly reports of Bruce using his fists to keep the kids in line. They seemed to focus their so-called discipline particularly on Gery—if what you're saying turns out to be true, my guess is that when he showed signs of gender problems, they tried to 'beat' it out of him. I don't think the adoptive grandparents are the way to fly with a boy who's already been through this much trauma, and I doubt I'll get much of an argument about that from the family court judge. It might take some persuading, but I'm willing to bet they'll give Hannah a try over the Rutlands.

"Detective Jedrek, I probably don't need to remind you that like you said, no one knew where to reach Carrie Rutland. Therefore no one actually told *her about her sister-in-law's death, plus your department really put a lid on it with the press. That means there's only one way she knew about it. And I bet it wasn't from chatting up the neighbors."* If she'd thought she was surprising him, she wasn't; that was the first thing that had hit home when she'd told him Carrie had Ben. *"My suggestion is that we get the hell over to Budlong Elementary School and get that boy back in departmental custody before he gets hurt."*

Greg had the receiver back in its cradle before the caseworker had even finished her sentence.

««—»»

"It says here that Carrie Rutland works as a nurse at the University of Chicago Hospital," Quesada said as he paged through the pile of papers that Greg handed him. The senior officer's expression had gone from doubt to shock to anger as he'd listened to Greg recount an abbreviated version of the saga of Tony, Carl, and Hannah, the childhood abduction and the murders—at least the ones Greg could explain … minus a few not-so-explainable details, of course. "Can we pick her up there?"

"No," Greg said grimly. He knew what the lieutenant was thinking—cops were always all over hospitals and they might be able to catch her by surprise. Not so this time. "She's on the run again. I already sent a couple of squads over, but the head nurse reported that Carrie took a six-week leave of absence after her brother's death. She hasn't been in to work since then." He leaned over the other man's desk and jabbed angrily at an address scribbled on a Post-It note. "See that? That's the 'new' home address she gave Child Services when she came in to pick up Ben. Unfortunately, not a single one of those quarter-wits checked it out—the place is a fucking abandoned building on the near west side. The only things in there are rats and junkies."

The older man's eyes narrowed. "This means Tony's son is where, exactly? With Carrie Rutland?"

Greg glanced at his watch and gave his superior a grim but triumphant smile. "Nope. We checked and he was marked into school attendance this morning. Right about now, I'd say he ought to be getting into Monica Kenweigh's car."

«««—»»»

She didn't make it over to the elementary school in time.

Carrie had planned on going by work and picking up her paycheck, because you just couldn't count on those idiots in Human Resources to mail stuff out with anything resembling promptness (she certainly wasn't going to make a record of her life by doing something as stupid as automatic deposit). She'd dropped Ben off at school this morning with the resolve that they were going to make a fresh start. Yeah, maybe she wasn't so good at this parenting thing just yet—the boy's constant sniveling was really driving her up a wall and she'd already lost her temper a couple of times and yanked him around a bit—but she could, no *would,* get better at it. It just took practice, that's all. So what if she hadn't exactly been born to be maternal; she could learn.

It didn't help that the boy—*Benjamin,* she reminded herself, she had to stop thinking of him as some third party outsider—treated *her* as if she were a space monster. Obviously he didn't remember her, and Carrie tried to put herself in his shoes on that matter. He'd only been two when she'd gone through her change, such a big thing for the whole family, so how could he know anything now, when Tony had forbidden her to see him or Dara afterward? Six seconds of confusion at the back door, then Dara had recognized her—really, the facial features were still there beneath the makeup—and let her into the house. Benjamin, of course, lacked the knowledge to make the transition that had ultimately cost his mother her life.

But a simple call into work on her cell phone had changed everything. Carrie had known instantly that something was wrong; maybe it had been the tone of the head nurse's voice, a few carefully placed pauses, that cagey question about exactly when she might come in to pick up her paycheck when no one on the floor would have ever cared about such a thing. She didn't need that paycheck all that bad—she had some cash saved up at the apartment—but that kid was all she had left of her family, her own flesh and *blood,* and she'd been damned if anyone on the face of this planet was going to take him away from her. She'd turned the car right around and gone back home, then dug her suitcases out of the storage locker downstairs. Inside of two hours, she had pretty much everything she needed packed into her car along with the few belongings of Ben's the Department of Child Services had given her. A last look around, and she'd hurried off to Budlong Elementary. She'd just tell them it was a family emergency, and God knew there'd been so many of those in the kid's life these last few weeks they'd probably be glad to see him go.

But almost only counts in horseshoes and hand grenades—wasn't that the old saying that was supposed to be so funny? Well, hardy-har-har, but Carrie'd be damned if she understood the humor now as, heart thudding, she turned into an alcove containing a water fountain and acted like she was taking a drink. Only six feet beyond, her nephew walked past, never seeing her and with his hand tucked into that of a gray-haired woman who was flanked on either side by a uniformed Chicago cop. Benjamin was so close she could see a piece of lint on the collar of his jacket, yet he might as well have been on the other side of the world, because it was obvious she'd never have him again, never have this last living piece of her family.

She straightened slowly, watching from the corner of her eye as the three adults and the child, her nephew, moved farther and farther away from her. The hallway was long and not very well lit, a typical inner-city school with highly polished floors and walls full of industrial-green lockers, the requisite door and windows at each distant end. That was where the group headed now, the brightness beyond making them into receding silhouettes giving off sadly echoing footsteps, with each fading *tap tap tap* of a heel another dig, another reminder of the mess, the failure, that Carrie's life had become. And why?

Because of Hannah.

That was it, Carrie thought. That was *all* of it. At the far end of the hallway one of the cops pushed open the school's double doors and they all filed out. The doors closed again with a bang that was surprisingly loud, final enough to make Carrie shudder. Yes, Hannah had done this—it was all her fault. She had been the one with the invisible tie to Tony, the one who had drawn too much attention his way and revealed things about him that should have never been known. She'd been like a living spotlight for Tony's deeds, a big arrow of evidence for that policeman-boyfriend of hers to use as a way to torment the man she hadn't even known was her own brother. Because of all that—

Hannah had been the one who caused his death.

And, by association, she had also been responsible for Dara's death.

But Hannah's biggest sin of all, her most unforgivable, was that she had separated Carrie from the last of her family, forever and ever, amen.

And for this, sister Hannah was going to pay dearly.

«««—»»»

"Hey, girlfriend. I can't remember the last time we pulled a shift together. Ought to have a good time today—what do you say we get a little live action going?"

Hannah grinned at Winnie's wicked little smile, then shouldered past her friend to reach for a milk shake glass. "Thanks, but I have all the live action in my life I can handle right now. A nice, ordinary day at work is just what the psychiatrist ordered. Besides, Greg and I offered you a threesome and you turned us down."

Ignoring the joke, Winnie regarded her in between totaling up a couple of checks. "Why are you seeing that guy again?"

"I'm not, fool. Figure of speech."

"I knew that."

Hannah smirked at her, then quickly dumped the makings of a chocolate shake into a metal cup and snugged it in place on the mixer. "Place is hopping for a Tuesday," she said, raising her voice to be heard about the whine of the machine. "Or did I miss some kind of work holiday?"

"Don't you know?" Winnie snatched up a setup for a threesome—silverware, napkins, water glasses—and loaded them onto her tray. "It's National Turkey Day. Gobble gobble."

"Honey, you're five months off," Hannah told her as she pulled out the cup and poured the shake into the waiting glass. A dollop of whipped creamed completed the picture.

"What?" Winnie lifted the tray and gave Hannah a look of mock surprise. "Oh, I get it—" She turned and headed toward her table, tossing her final comment back over her shoulder. "You thought I was talking about the *bird* kind of turkey!" Hannah laughed as she got her own tray.

"Hannah, customer at table six," Zubro snapped as he hurried past. She resisted the urge to tell him she wasn't blind—the hostess had only seated the table ten seconds ago. Instead, she just shook her head, dropped the milkshake off at the booth by the door, then went to wait on the woman at table six.

««—»»

"Dead end at work, dead end at home, dead end at the school."

Greg tapped his pencil on the paper in front of him, then realized with a start that he'd said the words out loud. He glanced around, but none of the guys in the squad room had noticed, so at least he hadn't embarrassed himself too badly. If he were Carrie Rutland, what would he do now? Run, probably. The life she'd put together for herself in Chicago was destroyed, and there was no going back. Her brother was dead, her identity was revealed, she was under suspicion for the murder of Dara Rutland, and she would never, *ever* get her hands on her nephew again.

Greg had seen Ben Rutland a little while ago, had stopped in at the facility where they were keeping him for the next few days—no release options at all—to introduce himself and broach the idea, gently, that there was another family member who would be stepping in to offer him a home. The child was pretty withdrawn and mistrustful, and who could blame him? His arms, wrists and shoulders had been pocked with the same dark-colored bruises that had repeatedly marred Hannah's skin over the last couple of days. His parents were dead and the person into whose custody he'd been placed had, as he'd related in a halting voice, "turned mean," yelling at him if he cried about losing his mom and dad and pulling him around her apartment if she thought he wasn't doing something just right. Greg's biggest hope was that Ben would be at least a bit more likely to trust him because he knew that Greg had been his father's partner on the job.

In the meantime, Carrie Rutland née Gary Rutland née Carl Danior was out there somewhere. They didn't have an address—Ben hadn't had a clue about that, just that they'd driven "for awhile" to get to school this morning—but it wasn't hard to guess that she'd probably cleared out her belonging and hit the road. She might think things were over and that she'd start new somewhere, but they'd never be over—clearly Hannah was as tied to Carrie as she had been to Tony.

So she had to be found.

Greg sighed and looked around the squad room. Most of his coworkers had families like Tony's, a wife or a husband and kids, siblings, parents. How would he have reacted if everything that he had and had struggled to get—which maybe hadn't been so much to begin with—was taken away, all in the course of a couple of months? No matter what the reason, right or wrong, how would he feel?

Angry.

Suddenly Greg stood, so quickly that the heavy metal desk chair toppled over behind him. This time, his coworkers did turn to stare at him.

Angry? Not even close. He'd be *furious*. And if he were a certain kind of person, a person whose past history had included a little too much going overboard in the mental instability department…

He'd want revenge.

Hannah!

««—»»

"Hi," Hannah said. "Welcome to the Diner. My name is Hannah." She slid a menu onto the table and pulled out her order pad. "I'll give you a few minutes to look over the menu. We have lunch specials, and the soup today is cream of chicken. In the meantime, can I bring you something to drink?" Finished scribbling down the table number and time—

God knows why, but Zubro insisted they record it—Hannah glanced up from her pad and focused on her customer.

The woman didn't look up at her, just pulled the menu over and opened it. "I'll have a Diet Pepsi. Large."

"Great," Hannah replied, blinking at the unfriendly tone. Her customer was focused on the menu with her hands on each side of her forehead as though she had a headache; Hannah couldn't see the woman's face, just the top of her head. "I'll bring it right back." Back at the drink station, she couldn't help shuddering a bit as she scooped ice into the glass and filled it.

"What's bugging you?" Winnie asked from behind her. "You look like a cockroach just crawled up your underpants."

Hannah made a face. "Oh, disgust me out, you silly twit." She hesitated. "It's just... *her.*" She nodded toward table six. "Serious mean queen. I don't even know her and she's acting like I beat up her favorite kitten or something—I can *feel* her animosity."

Winnie's mouth twisted. "Yeah, well, face it. Some people just wake up on the wrong side of the bed... every day. Don't take it so personal, Han. Give it a half hour and I promise you she'll be out of your life forever."

Hannah had to grin. "So true. Especially if she orders that meatloaf lunch plate. One taste and she'll never set foot in here again." When she peered into the dining room, she saw the woman had closed the menu and was digging through an oversized black purse, apparently trying to find something way down at the bottom.

She felt a little better, but she still stalled on going back to the table, unable to explain why this woman's apparently random hostility should unsettle her so badly. Finally, knowing she'd already left the woman to wait far longer than was acceptable, Hannah headed back over to see if Mrs. Grumpy was ready to order, scanning the rest of her station on the way to assure herself that no one else needed anything. So far, so good.

"Hi," she said as brightly as she could. "Sorry it took me so long to get back. Are you rea—"

She never got to finish her question.

As Hannah came to a stop at the table, the woman abruptly pushed back her chair and stepped to the side, grabbing Hannah around the neck. Hannah squeaked in surprise as she was dragged backward, then gagged and clawed uselessly at the forearm jammed under her chin. Something slapped against her side—the woman's black bag—and as she strained to breathe, she realized that only an inch away from her face was a large, wicked-looking pocket knife. Oddly enough, she wasn't really afraid. Instead, she thought quite clearly, *Damn it, why is someone always trying to* cut *me?*

Her feet scrabbled across the floor and there was shouting and screaming all around her—her coworkers and the other customers in the restaurant. The grip around her throat only tightened and Hannah could feel the blood backing up in her head, making it pound. She wished she could bite but her mouth was smashed solidly closed by the upward angle of her jaw.

"Get away from me!" her captor shrieked. *"Get away and stay away and don't anyone come near or I'll kill her, I swear I will!"* The voice exploding next to her ear was strange, fluctuating between high and low tones as though it couldn't decide at what pitch it was most comfortable. *"I said get back!"* More chairs and a table crashed over as Hannah's attacker bulldozed a path for herself and her prisoner, obviously headed for the front door. She swung Hannah in a circle, hard, and Hannah's arms and legs flopped around like a rag doll, sending dishes of food to shatter on the floor. Hannah felt some of the broken pieces splatter against her legs, little crockery bee-stings, and it wasn't until the woman turned her around again and she saw the door flash by that she actually started to get scared—if this maniac actually got her outside and hauled her away, what would happen to her, where would her kidnapper take her—

A cave, maybe, where it's dark and damp and cold, filled with shadows while the rain pounds so loudly outside that no one can hear while she screams...

—and now Hannah *did* try to scream, *did* try to fight, but it only got her neck wrenched even harder. The entrance door was coming up fast, only a few feet away, and the woman glanced behind her and reached to turn the doorknob with her other hand—

—and Winnie clambered over one of the overturned tables and leapt on top of the both of them.

They went down in a pile of flailing arms and kicking legs, with Winnie screaming like an outraged lioness as she fought to control the larger woman's knife hand and tried to pummel her in the face at the same time. In the background, amidst the yelling and crashing around, Hannah thought she heard a siren, but that was probably only someone else wailing—God knows, everyone in the restaurant seemed to be yammering at once. Hannah got hold of the woman's hair and pulled, half expecting it to be a wig that would come loose in her hands; it didn't, and the woman snarled in pain and jerked her head to the side, leaving Hannah with two fistfuls of dyed blond. She punched Winnie in the face and Hannah heard a sickening *crunch*; Winnie let go of the woman's knife hand and her eyes rolled back until only the whites showed, then she toppled sideways.

"Winnie!" Hannah cried. Her attacker had twisted one leg over hers and she tried to claw her way free, but without Winnie to distract her, the crazy woman's attention turned fully back on Hannah.

"You!" she spat in that uneven voice. "You wrecked *everything*, you clairvoyant little *bitch!"* She had makeup on, black mascara and tawny-colored eyeshadow, but now it was all smeared from crying. Her left hand shot forward and before Hannah could pull out of range, she'd gripped the collar of Hannah's uniform. She struggled up from the floor, hauling Hannah with her, then shook her like a dog shakes a bone. "You were dead to us, damn it—why couldn't you have *stayed* that way?"

"I don't—"

"Shut up!" she screamed into Hannah's face. Someone nearby moved and the woman spun Hannah around until she could use her as a shield, waving the knife menacingly until the person, one of the busboys who'd been trying to inch up on her, backed away again. Her forearm was once more across Hannah's throat. "It's too late now, Hannah, it's all too late—"

"Carrie," Hannah said desperately. *"Carl.* Please—we can talk about this, we can—"

"Don't *call* me that!" She was nearly sobbing now. "I'm not Carl anymore, I'm *not*, I haven't been for *years*. You're the last person who even knows that." Crushed against her, Hannah felt the woman's chest hitch. "I was okay, I was, and then you…" Carrie inhaled sharply. "I'm going to start over, Hannah. Somewhere else, with a clean slate. And I'm going to make sure that you aren't around to ruin it."

Hannah saw the knife blade shine as Carrie lifted it. The people staring at them gasped at the same time she opened her mouth to scream one last time—

And the glass in the door behind Carrie's head exploded.

«‹—›»

Greg yanked open what was left of the Diner's door and stepped inside, the sound of his revolver's discharge still hammering in his ear drums. Inside the restaurant it was oddly silent. The shot through the glass had made everyone reflexively dive for the floor—maybe there was something to be said about being trained by the boob tube after all. Carrie Rutland was lying face-down on the floor and he kept his gaze trained on her, though from the looks of what was left—or not—of the back of her head, it was highly unlikely she was getting up. Ever.

"Hannah?"

No answer, and Greg felt panic course through him as he moved closer. What if she had landed on the knife as they'd fallen? He'd seen Carrie raise her weapon, had known he'd never get inside in time to stop her… but had she been able to cut Hannah before he'd gotten off his shot? Or, sweet Jesus, had his bullet scored a horrid two-for-one?

"Hannah!" Around him people were starting to get up off the floor, while outside a couple of squad cars skidded up to where he'd left the Jeep, bubble light flashing on the front dashboard, double-parked on Sheffield. The noise level was building, inside and out, as everyone began talking excitedly at once.

Greg barely heard them. He reached down with his left hand and—

"Shit."

He barely caught the mumbled curse, but it was enough to make him able to breathe again. He pulled on the dead weight of Carrie Rutland's left arm until that side of her body came up enough to let Hannah squirm free. The back of her head and uniform was splattered with blood and bits of bone, though Greg thought he'd probably wipe her down and not mention that part. "Are you all right?" he demanded as he pulled her up and into the circle of his left arm. "Did she—"

"I'm fine," Hannah insisted, pushing away from him. "Where's Winnie?"

"I'mb here." They turned at the sound of the thick voice and Hannah knelt next to her friend. Winnie's face was a mess—both eyes were already black and her nose had spread to twice its size. "I ding dad bidje broge my nodse."

"Oh, she sure did," Greg said sympathetically. "You're gonna have to get that set right away or it'll end up crooked."

"Bunderful."

They helped the dark-haired waitress to her feet as four cops piled through the entrance, with more arriving outside. It wouldn't be long before the wheels of procedure stepped in to clean up this mess and the paperwork started. In the meantime—

"Hannah!"

Hannah twisted her head to where a sweaty-faced man wearing a name tag that said *D. Zubro - Manager* stood glowering at them. "Uh-oh."

Zubro's mouth worked, but for a few moments, he couldn't get anything to come out. Then finally—

"You're *fired.*"

He turned and stomped off as Hannah stared at him in amazement. When she started to go after him, Greg put his hand on her shoulder and stopped her. "Forget him, Hannah. That's the second best thing that ever happened to you."

"What?" Hannah only looked bewildered.

Winnie wrestled her way up to stand next to them, wincing at the pain in her face. She elbowed him. "Do ahead, Greg. Da girl's dense—dell her whad da firdst is."

In spite of the carnage and the sad, dead woman on the floor at their feet, Greg had to grin just as little as his hand slid down and he squeezed Hannah's fingers.

"Me."

Epilogue

Thursday—March 13th...

"Will the parties please stand."

It wasn't a request and Hannah shivered as she got to her feet along with everyone else. Gripping Greg's hand so tightly that it hurt, she found she was powerless to stop.

"I've read through the case file—quite extensive—and heard testimony both for and against Ms. Danior by Dr. Gorrado and Dr. Tansey, plus testimony by Detective Jedrek. I've also listed to Bruce and Erma Rutland, as well as Monica Kenweigh. It's been an interesting and complicated narrative, but I've come to a decision."

Judge Ita was an attractive middle-aged woman with graying, wavy brown hair and a face that was overly lined for her age, evidence of the responsibilities she dealt with on a daily basis. The brown-eyed gaze she leveled at Hannah was piercing and unflinching; Hannah wished she could be as strong and sure of herself as the woman sitting up there in those black robes.

"The decision I make today is going to affect the rest of a young boy's life," the judge continued. "So it isn't made lightly. I can send Benjamin Rutland to live with adopted grandparents who have until now not taken any interest in him and who clearly see raising him from here on out only as strict religious obligation. Regarding them, I've noted complaints regarding abusive behavior toward their prior adopted children, including Benjamin's father. Frankly, I'm disinclined to make that choice.

"My second alternative is to give this child over to a natural aunt who until recently didn't know she was related and who has in the past been subjected to the kind of abuse most people prefer to believe doesn't happen in the real world. There are those—" she inclined her head toward a grim-faced Dr. Tansey, "who believe the aunt to be mentally unstable, but her own doctor, a specialist in traumatic psychiatry treatment, believes she has more than recovered and can lead a fully functional and productive life, including caring for her nephew.

"Finally, I can keep the boy in the system and place him in foster care, with the hopes that he might someday be adopted. I think we all know that an older child's chances of adoption are slim at best."

Judge Ita flipped through the thick stack of papers on the bench before her. "According to the testimony of Detective Jedrek and the Chicago Police Department's evidence records, Ms. Danior's statement that it was her brother Tony who was doing her physical harm does appear to have some validity. It's a well-documented fact that abuse victims will often not name their attackers out of fear and the misplaced feeling that they should protect them." She sighed and closed the file, then folded her hands in front of her. "Ms. Danior, step to the bench, please."

Hannah swallowed and Greg squeezed her hand briefly before he let go. It was only a few feet, but she felt like she was walking a swaying plank over stormy, shark-infested ocean waters, and she was trembling by the time she got up there.

"You're asking me for custody of Benjamin Rutland. This is a *huge* thing—you're young, single, and you work as a waitress. This boy has lost both his parents to violent deaths, he was mistreated afterward, and he may have psychological damage that could manifest at any time. This isn't a matter of changing your mind once you try it out for a few days, and what you say to me in the next few seconds will determine the course of the *rest of your life.* Are you absolutely sure you're prepared to deal with being the legal guardian of Benjamin Rutland?"

Hannah lifted her chin. Her trembling had stopped, and she had never been more sure of anything in her life. "Yes, your Honor."

A corner of the woman's mouth turned up. "All right, then. Custody of Benjamin Rutland is granted to his aunt, Hannah Danior, on the condition that you both meet with the caseworker, Monica Kenweigh, once per month for a term of two years. At that time Ms. Kenweigh can either recommend additional probationary time, or permanently close this file." She raised her gavel and it came down; Hannah saw it happen in slow motion, and savored every millisecond.

When she turned she saw Ben standing next to Monica Kenweigh. He was smiling slightly, even if he still looked a little scared. But it would be all right—he would be all right, she would be all right, they would *both* be all right. Greg came around the table and hugged her as Dr. Gorrado and Monica Kenweigh shook hands; Dr. Tansey and the Rutlands were already on their way out, ready to leave this nasty little business behind them. She was sure the Rutlands were secretly relieved that they wouldn't have to raise Ben, even if they did think she was—what had they called her in their testimony yesterday? *"The devil's spawn, of course she is, being related to them two boys."*

She and Greg met Monica and Ben at the end of the table and she smiled down at her nephew. "Looks like it's the three of us, kiddo. That's not so bad, is it?"

"Okay."

Not bad—Monica had said Ben wasn't talking much these days, so at least he'd answered her. It would take time to build up his trust, but she had a good feeling about this, a good feeling about the family the three of them could be once they got things all sorted out. The Rutland house would be sold and Greg had decided to buy a place of his own, somewhere big enough for all of them plus the dogs. And what little boy who'd had a shortage of fun and affection couldn't use the friendship of two furry and fun-loving pooches?

As the last of the people left the courtroom Greg put his arm across her shoulders and, on a whim, Hannah offered her hand to Ben. He stared at it for a long moment and Hannah realized that she, Greg, and Monica were all holding their breath. At last, Ben reached out and carefully tucked his smaller hand into hers.

Yes, she had a *very* good feeling about all of it.

www.ingramcontent.com/pod-product-compliance
Lightning Source LLC
Chambersburg PA
CBHW020258030826
48979CB00026B/1392/J

* 9 7 8 1 8 9 2 9 5 0 6 9 7 *